Buried Truths

A DAUGHTER'S TALE

Enjoy the journey

Elsa

ElsaWolfBooks.com

ELSA WOLF

Cover design by Sarah Hansen
http://www.okaycreations.com

Interior design and formatting by JT Formatting

Wolf, Elsa
Buried Truths: A Daughter's Tale / 1st ed
ISBN-13: 978-1-7327774-0-8
United States of America

This story is dedicated to all adopted children
trying to find their way.

Adoption is a gift that is hard for many children to comprehend. There are feelings that emerge that are often impossible for them to understand or explain. Feelings of rejection as well as feelings of gratitude. The process of accepting adoption from a child's point of view can be long, complex and difficult to grasp in rational terms. Each person's story is no less important than the next. Every soul deserves a chance in this world to make the best of themselves. No one takes the journey alone, no matter how lonely they may feel. Their path is unique and should be embraced.

"I have been impressed with the urgency of doing.
Knowing is not enough, we must apply.
Being willing is not enough, we must do."

Leonardo Da Vinci

Chapter 1

1958...

Nathan fidgeted in the back of his chauffeured car while the driver pulled in front of the red sandstone building attached to the Mainz Cathedral, in Germany. As he looked through the car's side window at the angels carved in stone above the portal entrance, nuns hurried past on the street and into a courtyard edged with roses. His curiosity piqued, but he couldn't take his wife inside to meet the baby until the appointed time. He knew Reverend Mother Agnes needed every spare moment to set the stage for their 'noble deception.'

Michel, the chauffeur, opened the car's rear passenger door. Only Nathan stepped out. After positioning his fedora on his head, he inspected the side of the black Mercedes. Then, pulling a handkerchief from his lapel pocket, he wiped off a spot. He folded the handkerchief into thirds and slipped it back into his pocket as he peered inside the car door at his wife, Gwen.

Gwen flipped open a mirrored compact, patted her face with powder, and reapplied her lipstick and eyeshadow.

"Come, dear, you look lovely." Nathan tried not to show his frustration with her excessive preening.

She put one leg out of the car and hesitated. "Nathan, I'm off balance," she complained. "Let me take your hand. My new high heels are a little precarious." She slid across the seat and twitched her three-quarter length, full skirt back into place.

"Everything is going to be fine." He took her hand in his and pulled her up. "We're a bit early. I need a walk before our meeting."

"Do you think the straps on my new stilettos look all right?" Gwen's voice quavered. "They're the latest fashion, but maybe they make my ankles look too thick."

"They're quite attractive. Please, let's get moving," he pleaded. "We need to go. Sitting in the car for six hours has made me restless."

"I can't go for a walk! These are the only shoes I have with me. I left my other ones at home in the front hall."

"Wait a minute, stay here." Smiling, he went to the back of the car and signaled Michel, who hurried around with the keys and unlocked the cavernous trunk. Pushing aside their overnight cases, Nathan plucked out a small-handled, brown shopping bag and held it up. "Will this help?"

He passed his wife the bag, and she peeked inside.

"My walking shoes!" Gwen exclaimed with delight. "I was so flustered when I left the house. Thank you for bringing them." She sat on a nearby bench and exchanged her narrow heels for her practical square-heeled Mary Janes.

While Nathan waited, he took a pack of Lucky Strikes from his suit pocket and lit a cigarette.

"May I have one?" Gwen asked.

Nathan admired how delicately she stood up from the bench with the shopping bag's handle resting in the crook of her arm as she tugged off her white gloves and pushed them into her dainty purse. He passed her a cigarette and then held up the lit butane lighter. She placed the cigarette between her lips and leaned forward into the flickering flame. He thought she appeared pensive as she drew the fire through the tobacco. While he put the lighter and cigarette pack back in his pocket, they began to walk. To free up her other arm, he gently took the shopping bag.

Pulling the cigarette away from her lips, she said, "I love that you can get an American brand in Paris. I do prefer them over the French Gauloises cigarettes."

"One of my many talents," joked Nathan, with a sly grin. He had struck a deal with Sergeant Kane at the Embassy. For a small fee, every couple of weeks, the sergeant gave him a new carton at the guard station.

With her cigarette resting between her slender fingers, Gwen held her wrist up to her brow, shielded her eyes and squinted into the distance. "The Rhine isn't too far away. How much time do we have?"

Nathan looked at his pocket watch before replying, "They aren't expecting us for another thirty-five minutes." He treasured the silver etched case and connected chain that always reminded him of his long-departed father. The inscriptions within had both their initials and a saying; *carpe diem*. Smiling he realized he should 'seize the day' and treasure the moments to come.

"Oh my, the sun is especially bright out today," Gwen exclaimed. He watched her rustle through her purse and pulled out a wad of Kleenex tissue. She unrolled the edges and plucked out a pair of dark-rimmed sunglasses, and slip them over the bridge of her nose. He wondered why his wife never chose to put them in an appropriate case. Inwardly he chuckled at the practicality of having a dual-purpose tissue handy, although he couldn't imagine her wrapping the glasses back up in the tissue after using it on her nose For that reason alone, he always kept two handkerchiefs in his pocket.

Nathan turned toward the chauffeur and spoke in French, "Michel, find something to eat. Be back in two hours. We'll stay at Steinberger Frankfurter Hof on Kaiser Platz in Frankfurt tonight."

"Oui, Monsieur Schwartz." Michel stepped into the car and drove away.

Gwen took Nathan's arm, and they started to walk. She set the pace. "So, sir—my walking encyclopedia—how long is the Rhine river?"

He loved how she stroked his intellectual ego. Nathan chuckled and said, "The river is about 765-miles long, which translates to around 1233 kilometers."

"I knew I could count on you for an answer." Gwen rubbed his arm and began talking about the adoption. "Our friends will be ecstatic if we actually go through with this and decide to adopt the baby after the interview." She giggled. "We're in our late forties, and old enough to be grandparents! I'm afraid a woman of my age might be too old to learn new tricks. I don't know if I can handle a baby. My mother was never maternal, what if I'm not suitable to be a mother?"

"You'll be fine, and we're still young enough. Besides, the doctor gave us a clean bill of health." Nathan tried to calm himself and reassure his wife at the same time. Our friends are delighted we're trying to adopt, and they wrote such nice letters on our behalf. We shouldn't worry."

"You're probably right," Gwen said with a sigh. "In our circle of friends, age is rarely discussed. The diplomatic wives love to brag about their children. We've wanted a child for so long. It'll be nice to talk about ours for a change."

The corners of Nathan's mouth turned up ever so slightly. "We'll be fine." They passed by three of the building's towers, each a different size with a pointed turret.

Gwen looked up at Nathan. "Did I tell you Mrs. Kendrick's nanny won't be joining them at their next post in South Africa?"

"No, you hadn't mentioned it."

"We had a little chat, and Madeline said she'll be happy to work for us."

"That's splendid, my dear." Nathan sighed with relief.

"Yes, it is." Gwen squeezed his arm as they walked further away from the buildings. "Why do you suppose Germans call orphanages asylums? It seems rather harsh and makes the children sound like lunatics."

He laughed at his wife's comment. "They're more of a sanctuary, I think. The Germans only use the term in institutions that are exclusively for orphans. This cathedral and the connected buildings aren't the same kind of place." He encouraged Gwen to move a little more quickly by picking up his own pace. At the river, he breathed in the fresh, moist air.

"Dear me, this wind is fierce. Better hold on to your hat," she cautioned.

Maybe she wasn't trying to be metaphorical, but Nathan couldn't help associating the phrase directly to what their life would become with a child. They walked for another five minutes until he found a suitable bench. "Wait a minute," he said, stopping. Pulling out his handkerchief, he brushed off the seat. "Let's sit here and enjoy the view."

"I'm surprised it's so chilly out here." Gwen looked at the bench and adjusted her shawl. She spun around and began to sit down but fell hard on the seat. "Well, that was unladylike."

"Don't worry." Nathan presented her with an impish smile. "I won't tell anyone."

"Thank you, this needs to be washed." Gwen took his handkerchief by the corner and tucked it in the bag with her shoes. "So… yesterday, you said we shouldn't say too much about our first marriages since Catholics frown upon divorce. I'm uncomfortable with our script. Can we practice our lines?"

Nathan expected Gwen to be on edge, but he didn't really want to rehearse. Composing his thoughts carefully, he tried to reassure her. "I don't know if she'll ask us for our family history." He hesitated, then added, "This isn't meant to be one of your plays."

"Remember, I cope better if I know what I should say for important moments in our lives," protested Gwen.

"Yes, I know you well," he acquiesced. "All right, I'll run my lines. Ahem... I lived in California before the war, with a successful law practice and marriage. After I enlisted, my wife was unfaithful, and we couldn't stay together." He rested his hand on Gwen's knee, his eyes held hers. "Now, it's your turn."

She squared her shoulders and recited primly, "My former husband was a man I met in my hometown. We traveled to New York City for work and were both successful in classical theater."

He interrupted, "Why the classical remark?"

"Let me finish." She touched his cheek. "I plan to mention it because I don't want the nuns to think I was a movie actress."

"I see. You must be clear on that point," Nathan teased. "And the rest of the story?"

"Liquor took over his soul, and he became aggressive. I couldn't possibly stay with a man like that!"

Putting his arm around her shoulder, Nathan said, "Well done. She might also ask us about our religious practices. It seems sensible for you to answer those questions."

"Yes, I assumed so," she replied earnestly. "You don't even follow your family traditions."

"Well, nevertheless—in my family, mothers always define the children's heritage. I see no reason to change those rules."

"We'll raise the baby as an Episcopalian," Gwen announced. "I don't think the nuns will object, it's close enough to Catholicism. We don't have to reveal all the details."

Nathan snickered. "We are quite a pair. If we can let's continue to keep our personal lives private, just like I do with my professional life." He wanted to tell Gwen why this particular baby was so important to adopt, but he didn't dare. Gwen would never accept the truth.

"Your work has more secrets than I can imagine," Gwen grumbled.

"Yes, you are wonderful to put up with me." Nathan leaned over and kissed her. "I suspect Mother Agnes won't ask too many questions." Winking, he pointed toward the cathedral. "Let's go back up. With any luck, we'll be parents soon. I hope we like the baby."

They walked toward the building, and Nathan felt both nervous and excited. Gwen sat on the same bench by the entrance, removed her Mary Janes, dropped them in the bag, and put on her high heels. As they walked up to the portal door together, a gust of wind brushed by them, but Gwen's blonde, hair sprayed bouffant didn't move. The hollow sound her heels made on the stone steps announced their arrival.

After Nathan straightened his suit, removed his hat, and smoothed down his black hair, they passed through the double doors into a dimly lit hall. He ran his hand down the back of Gwen's tailored Christian Dior top and rested it in the small of her back. He gestured at the ceiling with his free hand. Softly, he said, "Look, darling, the keystones are carved roses."

"I see, they're beautiful." She wrinkled her nose. "It smells musty in here."

"Your senses are remarkable. Shh, someone's coming."

A young nun greeted them. "Hello, my name is Sister Claire. Are you Mr. and Mrs. Schwartz?"

Gwen removed her sunglasses. "Yes, yes we are."

"You're right on time. Come this way. I will tell Reverend Mother you are here. You can place your things on the chair in the corner." Sister Claire led them into an office with a vaulted ceiling. The walls were covered with bookshelves and tapestries. With a slight bow, Sister Claire closed the door, leaving them alone in the room.

Nathan and Gwen stood together by an expansive stone fireplace large enough to roast an entire pig. Nathan felt the urge to grab Gwen's hand when she began rubbing her index finger on the cuticle of her thumb again and again, but he chose to ignore the gesture. She stopped as abruptly as she'd started, peered at her watch, and began to complain. "I'm not sure, but it seems we've been here a quarter of an hour. What is taking them so long?"

"Come now; it's only been five minutes." Nathan flared his nostrils as he adjusted his thick-lensed black glasses with his right hand. "We've been in Europe for years. You know we can't rush anyone."

"I realize, but I'm a bundle of nerves. Tell me more about Mother Agnes." Gwen dropped her hands to her sides, tugged the corners of her shawl, and commenced tapping her toe.

Nathan grasped both of her hands and kissed her knuckles. "Oh, my dear, you *are* nervous. Mother Agnes is in charge of this congregation. She's a kind, yet stern woman, who is known for her compassion toward couples in our predicament. Darling, don't worry so much."

"I'll try not to, but it's not easy."

"I need to leave a minute to find a toilet. Try to relax while I'm gone."

"Nathan, please remember to wash your hands—the ones away from home are so dirty. Leave your hat here."

He gingerly set his hat on the nearest chair and scowled at Gwen before leaving the room. Down the hall, he found the door to a lavatory and went inside to relieve himself. On his way out, he turned a corner and almost ran into a woman he assumed was Mother Agnes. They spoke in hushed voices in German.

"Hello, Reverend Mother?" Nathan asked, hoping that he was correct since they'd only spoken on the phone.

"Yes. You must be Mr. Schwartz?"

He extended his hand, and she lightly clasped it. "I'm sorry, I didn't mean to startle you."

"You didn't, Mr. Schwartz," she responded sweetly. "Let us walk together."

"Thank you for all of your help," Nathan said. "How was the transfer from the hospital?"

"The baby's mother was heartbroken, but she agreed to the arrangements. I sent a private nurse to transport the child, as you and Captain McGwire requested. Other than Sister Claire, the nuns here don't know the details. Sister Claire and I would do anything for him after he saved our lives."

"He never told me the specifics." Nathan kept a mental note to be sure to ask at their next meeting because he had no idea what Mother Agnes was referring to. During the war, he and McGwire had become good friends, and they'd worked well together ever since.

In a soothing voice, Mother Agnes continued, "The war has been long over, but it created all kinds of problems for many people."

"Yes, so true. Thank you for being so discreet. The fewer people who know our adoption scenario, the better. Our wives aren't even aware of the circumstances. We want to protect everyone concerned."

"It's a difficult situation." She pursed her lips. "Even so, I'm glad I can help place the baby in your home. Let's go into my office and not keep your wife waiting any longer."

They walked into the room together. Mother Agnes stopped speaking German and addressed Gwen in English, "Welcome, Mrs. Schwartz. Please sit down. I found your husband lost in the hallway."

"Thank you." Gwen sat on the stiff-backed mahogany chair.

"How was your drive from Paris? I hope the border crossing wasn't a problem?"

Nathan smiled, picked up his hat, and put it on the desk, before settling into the chair next to his wife. "I have diplomatic plates on my car, the guards just waved us across the border. We're thrilled to be here."

Sister Claire returned carrying a handled wooden tray and placed it on the desk. The aroma of coffee filled the air.

"Help yourself," said Mother Agnes. "The sisters love to make sweets for our visitors. Enjoy them. I need to go over your file again."

"They look delicious." Gwen selected a pastry with a pair of tongs and placed it on a napkin for Nathan. "Here's one for you, dear. Be careful, I think it's cream filled."

Nathan enjoyed his strong coffee and pastry while observing Mother Agnes. She matched Gwen's height, around five-two, though her round middle made her appear much shorter in her black robe. She resembled a bird perching on a chair with her liver-spotted hands riffling through the papers. Her habit covered her head in two parts. The first white portion concealed her hair and neck in multiple creases that almost matched her many wrinkles. The second portion was stiff as cardboard and covered in black cloth that bent over her head like a mantel.

Mother Agnes tapped a pen on her desk, the sounds echoed throughout the room. She said, "Excellent, you come highly recommended. So many children in Germany need to be relocated." She eyed Gwen. "Do you speak German, Mrs. Schwartz?"

"A little. My father spoke to my aunts in German, but I never learned how to follow the conversations." Gwen submissively tilted her head.

"I understand. I only ask that you teach the baby about Germany as this is her first home. Heritage is an important part of a person's makeup; one must know where they came from even if their birth story isn't revealed. I think it's healthier to keep the details concealed and focus on their new family." She put down her fountain pen and pushed back her chair. "Do you have any other children?"

Nathan placed his hand on his wife's. "We don't have any other children in our home."

"Who will be the godparents?"

Gwen drew in a deep, audible breath. "The McGwires, David and Sadie. They have already agreed, and we couldn't be happier. They're such dear friends."

"Good, good. How did you and Mr. Schwartz meet?"

"After the war, Sadie introduced us at a party she hosted in Washington, D.C."

Mother Agnes rested her hand on the application form. "I see. Were you both working at the time?"

"Yes, we were. My husband was an Army Air Corp officer when we met and then became a legal adviser in the State Department." Gwen placed her empty napkin on the desk. "Before the war, I was a classical actress. During the conflict, I worked for a non-profit group called the United Services Organization as a recreational manager for the soldiers." Gwen paused. "I'm no longer with the USO."

"How long have you two been married?"

"Our ten-year anniversary is next month," Gwen answered.

"Congratulations. You have been together many years."

Nathan cleared his throat. "Yes, yes." He was relieved that Mother Agnes had held up her part of the agreement and had not asked about their former marriages. He'd just discussed it all with Gwen along the river to keep up appearances.

"Supporting your husband's work and taking care of a baby is challenging. Will you be hiring a nanny?"

"Yes. Nathan has quite a few evening engagements I have to attend. One of our friends is leaving Paris and their nanny, Madeline, will work for us instead."

"That is good to hear. Your forms say you live at 22 Rue Desbordes-Valmore in Paris. Is that still correct, Mrs. Schwartz?"

"Yes, in the 16th Arrondissement. We have lived there for the last five years and hope to stay a few more."

More scribbling on the documents.

"Mr. Schwartz, where will you move after your current post?"

"That will depend on the status of NATO at the time. I can't say exactly." Nathan furrowed his brows.

"I'm not surprised. Let's hope your next home is as safe as Paris has been these last years." She picked up the phone, dialed, and waited for a response. Speaking in German, she said, "Sister Claire, move the Schwartzes' baby to the vacant room across from the dining hall. We are on our way."

Nathan took his wife's hand in his, and they followed Mother Agnes silently down a dimly-lit, barren hallway with a few doors on either side. She stopped at the only double door, which had multi-colored stained-glass pieces randomly combined within the panels.

Perspiration dripped down Nathan's back and his stomach tensed. He prayed his wife would accept this particular baby.

Mother Agnes put her hand on the protective door plate and pushed. "Here we go. Sister Claire is waiting for us."

Glancing at each other with anticipation, Nathan and Gwen entered the room and gasped in delight. There before them laid a beautiful wide-eyed baby, swaddled in a pink blanket, in a bassinet. The distinct scent of lavender filled the air from freshly shaken powder, and Nathan felt Gwen squeeze his hand. His heart leapt as the reality of the situation sunk in.

Mother Agnes said something indistinguishable to the sister, and she scooped up the baby.

"Sister Claire has been with us since the end of the war. She's one of our best providers."

Nathan extended his hands. "May I hold her?"

Sister Claire rested the baby in his arms and backed away into a corner of the windowless room.

The moment he held the little girl, Nathan became enchanted. "Hello, Mousey. Would you like to come home with us?" he asked the little face peering out from the blanket. He walked away from the women and along the tapestry-covered walls mesmerized by the baby's eyes that appeared to be staring directly into his face as he talked jibber-jabber to her in a hushed voice. He directed his next question toward the nuns, waiting for the answer he already knew. "When is the child's birthday?"

"The fifteenth of March," responded Mother Agnes.

Gwen hurried across the room to Nathan. She grasped his forearm and whispered, "The baby has the same birthday as my mother. She must be meant for us." A bit louder she said, "Reverend Mother, does she have a name?"

"Mrs. Schwartz, you are welcome to choose for yourself. She was brought here with a name, but since she's only two weeks old, she won't know the difference."

"My turn to hold her," Gwen said, reaching out.

Nathan gently positioned the baby into his wife's arms and a light from the wall sconce reflected off her eyes.

"She's precious, I'm sure everyone will love her." Gwen gazed into the baby's eyes for the next twenty minutes cooing. Finally, much to Nathan's relief, she nodded in his direction. He knew then she'd accepted the child.

"Reverend Mother, this baby is just right." Nathan paused, and his stomach relaxed. "Darling, we should name her after your mother."

"Yes, my mother's name—Heidi—that's a lovely idea."

"I think her middle name should be Rose," Nathan added. Thankfully, his wife didn't object.

"Excellent! Sister Claire will take care of her until you return." Mother Agnes motioned toward the hall, indicating it was time for them to leave. "Sister, I will see you this evening."

With obvious reluctance, Gwen passed her little bundle back to the sister.

"Yes, Reverend Mother." Sister Claire put the baby back into the wheeled bassinet and rolled her away.

Nathan followed them with his eyes until they disappeared through an archway. Turning toward Gwen, he saw a tear trickle down her cheek. He wiped it away with his thumb and pressed it to his own lips with a reassuring smile.

Mother Agnes encouraged them back down the hall toward her office as she spoke. "With our attorney's help, I'm sure the adoption documents can be completed in about six weeks. We can mail or courier things back and forth if necessary. You can take Heidi Rose home during the second week of May. Will that be enough time to prepare?"

Nathan pulled on his ear. "Yes, I have a lengthy meeting I can't miss in Brussels before that, but I'm sure we can manage." He paused. "Excuse me, I need to grab my hat. Gwen, I'll collect your things as well."

"Thank you," Gwen replied.

He left the women in the hall and ducked into the office. After taking a few deep breaths, he reemerged with their belongings and handed them to Gwen.

Mother Agnes extended her hand to Nathan. He clasped both his hands around hers and said, "Bless you."

Nathan and Gwen left the nun at the doorway and walked to where Michel was already waiting outside their car. With a tilt of his head, Michel opened the door. They stepped into the warm vehicle, and he closed the door behind them as they settled into their seats. With a reassuring smile, Nathan patted Gwen gently on her knee as she pulled a moist towelette from her purse and wiped her hands.

On the way out of town, Gwen remarked that it was strange Mother Agnes never inquired about their previous marriages. She seemed perplexed, but Nathan remained silent.

Chapter 2

Six long weeks passed, and the adoption paperwork went through the appropriate channels in working order much to Nathan and Gwen's delight. However, the day before they were scheduled to leave, Gwen announced she would no longer be joining Nathan, and insisted he collect Heidi in Germany without her. Not choosing to argue, Nathan made a few phone calls and arranged for her to sign a Power of Attorney, allowing him to sign any last-minute documents on her behalf. He also arranged for their new nanny, Madeline, to accompany him. It was odd that Gwen decided not to come along, but Nathan assumed her nerves were getting the best of her and that she needed a little more time to prepare.

With the long journey ahead of them, Nathan and Madeline left with Michel before the sun rose the next morning. Hours later, they arrived in Mainz and stopped for a quick lunch. Afterward, Michel went back to the car for a nap while Nathan and Madeline walked up to the red sandstone building next to the cathedral. He took the opportunity to privately talk to Madeline in French.

"From time to time, there will be things I need to ask you to do for me. You won't be able to tell Madame Schwartz. Things like accepting packages or letters. Will you be able to keep these exchanges confidential?"

"*Oui, Monsieur.*"

"*Trés bien.* I'm glad I can count on you."

As they continued walking, he smiled to himself realizing it was Mother's Day weekend. They entered the side portal door and went straight into the open door of the Reverend Mother's office.

"Good morning, Mr. Schwartz."

Nathan shook Mother Agnes's extended hand.

She appeared confused and tilted her head. In English, she said, "And, you are? Nanny Madeline?"

"Yes, I am. *Bonjour,* nice to meet you." Madeline stood next to Nathan in her muted blue sweater and striped, knee-length skirt. Her brunette hair was tied up and accentuated her severe bangs, which made her look younger than her twenty-two years.

"Mr. Schwartz, I'm surprised to see you without your wife."

Nathan bowed his head. "Forgive me. She needed to finish preparing a few details. I should've called and told you in advance."

"I understand. Do you have the authorization documents?"

"Yes, I have." He sat down in the familiar straight-backed mahogany chair, unsnapped the two locks on his monogrammed briefcase and placed a folder on her desk.

Mother Agnes peered at the papers inside. "It looks like the attorney took care of everything." She pushed another document across her desk. "Sign this release form for your wife and yourself."

"Of course." After signing, he reached back into his briefcase and pulled out a manila envelope filled with Deutsche Marks. He slid both the document and envelope across the desk before snapping the locks shut on his case. "I hope the contents will help your work."

She opened the envelope and peered inside. "Mr. Schwartz, *Vielen Dank,* how generous! This gift will certainly help."

"Consider the sum an anonymous donation. Please divide it equally between the cathedral, the rose gardens, and the sisters' charitable work."

"That can be arranged."

Sister Claire hurried into the room holding her charge, with tears in her eyes. Her lower lip quivered. "Goodbye, my little one." She kissed Heidi's head, placed her into his arms, and backed out through the doorway.

"Hello, Mousey. You look lovely in pink. What is this?" He pulled the blanket away from her body. "A little, stuffed bunny. So sweet of Sister Claire, I'm sure she will miss you." He sat mesmerized by his new daughter.

"Sister Claire kept Heidi in her cell all this time. I warned her not to grow too attached, but I was ignored." Mother Agnes paused. "You look perplexed, Madeline."

"I'm sorry, what is a cell?"

"It is what we call a bedroom. Where will Heidi Rose be sleeping?"

"In a room on the third floor near me," Madeline replied. "When she's older she'll move to her own room across from her parents on the floor below mine."

"Very nice."

"I was wondering if you could provide us with some of the formula Heidi's been taking for the ride home."

"Yes, of course, I should have thought of that." Mother Agnes dialed the phone on her desk. After a moment of silence, she said, "When Sister Claire gets back to the hall, ask her to bring Heidi Rose's belongings to my office, with six bottles of formula."

Sister Claire returned ten minutes later with a canvas bag stuffed with clothing and cloth diapers. The glass bottles were nestled in the middle to keep them secure. Madeline took the bag and checked the bottles. "Thank you, for your help."

Nathan stood up a bit awkwardly with Heidi in his arms and readjusted the blanket around her tiny body. "I will always remember your kindness. You have both been a tremendous help. *Vielen Dank*, Sister Claire. Many thanks, Mother Agnes."

Sister Claire escorted them out through the side of the building where Michel waited by the Mercedes. At the door of the car, Nathan passed his new daughter over to Madeline. He turned toward Sister Claire and waved goodbye. She stepped backward, vanishing through the portal door.

He smiled and decided right then and there, after one look at Madeline rocking Heidi in her arms, that they'd hired the best nanny within his diplomatic circles.

"Monsieur, will you sit in the back seat?"

"No, you need to be able to spread out," Nathan said in French. "I will stay in front with Michel. You can pass Heidi to me whenever you like. Don't mention I sat up front to Madame Schwartz. We'll shift seats before we arrive in Paris."

"*Oui, Monsieur.*"

Nathan handed Michel the canvas bag. The chauffeur placed it on the floor of the Mercedes behind his seat where Madeline could easily reach it.

"*Merci beaucoup*, Michel." Madeline adjusted Heidi in her arms and scooted across the seat behind Nathan.

Half-way into the journey home, Nathan asked Michel to stop in Reims, so they could all stretch. Nathan took a quick stroll down the street and bought a single yellow rose. Back at the car, he didn't get into the front seat again. Madeline moved a few things over, and he got in next to her. The remaining two-hour drive back to Paris was uneventful, and the traffic in the city was as congested as always.

Upon reaching Rue Desbordes-Valmore, Nathan got out of the car with Heidi cradled in his arms and walked up the path toward the row house. Gwen hurried down the worn marble steps. She looked like she would burst into a run if he didn't hurry up and reach her first.

"I'm so glad you're back, darling. I've been waiting by the living room window for hours. I tried to read my book, but I couldn't. I should've gone with you!"

He gave her the yellow rose he'd picked up in Reims, then passed Heidi into her arms and enfolded them both in his. Nathan kissed each of their foreheads one after the other and said, "This baby is our little miracle."

"Yes, it is a beautiful day to become a mother!" Gwen put her nose to the blossom. "The rose smells lemony. I could eat it right up!" She pulled Heidi's tiny hands from under the blanket and gave each one a tender kiss.

In the living room, Gwen turned toward Nathan. "How was the trip home?"

"All in all, quite peaceful. Heidi had moments of restlessness and a few tears, but we got through with a couple of bottles."

"She's so calm," Gwen remarked. "I hope she won't be like my sister's son at night. I remember Edward being so cranky and strange. He didn't sleep well during the first months of his life. Eileen said it was colic."

Nathan watched as his wife cooed and cuddled their new child with a blissful gleam in his eye. He hadn't seen her this ecstatic in years and it brought renewed hope that everything would work out for the best.

"It's hard to believe my nephew is in high school and his new cousin is only a baby," Gwen exclaimed.

"It is quite extraordinary."

Madeline walked into the room.

Gwen said, "Dorothea cooked a lovely dinner, and she saved some for you. Madeline, hurry on over to the kitchen and eat.

Afterward, I want you to give Heidi a bath and put on the new outfit I left in the crib."

"Yes, Madame."

Nathan caught a glimpse of Madeline as she darted her eyes toward the hall and back at him. He thought this was her way of signaling him, and that she might need to speak with him privately.

"Gwen, I'll be right back." He followed Madeline out of the room and down the hall to the kitchen.

"Madeline, what is it?" he said in a strident whisper.

"Monsieur Schwartz, I just fully unpacked Heidi's things from Mainz and found a letter tucked under a flap in the bottom of the bag. It's not from the nuns, and I didn't know if you wanted Madame to see it right away." She held out a parchment paper envelope.

Nathan took it from her, pulled out a piece of paper the size of a thank you note, and read the contents. "Hmm, I don't have time to transcribe the German text. I know Madame won't like it, but she needs to see it written out in English. I'll telephone Mr. McGwire, stay nearby."

In the kitchen, he grabbed the receiver from the base of the phone that hung on the wall. As he dialed each number, the rotary clicked around and around. A ringing began, and soon the line on the other end was picked up.

"Bonjour?"

"Hello, David, this is Nathan."

"Hello, old chap."

"I'm back. Everything went well, except—for some reason— there's a signed letter from *you know who* in the bottom of Heidi's bag. Madeline found it…"

"What? The mother agreed to remain anonymous."

"Regardless, can you look at it tonight and write it out in Eng-lish for Gwen?" Nathan voice lowered and cleared his throat. "I'm not going to hide this from her. I need you to have a look before she tears it to pieces."

"Sounds risky to show it to her at all." David sounded distracted and irritated. "Are you sure?"

"Yes, I know it doesn't make sense, but I'm sure."

"Send it over with Michel. Is he still awake?"

"I don't actually know. The car's out front."

"Wake him and send him over."

"Yes, all right." Nathan's jaw twitched.

"I'll see you for lunch on Monday?"

"Yes, at Café Magots around noon." Nathan sighed. "I'll call you in your office to confirm once I'm sure there's nothing more critical to deal with at that hour. Good night." Nathan hung the receiver back in the cradle.

He turned around, directed his attention to Madeline, and said, "Please put some food in a bag for Michel and take it out to him. The car's parked by the curb, try not to startle him when you knock on the glass, he might be asleep. Tell him I said to drive the letter over to Mr. McGwire in the strictest of confidence and wait for a response. The chore will take a half-hour at most. When he returns, place the letter on the coffee tray when Dorothea brings it into the living room."

"Oui, Monsieur."

Nathan returned to the living room. He gazed into Heidi's eyes, and they were wide open. She looked adorable swaddled in the cotton blanket.

"Nathan? Why is Madeline out front with a bag in her hand?" Gwen inquired haughtily. "I want her to eat."

"I'm sorry, darling, it's my fault. I asked her to take Michel some supper before he left."

As the sun was setting, Madeline walked into the room and over to the window. "Madame, is Heidi ready for her bath?"

While Nathan looked on, Gwen shifted Heidi over to Madeline.

"Yes, she is." Gwen touched the baby's nose. "You're a cute, little bunny. Madeline, when you're done, I'll be up to give her a bottle."

"Yes, Madame." Madeline passed by Dorothea as she came in with the coffee tray.

"Oh—there you are, Dorothea—I didn't think you heard the bell when I rang earlier." Gwen paused. "Lovely; it smells like freshly ground coffee. Just put the tray on the table." She turned away from the maid and faced the window.

"Yes, Madame," Dorothea replied.

Having seen Madeline place the envelope on the tray as Dorothea passed into the room, Nathan discreetly slipped it off the tray and slid it into the breast pocket of his suit jacket. He stepped aside, toward the window, and leaned his shoulder against the sill. Without orchestrating his wife's next movement, she sashayed across the room and poured the coffee into the two cups on the tray. While she was distracted, he pulled the envelope out of his pocket and scanned the contents.

Satisfied with David's translation, he took a deep breath and casually stated, "Darling, this note was in Heidi's travel bag. The outside reads, 'For my baby.'"

"What? Let me see." Gwen traveled across the room and snatched it out of his hand. Her eyes noticeably darted back and forth across the page. "The woman says she gave her baby up because she didn't have enough money. She wants *her girl* to have a new life, and that's what we will give *our* Heidi." A mascara-filled tear rolled down Gwen's face. "I can't read another word. That woman gave up her rights. I don't want our daughter to read this letter, not ever. Throw it away!"

"Gwen, you sound attached to Heidi already." A wide smile spread across his face. "I'll dispose of the letter later." He coaxed it out of her tight grip and brushed her forehead with a kiss.

"All right, just get rid of it. The literature I've read on adoption says children should only focus on their new families. Their past should be forgotten. I don't know how Mother Agnes could've approved of this—this letter."

"Yes, I think you're right." Nathan kissed her on the cheek. "Excuse me, darling, I'll take care of it right now." He carried the letter upstairs to his office and locked it in a concealed compartment within his desk, then collapsed in his leather chair. After reflecting on the entire adoption ordeal, he reminded himself that he had everything he could ever want. A beautiful wife, a fulfilling career, and now an adorable daughter.

Chapter 3

Nathan arrived at work bright and early on Monday morning. He was looking forward to talking with David over lunch and finalized the arrangements over the phone. They agreed not to meet at their usual spot near the American Embassy. Instead, they decided to cross the River Seine separately, and arrive at Café Les Deux Magots, in Saint Germain, promptly at noon. As the minutes ticked by, Nathan filled them busying himself with minor tasks at his desk. Finally, the appointed hour was near, and he walked off the embassy grounds taking a circuitous route to clear his head. He arrived a little behind schedule and found David sitting at one of the small outdoor café tables under the shade of an emerald-colored umbrella.

"Bonjour." David stood and firmly shook Nathan's hand. They sat down across from each other. Since their last meeting, David's dimpled chin had grown an auburn tuft of whiskers.

"I haven't seen you in weeks." Nathan chuckled. "Your new disguise suits you."

"Well, I was feeling rebellious. A goatee added to my mustache and voilà, a Van Dyke." David's head bobbed left and right nervously while stroking his chin. "You chose an interesting spot to meet. It's more private, and we won't likely see any of our State Department pals, who would undoubtedly overhear our conversation."

"If it's good enough for Hemingway, it's good enough for us." Nathan joked. "These last weeks have been exhilarating, but exhausting."

The waiter appeared in a black suit resembling a tuxedo, complete with a white bow tie and apron. He brought each of them a glass of red wine and a plate of cheese. The smell of fresh bread wafted past them from a bakery up the street.

"How's our widdle baby?" David lit two cigarettes and passed one to Nathan.

"Oh please," Nathan grimaced, "don't use playful baby remarks. And, certainly, don't say *our* baby. People will start asking questions we don't want to answer."

"Sorry mate, you're right." David pulled out a trinity cap from his briefcase. "Here's a new hat for you."

Nathan laughed at the metaphor. "Oh, very nice." He tucked the cap into the folds of his trench coat. "Well, you'll be glad to know, Heidi is settling in beautifully. We pulled it off. I wish we could tell our wives what actually happened."

"I know. I'm sorry, we can't risk telling them the truth. To make things less complicated, I didn't tell the birth mother I was involved with the adoption proceedings, either. She believed the nuns were in charge and agreed it would be best if she wasn't aware of the details and could go on with her life." He put his head in his hands. "A fine friend I turned out to be to her! I got too involved from the beginning."

Nathan tried to comfort him. "Take it easy. Everything's all right now."

David continued, "This entire situation was a mess from the start."

"Yes, yes. Nevertheless, Gwen and I have wanted a baby for years."

"The nuns were truly a godsend, but—still—I feel horrible. No woman should have to give up her child. There just weren't any other reasonable options." David put his hand inside his dark-blue suit jacket, pulled out a handkerchief, and wiped his brow.

"Ack!" Nathan exclaimed. "I was the one who recommended you and her husband for those activities in Wiesbaden."

Nathan regretted helping the CIA with selecting the pilots for the U-2 missions. One ill-fated flight tore apart a family and created chaos that was only beginning to ebb. Yet, at the same time, his remorse was subdued by the realization that, had those events not occurred, his life wouldn't have changed for the better.

"We deal with stress—life and death situations—regularly at work, but this situation with the baby has undone me!" David countered.

"We are used to keeping secrets."

"Yes, but this is personal! I wish I'd never been sent to Germany. Going home to Sadie and acting like nothing happened was more challenging than I expected."

"I'm sure she didn't notice anything unusual." Nathan signaled the waiter and ordered two roast beef sandwiches.

"When I first returned home to D.C., she kept asking me if something was wrong. All I could say was that my assignment was more difficult than usual, and we'd lost an officer. I couldn't risk telling her anything more."

"I think you made the right decision."

"Not too long after that, I bought Sadie her favorite perfume. It was a bottle of CHANEL N°5. I said it was a hint about our next duty station. At first, she was puzzled, but then ecstatic when I told her work would be moving us to Paris. It's hard to believe seven months have already gone by."

Nathan shook his head. "Tsk, tsk."

"What are you smiling about?" David loosened his burgundy tie and adjusted his suit jacket.

"Did you realize Chanel's real name is Gabrielle Bonheur, and she was an orphan?"

"That's an odd tangent! You and your eidetic brain. Do you always have to remember everything you read?" The corners of David's mouth turned into a wry smile.

"I can't help myself. You know, you really need to relax. Gabrielle turned out fine and so will Heidi. As for Sadie, I'm sure she's better off not knowing how the baby came into our hands." The sandwiches arrived, and Nathan took a bite out of his.

"How is that perfume lady related to Heidi? You're not making any sense," David scoffed. "Oh, never mind, I'm taking things too seriously today."

After an awkward lull ensued, Nathan said, "What was Mother Agnes talking about when she told me you had saved her life?"

"God! That was a bad day." David summoned the waiter, and said, "*L'addition, s'il vous plait.*"

After settling the bill, they silently sat at the table for another twenty minutes, emptied their glasses, and finished their sandwiches.

"We need to go back to the office," Nathan encouraged as they both stood up. "Are you going to tell me about the nuns?"

They headed down the road toward the embassy. David began. "Aaah, yes. The story—detestable—I'll keep it short. In 1951, I was on leave in Frankfurt and had just finished an early supper in a beer house. I walked out and noticed two nuns across the street. When they passed by the end of an intersecting alley, a couple of men staggered toward them. They grabbed the women and dragged them away struggling.

"I bolted across the street in between congested, oncoming traffic, which took me longer than I'd hoped. I found the older nun sitting up against the wall with blood on her face and a young nun on the ground. One drunk was holding the girl's shoulders down while the other dropped his trousers... I lost my mind and threw the guy up against the wall. He hit his head on a couple of uneven bricks and was out cold. I started on the second guy and, before I knew it, my hands were around his throat. I didn't kill him, but I came close.

"The young lady's habit was torn. She hadn't been raped, but she was stunned and bruised. I covered her with my coat and gave the older nun my handkerchief. I offered to escort them to a nearby hospital or to their church, but they were visiting the city and wanted to return to their hotel. They'd been exploring the area before the girl took her final vows at the Mainz Cathedral. She was fourteen at the time. You know her—Sister Claire."

Nathan was aghast. "Aw, thank God you were there. Now I understand why the nuns were so willing to help us with our adoption scenario." Nathan squinted one eye and wiped something out of the corner with his finger.

"I kept up with the nuns over the years. When I told them about the baby, they offered to help because of the debt they felt I was owed. Odd how everything turned out."

They stopped at the far corner of Place de la Concorde and waited for the traffic to clear before they crossed.

Nathan said, "I presume you've heard from your wife that Gwen's arranged Heidi's baptism for three weeks from this Saturday?"

"Yes, yes, she did. The American Church on Quai d'Orsay is perfect for the occasion. It's wonderful how everything's worked out. Sadie and I are so excited to be her godparents." David rested his hand on Nathan's shoulder. "I'd rather not be in a group every time I see Heidi. This Sunday, I'll figure out how to walk by your place when Madeline comes out with her. Will that work?"

"No, Madeline has the day off. Besides, she hasn't met you yet." Nathan mulled it over. "Since Gwen sleeps half the morning away, and I plan to tend to Heidi on Sundays, I'll bring her out to Jardins du Gallagher after breakfast. You'll find me there around nine o'clock."

"Very good. Back to work we go, there are countries to be saved." David sounded melodramatic.

"Always a battle to be won," responded Nathan.

"Before going back to my desk, I need to walk a little more over there." David pointed toward the Tuileries Gardens.

"All right. See you later." He left David standing on the crossroads.

Chapter 4

Four months later…

G wen got the last touches ready for Heidi's afternoon party which included propping her daughter between two pillows in the living room playpen.

"How's my little bunny?" she cooed. "I want everyone to see you when they walk into the room. The last four months have gone by so fast. You'll be sitting up all by yourself soon!"

Gwen straightened the edges of her daughter's pink, ruffled party dress and put a rattle into her little hand. There was a knock at the front door, and Gwen hurried over to the archway out of site to eavesdrop.

Within earshot, she heard Dorothea say, "*Bonjour.* Madame is waiting for you in the living room. Please follow me."

Not wanting to appear too anxious, Gwen moved back over to the playpen.

A moment later, Dorothea came around the corner. "Madame, excuse me. Your sister and nephew have arrived."

Eileen entered the room with Edward close behind her heels.

Gwen kissed Eileen once on each cheek.

Approaching with her arms open wide and a smile on her face, Gwen embraced her nephew. "Come, come, Edward." Gwen led him across the room. "Heidi is eager to meet a new young man."

"Ha, ha, that's funny, Aunt Gwen. It's good to see you, too." He straightened the lapels of his school blazer. "She's so little." He turned and faced his mother. "Mum, why didn't I get a baby sister?"

Eileen didn't respond to his inquiry. Instead, she said, "Aw, Heidi, you're adorable. Come here, sweet girl. I must scoop you up." She bent over the playpen and pulled Heidi into her arms.

Gwen noticed her outfit and gasped. "Oh, for heaven's sake, Eileen, you're wearing trousers! The newest American fashion for women, I suppose? Awful things! You'll never catch me wearing a pair."

"I made the trousers. They are quite comfortable." Eileen glanced down at Gwen's feet. "You're still wearing heels. I thought you would have moved to flats with the baby."

"Oh, don't fuss over my shoes, Eileen." Gwen took Heidi from her sister.

"All right I won't if you leave my trousers alone." She adjusted the waistband in an exaggerated manner. "By the way, Edward and I are enjoying our rooms at the Alba Opera Hotel. Staying there in the 9th Arrondissement for the month will be a pleasure."

"I'm not sure about that—but then again, you're not used to having a baby underfoot. So, I guess, the hotel is better than here." Gwen pushed a curl back into place behind her ear.

"Where's Sadie, and Claudia? Are they coming today?"

"No, I'm afraid not. Claudia has a runny nose, and I don't want her near Heidi. Besides I want all the attention on my little one today."

"Oh, that's a shame. I hope I can see them another day?"

"Of course. I imagine Claudia will be fine by next week and Sadie will bring her by."

"I see Nathan in the corridor." Eileen prodded her son. "Come along, Edward. Let's go say hello, and then you can tour the city with your uncle while I party with the girls. I know he wants to hear all about your university plans after boarding school."

Gwen gazed at her sister before speaking to Edward. "Enjoy your time with Uncle Nathan. He's been looking forward to your visit."

"Me, too. I'll see you later, Aunt Gwen."

Gwen placed her daughter back in the playpen and scanned the room before moving a small gift table beside it. With some effort, she dragged the broad Chesterfield chair to the other side of the table. Moments later, Dorothea and Madeline entered the room with two folding tables and set them up across the back wall. They walked in and out multiple times with different items. On each table, they spread an intricate lace tablecloth and tied balloons to the legs. In the middle of the first, Madeline placed a crystal vase with a dozen pink roses, a pink cake, and a bowl of red punch. On the second, Dorothea added trays of finger-sized toasted bread; some topped with cucumbers, some with pâté or caviar, others with beef tartar.

After glancing around, Gwen walked over to the table and readjusted the plates of food. Everything needed to be perfectly arranged. For the final touch, she went to the record player and selected a new 33-rpm record of a Mozart concerto, slipped it out of the sleeve by the edges, and put it on the turntable. Carefully, she dropped the diamond stylus down on the outer side of the record. The music began. Just for fun, she turned her back to the sun, and her shadow appeared. Raising her hands, she grabbed her imaginary shadow partner's hands and waltzed across the room.

"I'm back!" Eileen announced. Gwen was startled as Eileen caught her in mid-swing and commented on her performance. "You're such a good dancer. We strolled around the back garden looking at all of Nathan's plants before he took Edward to town. The roses are perfect, and the fragrances are divine." Eileen looked into the hall. "Dorothea just let a few of your friends in the front door. I'm going to hold Heidi so they can get a good look at her."

"That's a good idea," Gwen agreed.

Eileen lifted Heidi out of the playpen.

Gwen greeted each of the women entering the room with a light kiss on each side of their cheeks as they passed her a gift wrapped in pastel colors with oversized, bright bows. The women *oohed* and *aahed* over her adorable baby.

Gwen glanced at her sister. "Oh, Eileen! Be careful, Heidi's grabbing onto your pearl necklace."

"Not to worry, they're not my real ones. You're right though, probably not good to encourage such behavior." Eileen uncurled Heidi's fingers from the necklace.

After all the guests arrived, they chatted incessantly about local events for the better part of an hour until it was time for cake. After serving everyone, Gwen put a little icing into Heidi's mouth even though Eileen advised against it. The icing drooled down the corners of her mouth, and some of the bits landed on Eileen's shoe.

Gwen narrowed her eyes as Eileen grinned at her smugly. Exasperated, Gwen grabbed a napkin from the table and wiped the white, sticky mess off Heidi's face. Before her sister could say anything, Gwen took Heidi into her arms and moved across the room to the Chesterfield chair. There she sat and held her daughter close as she opened each gift. Methodically she pulled out one fancy dress after the other, along with some little toys and cardboard books. Once the items were all lined up on the table, Gwen placed Heidi back in the playpen among the pillows with a new stuffed rabbit. Gwen encouraged her friends to play charades or chat the remainder of the afternoon. She made sure they had plenty of hors d'oeuvres and rum punch before they left for the evening.

Chapter 5

Two years later, 1960...

Heidi was an easy-going baby starting from the first day they became a family on Rue Desbordes-Valmore. From the get-go, Gwen took it upon herself to take charge of Heidi's nighttime regime so Madeline could tend to her during the day without being exhausted. Every night Gwen stretched out on the Antoinette fainting sofa with a pillow behind her back in the guest room and read a book from her list. Each morning, around four, she would sneak into bed with Nathan before he woke up so he wouldn't notice her absence. Gwen realized she liked how peaceful the house was during the nighttime hours, so she kept up the practice even though Heidi had been sleeping through the night since she was six months old.

Wednesdays were the only day Gwen did not sleep until noon. Her ladies' book club meeting began at eleven in the morning, and she'd need several hours beforehand to prepare. Gwen dressed with the utmost care while rehearsing what she would say about the novel she'd finished reading the night before. She sat on the bench in front of her vanity table and gazed at herself in the mirror. The tufts of fine hair that escaped from the tightly wound pink curlers annoyed her. Slipping open the latch of each curler, her blonde hair spiraled loose and bounced down on her forehead. She positioned the curls on top of her head, secured them with bobby pins and applied a cloud of hairspray. Next, she added a dense layer of blue eyeshadow to her eyelids, followed by a thick coat of mascara on her lashes, and penciled in her eyebrows. For the *pièce de résistance*, she applied cherry-red lipstick.

From the bottom corner of her mirror, Gwen caught a glimpse of Heidi staring at her with doe-eyed awe and admiration, she supposed. With a smile, she asked, "Why are you always watching me? I'll put a little lipstick on you. Hold still." Gwen dabbed a bit on her daughter's tiny lips and added some pink rouge to her pale cheeks. "We must always look our best, even when our moods may be to the contrary."

Gwen's outfits were all the latest designs from the best stores. While her external appearance was that of a pillar of perfection, her internal reality was often full of tension and worry. To protect herself from the world's contaminants, she put on a pair of fashionable white gloves. Today she had to take a dirty taxicab to the book club meeting. She didn't have a choice because Michel was driving Nathan to various meetings around town.

Nathan and Gwen returned home that evening at about the same time.

"Hello, sweetheart, how was the book club meeting today?" Nathan asked.

"Sadie, my *bon ami*, didn't attend," Gwen announced. "I was disappointed, but she isn't feeling well. All the other women showed up, including our featherbrained newer member. Her comments were ridiculous. Sadie usually manages to re-route the woman's annoying prattling. This gathering wasn't any fun."

"Wasn't this round Jane Austen's *Emma*?"

"Yes, good of you to remember. I think I'll nickname the new woman, Harriet. It sounds appropriate since the character with the same name in the book isn't very clever either. I much prefer reading outside the group. At least, when Sadie's at the meetings, she has sensible things to say about the British. If it wasn't for her and my diplomatic duties, I don't think…"

"Well, you have to go," Nathan scolded. "Since Heidi arrived, you've stopped volunteering with the wives at afternoon charity functions, so you must at least keep going to the book club meetings. Regardless, I do appreciate you coming to all the evening events and parties I have to attend. You're always so charming, and everyone loves you. Partly, because of you, I know I get good employment reviews from my boss."

"Thank you for the compliment, dear." A long pause ensued. Glaring at Nathan, Gwen said, "Don't worry, I'll continue with the book club."

"You look a little pale. Are you all right?" Nathan touched her cheek.

Gwen grimaced. "Not really, my teeth are bothering me. I don't mean to complain, but I've been having some problems the last few weeks." She poured herself a glass of water. "I miss Eileen. It's been at least a year since our last visit. Writing letters back and forth isn't satisfying when I'm not feeling my best."

Nathan reached over and hugged her, but she pulled back from the embrace. He said, "Darling, we must get you some help. I'll look into finding a dentist or perhaps our general physician has some ideas."

"Maybe I'll feel better on my own. I hope I don't get another headache before your business party tomorrow night." Gwen ran her hand across her jaw. "I want the evening to go well for all our sakes."

There was a knock on the door around noon. Gwen stopped writing her to-do list for the party and walked over to the living room window. She plucked the curtain away to see who was there. Sadie stood on the steps. Gwen never liked surprise visits from anyone, and today that was especially true. There were only six hours left to prepare. She hurried back to her desk and sat down.

Dorothea walked into the room with Sadie and announced, "Madame, you have a visitor."

"Hello Sadie, what a surprise! Come on in." She scolded, "Darling, you should have called first and used the doorbell like everyone else."

"Calling ahead is so much more proper, but we're too close to stand on formality," Sadie announced. "Besides, you've said no one knocks. Everyone else rings the bell. I could I suppose, but how would you ever realize it's me?"

"You have a good point," Gwen conceded.

Sadie smiled and said, "Dorothea, be a dear and bring us a fresh pot of coffee."

"May I, Madame?"

"Yes, please," Gwen responded.

Dorothea disappeared. Her footsteps echoed down the staircase.

Gwen wagged her finger. "Sadie, you compromise my position with Dorothea when you ask her to bring something while I'm standing right here."

"Forgive me, darling. You know I'm incorrigible!"

"Today is not a good day to be difficult. I'm getting the house ready for one of Nathan's work parties. The seating chart and place cards aren't finished yet. It's my least favorite task, I worry about putting the right people next to each other at the table. I'm so behind. Didn't David tell you about the soirée?"

"Yes, I'm aware. I'm sorry I barged in on you. At my house, I like friends to feel they can walk in without warning."

Frustrated, Gwen replied, "Yes, I know you do. Rules are different here. We need to keep the doors locked. Don't forget we were robbed the year before you moved here. Where did the State Department send David this time?"

Sadie slid a chair up to the desk and sat down. "They didn't send him anywhere. He took Claudia to London to visit his aunt. Oddly, the sun's pretty bright over there these days. I told him to make sure Claudia keeps her hat on. Her blonde hair and fair skin seem to attract the sun. Last week, her face was a little red." Sadie's New England accent was more pronounced than usual. "I can't believe she's four-years-old already. Time flies! David suggested I come see you while they were gone. So thoughtful of him, don't you think?"

"Well, yes." Gwen crossed her arms above the belt on her form-fitting dress. "Why didn't you go with him? You like his family."

"He asked me, but I wanted a few days to myself. I'll go next time."

"I'm so happy David was transferred to Paris. The first years here were lonely without you."

"It's wonderful being together again in such a glorious city," Sadie replied.

Heidi ran into the room with Madeline at her heels and interrupted their conversation. Sadie scooped Heidi up and gave her a big, loud, puckered kiss on the cheek before putting her down. "She is so sweet."

Madeline ushered Heidi back out of the room.

"Thinking back, it was so difficult being away from David when he went on his mission to Germany when Claudia was only a year old. He missed Claudia's milestones—crawling, walking. I still think about the months we lost together."

"Yes, I know, we've talked about this before. You know he didn't really have a choice, he had to go. I thought it would have been fun for you and Claudia to come here during part of that time, but your mother needed you."

"Yes, she did. She was so sick, and now she's gone."

Gwen wasn't sure what she wanted to say, but after a lull in the conversation, she said, "I'm glad your mother had an opportunity to meet Claudia. I'm sorry she was so sick in her last days," Gwen sympathized. "I wish I could have been more helpful."

"You were far away," Sadie responded wistfully. "I didn't expect you to do anything. I'd rather not talk about my mother and don't start talking about yours. We always feel melancholy for days afterward." Sadie moved out of the desk chair and leaned up against the built-in bookshelf. "Gwen, I'll help you finish getting ready for the party and leave before it begins."

"Wonderful! You can prepare some of the hors d'oeuvres. I ordered most of the items from the caterer, but I wanted to make a tray of cucumber and cream cheese sandwiches as well as smoked salmon on toast. Dorothea is setting up the supplies in the dining room."

"Shall I get started?"

"No, wait until we finish our coffee."

"In the meantime, tell me why this particular soirée is more difficult than the others? You've successfully managed parties your entire married life."

"I have, haven't I?" Gwen smiled and then lamented, "I'm fairly certain the embassy is sending a finance inspector tonight." She stood up and paced around the room, moving things on the tables, adjusting pictures on the walls.

"For heaven's sake! Inspectors are always a possibility. They pop in on parties all the time. I can't imagine you ever violating State Department protocol." Sadie hesitated. "Is anyone new and important attending or are your nerves acting up today?"

"Oh Sadie, I love that you understand me. Charles De Gaulle and President Eisenhower are coming." Gwen lowered herself down onto the Chesterfield.

"No wonder you are jumping out of your skin, but the inspector shouldn't be a threat. He's only making sure you're using your entire party allowance efficiently." Sadie straightened a sofa pillow and sat down. "He couldn't possibly have any complaints, other than to say you don't spend enough. Your etiquette is flawless, and you're always charming. Besides, you've already met De Gaulle and Eisenhower."

"Thank you, you're right, I shouldn't worry." Gwen settled back into the chair just as Dorothea arrived with some coffee and cookies. "My acting career comes in handy when my nerves are raw." Hopping out of the chair, Gwen hurried over to the liquor cabinet. "A little Irish whiskey in my coffee helps. Do you want some?"

"Sure. A hot toddy at two in the afternoon sounds like a heavenly treat. A little early, but why not? It's the right hour somewhere in the world! Please, try and relax for half an hour."

"Sadie, a hot toddy is heated whiskey, honey, and assorted other things. You're goofy, but you always help me unwind. Between you and Nathan, I feel balanced most of the time. You two keep me grounded."

"How can you be gloomy when you have a toddler that keeps you on your toes? She's added so many new dimensions to your life—I know Claudia is my sunshine."

"You have an advantage over someone my age. Some days I hardly know what to do with her." Gwen's voice trailed off. "I'll be glad when Heidi can talk in full sentences, and I can tell her stories she'll understand. It's taken her longer than most since she'll be bilingual."

"You'll be fine. Nanny Madeline is a gem and quite the expert with young children. You were so lucky the Kendricks' moved, and she didn't want to go with them."

"I'm a little envious," moaned Gwen. "Heidi seems to prefer playing in the sandbox and the garden with Madeline. Sometimes it seems like she's more of a mother to her than I am. I realize I can't be all things to our daughter, so I bite my lip and say nothing." Gwen decided to stop complaining and sent Sadie into the dining room to make the sandwiches while she finished the seating charts for the party. Once the event was over, she planned to focus on Heidi.

Chapter
6

Gwen hadn't seen a dentist since they'd left their home in the States. She was afraid to go in Paris, but the reoccurring ache in her mouth didn't give her a choice. Nathan found her an English-speaking dentist who discovered two cavities and filled them during the appointment. He then declared her bite radically out of alignment, and she was—no doubt—grinding her teeth while she slept. The situation could be remedied by filing her teeth to a more even and balanced proportion. Gwen thought this was a reasonable solution since her smile was affected and her outward appearance was so important. She agreed to return for a longer appointment the following week.

After the next grueling two-hour session, Gwen was quite addled. As she got back in the car, she asked Michel in French, "Michel, please, take me to bed, quickly."

"Madame?" he replied, startled. "I think your French is…"

"Oh, my goodness! I'm sorry, Michel, I'm so embarrassed." Gwen's cheeks felt noticeably warmer. "My session with the dentist was quite difficult. I want to go home and sleep. It was not my intention to suggest anything inappropriate."

"*Oui*, Madame, I understand." Gwen noticed his smile in the rear-view mirror.

The traffic on the way home was worse than usual. Michel helped her out of the car and up to the house before leaving. After unlocking the door, Gwen went straight to the living room to rest on the sofa with a Vogue magazine. A half-hour passed. The Novocain was wearing off, and her jaw twitched. The throbbing pain that followed was unbearable. She struggled to rise from her reclining position and slogged across the room to the telephone. Grabbing the receiver off the cradle, it felt heavier than usual. The pain in her mouth increased, and she squeezed the receiver. She dialed Nathan's work number, but heard nothing on the line and began to panic.

Nanny Madeline walked in with Heidi. "Ohhh, Madame Schwartz, are you all right?"

"No, Madeline." Gwen's voice cracked. "My dental appointment was a disaster. My head is killing me."

Heidi reached out. A mischievous smile spread across her face.

Gwen frowned. "No, I can't hold you now, precious. Mommy is sick."

The toddler's smile turned into a pout.

"Madeline, the lines are down—I'm desperate. Go to the embassy and tell Mr. Schwartz I need him."

"Can Michel drive me?"

"He's left for the afternoon—you'll have to find another way."

"But, Madame, how will I enter the building?"

"Tell the sergeant at the desk who you are and ask him to phone Mr. Schwartz's secretary. Go, now! It's an emergency! You have to take Heidi with you. I can't possibly look after her."

"She just woke up from her afternoon nap and should be fine."

"Yes, yes—just hurry!"

Madeline was out the door with Heidi planted on her hip. She didn't want to waste time pulling out the pram or flagging down a taxi on the main avenue. Instead, she ducked into the nearest Métro station at La Muette. She knew she could never tell Madame she used the crowded underground rail, but it was the fastest way. Thirty minutes later, after one transfer stop, they were up on Place de la Concorde. Once they were across the busy road, Madeline put Heidi down so they could walk hand in hand into the American Embassy complex on Avenue Gabriel. They passed through the gates and stopped at the guard station.

"Excuse me…"

"Yes, Mademoiselle, may I help you?"

"*Oui*," she read his name badge, "Sergeant Kane, my employer works here. His wife is having medical troubles and needs him at home."

"His name and yours, please?"

"Monsieur Schwartz. My name is Madeline Lefevre. I'm the family's nanny. This is their daughter, Heidi."

"Of course." The sergeant lifted several papers on a clipboard. "Mademoiselle Lefevre, I will call his secretary right away. Sorry for the inconvenience." He signaled another Marine to take his place at the guard station.

Heidi began to pull on Madeline's hand. She leaned over, picked the toddler up and started to sway her hips from side to side in a soothing motion. She watched the sergeant dial the telephone on the desk before placing the receiver to his ear. A line of sweat beaded across his forehead, just below his cap. Cocking her head to the side to nuzzle Heidi's soft cheek, she listened to the sergeant's words as he spoke.

"*Alo? Mademoiselle De La Croix? Pardon*, can you please ask Monsieur Schwartz to come to the front lobby? … Yes… His nanny and child are here… No, Madame Schwartz is at home."

The sergeant hung up the phone. "Monsieur Schwartz is on his way. I'll escort you into the building."

"Thank you," Madeline responded with a smile. "You look familiar. I think I've seen you before when I've taken Heidi out for long walks."

"Yes, you have, but I didn't realize you were a nanny," he whispered. "I thought you were a married woman."

"No, I'm not."

"On one of your days off, would you like to have lunch with me?"

His baritone voice gave her teenage butterflies. She blinked her eyes a few extra times and smiled the biggest smile she could manage. "Lunch would be lovely, Sergeant Kane. I have a free day in two weeks, on Sunday. Are you able to come to the Schwartzes' home at eleven o'clock that morning?"

"Perfect. I look forward to seeing you then." He handed her a pen and paper. "Please, write down the address." Madeline eased Heidi on to her feet and wrote down the information. His voice returned to normal volume as they discussed the sites of Paris.

The three of them entered the building's lobby. Monsieur Schwartz came out of a corridor a moment later. He was dressed in his usual black business suit with a muted blue tie.

Sergeant Kane stood at attention.

"At ease, sergeant."

"Yes, sir."

Heidi reached out to her father. He grasped her hands and pulled her up into his arms. "Hello, Mousey. How are you today?"

"Monsieur Schwartz…" Madeline's voice wavered.

"I'm in between meetings, what's wrong?"

"The phone line isn't working at the house. Madame has a terrible headache from her dental appointment. She said it's an emergency and needs you to come home."

She watched him put his hand on his forehead, his cheeks puffed out and his lips pursed. "I need to work out a detail or two with my secretary. I can take Heidi with me. Go on home. Tell Madame I'm on my way. Put a cold washcloth on her head and give her some of the good Courvoisier Cognac." Monsieur Schwartz put his hand in his pocket and brought out a money clip. Putting some francs into her hand, he said, "Here, for a taxi."

"Yes, Monsieur, *merci.*"

Madeline turned to the young Marine. "Thank you for your help, Sergeant Kane." She hurried out to the street, signaled for a taxi, and hummed all the way home thinking about their upcoming date.

Nathan arrived home and saw his wife stretched across the Chantelle sofa with a wet washcloth draped across her forehead.

"Thank you for coming to my rescue! I feel positively terrible," moaned Gwen. "The Cognac and aspirin Madeline gave me helped a little. I'm feeling woozy. I guess you heard the phone isn't working?"

"Yes, yes, I did." He stood over Gwen. "You're quite pale. I'd say you have a migraine. My mother suffered quite a bit with them. Let me dim the lights." Nathan turned a few lights off and checked the phone. He laughed to himself, without telling his wife there was a bit of dried soap dabbed around the base of the buttons causing the malfunction. This wasn't the first time she'd put too much soap onto a surface. Using his handkerchief, he freed the jammed buttons and dialed his office. After talking with his secretary, he sat down in the chair next to the sofa. "I fixed the phone."

"Good, that can never happen again! I felt completely cut off from the world."

"Another one of life's challenges." Nathan briefly put his hand on the washcloth on his wife's head and moved a piece of wet hair away from her face. "Now, tell me what happened."

"The dentist took a grinding tool to my molars to level them. Last week's fillings on the back of my two front teeth were easy by comparison to today. I don't think I'll ever be the same again."

"I'm so sorry, sweetheart. You've had quite a jarring experience. Let's hope you feel better when the nerves around your mouth calm down."

"My ears are ringing on and off, too. How long do you think it will take for my head to stop pounding?"

"My mother's migraines lasted a day, but they weren't connected to a dental procedure. She had problems with double vision sometimes. I don't think she had ringing in her ears."

"My eyes are fine! I don't think I could bear it if they weren't. Can you stay home the rest of the day?"

"Yes, but I don't think my associates are sympathetic about this type of emergency."

"Don't give them the details." Gwen snuggled into the Chantelle sofa.

"I suppose." He rinsed out another washcloth in the bowl on the side table and exchanged it with the one on her head. "This cooler cloth should help. May I read to you?"

"Nooo!" Her words came out sounding like a child. "I love it when you read to me, but I'm in too much pain. Just sit here and read on your own."

Chapter 7

Gwen's migraines frequently returned over the coming months, although they were never as severe as the day Nathan had to leave work. Even so, he needed to make some decisions about his career that would alter all their lives. He arranged to meet David for lunch at Café Les Deux Magots.

"Here we are again at our old stomping grounds." David sounded gloomier than he'd been in months. "A few days ago, at our couple's dinner, Gwen didn't seem to be her usual exuberant self. Is everything all right at home?"

"For the most part. Gwen is still having a devil of a time with migraines."

"I'm relieved Madeline is there for Heidi. The situation with Gwen's health is disturbing." David flagged down the waiter. He ordered two bowls of asparagus soup, red wine, and corned beef sandwiches without asking Nathan's opinion.

"It's hard to watch her suffer. Although, that's not why I wanted to meet today. Both of our current positions are under review, and I felt we should talk away from the office. I can choose to stay in Paris, take a new post, or go back to the home office in D.C. I think I need to take Gwen home." The waiter brought the wine, and Nathan swirled it around in the glass. "David, according to the scuttlebutt in the embassy, they are going to offer you a promotion in Paris. You need to be aware that there is also a spot in Luxembourg if you chose the route of ambassador."

David sputtered, "I'm not going to Luxembourg. I love Paris! There is no chance I'll accept any other overseas post unless there isn't a choice."

Nathan moved his utensils around, picked up his napkin and draped it across his lap.

"What about your house?" David said.

"I have it all worked out. You can live there after we leave. We'll see if we can get Dorothea to stay on and help in the kitchen. I think Gwen will want Madeline with us."

"I wonder what my wife will think." David rubbed his goatee.

"Sadie loves this house already. It's a natural progression to move out of your apartment to a larger place after a promotion with a significant pay raise. When you're done in Paris, I'll rent it out to other diplomatic families."

"I've kept the secret, but why didn't you ever tell Gwen you owned the property?"

"I thought I told you the details?"

David looked perplexed. "Sorry—oh, yes, I vaguely recall. We had so many things going on at the time. It was something about family money and investments."

"After Gwen and I met, I realized she didn't have a problem spending money on clothing, but she was a miser about every other expense. Initially, I wasn't bothered, but I decided not to tell her about the art or the Paris house. Honestly, I didn't want her to marry me for my money. When we arrived here, Gwen assumed the State Department rented the house for us. I didn't correct her. And, by the way, the few things you and I have bought since moving here aren't as valuable as the wartime art. It's all legit, but Gwen would never understand why I didn't tell her. Deep down I have unresolved trust issues after my first marriage failed and I can't confide in Gwen the way I suppose I should." Nathan scooped several spoonfuls of soup into his mouth.

"Yes, that makes sense," David acquiesced. "I suspect Gwen would be furious about the house and art, but not as much as she would be if we told her about Heidi. There's no need to bother her with any of it. Especially now, with her migraines. Can't the doctor give her something?"

"Yes, but the pills make her sluggish, and then she gets irritable. An aspirin and a couple of gins or a Cognac seem to do the trick—I can't complain. But, I'm also thinking, Gwen's sister can help if we're in the States."

"Yes, I see your point. Eileen is a saint." David lit a cigarette. "I'm sure she'll enjoy spending time with Heidi, especially now that Edward's away at Princeton. How will I see Heidi?"

"Your new position will require periodic visits to D.C. If you arrange to be around over a weekend, we can meet for lunch on Sundays in Georgetown or somewhere else near the State Department. I'll plan to bring Heidi with me."

"I'm impressed." David's head bobbed up and down. "You're always one step ahead of me."

"I figure, if you play your cards right, you'll be stationed stateside in three years."

"Our wives are going to love this separation," David said sarcastically.

"They'll adjust. And, when we all get back together, our little girls can interact more and develop a real friendship."

"Nathan, What about your career aspirations?"

"I'm sure I can work out something with international travel. I'll be able to take business trips away from home whenever I need to." He winked at David, knowing full well either of them could do government intelligence work from almost anywhere. "The Cold War isn't going to end anytime soon."

"I have no doubt about that," David replied.

"Gwen will just have to entertain herself while I'm traipsing all over the world. Heidi will be fine, and I'll bring her dolls from each country, so she'll know I'm thinking about her when I'm gone. Then, when I'm home, I'll make sure to have father-daughter days with her on Sundays."

David snickered. "I'm curious since you've thought everything out, what happens to our art?"

"The back room of my office will remain locked with the tapestry over the door. Years ago, Gwen asked about it. I told her the owner of the house wanted it to stay in place. When you move in, Sadie won't be able to dispute that reasoning either."

"My art collection is small compared to yours. I wager many of mine will eventually sell for a large sum. Do you think we can ever get any of them out of Europe?"

"I can ship a few pieces back to D.C., but I'd like most of it to remain in Paris. I feel we owe our girls personal letters explaining our connection. I plan to put mine in the room with the art tonight. If anything happens to us, they'll know what's going on."

"The letters are a splendid idea. I'll write mine this afternoon since there isn't much going on at the office."

Nathan continued his detached explanation. "The authentication documents are in order. I suppose if we are ever in dire straits, we can sell some pieces, but I don't see that happening in our lifetimes. The girls will decide whether to keep or liquidate it after we're gone."

"How are they going to deal with our covert lives? I hope they'll forgive us."

"At least they'll be financially secure. I'm hoping they'll understand and love us anyway." Nathan glanced at his wristwatch. "Let's stroll back to the office. I hope our wives won't be too upset when we tell them about the move."

"Sadie should be fine since we'll be staying here, but even if we weren't, she's very good natured about things." David paused. "I'm worried about you."

"Don't be. This old man can handle himself. Come over to the house tonight, about eight. Tell whoever answers the door that we have a meeting and come upstairs to my office."

"Right, will do. I must say, I have thoroughly enjoyed most of our adventures."

Nathan paid his portion of the bill, David did the same, and they walked away separately to undisclosed destinations.

After work, Nathan stopped at a corner flower cart and a perfumery on his way home. He walked into the foyer of Rue Desborde-Valmore with a bouquet of red roses and placed them on the hall table. He caught Gwen inching down the main staircase backwards while she held onto the rail with one hand and spotted their daughter with the other. Heidi bumped her bottom down each step giggling.

Nathan mockingly put his hands on his hips. "Mousey, what are you doing? That is no way for a young lady to behave." Gwen moved aside when they reached the second to last step. He laughed and lifted Heidi up into his arms squeezing her affectionately.

"Are those roses over there for me?" Gwen gestured toward the table.

"But of course," Nathan said, in an exaggerated French accent.

"They're beautiful! I'm relieved to say I didn't have a headache today and can enjoy our evening." Gwen hurried over to the table, examined the bouquet and found the hidden bottle of L'Air du Temps. "Perfume! I love Nina Ricci fragrances. The crystal doves on the stopper are so delicate." She put the roses back on the hall table, dabbed a drop of the perfume on one wrist and rubbed it against the other.

"I received some news from the office today. Let's go into the living room and relax."

They left the foyer and settled down on the sofa with their daughter tucked between them.

"What's going on, sweetheart?"

"I've been offered an extension to stay here in Paris, but we have the option of returning to the States, and I'd like to take it."

"Oh, my, this is a surprise."

Nathan continued after giving his wife a few minutes to absorb the news. "Everything will be all right. I can fly back here or wherever work needs me for short periods of time."

"Yes—yes, I suppose you can." Gwen's eyes narrowed. "I hate the idea of flying, so you'll never get me on an airplane."

"Planes are so much quicker than ships. Don't worry, I won't force you to fly anywhere."

"Thank you. I really loved the ocean liner we traveled on when we came here."

"I'll book our passage as soon as everything's settled." He decided to tell her about his long-term plans. "I think I only want to work in the State Department for another ten years and then retire."

"You'll be sixty-two, that seems too young to leave," Gwen scoffed. "I imagine the State Department would appreciate your continuing to work with new recruits after you reach that age. After all, you mentored David and look how well he turned out. Or maybe some other work in a different division?"

"Perhaps, we'll see." He rubbed his nose. "Let's go back to the States and enjoy the home we designed before we left."

"Daddy?"

"She doesn't understand," Gwen said, stroking Heidi's hair. "I suppose you're right. We should go home and plan to have the house repainted after the current renters leave. But I don't like the smell of fresh oil-paint; it's so pungent."

"We've only had two sets of State Department families living in the house. It will be in good shape. If not, we'll hire someone to spruce it up; painting, carpeting and then airing it out afterward. Either way, we'll need to live at the Kenwood Country Club when we first arrive since our belongings will get to the house after us, and we'll need to buy a few pieces of furniture." Nathan gazed at their daughter. "I also think it will be better if we don't relocate her every few years like most foreign service children." Inwardly he believed Heidi could live anywhere, Gwen was who he worried about the most.

"The cherry blossom trees on Brookside Drive were so beautiful when we left. Bethesda is a nice place, but it's so different from here."

"I heard the area developed a bit more after we left, yet our street is the same. The trees are just more mature."

"A small, quiet neighborhood outside the city will be a refreshing change," Gwen said.

"We won't have a chauffeur anymore," Nathan replied.

"I imagine your daily commute will take some getting used to."

"I'll adjust, it's only seven-and-a-half-miles from the house."

"What will happen to Sadie and David? They've only been here a little over three years—I have enjoyed our time together."

"I have, too. The McGwires will remain in Paris. Another assignment for David's type of work isn't available in D.C. right now."

"Well, I hope we aren't apart for too long."

"I agree. I suspect they'll return to the States by the time our girls are the perfect age to play together."

Heidi slipped off the sofa and wandered over to her toys in the corner.

Nathan's eyes followed their daughter. Focusing back on his wife, he said, "Once we're home, you can drive into Georgetown whenever you'd like to see your sister."

"Mmm, that will be nice," Gwen announced wistfully and smoothed out her skirt. "I imagine Eileen can teach Heidi how to make clothes when she's older. I can only sew on buttons and darn socks. Sewing surely isn't one of my gifts."

"Darling, you present our guests with beautiful food and entertainment. You both have different talents."

"So true, so true."

Nathan pulled her close.

She cuddled next to him and put the inner side of her wrist up to her nose. "Thank you again for the perfume. The floral undertones are intoxicating."

"You're welcome." He kissed her wrist. "Back to our plans. Our move might happen more quickly this time since we are coming up on elections. Eisenhower's second term is nearing an end."

"Why will the presidential election affect you?"

"Eisenhower's a good man. We've worked together with NATO-related affairs for coming up on eight years, and I'll have quite an adjustment under a new administration."

"Oh Nathan, I'm sorry, I should've realized."

"We'll move soon after the new president takes office."

"I need to start making lists."

"We can do that later. I'm hungry." Nathan playfully winked. "I smell a delicious aroma floating from the kitchen—it must be my favorite roast."

"Yes, I think it is. That's odd I wasn't consulted about the menu, I'll scold Dorothea later." Gwen squeezed his forearm.

As they stood up, Madeline came into the room.

"There you are, please attend to Heidi while we eat."

"Yes, Madame."

Nathan took her hand and escorted her into the dining room. In accordance to his earlier instructions, Dorothea had covered the table with a white linen cloth and added place settings of French floral-edged china, sterling silverware, and crystal glasses. She'd also arranged the flowers from the front hall in a vase on the table. On either side, stood two tall silver candlesticks with 12-inch tapered candles glowing in the dim room.

"I wonder why the table's set so formally. Nathan, did you ask her to set the table like this?" Gwen's lips tightened. "Are we having someone important over and you forgot to tell me?"

He pulled out her chair, and Gwen sat down. "Yes, my darling. Someone important is already here. It's you!"

She blushed. "Oh! How sweet, it's me!"

Nathan moved around the table and poured some wine into their glasses before he sat down opposite Gwen. He tilted his wine glass and admired the ruby color of the Chateau Margaux. Not really expecting a positive result, he casually said, "Once we're resettled, I'd like to get a dog."

"Absolutely not! They scare me."

Dorothea entered the room with serving dishes and place them on the table. She filled their plates with a vegetable medley, pearl potatoes, and slices of roast beef.

"Yes, but having our own dog would be different since we'd raise it to be gentle. It would love us and never pose a threat to anyone we know." Nathan felt quite hungry and took more on his fork than usual while he thought about his childhood golden retriever. Whenever he left his parents' house, Laddy would follow him around the hills of San Francisco.

"It doesn't make any difference, if we had our own dog, I would still be frightened. Besides, they're dirty creatures."

"Well, that's a shame. I thought a dog would be a fine addition to our family. Having one around would make *me* feel complete."

"I have too much to think about now." She pushed the potatoes away from her vegetables and ate each pile separately. "Although, it would be nice to get a small animal of some *other* sort for Heidi when she's older. I would much prefer a cat like the outdoor ones my parents kept."

"Perhaps." Nathan savored his wine.

Gwen glanced around and whispered, "What about Madeline? Heidi will be devastated."

"Madeline can fly to D.C. after we take the ship home. Her paperwork will take longer than ours. Dorothea will have to stay behind in Paris, so maybe Madeline won't mind adding to her current duties."

"I'm sure I can't function without a nanny! I hope she'll agree to come with us, but I'll wait to ask until we get closer to our departure date," Gwen spoke in a hushed voice. "I'm afraid to tell her now because she might leave us before we can make alternate arrangements. Besides Christmas is in two months and getting a new person at this time of year would be impossible."

"Don't wait too long, we'll be moving in the spring."

"I won't, don't worry. I'll mention it to Madeline in January."

They sat in silence for the next ten minutes. Nathan breathed deeply in an effort to clear his mind of all distractions. Before he knew it, his plate was empty.

Gwen smiled in his direction. "Even with everything we have to do, I'm excited about going home."

He thought, for a moment, about how Heidi came to them and decided he needed to recheck her documents before the move. Then said, "The government will handle all the travel arrangements, including packing, like they did when we left the States."

"The entire process is so much work even with their help." Gwen picked up a bell on the other side of her placemat and rang it to summon Dorothea.

"It certainly is." Nathan couldn't disagree.

Dorothea appeared. "Madame, may I take your plates, and bring coffee and dessert?"

"Yes, thank you."

She came back with two coffees and bowls of crème brûlé.

Nathan tried not to rush, but it was almost seven-thirty. After a respectable amount of time passed, Nathan stood up. "Excuse me, I need to go to my upstairs office. David and I have a meeting in fifteen minutes."

"Darling, you hadn't mentioned that before."

"I'm sorry, my mistake. Please send him up when he arrives."
He kissed Gwen and left the room.

Nathan trudged up the stairs and stopped in front of his office door.
After struggling to untangle the key from the others in his pocket,
he unlocked the door and stepped inside. With a heavy sigh, he
closed the door and locked himself in before leaning his back
against the wooden panels. He Deciding not to waste another
minute, he walked over to the right side of the room, grabbed a
bottle of Jameson Irish whiskey out of the liquor cabinet, and
poured some into a nearby glass. Carrying it to the far side of the
room, he sat down next to the window in his overstuffed leather
armchair. Gazing out at the city he loved, he hoped he wasn't
making a mistake leaving. His contemplations were interrupted at
quarter-past eight by a knock on the door.

Nathan got out of the chair and lumbered across the room.
"David, is that you?"

"Yes, open up. Sorry I'm late, I was chatting with Gwen
downstairs.

He pulled the door halfway open, and David scooted through.
Nathan peered down the hall before closing and locking it again.
"Let me pour you a whiskey." He did so and handed it to David.
"Relax, I've got everything in order. Did you bring your letter to
Claudia?"

"Yes, I've got it." David unbuttoned his shirt and pulled out a
white envelope.

"In your shirt?"

"Yes, I didn't want Sadie to see it and ask questions I couldn't
answer. While I was in the foyer with Gwen, a question occurred to
me. I didn't ask her, of course. Will your neighbor continue to look
after the house after we've all left?"

"Oh, yes." Nathan smiled knowing he'd never have to worry about Monsieur Rousseau's loyalty. "The man loves his French wine, and I'll provide him with several cases each year. If anything is amiss, Monsieur Rousseau will be sure to call my contacts at the embassy."

"I guess I shouldn't be surprised since you two have known each other since you bought this place after the war."

"We can never be too careful, I'm glad you asked."

"Good then, let's get on with our work. No time to relax."

"All right, let's sort through everything." Nathan went to the liquor cabinet. Pushing on a corner button and nob simultaneously, a small compartment revealed itself. He took out a key. The two men went behind the desk, ducked around the tapestry, and entered the hidden room.

Nathan yanked a cotton light cord that hung down along the side of the wall. "I already put my letter to Heidi in here." Nathan turned to the corner and pointed at the Victorian parlor chair.

"I'll put Claudia's there, also." David slid his letter under Heidi's.

"Wait... I need to tie these into two separate groups. Here are some ribbons I put aside." Nathan pulled them out from behind the chair.

"Yellow ribbon, nice touch. What's the order?"

"This one—" Nathan held up an envelope— "as you can see has, 'Open Me First, Heidi Rose,' written on it, which will tell the girls the origin of the art. And then, 'Open Me Next,' on this oversized manila envelope, which contains a copy of the inventory list. The official authentication documents are in the bank safety deposit box on Rue Montorgueil. We'll wrap these by themselves. The more personal letters we'll put in another bundle. Look under the chair. I left them a bottle of Romanée-Conti."

David eyeballed the wine and pretended to swoon. "Oh, how romantic and extravagant. Don't you think they might need something stronger?"

"No." Nathan grabbed one of the envelopes and added to the heading in bold letters, 'A fine wine is under the chair. Enjoy it, and don't consider the cost.' Nathan continued, "We need to review the inventory. Everything must be in order before I leave Paris. One can never be too prepared."

David muttered under his breath, "So many secrets."

Paintings hung in orderly rows on the walls, covering every available inch. Nathan droned on in a monotone voice. "The paintings have catalog numbers on the back, but I put sketches on the front of the sealed crates so that the girls can understand the order of things." Nathan looked over some of the items. "Let's see—*Diana and Nymphs by Ruben, The Lovers: The Poet's Garden IV by Van Gogh, Portrait of Trude Steiner by Klimt.*"

"We are something," David interjected.

Nathan hesitated before continuing, "I'm glad I was able to acquire them to help the museums during and after the war." He didn't go over the oddly shaped crates down the center of the room or the ones they had purchased together.

David pointed at several of the crates. "We've had a jolly good time buying those at the auctions." Abruptly, David stopped talking and left the display room. "I think I've had enough of this tonight it's already nine-fifteen."

"That's fine with me." Nathan tuned out the light, locked the door, repositioned the tapestry, and meandered over to his desk. He sat down and said, "I pray every night that we haven't made a mistake with Heidi and Claudia or our wives."

"Don't worry, Nathan. As you're apt to say, 'Everything will be fine.'" David poured himself another whiskey and knocked it back. He walked over to Nathan with the bottle and placed it on the desk. "What are you doing?"

"I need to check some tax papers." He remembered the note from Germany. "Oh damn, I didn't leave Heidi's birth mother's note with the others!"

"Bloody hell! You still have that thing?" David slapped his forehead.

"Yes, well, I did take it away! We won't tell Gwen it wasn't quite the way she requested. I want Heidi to have a chance to find out the entire truth someday."

"I thought Gwen wanted you to burn the thing."

"I'm sure she did, except I didn't." Nathan unlocked the compartment in his desk and retrieved the letter. Going back into the tapestry room, he added it to the personal envelopes. "I'll write three, four, and five on the letters."

"They'll figure out what you're up to—I have no doubt."

"I wish we could see the look on the girls' faces when they learn our secrets. I plan to sort out the rest of the details with the estate managers in D.C."

"We're wretched men!" David's face looked grim. "Families shouldn't conceal things from each other the way we have, but with us it's impossible. It's a wonder we can find anything interesting to talk to our wives about at the end of each day that isn't confidential."

"At least our work at the office is for the betterment of mankind." Uncharacteristically, Nathan grabbed the Jameson whiskey bottle and took a quick swig without pouring it into a glass.

"You truly believe that?"

"Mostly." Nathan shrugged.

January, 1961...

Gwen stood in the front foyer looking up the staircase as Madeline brought Heidi down dressed in a wool coat with a fur collar and hat. It was hard to believe their daughter would be three years old in a couple of months. But even more difficult to accept was the fact that their time in Paris was coming to an end. Gwen hoped with all her heart that their treasured nanny would agree to go with them.

"Madeline?"

"Yes, Madame?"

"Before you two leave the house for your afternoon stroll, I have some news." Gwen wanted to get this over with. "We are going to move back to the States this spring; two months from now. Will you consider coming with us?"

"Madame?"

"I understand why you didn't leave Paris with Mrs. Kendrick. After all, their daughter was older, and you didn't want to go to Africa. Heidi is still young, and she needs you." Gwen paused. "What do you think?"

"I have never left Paris. I need some time to decide." Madeline turned a deep shade of pink. "I want to talk to Sergeant Kane."

"Hmmm, I didn't realize you'd become so serious."

"Yes, Madame." Madeline smiled sheepishly. "He's from South Carolina, and I know he'll want to go home at some point. Just the other day, he was talking about working in Washington, D.C. I will see him this weekend."

"This position will last for another three years until Heidi goes to school when she's six. You will have a private apartment on the lower level. We will not have a maid anymore, so I'll need you to help in the kitchen. Your wages will be increased to compensate you for the extra work. If you marry, later on, you will need to find other accommodations."

"Would I be able to work for you during the day if I marry?"

"Certainly, but we don't have to figure that part out today. I hope you'll come with us. Our nation's capital is very interesting. Please, let me know soon. My husband will need time to arrange a work visa for you."

"I will, thank you."

Gwen studied her daughter. "You look quite restless, and I'm sure you're hot in that adorable coat." She escorted Madeline and Heidi to the front door. "Go cool off outside. I'll begin writing letters to my friends in the States while you're gone."

Gwen closed the door behind them and walked into the living room. She sat at her desk and tried to relax after talking to Madeline, but found it was too difficult. A glass of Cognac would certainly solve the problem. As she sipped on the golden liquid, she busied herself with moving pieces of ivory writing paper and pens from one side of the desk to the other until the vertical spaces between each item matched every other gap. In her mind, she planned how to make each letter a page long and keep most of the content the same with several personal touches to each recipient. Most importantly they needed to be neat and precise.

Spring arrived, and the State Department scheduled their moving date for March tenth. Heidi's third birthday would be celebrated in the United States. The movers would come the first of March and Gwen planned to pack their clothing in suitcases the night before their arrival with Madeline's help. For the remainder of their time in Paris, they would sleep in the house on beds that would be left behind for the McGwires' move-in date at the end of March.

While all the commotion was going on, to keep Heidi from getting under their feet, Gwen gave her a pile of toys and a bag from Le Bon Marche department store filled with white tissue paper. Their daughter stood next to the bag pushing the toys and paper in and out. The bag would go with them on the ocean liner to entertain Heidi during the voyage.

On the day of their departure, Gwen sat on one of the remaining beds with Heidi and rustled through a suitcase. She found a fresh little dress and pulled it over her daughter's head. Brushing Heidi's tousled hair, she said, "We are going to have so much fun in America."

"Mommy, what is A-merica?" Heidi's legs wiggled over the edge of the bed.

"A faraway land. We will go on a big boat."

"Like the boat in my bath?"

"No, Heidi, a boat bigger than this house," Gwen laughed.

Heidi stretched up her arms and tried to touch the ceiling with her hands. "Sooooo big. Je suis prête. Maddie à venir?"

"Yes, Heidi. Madeline is coming. You speak French very well. In America, everyone speaks English."

"English in America." Heidi's hands collapsed into her lap.

"You are a smart girl. Get ready we are going soon."

"Maddie's going on the boat?" Heidi slid off the bed and planted her feet on the floor.

"No, she'll come to America soon, but not today. She's with Claudia for a few weeks."

Whining, Heidi scrunched up her face. A tear ran down her cheek. "When, Mommy? I want Maddie now."

"Soon, my little one, soon. Remember, Maddie said goodbye to you yesterday." Gwen bent down to her level. "No more tears."

Gwen took Heidi's hand and coaxed her out the front door. "Michel is loading our suitcases into the car and your shopping bag of toys. Come, let's go to your daddy. He's out front."

When they emerged, Gwen waved at Nathan. He came up to the door, locked it, and put the key in his pocket. Their neighbor stood on his own front steps. Nathan waved while calling out, "*Au revoir, Monsieur Rousseau.*"

The man tipped his hat, the same way he had done on the first day they moved in, but this time he spoke, "*Au Revoir.*"

Gwen squinted. "He's a peculiar character. He's never said a word to me. Eight years here on Rue Desborde-Valmore and nothing!"

"Too late to do anything about that now. Besides, he's young and a bit socially awkward around women. I understand he's lived in that house his entire life. Come, darling, let's be on our way. Michel is driving us directly to the ferry."

After a two-hour drive from Paris, they arrived at Dieppe on the coast and got out of the car.

"Thank you for everything, Michel," Nathan said, while Gwen looked on. "You have been a godsend and done so much for us beyond the call of duty. I hope to see you again." He shook Michel's hand crisply while simultaneously slipping some French francs into his palm. Gwen smiled knowing Michel would appreciate the tip.

"*Merci.* It has been an honor to assist the family all these years." Michel lifted their four suitcases out of the car and slid them onto a luggage cart. A porter from the ferry rolled their belongings on board.

After they settled themselves in seats with Heidi, Gwen said, "So, Nathan—my walking encyclopedia. What are the specifications of the ocean liner we're going on after this boat?"

"Well, let's see. It's five city blocks long which is about 990 feet long. It can hold 1,972 passengers and 1,011 crew members. The best part; it's the fastest ocean liner in the world at 35 to 40 knots per hour which translates to approximately 40 to 45 miles per hour. Her sister's name is the HSM Queen Mary, but she's not as fast. Once we board, we'll be in New York City in under four days and into D.C. the day after via the train. We'll be home before you know it."

"Good, that's good. I'm in a hurry to get home." She leaned into Nathan. "Here take Heidi, she's too much to carry."

They took the three-hour ferry across to Southampton, England and spent the night in town. In the morning, they boarded the SS United States. The ocean liner slowly pulled out of the harbor, before increasing her speed to thirty-five knots per hour. Gwen and Nathan spent most of their waking hours chasing Heidi around the deck. Gwen worried she'd fall through the rails and Nathan dropped to his knees many times rescuing her by the edge. At times, to both Gwen's and Heidi's delight, he'd whisk their daughter up on his shoulders for a 'horsey' ride. His ridiculous neighing made them all laugh.

Chapter 9

Three years later, 1964…

Heidi sat with Madeline on a stone bench listening to the birds in the garden among the waist-high rose bushes her father had planted three years before. She watched Madeline take a deep breath and begin in her usual French, "I need to tell you something."

"What is it, Maddie?"

"I remember when you started calling me that. You tried so hard to say Madeline and all that came out was Maddie."

Heidi smiled. "You call me Rosie. I like Rosie."

"When I say your name, there is no mistake it's me. I started because your middle name is Rose, and your dad likes roses." Maddie stopped talking, and Heidi waited for her to continue. "You have seen me leave with William—I mean Sergeant Kane—when I'm not with you."

"You have fun. When you come home, you're smiling."

"We are getting married in four weeks. I can't live with you anymore. There isn't enough room in this house for two married couples."

Heidi's shoulders drooped, and she nuzzled in against Maddie's arm. "I don't want you to go."

"You know I love you."

"Why are you leaving? Aren't people supposed to stay together if they love each other?"

"Many people can't stay together. There are lots of reasons. Sometimes life changes in ways we can't control."

"Why?"

"You will understand when you are older."

"I want to know now!" Heidi pulled away, hugging herself. A sob started to emerge.

"I'll stay around here for a few months after we're married. Then we'll move to Sergeant Kane's hometown in South Carolina to be near his parents and sister."

"Will you come visit me? We can play hide-and-seek." Heidi relaxed a little and uncrossed her arms. She slid sideways across the bench and snuggled next to Maddie again.

"Dear little Rosie." A tear ran down Maddie's cheek.

Heidi reached over and wiped it away. "Don't cry."

"Yes, I can visit when I'm first married. But, when we move, we will be a long way from here. I will write to you on your birthday every year and visit when I can."

"I'm going to miss you every day!" Heidi's voice trembled, and giant tears rolled down her six-year-old face. "Send pictures!"

"I will. I don't think you need a nanny anymore."

"You're my friend."

"Maybe you will only miss me a little, but your parents are here. You will make new friends in first grade at your private school."

"I forgot, what's it called?"

"Maret. It's not too far away on Cathedral Avenue. There isn't a bus so your mom will drive you or she'll take turns with other parents."

"Oh." Heidi pulled on the edge of her dress. "Do I have to wear these clothes?"

"No, the school provides uniforms so that will be easy, everyone will wear the same type of clothes. The boys wear suits, and the girls wear skirts and blouses. Every day will be an adventure."

"I don't think so." Heidi's tears formed a puddle on Maddie's blouse. "*Je t'aime.* I wish you could stay with me."

"I know, but life's always changing. The weeks before I leave will go by fast. Be strong. Everything will be all right."

"You are with me all the time. Mom sleeps so much, and her head hurts. How is she going to take care of me?"

"Your mom bought some new things to keep you busy."

"That's not the same. Playing teacher and games with you is better."

"We'll just have to adjust." Maddie rubbed her back. "Claudia's family is moving here soon. Your families will spend a lot of time together."

"Claudia, yay. She sends me pictures and cards. I like it when you help me read them. I'm still learning. Reading is hard!"

"You will learn faster with more practice. Claudia liked to spend time with you when you were little in Paris. I'm sure you two will have good times together. I'm sad that I will miss seeing the McGwires."

"McGwires?"

"Sorry, that is their last name. You need to memorize everyone's full name when you meet. Sadie and David McGwire are Claudia's parents. Their house is nearby so you and Claudia will grow up together."

"Maddie, I don't want you to go away. You can explain stuff I don't understand." She stood up and broke a budding rose off the bush and peeled the petals. "I'll forget how to speak French."

"No, no. You'll have a French class at Maret every day. Talk to your dad when you want to practice or with your classmates. You'll learn many things from many people in your life."

"I know." Heidi tried to smile. Soon the effort was too much, and her face stiffened.

"Come on, try to cheer up. Go inside and find your mom. While you're looking, I'll go in the kitchen and scoop some ice cream out of the cartons. When we're done, we can make a cabin with your new Lincoln Logs."

Maddie and Heidi separated. Within a few minutes, Heidi found her mother in the sunroom. Shortly afterward Maddie walked in with bowls filled with chocolate and vanilla ice cream. They began to eat but the feast was interrupted by the doorbell. Heidi peered at the two grownups and wonder which one would respond—Maddie left the room.

Maddie opened the front door and a delivery man was standing on the other side with a slim wooden crate addressed to David McGwire care of Nathan Schwartz. Madeline signed for the package.

"Please, go around to the basement door on the side of the house. I'll meet you there."

The man pointed to his clipboard and said, "This is the last of three scheduled wooden boxes from France."

Madeline flinched. "Yes, yes, I know, and you're the third carrier over the last few weeks. Hurry, my boss doesn't want his wife to see the crates."

They both arrived at the basement door—it was stuck. Madeline pulled, and he pushed. The door flew open, and she stumbled backward.

"Hurry, please. Put the box by the others." She pointed across the hall.

"Yes, Miss." The man pushed the package under the stairs before sprinting outside.

"Wait!" She followed him and pulled an envelope out of her pocket. "Mr. Schwartz said to give you this."

He took the envelope, jumped into his van, and drove away. Back upstairs, Madeline told Madame the package belonged to her.

A month later, Heidi watched Maddie pack all her things and move out. She reappeared once a week on Friday nights for a few hours, but by spring she'd left for good with Sergeant Kane to South Carolina. Afterward, Heidi's parents hired a live-in maid. The woman cooked and cleaned, but didn't interact with Heidi unless it was absolutely necessary. Most of the time, Heidi read books or worked on puzzles and models by herself when she wasn't with her parents or friends.

Chapter 10

Four years later, 1968…

In the afternoon, Heidi stood at one of the open swinging kitchen doors watching her mother tell the maid how to cook each dish for the dinner party that night. Heidi cherished the smaller parties as she felt like the' bell of the ball,' but even better were the times Claudia came along with her parents.

Several hours into the evening, after the guests sat talking in the living room eating hors d'oeuvres and drinking wine or mixed drinks, they went into the dining room for the main course and dessert. Heidi sat at the table between two guests on one of the long sides, and her parents arranged themselves at opposite ends. During the meal, usually between courses, her mother summoned the maid by ringing a small golden bell, which resembled a skirt with a stem-like handle coming up out of the top. The maid entered the room and dutifully carried in or out whatever dishes were required.

During this particular dinner, Heidi and Claudia sat opposite each other making google-eyes, grinning like Cheshire cats. She laughed at her friend's expressions while plotting their next move. After dessert, Heidi dragged Claudia back into the living room ahead of the adults. Claudia hid behind the couch, and Heidi wiggled under the two cushions on the oversized armchair. She pivoted her head slightly to the side and saw her father hovering next to the chair.

He said, "Where did Heidi go? This armchair is awfully lumpy. Let me fluff it up a bit."

The fabric pushed against her nose and smelled dusty as he kneaded the cushion. She jumped out and said, "Surprise!" Maneuvering around she fell back onto the cushions, and her father squished into the remaining space by her side.

"Glad I listened to my doctor and stopped smoking cigarettes," he said. "Now I can sit here without the incumbrance. This is much better."

"Yippy," Heidi exclaimed. "No more heavy glass ashtrays or giant silver lighters to put out."

"Sorry, you'll have to keep doing that. Many people are ignoring the new warnings that say smoking can cause health problems."

Claudia popped up from behind the couch. "Hey, what about me?" She waved frantically. "Dad, you were supposed to find me."

Uncle David lifted up his daughter, lost his balance, and thudded down into the soft cushions. Recovering, he tweaked Claudia's nose and pulled her close. Their mothers entered the room laughing.

"You boys are so stuffy," Heidi's Aunt Sadie said playfully.

After listening to the adults talking for a little while, Heidi and Claudia went upstairs to get ready for bed. They changed into pajamas and brushed their teeth. Claudia pulled a book off of Heidi's shelf and started to read without saying goodnight. Within ten minutes the booked dropped down on her chest. Heidi couldn't get comfortable and got out of bed. She went halfway down the stairs, sat on the pink-carpeted steps and listened to the grownups talking. Peering through the white wrought iron railing, she unsuccessfully pretended to be invisible.

"Heidi, you shouldn't be listening to our adult stories. Go to bed!" Her mother took a sip of something out of a small glass. "Is Claudia asleep?"

"Yes, Mom, she fell asleep reading a book."

Heidi wondered if her mom was drinking 'silly' water. It made her dad fall asleep, and her mom giggle over stupid stuff with their friends. The last time there was a glass of the stuff around, Heidi took a sip of the bitter liquid by mistake and then discovered that the bottle nearby said Gordon's gin. Why any adult would drink it, she didn't know, but they seemed to like it a lot.

"Is Claudia on the cot?"

"Yeees, Mom, she's always there for sleepovers."

"Claudia will have to go home with her parents when they leave tonight."

"Oh, okay." Heidi's lips fell into an exaggerated pout.

"Come here, give us all a quick kiss and go straight to bed. You need your sleep."

Heidi obeyed, went back to bed, and soon heard singing. For an instant, she covered her ears, but then realized her mother was mimicking her favorite German singer. Her mother's voice was not off-key like it was when she sang Christmas carols. Instead, it came out deep, guttural, and saucy as she sang her own rendition of Marlene Dietrich's song, *Falling in Love Again*. Heidi crawled back out of bed and stood at the top of the stairs listening. Sometimes Heidi thought her mother looked like Miss Dietrich with her curled blond hair bobbing around her face and make-up that made her look like a porcelain doll. After the song was over, the adults began to talk again. The men's laughter resonated up the stairwell. Heidi started to nod off while leaning against the wall and scared herself awake before she toppled over. Sneaking back to bed, she fell asleep almost instantly.

At midnight, Heidi was awoken by the click of the light switch as her parents entered the bedroom. Her eyes flickered open, and she caught a glimpse of Uncle David gently coaxing Claudia from the cot beside her. While Claudia seemed to comply, her friend appeared to be sleepwalking, shuffling forward through the doorway with Uncle David directing her moves from behind with one hand. Once they were gone and Heidi's room returned to darkness, she moved over toward the window and watched as the McGwires' car disappeared down the street beyond the street light. Since Heidi was wide awake, she organized her stuffed animals along the length of the bed. When the task was done, she curled up under the blanket. Her body heat filled the cold spaces within the air pockets. It wasn't long before her mother came back in to wish her a good night sleep.

"Mom, can I have some ginger ale and a salted bread ball?"

"No, not tonight. You know that's only for when you're sick in bed with a sore throat. Do you have one?"

"No, I'm hungry." It occurred to Heidi to tell a white lie, but she didn't want to get in trouble.

"Go to sleep, the morning will be here soon." Her mother pecked her on the cheek. "Remember the magic dome will protect you and your animals during the night. If you need anything else, I'll be downstairs reading the newspaper." Her mother switched on the nightlight on the dresser.

Rolling left and right, Heidi managed to twist her footie pajamas around her legs like a boa constrictor. She struggled and eventually freed herself. Sleep didn't come. Gazing up at the ceiling, the dome encased her like a glass, oversized, upside-down teacup. On the outskirts of the curve, she envisioned white wisps floating past. For protection, she recited the Lord's Prayer.

Maybe, at most, a half an hour past when her mother returned, switched on the ceiling light and started to hunt for spiders. Most nights Heidi slept through this nonsense, but sometimes she'd open her eyes a tiny bit to observe the ritual without being discovered.

Tonight, she was awake and peeking. Her mother peered behind dressers, doors, under the bed, and up at the ceiling.

Oh, Mom found one. There she goes, she'll be back with Dad. I'm going to be rolled out of my cozy bed or, if I'm lucky, the spidey creature is on the other side of the room. No, here we go.

"Get out of bed. Your dad has to get the spiders."

Heidi didn't say a word while she stood there watching. This time her father swept away real spiders and webs, but other times there were none, and he just went through the motions of getting rid of her mother's imaginary crawly things.

"Sleep tight, Heidi, back to bed you go." Her mother re-arranged the blankets. Heidi wriggled back under them and groaned pulling the pillow over her head. The room went dark again with a flick of the switch.

Her father lumbered into the hall grumbling within earshot. "Darling, you know I have to sleep at night and wake up with the dawn regardless of how many hours I've slept. Ask the maid to vacuum more often to keep the spiders away." A second later, they were gone. Heidi didn't hear the rest of their conversation.

Most Saturdays, around ten in the morning, Heidi ate breakfast with her father while her mother slept. This morning's meal began with Heidi staring at the back of the *Washington Post* that her father held up in front of his face. The maid walked in with a plate of scrambled eggs, bacon, toast and a glass of orange juice and put them on her placemat. Heidi pulled the plate closer and placed a napkin across her lap. Midway through the meal, she stopped eating and started twisting the napkin in her lap until she couldn't take being ignored another second. Getting up from the table, she walked over to her father's place and touched his arm. A faint smell of Old Spice surrounded him. She silently pouted up at him and scowled.

A minute later, her father put the newspaper down next to the placemat. "I shouldn't talk to you until I'm finished reading the world news. The information is vital for my job. I must keep up with what the reporters think is going on." He pulled out a section of the paper. "Here, take this and read about the arts while I finish up."

"How do you remember everything?"

"Born with an eidetic memory."

"What does that mean?"

"Means I hear things, read things, and easily remember most it. Really helps me at work. A lot of people just say they have a photographic memory, which is similar enough to eidetic."

"I wish I could do that, school would be much easier."

"Yes, it would, but for some people it's a curse, not a gift. I've learned how to take it all in without being overwhelmed. Your mother remembers many things as well, but she has a difficult time with the gift."

"How?"

"I handle it with logic and analyze information. Your mom gets emotionally involved." He took hold of the egg cup that the maid placed in front of him and lopped off the top of his soft-boiled egg. Then he added a pinch of salt before he scooped out the eye. The rest disappeared in three bites. "You're quite the little thinker... read your section of the newspaper, so that I can read mine."

"Sorry. Where are we going on Sunday?"

"Zoo or hiking on the C&O canal. What do you think?"

"How about fishing? I remember going when I was too little to fish with real worms, and you put a fake fish on the end of the line. Dad, I don't know, you pick."

"Let's go to the zoo. We'll go hiking and fishing another time. I have to skip next weekend since I'll be out of town on a business trip."

"Anywhere interesting?"

"No, not particularly." He lifted the newspaper back up in front of his face.

"Dad?"

"What? I'm trying to read. Stop interrupting."

"Sorry, I forgot to ask you something. Are we going to church too?"

"Yes, the eleven o'clock service. We'll make our own oatmeal tomorrow since the maid is leaving earlier than usual."

"I wish Mom would go with us."

"I do too. I think we'll head up the road to the Norwood Parish, and then grab lunch on the way to the zoo. I'll call the McGwires and see if they can meet us in front of the elephant house after church."

"Okay, Claudia likes the zoo."

"When I come home from my trip, we can go to the National Cathedral with the McGwires."

"Why do we go to both places?"

"I like Norwood's Sunday school for you. Going to the cathedral once a month is plenty. If we go too often, I might become numb to the inspiring architecture."

Soon after her father left town, Heidi went clothes shopping with her mother. Heidi preferred wearing casual clothing, but she was only allowed to wear such things for outdoor activities like gardening or hiking. Today's shopping trip was a little different, and Heidi lost her patience. She wanted to pick out her own clothes even if they were at Saks Fifth Avenue instead of her favorite Woodward & Lothrop's department store.

"Mom, I don't want to wear dresses all the time. I can wear this with you, but not with my friends. They think I'm a dork. I need some jeans."

"For heaven's sake, why not? Dresses are so pretty. I don't want my daughter wearing those things in public. They aren't feminine." Her mother wiggled a finger at the rack of jeans.

"Lots of girls wear jeans after school. We get tired of wearing uniforms."

"Mmm, what is the world coming to? All right, pants then. I'm buying them in a bigger size than you need. You're at the right age to have a growth spurt, you'll fit in them soon enough. I've seen girls with those tight pants, showing off every inch of themselves on purpose, I'm sure. I won't have you wearing tight pants, not ever!" Her mother handed her a pair. "Here, take these. You can try them on at home before your bath."

Heidi held the blue jeans up by the belt loops. "I think two of me can fit in these. I should try them on now."

"No, they're unsanitary! I don't want you to get exposed to other girls' germs. You'll have to put them on over tights, then wash the tights during your shower. If I approve of the pants, they'll go through the laundry before you wear them."

"What?" she whined. "You're kidding?"

"No arguments. It is either that or I won't buy them, and you will have to keep wearing dresses."

"Yeees, Mom." She thought; *has Mom always been this way and I never noticed?* "You're such a pain. I have to go to the bathroom."

"You were supposed to go at home," her mother snapped. "We've only been gone a couple of hours."

"Oh, fine! It's an emergency. I'll be right back." Heidi strutted away.

"No, you don't. I'm going with you."

"Mom, leave me alone."

They both went into the bathroom.

"Everything is dirty," her mother said haughtily. She turned her back to Heidi and held open the stall door with a Kleenex tissue and handed over a wad of toilet paper.

"Mom! Stop it, go away! I use the toilet at school by myself every day."

"No, I won't! And don't sit on the seat. Put some of the paper down or squat since you're tall enough."

"Leave me alone!" Only partially out of view, Heidi finished her business.

"Here, use this Wash-N-Dry to clean your hands. Hurry up, this place is disgusting."

Back out in the clothing department, Heidi said, "Mom, it looked okay in the bathroom. It smelled like oranges in there, not anything yucky. Everyone stared at us. I'm not a baby anymore. I know how to behave in public bathrooms. Why did you make such a fuss?"

"Nasty germs, they're hiding everywhere."

Things got worse in the lingerie department.

"Don't touch anything!" Her mother exclaimed, holding her credit card in one hand and only touched a corner of the underwear with the other. They made their selection, with Heidi pointing at what she wanted, and walked to the counter. Her mother handed the clerk the card and took it back with a Kleenex tissue. The clerk grimaced, and Heidi presumed it was an expression of pity. They walked out of the store.

"Mom, the clerk looked offended. No one else I know is scared of germs. Not even Aunt Sadie when she takes me out shopping with Claudia."

"I'm not anyone else. Maybe we can try again, and next time will be more fun."

"I don't know, Mom." Heidi was sure shopping wouldn't get any better.

Chapter 11

Now that Heidi was almost eleven, three months and counting, her parents allowed her help during the Christmas season. Up until this point, she had helped with simple things like putting an ornament or two on the lower branches of the tree.

Heidi and her father bundled themselves in their winter coats and gloves before driving down the road to search for a Christmas tree. In front of the Farm Woman's Market on Wisconsin Avenue, they walked down the narrow corridors in the lot by the road. The branches of the trees left pine scent on their coat sleeves.

"How about this one, Dad?"

"No, its needles are too long. Your mom wants a tree that looks like the ones in our yard, only smaller. I have to be able to reach the top to put on the angel doll. A six-foot tree is just the right size. Here, this is from last year." He reached into his cashmere coat and pulled out a photograph.

"I know," she complained. "We have the same one every year. I wanted something different."

"Spruce trees are your mother's favorite from her childhood. It's a tradition we're not going to change."

"Okay, Dad. How tall are you?"

"Five-foot, ten-inches. Let's keep searching."

They walked around some more.

"The trees looked a hundred-feet tall when I was little." Heidi continued, "I'm happy I could come with you this year."

"I'm enjoying your company."

"Did Mom ever go tree shopping with you?"

"Only a few times when we were first married. She handles the gift shopping, and I buy the tree. Seemed strange at first, but that's okay, you're here now to help."

"Dad, let's buy this one." She pointed at one wedged between two others. "I like the bird's nest in the branches."

"It's a fine tree," he exclaimed with a grin. "I'll pay the man, and he'll tie it on the roof."

At home, Heidi spread out an old sheet on the floor. Her father lay the tree down on top, and they pulled it into the living room by the sheet's corners. He shoved a metal tree stand onto the base of the tree and tightened the bolts into the trunk. Once that was done, he stood it up and wove two strings from the midsection of the trunk over to hooks in the wall. The strings kept the tree from falling over if it became unbalanced. Heidi ran off to the kitchen for a pitcher of water to fill the reservoir in the stand. It would be her job to make sure the tree didn't dry out.

Her mother entered the room and said, "My shopping today was successful." She paused and walked around the room. "Oh, my! The tree is beautiful, except it's rather naked. Nathan, can you get the decorations in the attic and put the lights on with Heidi. I'll have the maid make dinner. There's plenty of time to put the glass ornaments on tomorrow. The angel, soldiers, and miscellaneous little people can wait until later in the week."

Her mother put on her pince-nez eyeglasses and examined the branches. "Take the bird's nest out. There must be spiders or some other bugs hiding in there. You know I despise crawly creatures."

"Mom, please don't worry."

"That's my job. We can't have alien things in our house." Her mother stepped out of the room and brought some bags back in. "I bought some gifts to wrap for friends and family I'll take them upstairs in a few minutes. Heidi, since you've never wrapped anything before, I will teach you after dinner. But we'll need to go through the gift closet first."

"Okay, Mom." Heidi wasn't eager to help. In the past, she'd watched her mother wrap gifts, and it looked repetitive and tiresome.

Once the meal was over, Heidi trudged up the stairs behind her mother, exaggerating every movement while pretending to propel her forward until they arrived at the walk-in closet in the guest room. With a twist of the handle, the door came open and, a strong odor of mothballs spilled out. Her mother stood inside, turned her head left and right, and moved some things around on the shelves without any apparent reason.

"Mom, this stuff is too old to give to people, and some of it's broken." Heidi pointed at a music box with a creepy clown dangling out of the top.

"There are plenty left in the closet, but I did buy some other things at the store earlier today. Here take these trinkets over to the table. I'll give you one at a time to carry. We'll wrap them with the rest."

Bored to death, Heidi took the items and placed them in rows across the table. This ritual seemed so dumb and wasn't fun. She bit her thumb while staring at a glass snow globe. The water level was half of what it was supposed to be.

"Heidi, pay attention! Stop daydreaming. We don't have time to play around." Her mother put her hands on her hips. "Let's start wrapping."

"Okay." Heidi focused on the task while listening to the instructions.

"Each gift must be placed in a white box with tissue paper. If it came with a box from the store, skip that step." A large green bag filled with folded gift boxes sat on the floor next to the table. Her mother sorted through the plastic bag until she found a matching top and bottom combination. "Unroll some gift paper, wrap it around the box, and use the ruler to measure four-inches extra on the ends for folding before you cut anything."

Heidi began the process.

"Careful, careful, each one needs to look like they were professionally wrapped," her mother interjected. "I learned how when I worked in a bookstore. It was an intermittent job between theater productions. You can snip a little off the folds inside the end triangles to make the paper sit smoothly against the ends. Like this…" Her mother demonstrated.

By the time they'd worked through three gifts, Heidi understood, but some of the packages still looked lopsided. After a great deal of frustration, Heidi learned to fold each corner to the correct specifications. To complete the process, she rolled pieces of tape and put them invisibly under the cut edges. The ribbons and bows were as easy as tying a pair of shoelaces. Next, came laborious instructions on how to print precise labels.

"On a scrap piece of paper, trace the card and within the borders write, 'To Mr. And Mrs. Pendergast.' Below the names write, 'Love from the Schwartz Family.' Once the script is perfect, you can write it on the real card."

"Mom, it's just a card."

"No, it isn't! Everything we do reflects our personality. The gift cards are just as important as the letters and thank you notes I make you do over and over. This is especially true for the gifts I'm sending to your dad's work. Write!"

Annoyed, Heidi put her pen to the paper and soon held up the completed product for inspection. "How's this?"

Her mother examined her writing. "Heidi, make the loop on the 'g' a little bigger and don't squish the letters together. Space them out evenly and write straight across, not diagonally. You'll have to trace a new card and start over."

Four drafts later, Heidi wanted to give up. She whined, "Is this correct?"

"Yes, good. Write it on the gift card in the same way, tie it onto the ribbon, and then you're ready for the next package."

And the next, and the next. Heidi couldn't wait to get the job done and escape.

On Christmas Eve, the family went to church. It was the only time of the year her mother attended services, and she didn't explain why—Heidi never asked. They stuffed themselves in the over-crowded Saint John's Episcopal Church at Lafayette Square in D.C. and sang Christmas carols.

"Dad," Heidi said in a hushed voice. "If this is the president's church, where is he?"

"He could be hiding among the crowd with his family and the Secret Service or, more likely, they have a private ceremony. Do some research next time you go to the library. I do know that every president has come here at least once in their term."

Her mother sang with gusto, even though her voice cracked and went off key. At the end of *Silent Night,* she pulled out a Kleenex tissue from her dress pocket.

"Mom—" Heidi touched her arm— "why are you crying?"

"We come here for the carols—" she patted her eyes with the tissue— "because they remind me of my father. He loves to sing. This year has been very difficult because he's not well."

Heidi pulled on her father's coat sleeve. "Dad... Mom hates small places! How can she stand being stuffed into this church with so many people?"

"I don't know. Now isn't the time for questions. Shh, stop talking and pay attention to the nativity pageant." He raised his finger ever so slightly in the direction of the altar.

A woman dressed up as the Virgin Mary carried a plastic baby Jesus, wrapped in a cloth, down the aisle. Followed by four wise men, each with a real sheep on the end of a rope.

Her father slid an offering envelope out from the back of the pew in front of them. Heidi watched while he wrote on the outside, 'My roots aren't here, but in the archives.' He wedged it between the pages of a hymnal and pulled out a fresh new envelope. He wrote his name, added some money, and sealed it shut using some saliva on the tip of his finger. The offering plate cycled through the crowd, and her father dropped his contribution on the top of the others. Heidi noticed that some parishioners used the envelopes and others tossed loose change, bills, and checks onto the pile.

Heidi mulled over the cryptic message her father had written on the first envelope before he inserted it into the hymnal. She wondered about its meaning but decided she'd been reading too many Nancy Drew mystery books. The note probably meant nothing. Her thoughts were interrupted by the minister talking about charity, and she refocused on him.

Once the service was over, her father became distracted and left them standing in the church's vestibule. He came around the corner thirty-minutes later with the car. Heidi barely closed the door before he drove away and ran through a red light. Her mother didn't seem to notice from the back seat. Heidi cringed and didn't say a word.

At home, they ate a quiet dinner. Heidi had enough of the dampened mood that hung in the air. "I'm going to my room. I hope Granddad feels better soon. The last time we visited him, he didn't even know our names."

Heidi walked up the stairs to her room, grabbed Baby Bear off her bed, and diverted around the corner to the attic door. She had been there before with her parents, but it was yet another area in the house she wasn't permitted to go without a chaperone. Heidi placed her foot on the first of eleven steps and stopped for an instant when one squeaked. At the top of the stairs, she glanced over piles of old gift boxes, packing barrels, suitcases, used toys, old school books, broken furniture, and boxes filled with empty shampoo bottles. On her tiptoes, she maneuvered around the mess and found new toys stacked neatly together with only one wrapped. She snuck around the largest box and fingered the label taped on the corner— "To Heidi Rose, From Santa." Her head dropped onto her chest, and she hurried down the attic stairs to her room. Heidi didn't want to accept that her parents—and all the stores—had created a make-believe world for children. She still hoped Santa hid the toys in the attic or maybe his elves.

"Baby Bear, do you think it's all pretend?"

The bear said nothing.

She buried her face in his fur. "The grown-ups…"

"Heidi, come back," her mother called from somewhere far away. "We need to put cookies out for Santa."

Heidi started down the stairs and pushed on her cheeks with her palms while rubbing her eyes. "Coming, Mom."

"What's wrong?" her mother asked. "Your eyes are red."

"Nothing, I just figured out something."

"Tell me."

"Nope, don't worry." For the first time in her life, Heidi didn't tell the truth. She couldn't confess she'd gone into the attic without permission or that she'd seen the gift from Santa. Even though she felt betrayed, she wasn't going to make a fuss.

"If you're sure." Heidi's mother handed her the cookie plate. "Take this to the hearth and come back for Santa's beer. After that, we can read your favorite illustrated Christmas book."

"No, Mom, I can read *T'was the Night Before Christmas* by myself." Heidi wasn't going to give her mother the satisfaction. "Besides, the chimney doesn't work."

"We don't have fires, but it's safer for Santa this way. Are you sure we can't read it together?"

"Yes. Good night." Heidi stomped up the stairs and flopped into bed.

On Christmas morning, while Heidi's parents slept, she took the needlepoint stocking off her doorknob and poured the little individually wrapped gifts onto her pink blanket. The wrapping paper was delicate and easily ripped away.

"Baby Bear look at these things. Toothpaste, toothbrush, socks, and chocolate bars. Nothing fun this year." She hugged Baby Bear and ignored the nine other animals, except for her rabbit, which she pulled into her arms next to the bear. "I wish you'd say something to me. Silly things. You're such good listeners." She carried Baby Bear and the rabbit down the stairs to the living room and peeked around the edge of the sheet that covered the entrance. By the tree stood a pile of gifts two-feet tall extending around the base. None of them were there the night before. Santa's cookie crumbs remained on the plate. The beer glass was empty.

Heidi stared into Baby Bear's glass eyes. She spoke mournfully, "The box! The box I saw in the attic is next to Santa's plate by the fireplace. My friends were right. Mom and Dad staged it all, they even ate the cookies and drank the beer." Her voice sagged even more. "Santa is a parents' game. This is stupid. I guessed last night, and now I'm double sure."

A noise somewhere else in the house startled Heidi. She backed away from the sheet. The new maid wagged her finger at Heidi from down the hall. She wondered how long this woman would stay around—Heidi didn't bother to remember their names. There had been a new one each year since Nanny Madeline moved away nearly five years ago.

Heidi knew it would be another hour before her parents appeared for breakfast, and another two before the gift exchange began. This was how it was every year. Heidi crept up the stairs to the laundry closet and grabbed a cotton bag. She marched into her room and put almost all her stuffed animals in the sack and threw them in the closet. She was done with all of them except Baby Bear and the rabbit. They were spared the indecency of being stuffed in a bag. Pulling out her book, *Edith and Mr. Bear* by Dare Wright, Heidi sat on her bed and read out loud to her two friends. She hugged the bear and rabbit as if they were the last bit of hope in a desperate world.

Finally, the unwrapping began while they all sat on the living room couch next to the lit tree. Each package was rattled and examined before the paper was ripped away. The content of each box was admired. A sweater or piece of jewelry was tried on, a board game was played, a bicycle was assembled, and an easy-bake oven tried. Once everything exchange was over, Heidi helped her parents put more gifts under the tree for the evening guests who would stay for dinner. This year, though, the usual sparkle and excitement of the holiday was missing for Heidi. Santa was dead to her.

Spring arrived with the cherry blossoms in full bloom. Heidi and her father went out to do some errands. At her request, he agreed to dropped her off at the library armed with a pen and notebook, while he went across the street to the grocery store. Inside the Bethesda library, she sauntered over to the shelves in the reference area and searched through the books. Nothing relevant caught her eye, she gave up and went over to the information counter.

"Excuse me, this is my first time alone in the library. Can you help me?" Feeling a little foolish, she said, "I'm trying to understand where the story of Santa Claus started."

The librarian pulled her glasses away from her eyes. "How old are you?"

"Eleven. My birthday was last week."

"I see. We can look for some reference materials together."

"Last Christmas, I figured out Santa wasn't so magical."

"Aw, I understand your concerns." The librarian smiled, flipping her pencil between her fingers. "He came from another country and was known as Saint Nicholas there. As history evolves, names and events sometimes change a little."

"Wow! So, he was real?" Heidi's voice rose a little higher, and she covered her mouth.

"Absolutely! Watch how I look the books up, and you can do it on your own next time."

"Oh, thank you," Heidi said, leaning in to watch the woman's fingers move over an open drawer in one of the many cabinets filled with similar drawers. It looked like there were hundreds of cards behind alphabetically ordered dividers.

The librarian slid out a blank piece of paper from a tray and wrote a series of numbers down from several of the cards. Heidi followed the librarian down the aisles while the woman searched the shelves.

"Here are the books that should help you in your quest."

"Thank you!" Heidi put her hands out, palms up, and the librarian rested the books there. The pile of five thick, massive books weighed her down.

"Anything else I can help you with?"

"Um, um…" Heidi took in a deep breath. "Do you have any new mystery books? I need some for my dad, something like the Sherlock Holmes stories. He's read them all and needs something else. Something, something more modern."

The librarian plucked some new arrivals off a cart at the end of the aisle and placed them on top of the books in Heidi's arms. The woman said, "The ones on Santa Claus are reference books so they can't leave the building. However, you can check out the mystery books."

"That's okay, I don't have a library card. I'll write down the titles for my dad to get later." Heidi's cheeks flushed.

"Bring your father in some time, and he can help you get a card."

"I'll ask him, thank you."

The librarian went back to her desk, and Heidi sat down at one of the community tables. First, Heidi wrote the mystery book titles and authors down in her notebook. Then, she skimmed through the reference books on Santa Claus. There were many pages of helpful information which included facts as well as legends, but she didn't have enough time to go through every page. Instead, she chose a few key points that interested her.

The first Santa Claus or Father Christmas was called San Nicola. He was born in 374AD in Greece and grew up to be a Bishop of Myra; a wiry man and not large at all until he was commercialized and renamed Santa Claus in the Modern World. In the old stories and the new, he's known as the protector of children who brings gifts. He was buried in a tomb in Bari, Italy. In modern times Clement Moore wrote a poem about him.

After Heidi was finished, she turned the books back into the librarian and went outside to wait for her father. He drove up to the curb, and she jumped in the front seat of the car.

"I'm all done," he said. "How'd you do in the library?"

"Dad, Dad, I figured it out. Santa Claus was a real person. I'm going to read *The Night Before Christmas* at home, again."

Her father wiped his hand across his brow. "Phew, now I understand what's been bothering you these past months. I thought you and Claudia were having some sort of difficulty."

"Nooo, Dad, Claudia is fine and so am I." Handing him a sheet of paper, she said at a rapid pace, "And I found some new mystery book titles for you by Agatha Christie."

"Lovely! I'll get one and try it out." Her father started to drive down Arlington Road. "You are so like Sadie, always doing things for other people."

"Hey, Dad, I'm like you too. I read mysteries," Heidi sassed.

"Yes. I know. You like Nancy Drew stories. We can go to the bookstore now since the weather's cool enough to leave the food in the car. I'll buy a book from your Agatha Christie list if they have one."

"Love you, Dad." Heidi scooted closer to him in the middle of the front seat. Enthusiastically, she said, "Let's go!"

The car squealed around the corner onto Bradley Boulevard. Heidi liked the sound, it made her giggle.

Her father parked the car in the lot next to Waldenbooks. They hopped out and went around the front of the building. Heidi stalled to looked at the display window before going in. She loved seeing how the shopkeepers set up displays and thought about the ones she'd seen during the Christmas season at the department stores.

Inside Waldenbooks, she said, "Dad, look, Uncle David is here."

"So, he is. Hello David, I see you had plenty of sleep last night," her father joked and shook her uncle's hand.

"Two hours." Uncle David's eyes were red and his hair askew. "What are you two doing?"

Heidi bounced in. "Getting an Agatha Christie book. I made a list of books at the library."

"Why didn't you sign one out?"

"You know Gwen," her father replied. "She only likes books in pristine condition around the house."

"Dad, what's pristine?"

"New and clean, in perfect shape," her father answered.

Her uncle raised his hands up to surrender and said, "Not touched by the general public. Your wife is a pickle. Sadie goes to the library constantly and forgets to take the books back."

"I heard that, Uncle David," she scolded.

Her father bent down next to her. "Please, go sit and read something until we're done talking."

"Okay." She grabbed a book off a display table in the center of the store and cuddled into a big stuffed chair. Pretending to read, she glanced over the top of the open book and watched the men standing a foot away from each other talking at the end of an aisle. They were three rows away, and she couldn't hear a word. Just before they separated, her father passed a tan manila envelope to Uncle David. Then they went out of her line of sight.

Her father walked back over after she'd read five pages of the book she'd chosen. "We're done talking, say goodbye. I already bought Ms. Christie's book called *By the Pricking of My Thumbs*. It was published last year." He held up his package.

"Such a funny name for a book," Heidi squeaked a bit louder than was appropriate. "Bye, Uncle David."

"See you soon," her uncle replied.

"Oops, did you want to buy that book?" her dad asked.

"Yes, please."

He took the book from her and handed it to the cashier with some money. After the register's bell sounded—*ding*—a brown bag that matched the size of the book was passed back over the counter.

Her dad said, "Here you go."

"Thank you." Heidi took the bag and smiled up at him. She tried to stop thinking about the envelope.

Out on the sidewalk, she pulled on her father's sleeve. "I saw you give Uncle David an envelope. He stuffed it in his coat. What was it?"

"Just something for work. Time to go home."

Chapter 12

Three years later, 1970...

In the night, her mother's father passed away, a man Heidi barely knew except in dementia. Her mother's moods drastically changed, her sadness infected everyone. Even the house seemed to groan along with her. Heidi's twelfth year became clouded by her mother's bouts of depression and explosive temper tantrums.

On their way home from the grocery store, her mother drove past their pine trees and honked at a neighborhood dog by the trash cans. At the top of the driveway, she put the car in neutral. Heidi's mind didn't register the problem, even though her father had given her unofficial driving instructions in a vacant lot for fun on her birthday. They got out of the car, the balance shifted, and the vehicle rolled back down into the street just missing the dog. From that day on, they depended on her father, friends, and taxis for transportation.

On a daily basis, she watched her mother walk around the house wringing her hands together. She repeated the words over and over, "Mmm uh, mmm uh." Then started to talk to herself while Heidi stood a few steps away.

"Mom, I'm right here. What's wrong?"

"Nothing, grown-up worries." Her mother's voice lowered. "Go play with your rabbits. I need to be alone. Take the bag of carrots on the maid's table with you. And, while you're outside, clean the cages. I left a new bottle of fresh Lysol in the garden shed."

"Mom, the rabbits are sweet, and they smell really good, but I still want a dog."

"Oh, don't go on about a dog. They're such dirty, scary things. You saw the one by the garbage can. I need to call the neighbor and complain." Her mother let out a long breath. "The beast keeps getting out, and he makes such a mess for the maid."

"Yeah, well, I still want one. I'll leave you alone." Heidi turned away and hesitated with her hand on the back doorknob. Lately, her rabbits had been much more affectionate than her mother and certainly easier to understand.

"You and your dad did a wonderful job making a strong cage to keep the dogs at bay. Be careful, the bunnies are so fragile. Keep your fingers away from their mouths. I'll check on you in a little while." Her mother's voice elevated. "Just go outside!"

"Yes, Mom, I know. See you later." Heidi rolled her eyes and stormed out the door. Her mind began to roam in many directions so she wouldn't have to confront the sadness she was feeling. She couldn't figure out how to talk her mother into anything, much less a dog. Every conversation was awkward, every effort failed. When things were exceptionally unbearable, Heidi wished Madeline was around to help keep the feelings of suffocation from overwhelming her, but they hadn't talked or seen each other in quite a while.

Heidi took a carrot out of the bag she had grabbed from the kitchen table and, as she devoured it, she recalled a funny thing Madeline had once told her. As a toddler, her skin turned a tint of orange from eating too many jars of carrot baby food. She popped the last bite of her carrot into her mouth as she worked her way into the twenty-by-thirty-foot fenced in rabbit pen that she'd made with four-foot high bamboo sticks. With a sigh, she dumped the remaining carrots from the bag into the rabbit hutch and began raking up the area surrounding it. Behind her, the starlings arrived and landed on the bamboo grove. The place was buzzing with hundreds of the black birds that her mother had tried to get rid of by playing a reel-to-reel recording of hawks. Claudia kept saying the boogeyman was in the bamboo with the birds. Heidi had been scared when she was little, but not anymore. The grove had become an imaginary oasis for her, a place to read wonderful books while perching on a crook of a tree that had grown and then fallen within the thriving bamboo stalks. She was happy it wasn't the right kind of bamboo for the pandas at the national zoo. Her mother wanted the zookeepers to take the bamboo away because it was trying to take over the entire backyard. Instead, with her father's encouragement, Heidi stomp on all the new shoots in the grassy areas as they emerged.

After cuddling with the rabbits—Peter and Kate, she cleaned their cages. Heidi went back in the house and up to her room. Her mother was fussing with a box of powdered soap.

"Mom! Why are you putting soap powder around my bed?"

"Spiders don't like crossing over this new type of powdered laundry detergent. I'm doing this to protect you and keep your dad from having to wake up in the middle of the night to catch them."

"If you say so. I don't like the smell; the powder hurts my nose." Heidi groaned. "None of this makes any sense!"

"But it does. Go take your bath since you're done playing with the rabbits. I'll be downstairs supervising the dinner preparations. The new maid doesn't seem to know how to cook."

Heidi wandered off to the bathroom and found soap powder caked around the sink's handles. It seemed there was two or three cups worth across the area where she usually left her toothbrush. It looked like the top of the sink was wet when the soap was added, and it was already rock hard. Ignoring the mess, for now, she turned on both bathtub faucets and waited for it to fill up to the halfway mark. As she got in, the hot water and bubbles tickled her nose. After a while, the water cooled, and she added more hot water to delay having to clean the sink. Finally, she gave up and pulled herself out of the tub, drained it, and wiped off the bubble ring. She wrapped a towel around her torso and tucked in a corner above her developing chest. Deeply sighing, Heidi grabbed her dirty jeans and shirt off the floor. She walked out of the bedroom into the hall supply closet and threw the clothes into the laundry chute. They slid down the slick metal tube to the basement. Next, she grabbed a bucket, a clean rag, and a scraper. Back in the bathroom, she got to work. The smell of the scented soap stuck in her nose and overpowered her senses as if she'd just sliced an onion. Her eyes misted. Before her tears dripped into the basin, she wiped them away with the back of her wrist and stuck her tongue out at her reflection in the mirror. She scraped and scraped. The quarter-inch thick crusted layers didn't come off easily. *Stupid soap*, she said to herself, not understanding her mother's peculiar behavior.

In the bedroom, Heidi pushed her clothes around in the bureau drawer and selected a casual long skirt and top to wear to dinner. After she got dressed, she went down the stairs holding the railing, hopping from one step to the next, thumping loudly. From a distance, she heard her mother talking in staccato pidgin English to their South American maid in the kitchen.

"Heidi," her mother called out. "Are you all clean? I heard you trotting down the stairs. Dinner is ready."

"Yes, Mom, coming." She sat down in the chair at the faux gray and white marble table. "You're funny. You don't speak Spanish any better than French."

"True, I just can't be bothered." Her mother put a glass of water on the table. "I can memorize many things, but other languages are…" Her mother's voice trailed off. She opened the swinging kitchen door and gesticulated at the maid. "*Café aquí, por favor.*"

"Maybe I can learn Spanish—can't be much harder than French."

"You can try, but I'm done with learning languages."

"Where's Dad?" Heidi didn't really want to talk about languages.

"He's working late tonight so he can go to the doctor's office tomorrow for a check-up. He has to take the day off."

"Oh." Heidi cut the hot dog in the bun on her plate in thirds while her mother sat and examined the daily mail. "Mom, why did you put soap powder on the edges of my bathroom sink? More spiders?"

"As a matter of fact, yes. What about it?"

"Nothing, I cleaned the soap off after my bath."

"That's fine. Did you use the goggles and gloves to clean the toilet, too?"

"No, and it's not hazardous waste, why all the protective gear?"

"I don't want you to get toilet cleaner in your eyes."

"That's silly. If you're worried, why not ask the maid to do it?"

"She has other assignments, I want you to be responsible for your areas of the house."

"Yeah, okay, you're the boss." Heidi bit into the hot dog meat, and her stomach almost turned inside out. Eating them stopped being appealing after her school field trip to the factory. She didn't like seeing how the meat was mixed and forced into the sausage sleeves.

"That's fine, the sink is sterilized, and the spiders shouldn't come back."

"What? Sorry, I don't understand."

"The spiders don't like soap. They won't worry you again."

"They don't. I think they're beautiful outside in the morning with the sun glistening on their webs."

"Outside is all right, but inside isn't. Spiders give me nightmares. I'm not discussing this anymore."

Heidi glared at her plate. The ketchup oozed from the edges of the bun. Her throat constricted, and she pushed it aside. "Can I go to Claudia's this weekend?"

"I'll check with Sadie and see if she can pick you up Saturday morning. We're going to their house that night for dinner and can bring you home."

"Thanks, Mom. Can't I spend the night?" Heidi hoped they'd have macaroni and cheese or peppered fried chicken for dinner instead of nasty hot dogs.

"Yes, if they're not too busy."

"Mom, what are you and Dad eating tonight?"

"A roast, he's not home for another two hours." Her mother turned away and walked into the den.

"I'm going back to my room to study," Heidi got up from the dining room table and called after her.

"I'll check on you later."

"It's okay, you don't have to." Heidi didn't want any company. She worked on her geography and math homework at her desk for the next two hours. The math annoyed her, and she slammed the book closed, grabbed her blanket and carried her reading assignment into the closet cubby and snuggled into the corner hoping to forget about the world.

The next day wasn't much better. Heidi returned from school in a taxi she'd shared with a friend, unlocked the front door, and stepped into the foyer. Her dad's clothes were in a pile on top of a piece of plastic. Heidi frowned and was glad it was the maid's day off. Everything he was wearing that morning; even his underwear, socks, and shoes, were by the door. Her mother stood by the wall that hid the staircase.

Her father's words floated around the corner. "Hello, Mousey, please stay by the front door. I'm going upstairs for a shower and will be out of your way in a minute."

Heidi stood her ground and called out, "Mom, what's going on?"

"I told you yesterday, he had an appointment with the doctor! So many germs at their office. Stay down here. I have to go up and turn the shower on for your father. I don't want him touching anything until he's clean."

"I don't get it, we never do that when I go to the doctor's office." Heidi had other toxic words rolling around in her head but didn't dare say them out loud.

"Yes, we do," her mother snapped. "You just didn't realize."

"If you say so." Heidi snuck around to the back side of the hall where she could hear them without being seen.

Her mother said, "Nathan, you are such a hypochondriac. Why do you go to the doctor's so often?"

"Uck, you know I have to have a check-up before the doctor will re-fill my blood pressure medications. He won't do it over the phone," he sneered. "Remember my father died at my age from a stroke. When was the last time you had a regular check-up?"

Heidi didn't hear her mother's response, but she'd heard enough and walked into the den to phone Claudia. She dialed the number and waited.

"Hello," Claudia said.

"Hi, it's me."

"Something wrong? You sound upset."

"What am I going to do? My crazy mother is up to no good. Her germ phobia is acting up again. God, I really don't know how to handle my life at home. I want to hide in my room. Maybe, I'll only come out for meals and school. Oh, wait, Mom is already coming back down the stairs muttering about something. I have to hang up. Sorry, I'll talk to you later."

When her mother acted irrationally, her father never seemed to put up a fuss. At least Heidi rarely heard him complain. He would sigh or say a word or two before he walked off, but he didn't yell. For the most part, he'd observe her mother's irrational outbursts and only respond when absolutely necessary. Heidi did the same when she could since she wasn't skilled at rebuttals.

Chapter 13

Her father left on a business trip. When he returned, his entire body appeared to be drooping. Heidi hugged him, but he said very little other than hello and disappeared into her parents' bedroom. She eavesdropped from the hallway and heard him talking to her mother but couldn't catch his words.

Finally, she heard him call out, "Heidi, come into our bedroom."

"I'm coming." Heidi popped around the corner. "I think I'm too old for dolls but did you bring me a new one?"

"Yes, and something for your mother as well." He handed the tissue-wrapped package to Heidi. "This one is from Iceland, and the last one."

"Thanks, Dad." She unwrapped her new treasure. "I'm happy you're back. I'll put it in my curio cabinet."

Heidi walked out of the room and heard her father growl. She held the doll against her chest and stood frozen within earshot of her parents, but not close enough to be seen.

"Gwen! What do you mean the perfume bottle isn't clean! Your germ phobia is driving me out of my mind!"

"I can't help myself. I need to wash the bottle before I use the perfume. I'm sorry."

"You need help! And—to top it off—I found out something devastating at work."

"Darling, please," her mother croaked. "What are you talking about?"

"We should've stayed in Paris longer, leaving early hurt my career. I just found out, I would have been put on the latest list of prospects for Secretary of State if we hadn't abandoned ship!"

"What? You said we could come home!"

Something made a crashing sound.

Heidi peered around the corner and saw her dad's suitcase spilled all over the carpet. He grabbed the luggage rack and threw it across the room.

"Dad, stop!"

"I'm sorry, I didn't mean… This was a mistake… I'm angry." He rushed past her and went down the stairs. The front door slammed. Heidi scrambled back to her room and wanted to bang her door closed but left it open.

Next thing she knew, her mother was standing in the doorway. "Your dad lost an opportunity for his dream job because of my health. At the time, he said it was for other reasons until I learned the truth much later."

"I don't understand." Heidi squeezed her new doll and then stopped abruptly. This doll and all the rest in her curio cabinet were for 'display only' and rather fragile.

"In Paris, I had trouble with my teeth. The dentist tried to help, but things got worse. That's when I started getting sick migraine headaches."

"Mom, Paris was forever ago."

"Yes, it was long ago, but some wounds don't ever heal. Your father missed opportunities. Give him some time, he'll calm down."

"Okay." Heidi wanted a distraction. "Mom, I need to label my new doll."

"Quite a collection you have. How many with Iceland?"

"Twenty-four in all." She proudly declared. "One from Morocco, Iceland, Egypt, Russia, South America…"

Her mother interrupted and said, "Yes, yes, you have quite a few. After you put the new tag on, read a book, and get some sleep. I need to wash the luggage rack and suitcase." She left the room without another word.

Forgetting about the doll, Heidi climbed into bed and focused on a book by Julie Roberts, called *Mandy*. In the story, Mandy found a private garden to call her own, beyond the wall of the orphanage she'd lived in most of her life. Today had been a bad day with Heidi's parents, and the story took her away from her own troubles. She finished five chapters, pulled the rabbit and bear against her chest, and curled around her soft pillow for the night.

Sunday started like most, except Heidi still felt a bit on edge after her father's outburst. She sat down at her usual place at the breakfast table with Baby Bear in her lap but didn't say a word.

His eyes appeared over the top of his newspaper. "Morning, Heidi, don't you think you're too old to be carrying a stuffed animal around? After all, you are twelve."

"Morning, Dad." She looked down at the bear and straightened his jacket. "Yes, I know, I'm not sure why I brought him downstairs."

"I'm sorry about my behavior last night," he said. "Really, there's no excuse, I have a lot on my mind."

She hugged the bear and glared at her father. "Throwing the luggage rack across the room was a bit extreme, don't you think?"

"Yes, I do," he said, sounding rather glum. "I'm retiring from the State Department soon, and I'm having trouble figuring out what I'm going to do next."

"Why do you have to leave? You love your work." She squinted into the morning sunlight streaming through the dining room picture window.

"It's just my time, that's all. Younger people can fill my slot."

"You know more than any of them, you're so smart."

"Funny, your mother and Uncle David said the same thing." He folded the newspaper into thirds and placed it on the table next to the placemat.

"Will you get a different kind of job?"

"I've decided to go ahead and take some time off, then look for something else."

"Dad, that sounds good." Heidi stared at him.

"Hope I can find something fun." He rolled his eyes. "Your mother plans to give me a *big* retirement party next month."

"Who do you want to invite?"

"I've worked with so many exceptional people. I wish I could ask my good friend Allan Dulles, but sadly he passed away a couple years ago. His sister, Eleanor, is still in our lives, so I hope she'll come.

"Dulles, like the airport?"

"Yes, the entire family is extraordinary. Mrs. Dulles is quite a modern woman and chose to keep her father's last name when she married Mr. Blondheim. In the '50s she managed the Berlin desk with her brother, John, at the State Department. She's an exceptional person with a long list of accomplishments. I'm sure you've met her before."

"All the people I've met at parties have interesting stories. I'll try to remember more of their names this time."

"If you want to learn about them, ask questions and write down the information. I don't know how many of them we'll keep in touch with after I retire, but hopefully quite a few."

"Okay. So, who else do you want to invite?"

"Let me think. Of course, we'll invite the friends who come around for our smaller parties—Mr. Leinbach and Mr. Cassidy, Mr.

and Mrs. Kendrick, Miss Kelly, and the Klays... followed by General Norstad and his wife, the Spiers, the Farleys, and Ambassador Holmes to name a few. Your mother has started lists to keep track of everyone and everything. There will likely be about eighty guests." Her father rubbed his temple. "We must not forget Sadie and David. I'd ask your cousin, Edward, but I already know he's traveling then. I'm sure his mother will be available."

"I love Aunt Eileen! Can Claudia come?"

"Of course, if your mother agrees, Claudia can be in charge of the guestbook at the beginning of the party. We're hiring a bartender for the drinks and a waiter to serve the catered food. It'll be fun. The hired help will dress in black uniforms rather than the white type the maid wears every day. You won't have to pass any hors d'oeuvres unless you want to."

"The job keeps my hands busy, so I don't get jittery talking to people."

"I'm sure you'll be fine with or without the trays. If you'd rather, you can carry around a tall glass of ginger ale or a Shirley Temple. It'll be a grand formal event."

"Formal! That means long dresses, fancy shoes, and men in suits. Will there be dancing?"

"Yes, we'll have a dance floor and tent set up in the backyard just outside the sunroom, and we'll hire a pianist."

"I remember when I used to put my feet on yours, we'd take each other's hands and pretend to dance with music on the radio. I'll ask Aunt Eileen to help me make a dress. But yuck, I don't like party shoes, they're uncomfortable."

Her father winked. "I'm sure what ever you two create will be beautiful, just like you. Your long dress will cover your feet, so you don't need fancy shoes, just keep your toes hidden, and your mom won't see anything. It'll be our secret." He chuckled. "I will be wearing uncomfortable shoes."

The evening of the retirement party arrived. The birch trees, edging the walkway leading to the arched front door were illuminated by spotlights for the occasion. Heidi greeted the McGwires halfway up the path. Claudia remained behind while her parents went inside.

"So, Claudia, my assignment is to greet each guest with a serving tray filled with champagne glasses from the table over there." Heidi pointed at the bottles, glasses, and trays on the other side of a holly bush. "The waiter will be standing there filling the glasses, and when I'm tired of holding the tray, he'll take over. I'll have to quote the same lines over and over to the guests." Heidi held an imaginary tray in her hands and practiced her lines in a sing-song voice. "Thank you for coming. Would you like a glass of champagne? My dad is looking forward to seeing you. Claudia is just inside the foyer and will ask you to sign the guestbook."

"Doh, very funny, now I know my assignment," Claudia smirked and disappeared into the house only to return seconds later. She said, "The food inside is amazing."

"Yep. Come on, I want to show it off." Heidi pulled Claudia back into the dining room. Silver and glass plates, each covered with paper lace doilies and topped with every imaginable finger-sized food, covered the faux marble table.

"Heidi, wow! There's so much food! I love steak tartar and caviar." Claudia picked up a tiny sandwich off one of the serving plates and stuffed it into her mouth. "Yum, cucumber sandwiches."

"Eat them now, they won't taste as good after people have been smoking around the food. I swear I could taste the smoke in the food the last time my parents hosted a party."

"When did you get so sensitive to cigarettes?"

"I don't know," Heidi whined. "Moving on, check out the ice sculpture of Poseidon and the congratulations sign with photos of Dad's work friends."

"So cool." Claudia giggled at her own joke.

"I know, I know. Mom went all out on this one. The ice is from the icehouse on River Road." Heidi picked up a piece of shrimp and dipped it into a silver-rimmed, glass serving bowl. "I'm trying not to eat all the shrimp, but it's so good." Heidi signaled to Claudia. "Take one of the small plates on the sideboard. Sample some of the other food—oysters, smoked salmon, pâté—check out the magnum-sized champagne."

"I've never seen such a big bottle!" Claudia wandered over to the bar around the corner. "Look at all these choices; gin, rum, whiskey, red and white wine, Coke, ginger ale, tonic water..."

"Claudia, Claudia, come on... We have to do our jobs. You stay here with the guestbook and catch people when they come in the door. I'll be outside sending them your way. Mom said getting everyone to sign the book is very important."

"Where's the book?"

Heidi pulled it off the sideboard and handed it to Claudia along with several extra pens. "I'm going out front, I'll be back later. Mom only expects us to do this for the first hour of the party and then we have to mingle. Leave the book open on the hall table with some pens when you're done."

Soon after the house became so crowded that people began bumping into each other. Heidi left her post outside and wove around the guests in the living room carrying a tray with an array of puff pastries filled with either crab or spinach. She smiled and answered questions about the food when she was asked. A waiter with a different selection of hors d'oeuvres passed things at the other end of the room. Every twenty minutes or so Heidi exchanged one tray for another.

A good number of the guests balanced a cigarette in one hand and an alcoholic drink in the other. Heidi wished there were fewer cigarettes, but she was happy her Dad had quit. A cloud of smoke hovered in the living room and was beginning to drift into the hall. Heidi stop carrying around hors d'oeuvres and put the empty tray back in the kitchen. She wanted a Shirley Temple and went around to the outside of the room to the hall where the bar was set up on the pass-thru. While the bartender made her drink, she noticed some of the guests had moved into the sunroom and others were going into the backyard. She snatched up her glass and went outside to listen to the piano music and watched some guests waltzing on the parquet dance floor under the tent. Just about the time Heidi began to wonder what her friend was up to, Claudia appeared by her side with a glass filled with iced Coca-Cola.

"Cute twinkle lights in the trees out here. Who did that?"

"Dad and I did." Heidi cleared her throat. "Balancing on the ladder was awkward."

"I bet. Hey, did you see those men in black suits wandering around?"

"Which ones? All the men are wearing suits."

"Oh," Claudia said and nudged Heidi's shoulder. "Really? You know what I mean. The men with the extra-short hair strutting around away from the guests."

"Right, them." Heidi giggled. "Don't worry. I asked Dad, and he said they're here for security because some of the guests are bigwigs."

"Geez, I didn't realize your dad had those types of connections," Claudia teased.

"Oh, yes you did. Let's go inside and see if they brought the desserts to the table." Heidi took Claudia's arm, and they sauntered through the guests, past the kitchen, and into the dining room. Heidi put her Shirley Temple on an empty tray that rested on top of a folding stand. She picked up a small glass plate and began to inspect the new trays of desserts; strawberry parfaits, bite-sized key-lime pies and cheesecakes, cream-filled ladyfingers, a Harvey Wallbanger cake drizzled with white glaze, and translucent green Jell-O molded into a ring embedded with sliced strawberries.

"Hang on, what's happening?" Heidi glanced past the faux marble table through the front window. She pulled Claudia out the front door so forcefully that her friend almost spilled her Coco-Cola on one of the guests. She was able to hear but not understand what was going on. "There's a guy over by a car speaking Russian to your dad. He must be up to something."

"Dad knows all kinds of people," Claudia retorted. "This one seems to be a problem. The guards are escorting him into a car. Problem solved, I guess."

"Yep, I see. I wonder what that was about?"

"You and me both. Hey, let's play a game and see if we can figure out who's who at this shindig."

"Sounds like fun and better than staring at mom's *Who's Who* publication. It's so dull with hundreds of important people's names and accomplishments listed like a telephone book. You cover the backyard, and I'll go into the house. Meet me by the inside staircase in an hour. We've got a lot of work to do on this mission. Do you have a pocket?"

Claudia's hands disappeared into the folds of her skirt. "Yes, I have a pocket. Why?"

Heidi pulled two spiral notepads the size of her palm, and two half-size pens, out from the concealed pockets in the side of her full-length flowered gown. "Here, take a set. I think we can stand around groups of people while they're talking and write their names down, along with some information about each of them. We can't be too obvious that we're taking notes, so we better do that off to the side when we leave each group."

"Cool, we can pretend to be detectives or maybe journalists." Claudia moved away.

Heidi caught Claudia's arm. "My parents aren't expecting us to socialize the entire evening."

"Good to know, because I want to watch some shows on television."

"Like what?"

"*I Love Lucy* reruns for starters. I'm thinking you might be Ethel and I'm Lucy."

"Go on, we have work to do." Heidi wandered off muttering, "Ethel, are you kidding me? I'm thirteen and Ethel's ancient."

After their mission was complete, Heidi rendezvoused with Claudia by the roped-off staircase in the middle of the house and meandered through the crowd back to the den. They collapsed side by side on the daybed feigning exhaustion.

"So, what's with the museum type rope across the stair railing?"

"Mom, put it there to 'tell' people she didn't want them wandering up to the bedrooms."

"Funny, lady."

Heidi shoved her friend over a smidge. "Okay, I found out my dad's a member of the, by invitation only, Cosmos Club. I asked Mr. Norstad what it's about and he said it's a place 'for people of distinction and intellect.' Sounded hoity-toity to me. He said the club's been around since the 1800s and some of the rooms look like a smaller version of Versailles."

"Mmm, the French influence is everywhere. I wonder if my dad was invited into the club?" Claudia stood up with her nose in the air. "I'll go ask."

Heidi jumped up and pulled her back. She snickered. "Claudia, stop, you can ask him later. What did you find out about the other guests?"

"Ambassador Holmes is here. I don't think he has anything to do with Sherlock Holmes."

"You didn't ask him, did you?"

"Yeees, I did!" Claudia snorted.

"Ugh, you're such an airhead."

"No, I'm not—I also learned more about the security staff. They said there're some interesting people around here."

Heidi wiggled to the edge of the cushion. Excitedly, she said, "Why? Who else is here that I haven't noticed?"

"I don't know. Got you going, though." Claudia poked Heidi in the side. "There's someone here called Mr. Abshire, whose first name is the same as my dad's."

"Great, Claudia, you're a genius," Heidi said sarcastically and stuck out her tongue. "Hey, maybe Henry Kissinger will show up or Vice President Ford. My parents are in a picture with Ford that mom put out on the hall table yesterday."

Claudia giggled. "Well, someone did mention they were coming."

"You're impossible. I don't want to be around if they show up. Too much pomp and circumstance, but even though Mom said we didn't have to stay around all night, we shouldn't hide in here for too long."

"Oh, come on, we can watch one show on the TV. Please?" Claudia pleaded.

"Well, all right." Heidi turned on the television. With her encouragement, they remained in front of the screen for an hour without another thought to their obligations to her mother or to the honors connected with meeting the vice president.

Chapter 14

Three months later...

Heidi walked into the den to watch television and saw her mother sitting at the desk writing.

"Hi, Mom, you startled me. I thought you were in the basement. Can I watch TV? The guide says reruns of *The Lucy Show*, and *I Dream of Jeannie* are coming on at three o'clock."

Her mother stopped what she was doing and turned around. "No, not now. I need to talk to you about something important. Please, sit down." Heidi rolled her lips together and slumped onto the La-Z-Boy chair that faced the television.

"Mom, pleeease, I want to watch my shows. What's going on?"

"No need to get snappy. What is the earliest event in your life you remember?"

Heidi's eyebrows went up, and she rolled her eyes toward the ceiling for answers. "Um, I don't know."

Her mother stood up and slowly began to pace back and forth across the room. "What I have to say is very important."

"What, Mom?" Heidi crossed her arms.

"Your dad and I were married to other people before the Second World War and then divorced. Later, we met in D.C. in our late thirties. By the time you were born, we were quite a bit older."

Heidi shrugged. "So?"

Her mother stopped pacing, pulled over the desk chair, and sat down across from Heidi. "We moved to Paris, and we still didn't have a baby. Our situation seemed impossible until we found help."

"Mom, what are you talking about?" She started to stand up, but her mother raised one finger in objection. Heidi sat back down.

"We had connections in Paris, and they helped us adopt a baby from Germany. You've brought us nothing but happiness ever since."

"What? You're not my mom? Dad isn't my dad?"

"Of course, we're your parents. There were so many children needing homes, it was just as well I couldn't become pregnant."

"How can you be a mom if you didn't have a baby?"

"I had one, just not in the usual way. A real mother takes care of her children, loves them, and makes sure they have everything they need."

"So, my first mother didn't love me?"

"I suspect she did, and that is why you had to leave her. Things were very different back then. Perhaps she didn't have enough money and asked the nuns to find you a new family."

"Nuns?"

"Yes, nuns. They helped us."

"And my other father, where was he? Why didn't he help with money?"

"I don't know. I'm only explaining this now because we need to go to court to get naturalization papers done for you. We tried to take care of this when you were a baby, but it wasn't possible."

"I don't understand." Heidi started playing with her fingernails and thought about biting them but didn't.

"We are U.S. citizens and you were born in Germany. Usually, that means you would automatically be a U.S. citizen, but because of the way you were adopted the circumstances are a little different."

"Adopted! You're unbelievable! You've kept the truth from me all these years!" Heidi launched out of her seat and clenched both fists at her side. She stared down at her mother. "I don't know how to speak the language, and I don't know much about the country. Am I going to get kicked out of here if I don't do what you're asking?"

"That's absurd." Her mother hesitated, linked her hands together, and kneaded her thumbs back and forth. "You have been here ten years, and for all practical purposes this is your country." Her mother's hands fidgeted even more. "Germany is a beautiful place. Regardless, we need to complete the paperwork."

Heidi turned toward the window and hissed, "I don't care about papers. I feel like a puppy." Tears welled up in her eyes, but she tried not to give in to the hurt and fury that was building inside.

"Don't be ridiculous, you're not a puppy!"

"Why didn't you tell me about this before now? I'm thirteen!" The tears began to roll down her face, and her chin trembled. She locked her gaze on a red cardinal outside the window.

"I believed you were our daughter from the moment we met." Her mother stopped talking for a solid minute. "We need to do this to make your life easier in the future. You can't get a job or a passport anywhere with your current status."

Heidi's voice elevated. "Who cares! What kind of mom gives away her baby?"

"That's a good question," her mother whispered. "Let's just say, we chose to adopt you, and that makes you special,"

"Special? I'd rather be normal." Heidi went over to the desk and picked up a pencil holder, intending to throw the contents on the floor. Instead, with a bang, she slammed it back on the desk. "Okay... now I know why you two appear older than all my friends' parents."

"I didn't realize you'd noticed."

"It's embarrassing. People have even asked me if you're my grandmother."

Her mother popped out of the chair and started to pace the floor again. "Now, you're being hurtful on purpose."

"Sorry." Heidi stiffened her back. "Can I be a U.S. and a German citizen at the same time?"

"We are going to apply for your naturalization papers," her mother said firmly and pulled a Kleenex tissue from the box in front of the leather-bound books on the built-in bookshelves.

"Why did I learn French and not German?"

Her mother turned around, went back to the desk, and leaned on a corner. "It made more sense for you to learn French since we lived in France, and Nanny Madeline was a native speaker."

"Mom, I need to know more." She shivered even though it was a warm summer day.

"Very well. You were born near Frankfurt. The nuns took you away from there a few weeks later."

"Why?"

"I have no idea, please don't interrupt. Our chauffeur, Michel, drove us from Paris to a cathedral in a small town in Germany. A nun interviewed us in her office. At first, I was worried we couldn't adopt through them because we weren't Catholic and had been divorced, but they didn't ask. Then, the nun took us into another room to meet you. That's when I found out your birthday matched my mother's, and I knew we should be together." Her mother's lips pursed. "Come to think of it, I'm not sure why our past wasn't an issue. Our doctor wrote a letter saying we were healthy, some of our Parisian friends wrote us lovely recommendation letters, and we paid an attorney to work out the details. A little over a month later, on Mother's Day weekend, Nanny Madeline traveled back with Nathan—your dad—to get you."

"I miss Maddie. She hasn't visited in a long time." Heidi paused. "Why didn't you go with them to pick me up?"

"My stomach was upset." Her mother's jaw twitched into a half smile. "She was such a reliable nanny, and wonderful when I had horrible migraine headaches. I'm sorry I wasn't much of a mother during those first impressionable years of your life."

"Sooo, I'm the last to know I'm adopted? Do the McGwires' know?"

"Claudia doesn't, but her parents do. The only other people are our friends from Paris because they were there when you came into our lives. Oh, and my sister."

"How did we get here?"

"We arrived on a gorgeous ship called the SS United States. It took about four days."

"Wow! This is all too much." Heidi started to leave the room. "Where is Dad?"

"Wait! Don't rush away." Her mother grasped her for an instant, and then let go.

"I can't believe you told me all this without him!" Heidi stomped out of the room and bumped into her father dressed in his gardening jeans and an Izod shirt.

"Dad, you're dirty!" She stood stock-still, staring at him. The tears welled up in her eyes, again. "I'm adopted? Why weren't you here when she told me?"

"Oh? No!" His face reddened. The rose he held by his side dropped to the ground headfirst. "Without me? I'm sorry, I wanted to be here." He glared past Heidi's shoulder, and his eyes narrowed.

Heidi held her sides, and her father wrapped his arms around her, but she didn't want any part of his sympathy. Her heart was melting and freezing all at once. She attempted to analyze the situation. *Now, what do I do? That woman deserves more than a grim smile. I can feel her eyes on my back. Why doesn't he say something? Why isn't he scolding her for leaving him out of the discussion? Why am I standing here?* She pulled herself away and ran up the stairs.

Her father called out, "Wait, let's talk about this."

She stopped in mid-step. "Maybe later," Heidi responded, before rushing the rest of the way up the stairs and into her room. Slamming the door, she flopped into her desk chair sobbing as the window in front of her sprung imaginary bars over the panes. Crying gave her a headache along with a stuffy nose and didn't solve anything. Blowing her nose hard on the nearest piece of clothing, she pulled her journal out from the desk drawer. One-Three-Six-Four, she clicked the numbers in place to unlock the pages and began writing.

Being thirteen is hard enough without my adoption being thrown at me. I will never trust 'Mom' again. But I feel sorrier for Dad than I do for myself. He was so angry standing there next to the broken rose. I was cast out of one family and put into another. My life is a blank slate before I came to Paris! Where did I start? What did I miss? I suddenly feel old and tired and trapped. Heidi Rose—a hollow void, forever to be lost in space. My family feels fake. I can't ever look at anything the same way again. And I thought learning the truth about Santa Claus was awful! Who am I?

Locking the journal, Heidi tucked it under her old school papers in the drawer. Picking up the receiver on the rotary phone, she dialed Claudia. The first number rattled around, the second, and finally the seventh—she hung up before the lines connected.

To refocus her mind, she snatched her copy of Charles Dickens' *Great Expectations* from the white bookshelf and noted the number on the bookplate inside the cover. She then found the matching number in the card catalog box and wrote down the date under the other four entries. It took days to stick the bookplates in each one of her 120 books and catalog them. Her library was dwarfed by her parents' collection of 987 books on the den's shelves—she'd counted.

Grabbing the Kleenex tissue box off the desk, she crawled into the corner of her closet, switched on the nightlight, and curled up in a blanket. She'd never connected with Pip in the past, but this time she felt inextricably linked. They were both adopted, and everything sort of worked out all right for him, but he'd had many more hardships. Maybe things would work out for her, too. She read through about fifty pages and fell asleep thinking about Pip.

The next morning, she woke cocooned in her blanket feeling stronger and determined to one day find her roots. For now, she would try to become whole again without her parents' help. She picked up the phone and dialed Claudia. Pacing back and forth from the desk to the bed, the long-coiled cord untwisted. "Hi, I have to tell you something in person. Can you meet me at the library? I'm going to walk."

"Sure, won't your mom have a fit if you do?"

"Yeah, probably. She's asleep. I'll tell Dad where I'm going, and he can pick me up later. I don't think he'll give me a hard time today. I have to see you."

"Okay."

"I'll wait while you ask for a ride." Heidi impatiently tapped her fingers on the table until Claudia returned.

"Mom's busy showing a renter the house across the street, but my dad will bring me. See you soon."

They arrived at the front of the library within minutes of each other.

Heidi pulled opened the door on the passenger side of the McGwire's car. Looking over Claudia, Heidi said, "Hi, Uncle David. Thanks for bringing her."

"You're welcome. Good to see you, Heidi. I'll be back in an hour."

Claudia wiggled out of the car, closed the door, and waved goodbye before he drove away. "You're all out of breath."

"I know, I ran." Heidi raked her hands through her hair.

"Right. Makes sense." Claudia put her hands on her hips. "So, what's going on?"

"While Dad was working in the garden yesterday, Mom told me something."

"What? Don't just stand there. Tell me."

"I wrote about stuff in my journal last night instead of calling. I tried, but I couldn't finish dialing your number. It seemed easier to crawl in the closet and read. I need your help."

"Sure, but what are you talking about?"

"My parents aren't what they seem. They're not like yours."

"Okay, no big surprise. Your mother's a fruitcake."

"Not what I'm saying. Listen to me."

"I'm right here, keep talking. What's the big deal?"

"Sorry, my head's all over the place. Your parents had you, mine adopted me from some cathedral in Germany! I'm not exactly a U.S. or a German citizen! I was only told because I have to get some naturalization documents done so I can officially become a U.S. citizen. I don't even understand how I could be here this long without having had this fixed, Dad must have done something."

"Cool story. Why are you freaking out?"

"They hid it from me all these years. This sucks!" Heidi tightened her ponytail. "Now I know why my parents kept exposing me to stuff about lost children."

"What stuff?"

"Um... the musical, *Annie*. Books like *Great Expectation* and *Mandy*."

"Don't forget *Peter Pan*. This is weird. Were they trying to tell you something all along? This new information explains a lot about them, too, I guess."

"Yeah, I suppose."

Heidi and Claudia passed through the double library doors and walked over to the reference section.

"Help me do some research," Heidi said.

"Liiiike?"

Heidi expression soured. "Like how to track lost parents."

"Are you kidding? This isn't a detective story out of your bookshelf!"

"Please," Heidi begged.

"We can try."

They searched through the library's endless catalog cards, and then the shelves.

"Well, sorry we wasted an hour," Heidi said.

"Maybe there's another way. We can try again when we have more time."

"I don't know." Heidi looked at her watch. "My parents...who are they? I feel like I have two sets, now. I don't know how to handle the new me."

"You're still you, just with a mysterious past. Your adopted parents take care of you. They get to be called Mom and Dad—get over it."

"Easy for you to say, but I'll try. Promise you won't tell anyone. I have enough trouble with my school friends without them knowing I might've been illegitimate."

"You don't know that."

"I'll be teased. Promise me!"

"O-kaaay. I promise."

"Hello, ladies—did I miss something?" Uncle David asked behind Heidi.

Heidi's heart leapt in her chest. "Hi, Uncle, you startled me."

He said, "Promise what?"

"Nothing Dad," Claudia snickered. "We were just talking about a story."

"Heidi, I'll drive you home." David adjusted his aviator sunglasses.

"Okay, thanks."

They left the building and got into the car. Heidi sat silently next to Claudia in the back seat pondering her situation.

Heidi and her father sat in the living room using flashcards to work through the naturalization questions. "Do you want to talk more about your adoption?"

"No, I wish you were in the house when Mom told me."

"I'm sorry she didn't wait."

"Hmm. Not sure I want to be an official U.S. citizen, but I don't know any other way of life." She pulled on her lower lip.

"You can always go back to Germany when you're older and explore the country."

"Like I said," continued Heidi. "I don't want to talk about my adoption, not ever. Let's do the flashcards. I hate taking tests, and this is going to be the worst one."

"I don't think so. They will give you multiple-choice questions on a form. I think you know most of them from your school history classes. After that, you will only have to stand up and answer a few more questions before reciting the same pledge you use in school every morning."

"Oh, it will be difficult in a different way. Never mind, I want to get this over with."

"Aw, I see. You mean emotionally challenging."

"Is Mom going to make me wear a dress?"

"Yes, you have to look neat, like a proper young lady."

She wrinkled her nose. "If you say so, let's start practicing."

"After I read the questions, I'll hold up the flashcard." He cleared his throat and began. "Here we go. What is the supreme law of the land?"

"That's easy, the Constitution."

"What are the first few words of the document?"

"We the People…"

"Excellent. How many years does the president serve?"

"His first term lasts four years, but he can be re-elected for a second term."

"Who is the current president?"

"Nixon."

"Here's a hard one. State one of the writers of the Declaration of Independence, and when was it officially declared?"

"Ugh, Thomas Jefferson." Heidi hesitated. "July 4, 1776."

Her father grilled her with questions for another half-hour. "All right, you've done well. Here are two more and then we'll go out for ice cream. Deal?"

"It's a deal. I'll have vanilla."

Her father smiled. "Aw, you have your life all planned out. I'll have chocolate. What is the nation's capital?"

"Dad, you're kidding!" She lagged and then said, "Washington, D.C."

"Where is the Statue of Liberty?"

"And the final answer is New York. Ding, ding, I'm done. Let's go, I want my ice cream." Heidi batted her eyelashes at him. "Please?"

"You betcha. That's what dads are for!"

A second before they stepped out the front door, her mother appeared. She said, "I could hear you practicing from the other room. It sounded like you had a productive study session. Don't leave yet, we have to pick a dress for court. I have a couple here I bought while I was shopping with Sadie. I'd like you to try them on."

"*Mom,* you pick one! I have stuff to do, and I hate modeling. Clothes aren't so important."

"Of course they are. Clothes reflect your character, and people judge you by your choices."

"That's dumb. I don't care about that!" Heidi put her hand to her mouth and started to bite her nail.

"Don't you dare bite your nails! Haven't I taught you anything? You're so stubborn!"

"Sorry." She took a bite and stopped, remembering the hot sauce her mother used to put on her fingers.

"Let's go with the white one." Her mother held up one of the two dresses. "It's a suitable color."

"I think I want the blue and red one."

"No, you don't want to stand out. The white one will work."

"Well, I guess you knew all along what was best for me," Heidi chided. "Oh, I mean, which dress is best. Dad, let's go for ice cream."

The following Monday, Heidi answered questions about the United States in court and recited the Pledge of Allegiance. Germany was lost to her, and she wondered what it would have been like to grow up with her other family and if she had sisters or brothers. Almost everyone she knew had siblings, and they never seemed as lonely as she often felt. Then, the thought struck her, she might have grown up in an orphanage.

Chapter 15

1974...

It had been three years since Heidi had officially become a naturalized citizen. Her relationship with her mother had changed. Her home life seemed to be different from what her teenage peers were going through. She compared notes with Claudia and other friends; arguments were prevalent, but nothing like what she endured with her mother. They started to argue more and more as Heidi struggled for her independence. The trouble was, neither of them backed down. They always argued about minor things like peanut butter sandwiches, bugs, soap, hair ribbons, bare feet, and which rags to use on different bathroom surfaces. The list of topics was endless and entirely pointless. At the start of each battle, Heidi had to listen to a long list of all her past sins before her present ones were revealed. Her mother recited grievances like a theatrical script. The fiendish rantings went on for what felt like hours—the staccato pitch of her mother's voice rising and falling.

This time, Heidi hoped she wasn't in trouble. She slumped against the nearest wall in the den. "Mom, make me sit in my room, I hate this. What's wrong?"

"Nothing's wrong." Her mother pursed her lips. "There are some new rules. Since you're driving on a regular basis, you can't go out alone with your girlfriends at night. Find some boys to spend time with, they will protect you…"

"What do you mean?" Heidi's voice became more strident. The argument escalated, and she tried to control her temper. "Most of my social life is built around my girlfriends."

"You can go out with them during the day. No sleepovers, no movie theaters, no concerts." Her mother's voice elevated even more. "They are dangerous without adult supervision."

Now, Heidi was shouting too. "Mom, what's left? All my friends want to do things together at night. Their parents are letting them go out, and they'll leave me behind. You're ridiculous!"

"No, I'm not. Surely, not every parent has consented. You'll work out something."

Unrelated topics and words flew back and forth for another half-hour. Finally, her mother's voice toned down and became more passive much to Heidi's relief.

Her mother said, "And don't bring any of those germ-infested library books home again. I saw one on your desk. I washed the area and the plastic library cover. They are such smelly things from all the people who handle them."

"The book isn't ours! You can't wash it! I love books, and I can't buy them all or sit in the library for hours reading. Wait! How do books relate to my friends?"

"Nothing, I was just thinking." Her mother wrung her hands. "You can meet your friends at the library. Don't forget, you have to wash your hands as soon as you get home."

Heidi squeezed her lips together and wanted to run. Imaginary chains created by her mother's rules crept around her chest. "We can't talk or have fun in the library! I can't fight with you anymore. I'm going to my room." She clenched her fists and went upstairs to write in her journal.

I don't want to get hung up on Mom's problems! She makes me feel so guilty when we argue—I can't stand her ranting. I want to please her, but I'm miserable. The fights make me feel abandoned. I should crawl into one of the rabbit's holes and disappear. Isn't that sort of what Alice in Wonderland did? Mom is unhappy no matter what I do. None of my friends' mothers act this way. I guess mine has always been abnormal. Aunt Eileen's normal, why are two sisters so different? I feel like I'm being eaten alive some days by my own mother. What do they say about praying mantises? They eat their young. No, that's not right, some fish eat their young. Female praying mantises devour their mates. My mother seems to take on our arguments as if they are a competition. She wins when I'm crying, and then she stands over me with a smug, victorious smile plastered across her face. Or maybe it's worse than that, and the battles are the only way she feels alive and not depressed. Now that would make a tragic script for a play. I'm rambling, but I can't help myself. I want to watch TV all night tonight; nothing better to do. Mom's not going to let me out. I think there's an old Frankenstein or Dracula movie

ReRun on television tonight and some new British comedies about crazy people.

She locked the journal and heard banging coming out of the connecting bathroom. Heidi peeked around the corner and saw her father sitting on the edge of the tub. A toolbox she'd never seen before rested at his feet on the tile floor.

"Dad, what are you doing?!"

"I'm trying to fix the leaky faucet," he said with obvious heartfelt exasperation.

"What about a repairman? You've always called them before. Besides, I like watching them work and learn a lot. For some reason, Mom lets me."

"Your mother has decided she doesn't want them around anymore. It's always been about those pesky germs." The side of his mouth twitched. "I've seen her walk around searching for microscopic creatures with a magnifying glass. She looks like a detective, but it's not amusing."

"Yeah, I know."

"Your mother doesn't want to be bothered with cleaning up around them. To keep her calm, I'm going to have to have a different toolkit for each area of the house."

"She's so peculiar. Why is this happening?"

"Remember the last crew that came through when you were on school vacation? Your mother washed the area they were going to fix. Then I covered everything in plastic with a hole cut out above the broken site—like a surgeon does. When the repairs were done, I had to take the plastic off, and she rewashed everything."

"Yep, yep. Dad, I watched her follow them around making sure they didn't touch any door handles. But why?"

"I don't know, Mousey. I'm afraid the house will end up in total disrepair since I'm not much of a fix-it man." He wiped his brow.

"Oh, Dad, this is too much! You only like working in the garden. Can you change her mind?"

"Not likely. I can't figure out how to push her out of this destructive cycle. My diplomatic skills of persuasion don't faze her. I can't even buy power tools to make repairs." Her father shrugged. "She thinks I'll hurt myself, and that battle isn't worth fighting."

"I guess. We made the rabbit hutches and bamboo enclosure without power tools. It took forever. You could do what you want and ignore her," Heidi scoffed, "but that tactic doesn't work for me. Every time I try, she guilts me into submission."

"Making someone feel guilty is a powerful tool. There certainly are better ways to change people's points of view." Her father looked at her and smiled sympathetically.

The wrench slipped and stripped off a thin layer of skin from her father's forearm half the length and width of a small banana. Pin-sized drops of blood formed instantly on the surface of the raw patch.

"Jesus! Dad, you just jinxed yourself. What should I do?"

"I'm all right." He flinched. "A bandage will distract me. My blood pressure meds make my skin thin and fragile. Shit, it hurts."

"Dad, you just cursed! You've never done that in front of me."

"Sorry, you're right. The wound's not that bad."

Heidi went over to the medicine cabinet by the sink and found some Bactine and a large bandage for his angry arm.

"You used to fix my scraped knees when mom was too squeamish." Heidi's shoulders hunched forward, and her throat filled with bile. Swallowing, she took a deep breath and covered the wound. Hoping to further distract him from the pain, she said, "Remember the time I was walking on a downed tree in the bamboo grove and skewered my inner thigh? You came to the rescue and put ointment in the gap. It itched for weeks."

"I do, but it could've been far worse. You were shaking and didn't even cry. Do you remember, the bamboo was inspired by Monet's garden in Giverny, France? There are many beautiful plants and flowers there, too, of course. The lily pond is splendid. When your mother and I went there years ago, she decided she wanted bamboo in our backyard, so I found some when we moved back from Europe and buried it in the yard."

"No, I don't think you ever told me. Thanks for patching me up when I fell on the bamboo, and for every other time." She smoothed the edges of his new bandage down and pretended to kiss the wound. "There you go. Now I've helped you."

"The tides have turned. I feel better already." He stood up and wiped his hands on his jeans. "I'm sure you remember stomping around on the grass breaking off the new bamboo shoots as they popped out of the ground. You used to say it was 'your homework assignment' so I wouldn't have to cut them down with a machete."

"It was my excuse to get out of doing my school work," Heidi confessed. "So, what do we do about Mom?"

"I'm not sure. I've been trying to figure out how to help her for ages."

"You've known her longer. I can't change anything." Heidi failed at being light-hearted about the situation. "You were doomed when she permanently kicked you out of the master bathroom."

"Very funny," he rebuked. "That was a long time ago. Your mother wanted privacy, so I respected her wishes. Now you and I are forever taking turns in the same bathroom. I'm sorry."

"No hard feelings, Dad. At the time, you were fighting bigger battles at work." Heidi liked how calm he was most of the time. "I think you should get busy finding another job. You're too smart to get consumed with household problems. What did you use to do anyway? You never talked about your work."

"Top secret stuff, Mousey."

"Really! You're so cool! Bet you can have any job you want."

"Thanks for the vote of confidence, young miss." He chuckled. "I'll get right on it. I plan to meet your Uncle David tonight at the Old Ebbitt Grill to discuss my options."

"Okay, that's good. I'm going to go downstairs and watch television all night."

"Maybe you shouldn't stay up too late. We're going to the cathedral with the McGwires tomorrow."

Sunday's cathedral service was a distraction away from her mother. After staying awake all night, it became difficult for Heidi to keep her eyes open during the sermon. She felt fortunate that Sadie didn't come to church this time. Heidi needed to talk to Claudia alone on their customary stroll around the cathedral after the service. Finally, the last of the choir members passed by the pews. The McGwires and Baileys slid out of their seats and went straight outside.

"Girls, we'll meet you by the car in half an hour," her father said as they walked away in the opposite direction.

"Claudia, what am I going to do. Yesterday Dad told me repairmen are banned from the house, and he hurt himself trying to fix a leaky faucet in our bathroom. To add to this, Mom is messing with my social life, and I haven't done anything wrong. Dad isn't much help on that front. Seems like he discounts everything."

"I doubt it, he's pretty sharp. What's going on?"

"Last night, Mom and I had a big argument over who I can go out with and when. She didn't 'ground' me, but she might as well have."

"You mean dates?"

"No, anyone. I can go out with girls during the day, only guys or double dates at night. This is going to put a cramp in my style."

"What a pain! Does she limit where you can go during the day?"

"No, not too much. She said to go out in groups and not alone."

"What's that about?"

They walked around the back of the cathedral.

"Safety, what else! The trouble is, I try to honor Mom's wishes, and my school friends want me to go to a concert Saturday night. I don't want to sneak out, so I told them I wasn't allowed to go unless the guys came along. They thought I was making it up."

"That's dumb. They should know you better."

"Probably doesn't help I flirt with the guys a little to get their attention. My friends see me and walk off in a huff." Heidi almost tripped over a crack in the concrete sidewalk. "Mom seems to like the guys I bring home, but they're not ones I'd date. Although, they are nerdy and fun!"

"I suppose that's a good start, so you can at least get out at night. I'm glad I don't have to watch your flirting, and we're at different schools. Not sure I'd stick around either. I think I'd get jealous."

"You've got to be kidding? You of all people. Every time we get together for a double date you always have the handsome and smart ones."

"Lah-de-dah!" Claudia stuck her tongue out. "You know I'm fat compared to you, Miss Twig."

"And you're an Amazonian goddess." Heidi tried to make it sound like a joke, but she really did feel that way.

"Am not!"

"Yes, you are! Then there's your golden hair and…"

"Really? Enough already."

"It's both our moms' faults, always comparing us. They say I did this wonderful thing. Yadda, yadda! Claudia did this and that, totally sickening." Heidi bit her nail. "Our mothers sound like they're having a boxing match over which one of us is better. I can't stand it!"

"You can't stand it?" retorted Claudia. "You should hear my mom go on about you while you're not around. She makes me feel like I'm a nothing, and you're a genius."

"Nope, not me." Heidi tapped her forehead. "No brains in here. Then there's my bulbous nose. Blah! I have to rely on being funny to get anyone's attention. Your blonde hair and blue eyes snare them in a heartbeat."

"Hey, I thought we were talking about our mothers."

"Whatever, the boy stuff's true. Anyway, I can't fight my mom and win, so I guess I lose a bunch of friends at school. The girls have their own issues and can't be bothered with mine, I guess. Thanks for sticking with me." Feeling hopeless, Heidi scuffed her shoe across the pavement.

"Sure, glad to help." Claudia poked Heidi in the side and made her laugh.

"Oops, we're already at the cars. The dads are coming."

"Here we are." Her Uncle David was grinning. "Your dad and I agreed the four of us should lunch together next Sunday after church. I mean the five of us, Sadie told me she'll be coming next week."

"Yeah, okay," Claudia piped in first. "Good idea. Bye, Heidi. See you."

There was a glimmer of hope. Two months later, Heidi's mother sent her to the basement after she got home from school. "Go see what we've done downstairs but stay out of the maid's room. Your dad and I made some changes while you were in school."

Heidi never went down to the basement after being punished for going down there years before. She thought about her little black rocking chair and wondered where it went. For the first ten years of her life, she sat in that chair in her room whenever she was naughty. Her legs would twitch, her tears would flow, and she'd chew her nails. The worst day was when she went into the basement after being told not to. She'd taken a flying ballerina leap right onto the freshly painted floor in the maid's room in an attempt to avoid the wet spots and landed wrong. Realizing her mistake, she ran up the stairs and left a trail of green footprints on every other wooden step and was caught. She hadn't been in her punishment chair more than five minutes when her mother came into her room and applied a horrible tasting spicy sauce onto her fingernails. After that event, her curious and somewhat defiant behavior ceased.

Going down the basement stairs today made her uneasy. On the landing, she hesitated before continuing. At the bottom, she cautiously peered into the first large room to her right. On one side, there was a pile of packing boxes stacked from floor to ceiling. On the other was a washer and dryer, which she had no idea how to work. The edges of the washing machine were caked with soap powder.

Yuck! Mom's hands are chapped and cracked from too much of this stupid soap. She's been wearing white gloves for the last month. No one wears white gloves anymore! God, come to think of it, she won't touch the escalator railing without gloves either, even when her hands aren't wounded. I'm surprised she manages to leave the house.

In the corner, below the laundry chute, there was a massive pile of unwashed clothes on top of a four-by-eight-foot table. Searching through, Heidi picked up one item and found a spider carcass and pulled her hand back sharply. Starting again, she found a few of her lost items and put them in a nearby pillowcase. Ducking out of the laundry room, she pushed the sack under the stairs by the wine bottles. She'd be brave and come down another day when her mother was asleep, grab the bag, wash the clothes in the sink, and hang them to dry in the bamboo grove out of sight. Opening the opposite door, she flinched when her mother appeared out of nowhere.

"Go on in," her mother prodded. "There's a new sofa, a sink with a bar, a foosball table, and a set of shelves with a 16-inch television and VCR movie player."

"Who's it for?"

"For you and your friends, it's a recreation room. Do you like it?"

"Wow! Yes!" Heidi wasn't quite sure how to deal with this new development. "Thank you, I can't remember the last time I had any of my school friends over."

"On your thirteenth birthday," her mother said.

"Yep, and that was over three years ago. Besides, I'm too old for balloon parties."

"Don't be silly, no one is too old for balloons. You can stay here with your friends instead of gallivanting all over the place."

"Gallivanting is fun." Heidi knew she should act more grateful, but she felt trapped. "All right, I understand."

"Ask your friends to enter the front of the house and say hello to me before heading down to the basement," her mother instructed. "Each and every one of them needs to wash their hands in the hall guest bathroom before coming all the way in the house. They may not use any of the other bathrooms and can leave through the basement back door. Is that clear?"

"Yes, Mom." Heidi's minor rebellious streak prompted her to walk into the hall bathroom whenever she came home and only pretend to wash her hands under the running water.

"That's a good girl."

"Speaking of washing," Heidi asked cautiously, "what's going on with the pile of dirty clothes in the other room? And the caked soap on the machine?"

Her mother put her hands on her hips. "You know the soap keeps the germs and spiders away. I don't bother with the clothes because they're old and they don't fit us anymore."

"Oh, I see."

"I do your laundry and give you a lovely new room, and you're criticizing me?"

"Sorry, I thought we could give them to a charity" Heidi lowered her head and decided not to press the subject. She was relieved to have a semi-private area since no one, other than Claudia, was permitted in her room upstairs. "What are the boxes in the laundry room?"

"Those are full of my memories. I have hundreds of letters and photographs, along with plates and other things I might want someday," her mother said proudly.

"Mmm, sounds interesting." Heidi flipped the braid that hung behind her back, and it landed on her shoulder. "Can I go call Claudia? I want to tell her about your gift."

"Go right ahead." Her mother's eyes lit up along with her smile. "Dinner will be ready shortly, so don't dawdle."

Heidi went to her room and phoned Claudia. "Hey, guess what? Mom cleaned out a room in the basement, and now I can have friends over."

"Cool."

"The old ratty curtains that hid the place from the outside are gone and replaced with wooden blinds. The walls have wood paneling, too. There are places to sit and a television. Maybe the rest of high school won't be so bad."

Chapter 16

Heidi and Claudia's parents insisted they go to a university after graduating from high school. Claudia chose to differ for a year and work in a nursing home, while Heidi completed her senior year. Once they were both free and accepted into a university, their parents rewarded them with a three-week paid vacation to Europe.

Days in advance, Heidi packed her bags and was ready for the adventure. A day before the trip, she drove over to the McGwires' to help Claudia pack her things.

"Heidi, I don't get it." Claudia put her shampoo bottle into her cosmetic bag. "Why is your mother letting you go on this trip?"

"I thought of that. Mom has always been so overprotective." She peeked in Claudia's bag. "Hey, you've got your toothbrush, but you're missing the paste."

"I got it, don't rush me." Claudia left the room and returned with the toothpaste. "Why do you think we're going?"

"Maybe it's because your mom found the group, and she's a travel agent. I guess she knows what she's doing. Besides, it's run by the University of Vienna." Heidi shrugged her shoulders.

Claudia laughed. "Your mom is letting you grow up after all."

"I don't know what to think. Mom tries to control everything."

"Yeah, I know. The tour is organized and chaperoned, that helps. It was only two years ago that she said you couldn't go out at night with your friends unless there was a guy in the group."

"Oh, whatever." Heidi bent down and picked some clothes off the floor.

"Leave them, I don't need any of those things. If you can't stand the mess, throw them on the chair.

Heidi scooped up more clothes and walked to the chair by the window. "Hey, someone suspicious is sitting in a car outside."

"What?" Claudia stopped packing and joined her. "Don't be so obvious."

"And you're not? You're staring right at him." Heidi marched away from the window over to the other side of the room. "Who is it?"

"Haven't a clue, but he's in a black suit." Claudia walked away from the window. "I wonder if our dads are up to something. My dad's new desk job doesn't sound interesting enough to warrant being stalked."

"You never know. Could be why our parents are in a hurry to send us away." Heidi twisted her newly cut shoulder-length hair around her finger. "Ignore the guy, maybe he'll leave."

"Yeah, we'll see." Claudia locked her suitcase and dragged it into the hall.

"Did you hear, Aunt Eileen is taking us to the airport?"

"This is getting stranger by the minute. I figured one of our parents would take us."

"Nope, the flight is early." Heidi shrugged her shoulders. "Everyone else is busy at their offices. Mom said she will get up and wish me 'bon voyage' at the door and go back to bed."

"Aunt Eileen makes sense since she drives, and your mom doesn't." Claudia went back over to the window. "That guy is still sitting in his car."

"Maybe he's just guarding the house. I'm more concerned about Aunt Eileen's driving. Last time I was in the car I felt like I was in *Mr. Toad's Wild Ride*."

"What do you mean?" Claudia smoothed the wrinkles out of her bed covers.

"You know the Walt Disney ride? When I went out to lunch with her last weekend, she turned a corner so hard I fell on the floor."

"Right, she used to be more cautious before she had cancer. I thought she was better after she ran off to Ireland for a new treatment."

"I don't know. I'd like to pretend she doesn't have cancer."

"Me too."

"Let's get out of here and go eat some lunch at Clyde's." Heidi's stomach gurgled.

"I'm right behind you, head for the back door. We don't want anyone following us."

"Sure, and then we fly out of here to England. We won't have to worry about strange men. At least I hope not." Heidi laughed and jerked Claudia out the door.

The European tour's itinerary included England, Belgium, France, Italy, and Germany. A Mercedes bus drove them around each country. A guide rode in the bus, filling each day with lectures, local cuisine, and cultural excursions with new friends. Heidi enjoyed each experience and every day seemed to disappear as fast as it arrived. She paid particular attention to every city and town they stayed in Germany, beginning with Munich, then Frankfurt, Cologne, and finally East and West Berlin.

"Wake up, Claudia. Everything out the window is gray and gloomy, like a black and white photograph."

Claudia stared outside. "Take a picture."

"I can't." Heidi fidgeted with the camera and shoved it deeper under the seat. "While you were sleeping, the guide said we couldn't take pictures or get off the bus. The guards can confiscate our cameras. I'm not going to risk losing twenty rolls of film. I have no idea what else they can do to us if we break the rules."

"Where are we? Hell?" Claudia rubbed the sleep out of her eyes.

"Soviet-occupied East Germany. We're going down the last part of a road known as the 'corridor' to get to West Berlin through the demilitarized zone. We've stopped a few times along the way while you slept. This section looks like a place right out of *The Twilight Zone*." Heidi wished they could get through faster.

"Now our parents should be worrying." Claudia rubbed her hand across the window to clear the fog, but it was on the outside. "The university must've gotten special permission for us to come through here."

The bus stopped, and they all disembarked on the West side of the wall. It was covered with graffiti and towered over their heads.

Heidi read the plaques. "Claudia, check out what these say about the people who tried to escape the East to rejoin their families. It says the wall is twelve-feet tall and ninety-one miles long and was erected in 1961. That was the year my parents took me out of Europe."

They stood and gawked at the concrete wall topped with coiled razor wire. "This doesn't feel the same as it did when we were taught about it in school." Claudia sighed.

"I'm having a hard time dealing with my German roots. I'm feeling torn up. I hope my other family wasn't really involved in the politics of the Wall."

"We haven't talked about your adoption for years."

"Standing here makes me wonder again."

"You're not from here."

"You're right, I'm from southern Germany. I keep wondering, do I have a sister or a brother? Was I first born?"

"So many questions. I'd go with firstborn." Claudia playfully hauled Heidi away from the Wall. "A bunch of our group is deviating from the planned tour tonight and traveling to a Heavy Metal concert. In the meantime, let's try to find some information in a government office about your other family."

"I've never listened to Metal music." Heidi stood paralyzed for a moment, then said, "I'd like to find out my roots. We need to plan."

Claudia grabbed Heidi's arm. "No, we don't, we'll just go to the local records office and see what they can tell us about adoption searches. I bet there's a procedure to follow."

"Ouch, let go."

Claudia released her grip. "Sorry. I'll ask the questions, and you just stand there."

Heidi thought the idea over. "Sounds okay, I guess."

"There's a phone booth over there." Claudia pointed to a little hut a short distance from where they were standing.

They crossed the road, and Claudia stepped into the booth. "I've learned enough German to be able to help you." She flipped through the pages of the phone directory. "Oh no, the page we want is torn."

"Let me see." Heidi held the two sides together. "There, now read. My heart is pounding. I still can't believe you speak German and I don't."

"Yeah, that's weird. Okay, I got an address. I'll wait here. Go get a city map from our bus driver and tell the guide we'll be back later."

Heidi left Claudia standing at the phone booth and returned to the tour bus where the driver sat on a step, smoking a cigarette.

"Hey, do you have a spare map I can borrow?"

The driver stared at her with a questioning look then snuffed out his cigarette with his thumb and index finger. "Vhy do you need zee map?" he asked in a heavy accent.

Heidi turned and pointed toward Claudia. "We wanted to check something out that our parents said we should see. So, can I borrow your map?"

With a groan, the driver stood on his feet and limped up the bus steps, one at a time. He opened a small, chipped cabinet near his seat and ruffled through its contents. With an "A-ha!" he produced a neatly folded, but coffee stained, map of Berlin. "Watch yourself, you don' vant to get in trouble."

Heidi thanked him before spinning on her heels to head back to where Claudia was waiting.

With a grin, Heidi waved the map in front of Claudia. "Here's a map."

"Cool, hand it over." Claudia unfolded the map and scanned the street grids. "Okay, found the place, off we go." They started walking down the pavement in single file. Claudia with the map unfolded in front of her. Heidi tagging behind. They found the office building and went inside, only to be turned away. They couldn't get adoption records from the office in Berlin since the files from the last decade were too fragmented. If they could be found, the clerk was reluctant to look—the rules were rigid. Most adoption records were inaccessible and deliberately sealed by some unknown entity.

"Claudia, this is hopeless. Why did we even try?"

"Hey, it wasn't a wasted hour," Claudia chided. "Maybe we should've tried in Frankfurt when we were there last week."

"I thought about it, I just didn't say anything."

"Heidi, really? You can be such a wimp. We were right there, and you did nothing! We don't have enough money to go back."

"I got scared. I'm an immigrant from Germany. This is so messed up. What if I find them, and they don't want anything to do with me? After all, they did abandon me. What if no one besides my birth mother knows I exist? What if they just don't care? What if no one is left alive who knows anything about me?"

"Whoa, don't be so hard on yourself. Yes, all that's possible, but you have to approach the situation with a more positive attitude." They walked down the street to the underground pubs for music and steins of beer.

"I'm happy you're my best friend," Heidi said. "I'm going to miss you after the summer is over. I wish we were going to the same university."

"Me too. Don't worry, you'll be okay on your own." Claudia put her hand on Heidi's shoulder. "Hey, we'll see each other during Christmas vacation."

The remaining three days of Heidi's travels with Claudia ended with a flight from Berlin to Dulles airport. For her, the adventure marked the end of living under her parents' rules. Legally, because she was eighteen, she was an adult but often still felt like a naïve child.

Heidi's belongings were packed and loaded into the family station wagon for the 450-mile drive to Bradford College in Haverhill, Massachusetts. Other than hearing about Aunt Eileen's years there when it was a private woman's college and glancing through the current brochures, Heidi hadn't seen the campus before applying. Thankfully, the school began accepting men in 1971, but that was only five years prior to her entrance. She wished she'd flown into Boston and taken a bus into Haverhill on her own, but her parents wanted to see the school, and her mother was afraid of airplanes. Leaving them at the airport would have been a quick goodbye but the hours in the car dragged out the separation anxiety she could feel ebbing out of her mother from the back seat. Sitting in the front with her father only allowed Heidi to avoid her mother's eyes, and she was glad to be up front with him.

Four hours into the drive, Heidi began to daydream as the car passed through a small town. She saw a young woman standing by a *stop* sign and thought about a news story. A girl was hitchhiking and hopped into a charitable driver's car and sat quietly in the passenger seat. When they arrived at the next intersection, the girl vanished into thin air. This happened to many drivers who picked the ghost girl up year after year. The local newspapers said the young woman had been murdered while catching a ride from a stranger. A lesson Heidi would always remember; be wary of strangers and never hitchhike. With that thought, trusting her father would get her safely to school, Heidi fell into a deep sleep for the remainder of the journey.

She woke with a start when the car came to a sudden stop. Her father looked in her direction and announced their arrival as she rubbed her eyes and looked out the window at a red-brick colonial building set back in a wooded area. A moment later, the car pulled into the semi-circular driveway of the Bradford campus. Heidi got out of the car and closed the door, ignoring her parents completely while taking in a deep breath. On the far side of the semi-circular driveway sat a collection of quaint colonial style buildings which resembled a miniature version of the photographs Heidi had seen in magazines of Harvard with both old brick and new concrete buildings surrounded by mature oak trees. Unlike Harvard, however, high grades were not required at this place. Coming back from her thoughts, she refocused on the mission at hand and moved around to the back of the car and unloaded her belongings with her parent's help.

Heidi and her father dragged her trunk and suitcase into the dormitory elevator. Simultaneously, across the hall, her mother duck through a door marked 'stairs' with a few light bags and reappeared on the third floor where Heidi and her father waited. Together they walked around until they found her name and someone else's written on an index card taped to the wall near the door jam. She took a deep breath and crossed the threshold. As Heidi stood surveying the room, a young blonde woman walked in with a guy in tow.

"Hey, how's it going? I'm Malinda. This is my boyfriend, Seth, he lives in Boston." He brought some boxes in and hauled them across the room. The space felt a bit overcrowded with five people in the dorm room.

Heidi's mother tugged her out of the room and said softly, "My first impression of Malinda isn't good. She's a bit rough around the edges. She's different than us, be careful."

"We just got here, how can you tell?"

"It's a feeling, that's all."

Her father interrupted, "We need to go soon."

"Please, make sure to call us when you are settled, and once a week every Sunday evening," her mother said. "I saw a phone on the wall about five rooms down in the next corridor by the stairs."

"Mom, it's okay. I'll talk to you soon." Heidi lightly kissed her on both cheeks. It was time to unpack without emotional distractions and to focus on the future.

Her father leaned in for a bear hug, and she welcomed his embrace. In her ear, he whispered, "Be safe, let me know if you need anything. I love you." He shoved cash into the pocket of her jacket which was certainly beyond the agreed monthly allowance that was already in her bank account. "Take this, it'll be our secret."

Her parents disappeared down the hallway.

The rest of the day was filled with orientation and organized social events. By the time the planned activities and dinner were over, Heidi felt exhausted. Back in her dorm room, she made her bed and tucked herself in. At midnight, she stirred in her sleep thinking she was at home and her mother was checking for spiders, but this noise was something else. The groaning and squealing sounds were unfamiliar, and they were coming from Malinda's side of the room. With a pillow over her head, Heidi struggled to fall back asleep.

Around nine in the morning, Heidi sat on her bed stretching. "Hello?"

Malinda and her boyfriend appeared from the other side of the room.

"Um… you two can't carry on like that while I'm in the room. What were you doing?" Heidi said tersely.

"You're kidding, right?" Malinda peered up at the guy. "We were having sex."

After eighteen years of excessive supervision, Heidi was having trouble coping with her current situation. She had never lived with a sister, much less complete strangers moaning on the other side of the room. Being adopted came to her mind once again. *Did my story start in a college dorm?*

She longed to talk to her mother about boys and relationships, except they never talked about such things. After Malinda's boyfriend left, Heidi heard all the graphic details of their encounter even though she tried to stop Malinda from talking. This wasn't really how she wanted to learn about such things. Heidi now believed her mother's warning and proceeded with caution from then on, seeking other friends beyond the walls of her dorm room.

Heidi phoned Claudia in December. "Hi, pal. Thanks for the letters you sent, sorry I haven't written. I've constantly got something going on and I haven't made time to keep up with anyone from home. So, get this—my roommate is, well, sleeping with her boyfriend every other weekend in our room!"

"It's okay about the letters, don't worry. Did you talk to her?"

"Yep, I complained. She explained everything she'd done with him. More than I wanted to know from a person I only met the night before. She said I should watch X-rated movies to see what to do. Then, she said if there is a tie on the door, I should go somewhere else."

"She sounds like a bitch, but did you find another place to stay when she's *busy*?"

"Yes, a new friend in the main dorm has a spare bed. This whole thing's so lame!"

"I know. Not sure what to tell you. *Sooo,* how are your exams going?"

"Changing the subject, I see. I don't blame you. I've learned how to study, and I'm actually getting decent grades on my exams!"

"What? I'm having trouble hearing you. There's lots of commotion in the dorm. We just finished exams, and I aced them."

Heidi raised her voice. "I said...I aced my exams, too, for the first time ever!"

"I need to find somewhere else to live next year." Music blared in the background, and Claudia shouted over the noise, "Hang on, let me close the door. Okay, I'm back. What did you say?"

Heidi talked fast. She wanted to tell Claudia everything before they had to end the call. Every minute cost ten cents. "I said... I aced my exams. During lectures, I take a piece of paper and write a clue word in the left column and a paragraph on the right explaining the terms. I review them every day. Someone said it's called the Cornell method. I don't know. Anyway, the night before exams, I went through stuff for an hour per class. Everyone else stayed up all night cramming, but I went to sleep. Yay, me!"

"That's great! See you in a couple weeks, and we'll celebrate," Claudia said. "Gotta go, bye for now."

Heidi went home for Christmas break expecting to be able to relax. Unfortunately, her parents were already deep into the holiday rush. She avoided getting caught up in the confusion and attended a matinee performance of Shakespeare's *A Midsummer Night's Dream* with Aunt Eileen.

Afterward, they stepped outside the Folger Theater on Capitol Hill, and her aunt stopped to talk to a couple outside the building. Heidi didn't know them, but she noticed the woman's eyes were puffy and red. They exchanged formalities which were followed by an uncomfortable silence. The woman had a yellow rose pinned to a pocket on her blouse. Heidi excused herself, saying she needed to pick up something at the market across the street to give them some privacy. She waited for the *walk* sign, then glanced back over her shoulder. The women were hugging.

In the aisle of the store, Heidi found some cookies and chamomile tea. She almost dropped the box of tea when her aunt walked up behind her and started to talk.

"Oh, you startled me." Heidi shook her head and refocused.

"Alexa is a friend from church, she's so upset."

"Why, what happened?"

"Her sister died of Legionnaires' disease a couple months ago in Philadelphia. They loved going to the theater together, particularly to Shakespeare. Today's experience was overwhelming."

"I can't even begin to understand what it's like to lose someone you love," Heidi said.

"Alexa seemed a little calmer after we talked."

"I'm not surprised, you have a way of making people feel more at peace. I think you're her angel."

"Thank you, that's a sweet thing to say."

They walked up to the register, and Heidi paid for the tea and cookies.

Upon leaving the market, Heidi took Aunt Eileen's arm, and they walked toward Constitution Avenue to hail a taxi. Half-way down the block her aunt stopped and grabbed her hip.

"Aunt Eileen? What's wrong?"

"My leg, it's spasming!"

Looking at her aunt, Heidi saw tears rolling down her cheeks. "Oh, it's that bad?"

After a few minutes passed, her aunt said, "No, it's stopping. The realization shocked me and brought me to tears."

"What realization?"

"It's—it's—the cancer has spread to my bones."

"Wait. What? Are you sure?" Heidi replied with a heavy heart.

"Yes, the doctor told me last week. The truth just struck me when the spasm hit. I'm sorry, I didn't want to tell you this way."

"I'm so sorry this is happening to you." Heidi found a Kleenex tissue in her purse. "Here, take this. With all your struggles, I'm surprised you were trying to comfort Alexa."

"Helping others keeps my mind off my own issues. Speaking of which, I have a gift for you at my house. Let's get out of here."

"A gift? You've been a gift to me. I don't need anything else."

They got into the next available Barwood taxicab, and the driver drove them to Dumbarton Street in Georgetown. Once they were in the house, Patches; a long-hair yellow Lab, bounded over and put his snout into Heidi's hand.

"Good boy." Her aunt stepped around the dog and rubbed his floppy ears. "Mmm, strange, I wonder where my husband is this time? Never mind, he'll appear eventually. Let's go into the living room."

"Can I make you some tea?" Heidi asked. "And open the cookies I bought?"

"You're such a dear. Both would be nice."

Heidi went down the hall, then into the kitchen. She found two plates with matching cups and saucers on the counter. At the sink she filled a pot of water, lit the stove, and waited for the water to boil—it took too long. Finally, she filled the cups with hot water and put two cookies on each saucer next to a chamomile tea bag. She was too distracted thinking about her aunt's cancer to bother about finding a tray. Balancing an arrangement in each hand, she slowly walked across the living room trying not to spill anything onto the beige carpet. Just as she reached the coffee table in front of the couch, she almost pitched one cup off the saucer and adjusted the cup before sitting down.

"Are you feeling all right?" Heidi asked.

"I guess, I'm never sure. The other day I found a fun picture of your dad, and it made me happy. Remember the dressmaking mannequin I bought you years ago?"

"Yep."

"Your dad was so funny. I laughed and laughed. The foam form must've been triple the size of the zippered case, and it was almost impossible to shove in there and close up. It was larger than any woman could ever be. He held it up in the air, and his eyes looked like they were going to pop out of his head." She took a Polaroid out of the end-table drawer. "Here it is. It's such a goofy photo of him."

"Wow!" Heidi put her fist over her lips and tried not to laugh, but it was no use.

Her aunt broke into laughter, too.

They laughed for a good long minute, and then Heidi said, "Dad isn't a comedian often, but that was a good day. I forgot you'd taken a photo."

"There's nothing like a happy memory. I feel better already." Her aunt finished her cookies. "I want to give you something else."

"Oh, the photo is enough, truly!"

"Come with me." Her aunt stood up slowly, and they went to the hall closet. She pulled out a satin-skirted gown, with a velvet jeweled bodice and large puffy sleeves. "This is for you."

"It's so fancy," Heidi said. "I could wear it to the Renaissance Festival or to meet a queen."

In a hushed voice, her aunt replied, "Either would be fine. It will need some alterations. Your chest is smaller than mine. Last time I wore it, I had to put a size double-D weighted falsie on one side to replace my missing breast, and the proportions never quite matched. I should have had a double mastectomy. I'm always off balance—my poor, broken body."

Heidi frowned. "Oh, I'm not sure what to say." She felt torn up inside and wanted to cry. Instead, she restrained herself and said, "You're amazing."

"The gown is no longer in fashion, and I know you love costumes, which most of my formal gowns could undoubtedly be at this point. This one was outlandishly expensive when I had it made." She glanced around the hallway. "Please, don't tell Rob I gave it to you."

"I won't tell; besides we don't talk. He's been like a ghost for years." Heidi felt quite discouraged about not knowing much about her uncle.

"I tried to tell him I wanted to give my things away before I die. He's very resistant to the idea, and would rather I live forever. He copes—or doesn't—by spending many hours away from home, and from me. At first, his behavior didn't make much sense, but then I decided it's good he has work to distract him. Maybe that will help him when I'm gone. He'll need a new wife, I told him so, and he shouldn't feel guilty about anything. We've had a wonderful life together."

"You've planned everything." Heidi felt overwhelmed with her aunt's blunt and matter-of-fact attitude.

"Remember the pearl necklace I gave you on your eighteenth birthday?"

"Of course, it's beautiful." Heidi pulled back her collar. "I wear it all the time."

"I don't think I ever told you the pearls are real, and they were your great grandmother's."

"Oh, gosh, I had no idea."

"I'm sorry, I should have told you at the time, so you'd be extra careful. Keep them to remember me. As for the dress, it's okay if you give it away in the future if it isn't useful."

"Of course, I'll keep the pearls and likely the dress, too. Life won't be the same without you." Heidi blinked hard, and a tear escaped as she hugged her aunt. "Aunt Eileen, I love you. Why are you doing these depressing things? Please try to find another remedy."

"I love you, too." She stepped away from the embrace. "No, I'm done. I've had too many surgeries and chemotherapy sessions. I've had enough pain and nausea over the last decade. Going to Ireland for alternative treatments helped a lot, until now." She took Heidi's hand in hers. "I can't search for any more cures. I've lost the battle."

"God will welcome you into heaven with open arms." Heidi cringed. Talking openly about faith always made her uneasy, but she needed to say something to comfort her aunt.

Aunt Eileen placed a hand on her arm. "Yes, faith in God helped me through my hardships."

The Labrador was pacing by the front door. "Patches is on edge. Maybe he needs to go out," Heidi observed.

"My leg is feeling all right now. We can take him out for a walk and get some ice cream to top off our cookies."

Heidi clipped a leash on his collar. They walked out the door and meandered toward the shops around the corner to an outdoor café. "Auntie, you're so brave."

"No, not really," She rubbed her thigh before sitting on one of the chairs and settling Patches under the table.

The waitress appeared, and they each ordered a bowl of vanilla ice cream.

Her aunt continued, "Heidi, I was just thinking about my old dachshund. Remember, how he used to sit with us when we made dresses together on my sewing machine?"

"Yes, he kept trying to sit on your foot while you were operating the machine petal. He was speedy little thing on walks, I like Patches better." Heidi slipped her hand into Eileen's. "Thank you for teaching me how to make clothes. I'm surprised you didn't sew the dress you're giving me."

"Not enough time in a day to make everything. Don't forget, I used to be a big woman, and it was difficult to find clothes from the stores that fit. That's really the only reason I bothered to make them. None of those garments fit anymore. They hang on me like bags, it's depressing."

"You're way too skinny. I wish I could do something to help." The ice cream arrived, and Heidi pushed hers across the table. "Maybe you should eat mine, too."

"No, I'll just have one bowl. Heidi, you have been wonderful through the years. Edward was off at Princeton when you came back with your parents from Paris, and I loved spending time with you. The years we've had together have been priceless." The dog curled a little tighter around Aunt Eileen's feet at the outdoor table. "After I'm gone, I hope Patches won't be a burden—he's an old dog, too, like me."

"Patches will miss you as much as everyone else will. And, you're not old."

"Dogs are a blessing. Patches is such a good companion, especially when I'm struggling. Maybe he should go to Edward when I'm gone. I'm tired, it's time to take me home."

They stood, and Heidi put her arm around Aunt Eileen's waist. She didn't want to let go.

"This isn't the best time, but I need to ask you a question about Mom."

"Sweetheart, you can ask me anything about my sister."

"Do you know why Mom goes around wringing her hands all the time?"

Aunt Eileen rested her hand on Heidi's shoulder for support. "Remember when your grandfather Herman died, and your mom stopped driving?"

"Yes, how can I forget. That's when Mom started walking around the house with swollen eyes wringing her hands and talking to herself or making 'um-um' sounds."

"She used to wring her hands and talk to herself when we were kids after traumatic events, but I haven't seen her do that recently."

"Mom does it all the time and hides it from everyone but Dad and me."

Aunt Eileen's lips scrunched together. "Losing our father was harder for her since she worshiped him. I think her nerves fell apart. I noticed a while back that she started drinking more liquor in the evenings to cope with the long nights."

Heidi blew a puff of air through her lips. "It's unbelievable. You've had far more to deal with in your life. You've never behaved in the bizarre ways she does. Oh, and then she tells absurd white lies to explain away why she shows up late to events. I just don't understand."

"Everyone's different." Heidi's aunt rubbed her leg, again. "Her behavior is confusing. She's always had issues, but they have become so much worse. I honestly believe she would cope better if she could regain her faith in God and trust Him, but the more I talk about it, the more she pulls away. I've tried other tactics, but..."

"I wish one of us understood. On the bright side, she's fairly calm after a few drinks. I guess that's not really a bright side. Anyway, Claudia thinks mom's an alcoholic. Every time I think about it, I just get angry. I don't have much patience for her nonsense, and Dad doesn't do anything."

"Yes, I know. Nathan's a brilliant man, yet he doesn't know how to get Gwen out of her neurotic behavior, either. I've talked to her about it a lot over the years, but she never wanted to go for professional help and lashed out at me whenever I suggested counseling." Aunt Eileen paused before continuing. "Your mother will never admit to having any problems. She's always right, and everyone else is wrong. I don't have the energy to try anymore."

"Oh God, no, I didn't mean you should. I'm sorry I brought this up, I'm being selfish." Heidi blushed and put her hand over her mouth.

"Don't worry about me, I know you're trying to be thoughtful. You need to go into the world on your terms, get a job, and start a family. Don't burden yourself with trying to figure out or fix anything. My sister's issues aren't solvable, and she'll drag you down with her if you don't stand your ground. I know this all sounds unpleasant, but someone needs to tell you the truth."

"What am I going to do without you?"

"You are strong. Besides, you can always talk to Sadie. After all, she's your mother's best friend. I don't think you're betraying her by asking for help to keep your sanity, no matter what she'd say to the contrary. You need to do whatever it takes to continue moving into your adult life without being controlled by her desires."

"I know. Thank you, I'll talk to Sadie if I need to." Heidi hesitated. "I'm going to have to go back to college next week. I promise I'll come see you over summer break."

"Yes, I know you will."

Heidi squeezed her aunt's hand. "You better be here when I get back. We're not done with you yet."

Heidi held onto Patches' leash on the way home. He sniffed at several tufts of grass and tree trunks along the way. The traffic noise had increased since they'd passed by earlier. Back at the house, her aunt fumbled with the keys, opened the front door and then kissed Heidi's cheek.

"Go on and enjoy the rest of the holiday with your friends. Please tell your mother, Rob and I will be at Edward's this Christmas and can't stop by. I'm going to go lay down now. We'll see each other in a few months."

"See you soon."

"Yes. Goodbye, Heidi."

In the summer, Heidi returned to Maryland. Nothing had changed at home, but Heidi didn't have anywhere else to go or any money of her own. She drove to the cathedral, a place she had always felt at ease when attending with the McGwires in the past. It was the safest place to think. She sat in a pew for a while and then recognized a familiar face on the other side of the nave. Sliding off the bench, she walked quickly across the cathedral.

"Mrs. McGwire?" Heidi tapped her shoulder.

The woman spun around. "Oh, hello, so formal. I thought you were someone else. You never call me misses."

"Sorry, Sadie," Heidi whispered. "I didn't mean to startle you. Why are you wandering around the cathedral?"

"I volunteer here. You didn't know?"

"No, I guess not. You're always so busy, I can't keep track. Are you still selling houses and working at the travel agency?"

"Yes, still earning a living." The corners of Sadie's eyes crinkled. "I started volunteering here, once a week, just a couple of months ago. I didn't realize you were back from Bradford."

"Yep, just got back. I'm not loving the school. It's too isolated from Boston, and the girl I live with is difficult."

"Sorry, can I help?"

"Thanks, but no. I'm just not used to spending so much time with my peers."

"Makes sense. Walk with me for a few minutes. I go around giving people information about the cathedral."

"Do you think you could introduce me to the gift shop manager? I'm looking for a summer job."

"Of course, I know they need extra help full-time now and part-time during the off-season. The last clerk left a month ago, and they are having trouble finding a replacement. When my shift's over, I'll ask the manager when's a good time for you two to meet."

"Sounds good. I'll get my resume ready. Thank you, you're a saint."

"You're funny, I'm no saint. What else is on your mind?"

"I think I want to leave Bradford and come back here."

"Oooh, are you sure? Dealing with your mother might be tough after being away for two years."

"Yeah, I know, but Bradford isn't D.C. I like it here better."

"Claudia has missed you. She's doing well at American University. Do you want to join her or go somewhere else?"

"I've missed her, too. Compared to high school, my grades are much better. I applied to Catholic University, and they accepted me as a transfer student for the fall term. I'm not sure if I'm going to take their offer because they don't have dorm rooms available for local students with families in the area."

"Well, if you do, Claudia will enjoy having you around again. Maybe she has a spare room you can rent."

"That would be super, I'll ask. It's so cool you let her live in one of your rental homes."

"I thought it would be an easy job for her to manage the place while living there and going to school. I'm close enough, she can get my advice if she needs it."

"I know she's happy you gave her the opportunity."

The altar caught Heidi's eye. She paused and said an internal prayer for Aunt Eileen.

"Thanks for your help, Sadie. See you later."

1978...

Heidi started working in the National Cathedral's gift shop and, by the end of the summer, she had officially transferred out of Bradford. She talked to Claudia about moving in with her, but her mother wanted to see the place first before committing as she would be paying the rent. They got in the car, and Heidi drove over to Claudia's.

"I talked to Claudia, she said there is only one room available. The other one was rented out last week. It isn't far from American University, and I could drive to Catholic U or take a bus."

"I'd rather you drove. The buses are a cesspool of germs."

"I knew you'd feel that way. I've taken buses before, and they're okay outside of rush-hour. They're not crowded then. I've been able to get a seat."

"Still dirty. You can use the Ford whenever you want since it just sits in the garage and I don't drive. Your dad and I are only going out in the Cadillac."

"But Dad gave me that car when I turned seventeen. At this point, it's funny you're giving me permission to drive it."

"Yes, well..." Her mother's lip stiffened. "In any case, be prepared to lend us the car if ours needs repairs."

"I can do that easily."

They arrived at the townhouse and Heidi parked out front. The door to the house was wide open. She called out, "Claudia, you here?"

Claudia stepped out of the kitchen, grinned, and began straightening the front room. Her brows furrowed. "Oh, hello, Aunt Gwen. I wasn't expecting you two until tomorrow."

Heidi blushed. "Sorry, my mistake."

The couch had clothes tossed all over the arms and cushions. The table was covered with dirty mugs, plates, and magazines. Heidi's mother fiddled with her sunglasses.

"Which room is available? Since we're here, can we see it?"

"Sure, but I have class soon." Claudia showed them the furnished carpeted bedroom upstairs. It had a window and a small closet, with a shared bathroom in the hall.

"How are your marketing classes?" Heidi's mother asked.

"I love them." Claudia led them back down to the cluttered kitchen.

"You should clean this up, it's not sanitary to leave all these dirty dishes around." Heidi's mother frowned. "And you shouldn't leave the front door open either."

"My parents never had any troubles with an open-door policy. I figured I'd do the same. My housemates don't mind either." Claudia shrugged. "Heidi, let me know if you want the room."

"Thanks, I'll call you," Heidi said as she and her mother stepped out onto the front porch.

"Okay. Bye, Aunt Gwen. If I don't hurry, I'll be late for class." Claudia closed the front door, waved, and hurried away in another direction.

They got in the car, and Heidi started the engine. She looked out the window on to New Mexico Avenue before heading down the road toward Brookside Drive.

"Mom, that was awkward. I'm thinking you won't pay my rent at Claudia's, will you?"

"No. Doors need to be locked. We were robbed in Paris, and then again here. We can't take any risks."

"Yeah, but regardless, there's always a chance of a break-in."

"I still want the doors locked. Your father suggested a dog years ago as a deterrent, but as you know they scare me."

"I know. I kept asking for a dog and ended up with rabbits instead. Did anything get stolen in the robberies?"

"My family jewels in Paris and my sense of security. The break-in here was soon after we'd moved back. They didn't take anything that time, but they threw a lot of stuff on the floor. Your father had an alarm system installed shortly thereafter."

Heidi tilted her head and twisted her lips. "Thankfully, no one was physically hurt. Anyway, nothing's foolproof. I'd still like to live with Claudia."

"I'm not paying for you to live in a dangerous place."

"God! Mother, we don't live in a bubble. Her townhouse isn't any more dangerous than our house. If someone wants to break in, they'll get around alarms and any other deterrents. Nothing is truly safe, and I can't live life properly if I'm always worried about safety. It was okay for you to inspect Claudia's place, but you can't inspect everywhere else I might want to live. People will think I'm a freak if you tag around with me analyzing every crevice."

"Well, I'm not going to pay for a place I haven't seen."

"You know I can't work enough hours to pay for a room near campus. I'm not staying in the cheapest places because I don't think they're safe. How about you loan me half, and I'll pay the rest without your inspections?"

"No. Either follow my rules, or you'll have to live at home."

"So much for being classified as an adult," Heidi scoffed. "You moved me into the Bradford dorms without a second thought."

"That was different."

"No, it was worse, but I guess I'll live with you and Dad for now."

"What do you mean Bradford was worse?"

"Never mind, I have to go." Heidi pulled into the driveway. "I'll be late for my lunch with Edward."

"Let's talk more tonight." Her mother stepped out of the car. "Don't rush, Edward can wait."

Heidi had the last word. "No, he can't. Please close the door." She drove away and stewed over her mother's unrealistic ideas.

The Black Rooster pub on L Street was dark inside compared to the bright sunny day she'd left behind. Heidi stopped by the entrance and waited for her eyes to adjust. She saw Edward sitting in a booth in the back corner and hurried over. As always, he was immaculately dressed in a black suit and red paisley tie.

Heidi greeted him. "Hey cousin, whatcha drinking at this hour?"

"Hello, always a pleasure to see you too," he joked. "Heidi, one glass of red wine isn't going to affect my brain; give me a break." Edward slid off the bench and kissed her forehead.

"Oh, stop with the kisses, just give me a hug." Heidi leaned in and gave him a gentle hug. "You know I'm teasing. Bet you're wondering why I asked you here today?"

"Nope, but I'm sure you'll tell me. Have a seat," Edward said.

"I've transferred out of Bradford, and I'm going to Catholic University this fall. Two years down, two to go. But, Mom is driving me crazy about where I'm supposed to live. She won't agree to pay for a room at Claudia's place. I'll have to live at home for a while unless I can come up with something else."

"Look on the bright side, I can visit you and your mother at the same time. Or you could move in with me. I've been lonely since my divorce."

"Oh, now... don't get weird with me, cousin." She smiled and batted her eyelashes playfully.

"What? Oh, right," he choked. "The spare bedroom in available."

"Thanks, but no. I can't afford anything at the moment."

"Let me know if you change your mind."

"Yeah, okay. Anyway, I want to talk to someone about my career aspirations. I figure you can help with that."

"Hmm, you're using me," he teased. "Sure, let's order first."

They scanned the menu and made their selections—one steak and one burger plate—plus a Heineken for Heidi.

"Hey, you picked on my wine, and now you're ordering a beer?"

"Well, Mom drives me to drink. I only have a couple a week, and that's the truth. My first two years in college are another story. Ugh, way too much."

"Now who's being dramatic? I'm happy you're going to be around. I know my mom will love it, too. Damned cancer!"

"Your mom is a gem. I want to spend lots of time with her while I still can."

"Point well taken. Are you going to tell me why you dragged me away from the White House or not?"

"Like you mind?" Heidi rubbed the back of her neck. "My choices for majors... I started out thinking political science would be cool. I could get a job like yours in the Executive Branch or Dad's in the State Department, but when I mentioned it to Mom, she laughed at me—don't know what that meant. But, whatever, I can't keep being emotionally controlled by her opinions." Heidi gulped down half of her beer. "Anyway, I tried a course in psychology, to figure Mom out and get a job helping people who actually want help, but I didn't sign up for another class. My psychology course books say Mom has obsessive-compulsive disorder, arachnophobia, claustrophobia, and germaphobia. I knew her symptoms, but now I get to put names to the stuff. Lucky me."

"What is this? Bash your mother day?" He laughed. "You're getting a mother complex."

"Too late, I already have one."

"She used to be much easier to get along with when you and I were kids," Edward grumbled.

"Yeah, yeah, we do still love her anyway. It's hard to believe our mothers are sisters. Mine seems to have a dual personality. What you see isn't real. She play-acts with her charming smile when you two are together, but—for me—it's another story. I've told you about her soap and spider obsessions. And she rants about Dad's and my sins at least once a week, for hours at a time. The person we used to know, when you and I were kids, disappeared. You know, our mothers are direct opposites—yours is an optimist, and mine only pretends to be."

"Your mom has fooled me all these years. I thought I knew the real Gwen, but evidently not."

"She's a talented covert operative." Heidi snickered. "I mean actress."

"Well, mine is definitely not, she's very genuine. I love her approach to life; always so full of fun and strong in the face of adversity. I missed her when I went away to boarding school, and then Princeton."

"Don't whine. A high school in Switzerland, for Christ's sake." Heidi puckered her lips. "Hey, your mom let you go. Being an only child isn't easy. Over there you learned how to live with your peers faster than I did here."

The waitress brought their food and disappeared without a word.

"Don't use the Lord's name in vain."

"Sorry, didn't mean to offend you. Some days I forget you're seventeen years older than me and more conservative." The French fries were salty, and Heidi guzzled down a glass of water. "Your mom is so easy to get along with. She's been like a second mother to me."

"What a nice thing to say."

"It's true. I love that she recognizes you're an adult and wants you to have your own life without making you feel guilty. Even with cancer, her opinion hasn't changed."

"Yes, I know. I love her for it. I call her every couple of days and go by the house frequently. It's so much easier now that I'm working in the area and sold my place on the West Coast. I'd rather not talk about her illness. Can we get back to your career choice?"

"Sure, I'm sorry." She took a bite of her burger. "This is yummy. I could go for marine biology, but I'm not qualified because I need exceptional math skills. I tried to study more, but my head goes blank when I see complex formulas. Way back, a male teacher at Maret told me girls don't need to know math beyond basic addition and subtraction. He said it was okay that I didn't understand because women are rarely in a job with anything else—rather judgmental or at least sexist if you ask me. I fell behind and never caught up."

"That's a shame. He definitely wasn't a progressive educator." Edward cut into his steak. "Remember when your parents took us to the Kennedy Center to see your mom's friends after a production of *Media*?"

"Yes, Mom's acting friends—Judith Anderson and Zoe Caldwell—were in the production. We had a late dinner with Dame Anderson after the show. Miss Caldwell was busy and couldn't come along. Aren't you impressed I can remember people's full names; wasn't always my strong point."

"Yes, yes, good job," Edward responded with a wink. "I thought it was wonderful your mom kept up with them.

Heidi took a sip of her warm beer. "And then, last month, Mom sent me off to Los Angeles to meet her friend, Mary Jackson, and we spent two days together—it was great! We walked a lot and had some delicious meals together."

"I heard that story. Miss Jackson is still in The Walton's television show. Your mom worked with her in New York in the early 40s."

"And your point for bringing up that time at the Kennedy Center now is because?" Heidi sighed.

"Oh, more drama." Edward wiped the back of his palm across his forehead.

"Please, stop. I'm not dramatic, leave that to Mom. She loves being the center of attention. I was just thinking about the private parties at home when I was a kid. After everyone else had arrived, Mom would appear at the top of the stairs. She'd smile and say, 'Hello,' while everyone watched her come down. A real Scarlet O'Hara."

"Okay, okay, that's true drama." Edward pouted. "Forgive me?"

"Uh-huh. Fall back, we're in sidetrack city. What type of degree should I go for?"

"Be patient, I'm getting there. Your mom exposed you to live theater and mine taught you how to sew. What do think about majoring in theater arts with a focus on costuming and history?"

"Well, maybe. I remember when I used to watch television with my parents on Sunday nights. The British comedy and Masterpiece Theater shows were our favorites. The costumes in productions like *The Six Wives of Henry the VIII* were fabulous. I think that was in the early 70s."

"It's still hard to believe that I'm in the middle of my career, and you're just getting started."

She smiled impishly. "Your old boss—Reagan—used to be an actor before he became the governor of California. I hear he's entering the presidential election the next round. If he wins... I bet he'll want you to work for him again."

"We'll see. Time's passing quickly."

"Year and a half to go."

"See you can do math." He snickered.

"Anyway, moving on. I can do something else after my degree if things don't work out, but I have to start somewhere, right?"

"Right. Who knows, you might run for president one day. Anything is possible in this country if you work hard enough."

"Yeah, but no. I'm going to go for an uncomplicated life." Heidi clenched her jaw and then relaxed.

Edward's pager went off. "Waiter, please, I need to use a phone right away." He stood up and went to the phone behind the bar.

Heidi finished her burger and wiped the juices off her hands with a napkin. Edward returned but didn't sit down.

"What's going on?" she asked.

"Nothing catastrophic, but I need to get back to the White House." He bumped a water glass before putting some cash on the table. "Oops, sorry. The meal's my treat today. I'll call you later."

Chapter 18

Spring 1980...

Today was a particularly stressful day in Heidi's last month at the university theater. She walked away from the costume shop and escaped into the student lounge. Finding a cushioned seat in the crowded room challenged her tired mind. Taking several deep breaths, she relaxed while staring blankly at the *General Hospital* soap opera on the television. Moments passed, she pulled her eyes from the screen, put her backpack behind her legs and nodded off into another world.

"Wake up." In the fog, someone moved Heidi's shoulder back and forth.

"Oh. Hi. Was I dreaming?" Heidi muttered and tilted her head up in the direction of the voice.

"How would I know?" Claudia grimaced.

"God, I'm stiff. Before I fell asleep, Luke and Laura were saying something on the show, but I don't remember what." Heidi reached into her backpack for a mint. "I'm stressed out, what time is it?"

"Half past three. I finished my classes early and thought I'd come by. The theater secretary said you'd taken a break from working on a costume and sent me here."

"She knows all—I need a cup of coffee. Let's go to the cafeteria. When you woke me from my dream, I was homeless and on drugs. I guess I'm worried about what I'm doing after graduation."

"With your skills, I'm sure you'll find work. I've already got something lined up in marketing at the Smithsonian."

"Have you? That's great!"

"Thanks, what's your plan?"

"I sent out applications a couple weeks ago with recommendation letters. Today, I'm just concentrating on my current projects. I finished my costume history report, the sketches of my designs, and the patterns from scratch. I still have more sewing to do."

"What are you making?"

"Two designs, well three if you count the monk's tunic, but that one was easy compared to the women's gowns. They are taking forever to finish. I was here late last night and came back early this morning. One of my friends let me sleep in their dorm room."

"Are you eating more than beans and rice for lunch these days?"

"Nope, still cooking on the costume shop's hotplate in Hartke." Heidi grinned and ran her hands across her midsection. "My favorite slimming diet."

"So, what gowns are you making?"

"One is medieval, with a corset and headpiece. The other has a stiff pleated collar straight out of Shakespearean times. Of course, they're all floor length." Heidi droned on. "They both have full skirts and fitted bodices. The skirts aren't difficult, but the other parts are detailed and labor-intensive."

"I'd like to see them," Claudia said. "Let's go—"

Heidi pulled back, and said, "Now's not good, I need to finish. After I get them back from my professor, I'll show you."

"Sounds cool. Did you get through the speech and acting class?"

"Yep, I'm getting through, but it turned out to be worse than I expected."

"Not surprising. You don't like speaking to crowds."

"You know me, I'm a behind the scenes kinda girl. Speaking of which, I have to get back to work."

Claudia pursed her lips. "Okay, we'll finish up our coffees and go to our separate worlds."

"Oh, the drama." Heidi put her hand on her forehead and swooned. "How are your classes?"

"All good. I'll tell you another time. *Ciao, Bella.*" Claudia waved as she left.

In the public bathroom, Heidi splashed her face with water and dried it with a paper towel from the dispenser beside the sink. With a quick glance in the mirror, she smoothed her hair back into a ponytail, then opened the bathroom door and strolled back to the costume shop to work on her project. Most days she felt secure with the thirty or so people who studied in the theater department, but today none of them were around. In the shop, she sensed something was wrong. At first, she thought she was alone until she caught a glimpse of a stranger in the corner by the emergency exit door, which was usually locked. He started to talk while she moved backward toward the shop door to get away from him.

"Have you ever had sex with, with a stranger?" he slurred. The man didn't appear to be a university student, but older with a long, pulled-back, unattractive ponytail and a bushy beard. He tilted to the right, perhaps drunk or high on drugs.

Heidi glared at him. "What!? No! Not my thing."

She left the shop and went to find a security guard. By the time they returned, the man had disappeared. After the guard did a quick walk through the area, Heidi went over to the hotplate to heat some water, and there was a thick manila envelope addressed to David McGwire. There appeared to be a drop of dry blood on the edge.

Heidi grimaced, wrapped the packet in a black plastic trash bag, and stuffed it into her backpack. On her way home, she would drop it off at the McGwire's house.

Focusing on the rest of her project became difficult, but she managed to finish. After manipulating the women's gowns and the monk's outfit onto hangers, she covered them with clear plastic garment bags and attached a label with her name. Her assignment needed to be dropped off by six o'clock at the costume warehouse. Carrying the heavy period costumes, sketches, and reports across campus would be too cumbersome. Her car was parked along the adjacent road. It took several trips to get all the items in the back seat. Each pass through the Hartke building made her skin tingle; the doors had new squeaks, and every corner revealed a potential hiding place for a stalker.

Heidi put her backpack in the car's trunk, then got into the front seat with her purse and tucked it next to her left leg on the floor. She drove to the warehouse and scanned the outside of the building before hauling the costumes inside. No one was there. She left her report on the professor's desk, along with a note, and hung the costumes on a rack in the corner. Again, her senses heightened, and she couldn't figure out why the professor wasn't there. The car might be a better place to wait for him. Flipping her keys from one finger to the next, she headed back out to listen to music on the car's radio. After she settled in the driver's seat, the passenger door opened. Before she could put her key in the ignition to escape, a different man in torn clothes with greased-back hair hopped in. He grabbed the keys out of her hand.

"Give me money, I'm hungry."

Heidi kept her eyes forward, her heart raced.

"Okay, just give the keys back." She reached into her purse and found a five-dollar bill. "Here take this." She pushed the money onto the dashboard.

"No, that's not enough, I'm starving."

Heidi struggled to stay calm and put up twenty more. He took the bills, tossed the keys onto her lap, and got out of the car. The second he left, Heidi reached across the car and locked the doors. For the first time ever, without her mother's insistence, she took out several Wash-N-Dry packets from the glove compartment. She ripped them open, pulled out the sanitizing wipes, and cleaned off her keys before putting the right key into the ignition. There was nothing to be done about the stench he left behind in the car, she wasn't going to open the windows for fear of someone else reaching in and grabbing at her. Gripping her steering wheel and eyeing the area surrounding her car to be sure there were no other surprises, an envelope on the floor of her passenger side caught her peripheral vision. She stared at it with a puckered expression, not wanting to touch it. Like the letter before, it, too, was addressed to David McGwire. *What the hell? How did the creep even know I was going to be in the warehouse?*

She tugged the steering wheel, but it was stuck. After a terrifying minute, the wheel released and the key turned. With steadfast resolve, Heidi decided to drive over to the McGwire's house and forget about waiting for the professor. The car squealed out of the parking lot onto the main road.

Driving through rush hour traffic took longer than usual. An accident, only three blocks from the McGwire's, slowed everyone's progress. The front end of a black Mercedes was crushed and steaming. Her mind wandered into a paranoid thought. *Could this be connected to Uncle David? Get a grip. The envelopes are playing with your mind. God, please keep everyone safe.*

When she arrived on Harrison Street, it was seven o'clock, and most of the curbside parking spots were full. The only opening was too small for the Ford. She drove around to the alley behind the house and turned into the McGwire's short private driveway. Abruptly she stopped in front of the two-car garage. On high alert, she got out of the car with her purse and retrieved her backpack from the trunk. There was no one in the area. She was alone, at least she hoped so. She walked around to the passenger side and wiped off the door handle with another Wash-N-Dry. In a panic, she realized she'd probably rubbed the alleged robber's fingerprints away, but there was no going back. She opened the door and, to keep from touching the warehouse envelope with her bare hands, pulled out a Kleenex tissue from the box on the back seat and grabbed the envelope.

The narrow path against the side of the house to the front of the McGwire's seemed darker than in the past. She wrapped her fingers around the front doorknob, but the sweat on her palm made it difficult to turn. Instead, she knocked, wiped her hands on her jeans and tried again. This time the knob turned, and she opened the door a crack.

A gruff voice called out, "Yes, who's there?"

"It's me, Uncle David. It's Heidi."

"Sorry, come on in. I didn't mean to snarl at you."

She pushed the door open the rest of the way and found her uncle sitting in his overstuffed armchair facing the front door. He had a pistol on his lap. She noticed that his hair had greyed considerably since she'd seen him six months ago. His once brilliant blue eyes had dulled, and his left eye was uncharacteristically twitching.

"Uncle David, have you been at the range? What's going on?"

"Nope, the range isn't an option today." He hesitated, then said, "I'm sitting for a bit. Getting ready to clean my gun, that's all."

Heidi wasn't sure what to make of the stern expression on his face. "Right, if you say so. You sound strange, Uncle David— distant."

"I'll be fine, just tired." His finger passed over the barrel of the pistol. "You realize I'm not your real uncle, right?"

"Yes, but you're my godfather." Heidi wondered why he was bringing this up now.

"I am, but I'm not Nathan or Gwen's brother. You've called Sadie by her first name for as long as I can remember. Since you're an adult now, can you call me David?"

"Feels weird, but I'll try to remember." At that moment, she had more important things on her mind and moved a little closer. "Sorry to bug you, but I'm on edge. Here…" She thrust the one envelope in her hand toward him and then dug into her backpack for the other. "These two things are addressed to you."

David squinted at the handwriting. "Christ! They shouldn't involve you in this stuff."

"Stuff? What stuff? I was terrified." Her face flushed. "Honestly, I didn't like how they appeared, and I don't want to be a part of whatever is going on. Envelopes, envelopes! I've seen them covertly being passed around for years between you and Dad. I think the first time was when I was a kid at the Waldenbooks further down on Wisconsin Avenue. That was easier than being around these creepy men today. I don't want to be involved!"

"What happened?" David said abruptly. He seemed more frantic than she'd ever seen him.

"You don't know? I'm surprised, or are you pretending?" Heidi was on the verge of screaming at a man she'd never been angry at a day in her life.

"I can't say anything, but I'll make it stop. I don't know why you were selected for this delivery." He coaxed her a little more, in a calmer voice. "Tell me the story."

"The larger manila envelope was on the counter in my costume shop next to the heating element where I warm up my meals. The guy made some lewd comments to get rid of me, I guess. Maybe he put it there when I stepped out to get the security guard. I don't know."

"Lewd comments?" David's jaw clenched, and the muscles visibly twitched.

"I'd rather not say. The other envelope arrived outside the costume warehouse. I had a scheduled time to turn in my projects and took them in the building. When I got back in the car, a strange guy reeking of sweat and booze jumped into the passenger seat. He snatched my keys out of my hand and wouldn't give them back until I gave him money. After I complied, twenty-five dollars later, he tossed the keys in my direction and left. I locked the passenger door and found the second envelope."

"Did either of them sound like they had foreign accents?"

"Accents? Yes, but I was too upset to notice what kind."

David pulled out his wallet and handed her a wad of money. "Here's a reimbursement."

"O-kaay, thanks. I guess." Without counting, she pushed the bills into the front pocket of her jeans. It felt like more than twenty-five dollars.

"As I said, I'll find a way to make it stop. I appreciate you bringing the envelopes."

"I should be angry at you, but I'm mostly worried. Your work shouldn't be forcing its way into your personal life. Can you put the pistol away! Please! You're making me more anxious by the minute." She noticed her hands were shaking.

"Will do. Let's have a glass of something strong—to cut the edge off our tension—before you leave. I'm going to have some Glenlivet Scotch. I want you to try my wine from Chateau Tourans. Wait here, I'll be right back." He put the gun in the holster on his side and took the two envelopes with him.

"Hey, I thought you were going to clean your gun, not wear it," she scolded.

But David said nothing and ducked into the kitchen. He returned with a glass of his Scotch and another of wine. Handing the glass to Heidi, he said, "I hope you like the flavor."

Heidi tasted the tannic, red liquid. "It's good. I'm too tense to sip the rest. I'm going to chug it."

"I'm sorry, I shouldn't expect you to try this particularly fine wine today." David threw his head back and finished his drink with one swallow.

"I've got to go. I have a date tonight."

"Anyone, I know?"

"Yep, I met him at one of your parties. Maybe I'll cancel. I'm not trusting your associates lately." Heidi snickered. "Today I was surrounded by…"

"I got your point. The Cold War continues to complicate life. I'll escort you to your car."

"No thanks, I'll manage."

"Remember, lock all your car doors when you're driving. Travel in groups, particularly at night, and be aware of who's around you."

"Sure, okay, yeah." Heidi hesitated. "I'm not feeling safe anywhere today."

"Try not to worry, I'll fix everything." David passed her a card. "Call this number and ask for me if you have any more troubles. I'll either pick up the line or one of my colleagues can take a confidential message."

Reading the number out loud, her eyebrows rose. "I see, 703-482-0…"

"It's a CIA exchange."

"Uncle David—David, I thought you'd only worked for the State Department."

"I have my hands in many things. Don't mention you have the number to anyone, you'd better memorize it. It's a private line, and I want to keep it that way." His face contorted.

"Thanks. Be careful with the gun. I'll keep your secret." Heidi slipped out of the house and hoped never to be involved with any of David's shenanigans again.

Chapter 19

On this particular visit with her Aunt Eileen, Heidi found her aunt stretched out on the living room couch at home. A blanket was tucked up under her chin, and she had a faint smile on her face. She was too weak to speak and even thinner than she had been at Heidi's graduation ceremony six months earlier. Heidi didn't know what to do or say but was glad her aunt had had these last few years to enjoy life, which was more than any of them had expected. She gently held her aunt's hand while staring at the dull cream-colored wall just behind the couch. She thought about how vibrant her aunt had always been.

Without warning her aunt squeezed her hand. Heidi came out of her trance and said, "You are fabulous. I will always love you, Aunt Eileen."

Patches pushed in, sat down on the carpet by her side and put his wet nose on his mother's chest. In the background, Edward and his father's voices hummed in the kitchen among the banging sounds of pots and plates.

Heidi sat holding her aunt's hand for another hour. "I have to leave now, but we will see each other again."

Two days later, Edward called to say his mother had died peacefully at home.

Heidi and her parents arrived at the Bethlehem Chapel of the National Cathedral for Aunt Eileen's funeral. Upon entering the church, a sense of peace and calm enveloped Heidi, and her thoughts drifted to how much her aunt would've loved the beautiful flowers. As they walked to their assigned pew at the head of the church, Heidi noted the several hundred attendees surrounding them and her heart swelled. Her aunt was very much loved and admired.

Once seated, Heidi repeatedly turned her head to the back of the church, hoping to catch a glimpse of Claudia. She had saved her friend a seat beside the aisle and wanted to wave her over before the service got going. Thankfully Claudia's bright blonde bob caught Heidi's eye just before the minister began, and she was able to signal Claudia over into position.

A glow seemed to surround Aunt Eileen's casket as the pastor's words floated all around them through the speakers in the corners of the chapel. He welcomed them in his speech, expressed his sorrow and joy in describing Eileen's battle with cancer and her initial success. But the tone changed to a somber one when he reminded everyone why they were there, to say goodbye to a dear wife, mother, sister, aunt, and friend. As the pastor continued, the realization that Heidi would never see her aunt again hit her full on. Instead of tears, her eyes glazed over in what she decided must be a type of grief. At the end of the hour, after the procession had filed out following the pallbearers, Heidi hardly noticed that Claudia had left her side to drive to the cemetery in her own car as they had planned the night before.

Heidi and her father emerged from the car without her mother, who had her palm on the back-seat window and didn't attempt to get out. Heidi would worry about that later and focused on Claudia walking toward her instead. Together, they went up to the graveside where an unknown man held Patches on a leash. She knelt down and hugged him and hummed words of encouragement in his ear. Edward put his hand on her shoulder and took Patches' leash. The poor dog whimpered as the casket was rolled over to the site.

When the graveside service was over, Heidi leaned into Claudia and said, "I've got to figure out what Mom's doing in the car. I'll meet you at Clyde's tomorrow."

"Sure, see you then. I've got to get out of here. Cemeteries give me the heebie-jeebies." Claudia turned away.

"Yeah, me too." Heidi watched Claudia walk down the hill before saying anything to her father. "I want to remember Aunt Eileen by her spirited love of life, not by a casket."

"Of course, Mousey. I agree but that's easier said than done." Turning to Edward he said, "Condolences again, if you need anything don't hesitate to call."

Edward moved his head left and right but said nothing.

Her father positioned his herringbone Gatsby cap on his head, leaned in toward Heidi, and quietly said, "Your mother has never been able to accept that life and death are interconnected. Every time someone dies, she becomes more anxious. Her sister's passing is another hurdle she may not be able to get over—I'll wait for you in the car."

Heidi watched her father walk away, open the car door, and climb in. When she turned to console Edward, she realized he was no longer standing beside her. He had wandered over to a bench under a tree with Patches. His face was buried in the dog's fur. She cautiously approached, and said, "Edward, I'm..." but he held up his hand to interrupt her without lifting his head to look in her direction.

Out of the corner of her eye, she spied Edward's father standing by another tree opposite the casket, and she wondered why he was always so aloof. As quickly as she thought that, she immediately felt a mixture of guilt and sadness that she had never really gotten to know him. He was never around and, when he was, he never really associated with her. In all honesty, he was just another face in the crowd.

Heidi stood at the graveside. Before dealing with her mother, she needed to close down her emotions and swallow the lump of tears that gurgled in her throat. Nothing would ever be the same without her aunt—she reached out to the casket, but stopped…

Stumbling down the hill, Heidi arrived at the car and got into the back seat. "Mom! Why didn't you get out? I needed you with me. Edward needed you!"

Her mother's cherry lips turned down and clinched. "I am sorry," was all she said.

"Why?" Heidi exclaimed through choked tears. "You're not the only miserable person here."

"I know, I know." Her mother's voice trailed away.

"While I was out there, something beyond belief happened!"

"Oh, don't be absurd."

The tears flooded down Heidi's face. "I reached out to touch Aunt Eileen's casket and drew my hand back—a force pushed me away. Her spirit seemed to be saying, 'You don't need to touch. I'm not here, I'm in a far better place.' I was startled at first, and then peaceful."

"All the more reason I wasn't there. Connecting to the spirit world doesn't give me any comfort."

"No one wants to be in front of a casket, but we all did it. Everyone but you. I feel ashamed." Heidi crossed her legs away from her mother, moved closer to the door, and adjusted the bottom of her skirt. "Why didn't you stand by Edward?"

"I was flashing back to our mother's death when I was ten-years-old. I couldn't move when it was time to get out of the car."

"What happened to your mother? Neither of you ever told me," Heidi protested.

Heidi's father turned the key in the ignition, bringing the car to a roaring start which broke the silence that reverberated throughout the car, then started driving away.

"My sister and I lived outside of Detroit in an area called the Indian Village." Her mother sat there filing her nails as she told the story.

"What?"

Her mother cringed. "It's a name of an area outside Detroit. Eileen and I were both born in that house. We were going to move into a new home my parents designed on the shores of Lake Michigan. Before that, though, they had planned to go alone on a European vacation, leaving my sister and me with our aunts. Everything was all set, and they went out to celebrate; the next day Mom felt sick. Within days she was bedridden and developed pneumonia. The doctor said it was another strain of the Spanish Flu. Eileen and I couldn't go in the room because the doctor said we'd get sick. I prayed and prayed, asking God to make her well. She died in a matter of days. God abandoned us."

"I don't think He took her away to hurt you."

"My father and I thought so. I still think so."

"I know it doesn't lessen your pain, but you weren't the only ones that suffered during those times. Millions died of the Spanish Flu." Heidi adjusted her skirt again. "I'm sorry, I shouldn't state facts you already know."

"Facts and feelings aren't related. As I was saying," her mother dabbed her eyes with a Kleenex tissue, "our maid ran sobbing around the house, covering all the mirrors with black fabric. Mother's body lay in an open coffin, in the sitting room, in the front of the house. I was hysterical when they closed the coffin and trapped Mother. My father said she was going to heaven, and she was in a *special sleep* for her journey. All the bedding and curtains were removed from her room and burned. I was such a

180

sensitive child, I never recovered from the shock, and I have lived with the memory ever since."

"Remember the book you gave me forever ago called *The Velveteen Rabbit,* I think it's by Margery Williams. I still have a copy."

"Of course, I got it for you for a reason."

Heidi recounted the story. "A small boy was given a stuffed rabbit for Christmas. They went everywhere together. Then the boy got sick with Scarlet Fever, and the rabbit stayed tucked in his arms. When he recovered, the doctor said the rabbit had to be burned with the bedding to kill the germs."

"Yes, that's right. The book was about love and death. I never told you what happened to my mother so you never connected the story to my situation."

"Oh, so this is why you clean stuff all the time?"

"Yes, and there's more. Then my father became absorbed in his own heartache. He didn't pay much attention to our grief. Eileen and I spent a lot of time with our aunts while he tried to put his life back together. He attended spiritual séances trying to find peace. Thankfully, Eileen was too young to understand what happened. She was five at the time. Being around us brought him some joy, but also great sadness. He was lonely and remarried, saying we needed a mother. I didn't want a new one."

"Losing Aunt Eileen must make you feel even more alone, but you're not. Dad and I are here, you have the McGwire's, and other friends."

Her mother stopped filing her nails and patted Heidi's hand. "You have a long life ahead of you; we're nearer to the end."

"Sounds defeatist—this is hard for me, too."

"Yes, but older people dying is very different."

"Edward is in a lot of pain. He barely said two words to anyone. We are all broken!"

"Perhaps he'll heal in time." Her mother stopped talking and turned away.

Chapter 20

Four years later, 1984…

All of Heidi's relationships with men had gone sour. The first love plucked one wing from her heart, and the second took the other. She wasn't in a hurry to start over and wasn't sure she knew how. Perhaps Claudia could help with a new strategy over a cup of coffee at Clyde's. It seemed like a good idea.

"Claudia, I don't know what's going on with me and dating. I can't seem to get back into the swing of things. I haven't been on more than one date in months, and that guy was so dull." The coffee mug felt like a heat-pack in her palms.

"When you least expect it, someone better will turn up." Claudia sneezed.

"Bless you! Okay, but is something wrong with me?" Sipping the coffee, she got burned. "Ouch!"

"Careful with that coffee." Claudia hesitated. "No, not exactly, but I think you deserve someone who will work with you when things get complicated. Your relationships are right out of a psychology book."

"Lucky me! You've decoded my brain after taking a couple of classes. Maybe I don't want to hear this after all." Heidi rolled her eyes. "Go on, do tell."

"When you get a boyfriend, you both stick around for a while to see how things go. After conflicts of one sort or another develop, you both give up. Maybe the initial glow of the romance fizzles or impatience sets in."

"Oh, great! That's such a help," Heidi said sarcastically.

"You're also craving attention from any man that can help you get away from your mother, instead of learning to be more self-reliant."

"Remind me, why are we doing this?" Heidi laughed at herself.

"You did ask." Claudia stuck the tip of her tongue out. "What are best friends for?"

"Geez! You aren't holding back," Heidi sneered, but then changed to a gentler tone. "But, yeah, the craving acceptance makes sense. It's all part of the person I am, I guess."

"Also, you're afraid to do what it takes to stay committed to a man because you're sure, deep down, that he eventually won't find you worthy enough. It's important for you to evaluate him, too. He could be unworthy. Maybe it's because your Mom spends so much time building you up with compliments and then smashing you down. You've become ridiculously humble and need to stand up for yourself when someone challenges your ideas. Shoot, this conversation is even deflating you, I can see it in your face."

"I suppose that could be it. An innate fear of rejection. Hey, it's proven to be true in both of the serious relationships I've had since I moved back home. I can't really explain it. I could say that I've watched Mom cut various friends loose when they don't do her bidding. Not sure that's it, but her behavior isn't a shining example of commitment through negotiation. It's amazing Mom and Dad are still together. I'm not sure when I became so weak hearted. Maybe it was when I learned I was adopted?"

"Not a bad guess since I never noticed you having trouble with your confidence before then. Things got even worse after your grandfather and aunt died. Your Mom started acting weirder than usual. Your mistrust is inevitable, because…"

Heidi interrupted, "What a mess! So, you're saying it's my parents' fault I derail relationships?"

Claudia wiped her hands on her napkin. "Pretty much, you never got help understanding what happened in Germany, and you haven't a clue how to have a happy, long-term, love affair after watching your parents' unhappiness. You're the type of person who needs tons of details to work through problems. Fact is, you have to rise above your mom's nonsense and take responsibility for your own behavior."

"That's what Aunt Eileen told me before she died. She said it differently, but it's basically the same idea."

"I don't know how it happened, but you act like your mom is your ruler and you do her bidding for fear of getting your head chopped off. Not literally, of course."

"Mom conditioned me well—you know I thrive on approval and collapse under pressure. What's worse is that my adult life is still affected. So, she has a 'Queen complex,' is there any such thing? What does that make me? A simpering idiot who does whatever she says."

"Sorry, I sound harsh." Claudia gulped down the rest of her iced tea. "Let's not talk about your mom so much and focus on the men."

"You're probably right about my mom."

"Okay, back to the men." Claudia chuckled. "Hey, I'm twenty-six and ready to find a husband. I haven't succeeded, so I'm not an expert, yet. Ugh, dating is for the young."

"You're still young." Heidi tried not to laugh, but she couldn't contain her amusement. "Anyway… Go on. What happened to my analysis?"

"Right, now you like my help?" Claudia teased.

"Sorry, go on."

"Stop apologizing! Think about the relationships you've been in that failed, and that should help make the next one better. The first would have worked except for a huge misunderstanding. Until that happened, I was so happy for you. In fact, I was doubly pleased since I introduced you to Tom after you got out of Bradford and transferred into Catholic U."

"Yeah, I know. Tom and I were crazy about each other, and he gave me one of his military dog tags before he was sent to Switzerland."

"That was a big deal; a promise to come back to you," Claudia said.

"We wrote each other every few days. He'd been gone almost a year, and then I said I couldn't write as often because my theater studies were taking up a lot of time. Next thing I knew, some Swiss bitch sent me a letter saying they were dating. Now that I think of it, I should have figured out if she was lying. He would have written the letter, not her."

"It never made sense." Claudia sounded like she was going to spit nails. "

"Every letter I sent was returned, and I never got another letter from him. I'm pretty sure the bitch sabotaged us, and he didn't have a clue what was happening. I don't know if I ever told you, but soon after I decided to confront him in person. Trouble was I didn't have enough money for the flight."

"I wish you'd ask me for a loan. Then, remember we found out later that his best friend, my boyfriend, knew he'd returned from overseas? He took forever to tell me what he knew. Jerk! He should've since we were dating. That was the beginning of the end for us. He got worse and worse about honesty."

"Yep, I know, you told me—Tom parked down the street from my parents' and saw me come out with a guy I'd just met. If he'd talked to me, we probably could've worked out everything, but for some reason, he didn't. I never understood why your boyfriend didn't help us."

"Ouch, I still regret that entire situation. He was so annoying and told me Tom was going to ask you to marry him until he saw you laughing with someone else."

"My relationship with Tom scarred me for life." After a deep breath, Heidi said, "I was twenty, and he was five years older. He should've made more of an effort to approach me. Anyway, that's long past, but he's still engraved in my heart. I shouldn't think about him anymore!"

Claudia hung her head down. "I wish I could've helped. I don't think I ever apologized, until now. I'm sorry."

"Thanks, but I never blamed you. Fate didn't deal Tom and me any favors. So, your evaluation of the next guy?"

"You two got along, but that relationship was doomed from the start. Matt had huge trust issues and imagined all kinds of bad stuff. My mom can attest to that since he used to visit her randomly. I know she tried to help because she was upset you'd met him at one of Dad's work parties. He definitely couldn't see anything beyond his own ego."

"I think there was a lot more to Matt than we realized." Heidi sat back in her chair. "All right, both failed, but at least each relationship lasted a few years. There's nothing you could've done to help with that situation. We had a fight, and both walked out. By the time he returned it was half a year later, and I'd already decided to block him out of my life, even though he'd taken another slice out of my heart." Heidi was more than ready to change the subject. "I think I've had enough relationship analysis for now... let's talk about something else."

"Okay, you're right," Claudia remarked in agreement and handed over a brochure. "It's time to move forward. I've got an idea. Here's a community group that goes on hiking trips. You should sign up."

"Thanks, I'll think it over."

"Your welcome. Let's get out of here and go to my place." Claudia stood up and pulled Heidi out of her chair.

"Right, we're done. You still have those VHS tapes of *Tootsie* and *An Officer and a Gentleman* in your film collection?"

"Yep, I'll vote for *Tootsie* today, it's just bizarre enough to lighten our mood. The other one is too romantic, and it'll make us cry."

"I'm not in the mood to get sappy. Dustin Hoffman, here we go; along with some popcorn and Coca-Cola. It's amazing how he plays the part of a woman on that day-time soap opera," Heidi said. "It's hysterical."

"Just what we need after this depressing talk."

It was spring by the time Heidi decided to go on one of the community organized hikes that Claudia had suggested. The walk she signed up for covered a span of ten-miles along the C&O canal. A mile into the day, a charming man with a short dark beard and brown eyes introduced himself, and his friend, Pete.

"My name's Walt," he said, tipping the brim of his safari hat in her direction. Right from the start, Walt seemed different for any man she'd ever met. He was quiet, with a mischievous, yet playful, glint in his eye. Pete was more of a snake charmer. Older and wiser, Heidi tried not to flirt, but she was intrigued by Walt's demeanor.

After the hike, all eight of the participants gathered at Clyde's in Georgetown. The waitress brought out three plates and put them in front of Walt.

Heidi gasped. "You're eating all that? It's enough to feed a small army. Three burgers, three orders of fries?"

"Yep, going to devour it all. Big hike, big appetite."

"Okay. Enjoy yourself." Heidi thought her own plate was too full. "If I ate like that, I'd weigh two-hundred pounds. I doubt you weigh that much, Mister Tall-and-Skinny."

"Hey, imagine what I'd look like if I didn't eat all this." Walt's mouth engulfed half the burger in one bite and chewed it up.

"Um, okay, I get your point. How tall are you?"

"A mere six-foot-two. You?"

"My lips are sealed. My mother says a woman should never tell such things." Heidi was enjoying the banter.

"Oh, come on. You're a modern woman."

"All right, I'm five-foot-two." She took a bite of her cheeseburger. "I'll watch you eat, maybe you'll grow rounder." Heidi laughed and fixed her eyes on his food as it moved off the plate into his mouth.

After he finished all three meals, he scribbled on a piece of paper, then pushed the paper and pen toward Heidi.

She read his words silently. *Can we go out next week?*

She wrote back, *Yes,* and added her phone number.

They talked several times on the phone over the following week. She made sure to give him her address and explain, unlike her peers, that she lived with her parents and wasn't comfortable about her situation. To avoid complications, she asked him to pick her up when they weren't around. At first, she thought it would be a good idea to warn him about her mother's idiosyncrasies, but decided she'd wait and see how the date went before revealing too much about her personal life. He arrived at the designated time, and she ducked out the front door and walked away from the house down the path with him.

Walt put his arm around her shoulder. "So... where should we eat?"

"You didn't figure that out?"

"I did, but I thought I'd ask anyway."

"Oh, you're a confusing man," Heidi said playfully.

"What do you mean?" he innocently responded.

"Not sure how to explain. You're not like most men." Heidi smiled, and butterflies jumped in her stomach.

"Thank you, I think." He winked. "So... where do you want to go?"

"Walt, I'm not particular. Did you pick one in Bethesda or Georgetown?"

"Neither. Anglers Inn by the C&O canal."

"Good choice. Will their food fill you up?"

"Likely. I don't always eat three plates."

The parking lot at Anglers Inn was almost full. It turned out he'd made reservations. For the next couple of hours, they talked and enjoyed each other's company.

After dinner, Walt said, "So, now that I've wined and dined you, what would you like to do next?"

"A walk would be good since we're across the street from the canal. You're interesting, no other man has ever asked me that before. They acted like dinner meant I owed them at least a kiss."

"I'm glad I'm not like the others. A little bird told me how to treat a lady. I'm a patient man, and I want to know all about you." Walt smiled and extended his hand. "A walk it is."

Heidi accepted and swung their hands between them to keep things light. "I'm glad I agreed to go out with you after the hike."

"My friend said he wanted to ask you out, but I told him you weren't his kind of girl."

"How'd you know that?"

"He's a player, and I didn't think you were."

"Thanks. The last guy I dated was... never mind."

"So, you're saying you'd like to go out again?"

"Yes, I think so."

"Sounds good." Walt squeezed her hand. "Although I need to tell you, I'll only be in D.C. for about four weeks before I have to go to California for six months."

"Thanks for telling me up-front."

ELSA WOLF

"You're welcome. I really like you, and I didn't want to leave out anything that could be important."

"Thanks, I like you, too. I'm pretty gun shy at this point, so I appreciate your honesty. Let's take one day at a time."

Heidi felt giddy when Walt returned from the Bay Area. They went hiking on the east coast, to movies and concerts. It didn't take long before they were dating exclusively. Ten months in, they went to the C&O canal for a five-mile walk, followed by dinner at Clyde's.

"Heidi, I was thinking—" Walt hesitated. "Do you want to move in with me?"

"Wait, what? That was unexpected. Really?"

"Yes, really. Will you?"

"I like the idea." Heidi smiled. "You're truly one of a kind."

"I hope that's still a good thing."

"Yes, I think so."

"I have confidence in you." He picked her hand up off the table and kissed it. "But I need an answer tonight."

"What's the hurry? Maybe I should think it over."

"You could, but if you want to live with me, just say yes. You might go home and get cold feet. I can't deny that your mother worries me. Her influence over you is strong."

"Yep, that's true. My parents are quite conservative, and I've always tried to make Mom happy. I don't like it when she's upset." Heidi twisted her napkin into a knot. "Enough about my mom, tonight is about our future." Heidi didn't need to think it over—she loved Walt. In her heart, she knew moving in with him would be the right decision.

Walt's puppy-dog eyes softened even more. "We have fun together, and I never want to be away from you again. I love you... and the answer is?"

"I feel the same way." Heidi's eyes glistened. "I feel giddy. Yes, I will move in with you."

"This will be great!"

After dessert, he drove her home. They parted ways by the front door after a passionate kiss.

Heidi wandered dreamily into the house. Her parents were sitting in the den. She approached them casually at first, then decided to drop the news bluntly.

"Tonight, was fantastic! Mom, Dad… I'm going to move out."

Her mother spoke first. "In a group house with your friends?"

Heidi thought; *so far this isn't creating too much chaos. I might pull this off, probably not though. Take a breath, my neck is tensing up.*

"No, in a three-bedroom house with Walt."

Her mother persisted. "With a group of friends?"

"No, only Walt." *I wish I could make them understand.*

An explosion followed, and Heidi cringed. She had been an adult for seven years, and her mother still treated her like a child. The next hour was filled with her mother's ranting. When Heidi had enough, she excused herself and went up the stairs to write.

My old friend, I thought I'd given up writing on your pages, but here I am again. I want to scream. I can't expect Claudia or Walt or anyone else to put up with Mom. What is she up to? This doesn't make any sense. She met Walt a year ago and never mentioned her concern, and there's nothing she can do now. It's too late. I am committed to him and now torn between the two of them. The last few months I've gone to his house on weekends, and she never questioned my intentions, nor my morality. I want Mom on my side, not pitted against me. I have no idea what Dad thinks about my decision since he didn't say a word, but I've made up my mind. Many times, I have given up and done what Mom wants. This is different. This time I will move out permanently. Walt and Claudia have saved me from self-destruction. Hopefully, things will work out with him, but—if not—I'll find another way to manage on my own.

Chapter 21

Walt and Heidi set up house in old town Alexandria. Their work wasn't far away, and they commuted to Washington on public transportation. Daily, just about lunchtime, her mother would telephone her at Arena Stage.

"Hi, Mom... You know, I shouldn't talk to you at work. I eat at my desk and plan out new costumes. Everyone around me can hear my end of our conversations. They're getting annoyed."

"Go into another room for lunch. I won't call you in the evenings at that place where you live with him!"

"Mom, you're unbelievable! Find something else to do with your life. Stop bugging me." *Oops, shouldn't have said that. Here she goes. Rant, rant. I should hang up on her, but I can't.*

During every conversation, her mother repeated herself in one fashion or another. Today she said, "Please, tell Walt he needs to find other people to live with you. This is embarrassing. I can't tell my friends you are living alone with a man!"

"Is that all? Nothing else concerns you? Maybe my rock climbing or my recent scuba diving? You don't fuss over those risky things." Heidi didn't give her a chance to answer.

"Everything's about appearances with you! Just don't tell your friends who I'm living with, if that makes you feel better."

"None of your friends approve of Walt," her mother said so loudly Heidi's ear hurt.

"Well, that's a blatant lie! If you're talking about my childhood friends, he hasn't met any of them, except Claudia. You don't know my adult friends."

Her mother was silent on the other end of the line, but only for about ten agonizing seconds. "He's taken you away from me, from the world I wanted you to be in. He's not..."

"He's not genteel enough for you?" Heidi imagined her mother's face twitching during the phone call.

"No, he's not."

"He has a university degree, a stable profession, and most importantly he's good to me. His father was a military officer and is now a respectable businessman. Yes, Walt is shy around you, but it's my fault. I told him how particular you are."

"I see, well he's still not for you."

"Oh, Mother, I've had enough! You're not in charge of my life anymore. I'm going back to work." She hung up the phone and rubbed the tension out of her neck.

The competition was fierce in the costume department, and there wasn't room for distractions. Once Heidi's contract was over, she tried to get hired on again, but the crew wasn't convinced she could manage with so many interruptions from her family.

After many failed attempts at getting work in another theater, Heidi did some soul-searching. It was time to transition into the corporate world—*arts be gone*. Besides, she needed a steady salary. Art would have to wait or become more of a hobby than a profession. After she settled into the idea, she began working for a temp agency to develop a new set of skills in public relations administration. She vowed to withhold any phone numbers or specific company names from her mother. Eventually, her mother gave in and started calling Heidi at home, but there was still a palatable tension between them. She continued to get agitated and wanted to cut off all communication. However, it wasn't possible to cut her mother out of her life and still keep in contact with her father. After a great deal of thought, she formed a plan. The next day she discussed the idea with Walt.

"Walt, I think it would be a good idea for you to meet Claudia's parents now that we're planning on getting married. I think they can help us with my Mom's attitude toward you. The McGwires are easy to get along with, you'll see."

"Good idea! Your mother's attitude is discouraging. It would be nice to find out if someone from your parents' circle of friends can like me."

"I should've introduced you to David and Sadie a long time ago, but I kept trying to separate my past from the present."

"How's that working?" he joked.

"It's not. I'll arrange a meeting." She shrugged.

Walt kissed her. "Past and present connecting. Let's go for it!"

"Okay, I'll call the McGwire's tomorrow. I think I'll also ask David some questions about my dad while we're there."

Heidi arranged to stop by the McGwire's over the weekend. She and Walt went to the front entrance, rang the golden bell, and waited. A hollow echo came from the new intercom box on the side of the door.

David's voice sounded strident. "Hello, can I help you?"

"Why do you have an intercom all of a sudden? You always leave the door unlocked."

"Yes, well... things have changed... Sadie and I will come downstairs, give us a minute."

The door opened, and David greeted them. "Hello, sorry about the lock."

Sadie explained, "There have been some robberies in the neighborhood, and the buzzer makes us feel better. Come in, come in."

"David, Sadie… this is Walt Bailey."

The two men shook hands.

"I'm glad we're finally meeting." Walt's voice sounded upbeat.

"The pleasure is all mine," David replied.

"I'm so happy you two were able to meet with us this weekend." Heidi played with the engagement ring in the pocket of her jeans and looked forward to telling the McGwires' their news later on.

David picked up a photograph off a side table. "I thought I'd share this picture of Nathan with you and Walt from our military days. We managed to find some comical moments in all the chaos." He passed the photo to Heidi.

She studied the small, black and white photograph. "It looks like you're trying to pull a rabbit in half with ropes."

"Gag photo; a bit of tomfoolery. The bunny won; no animals were hurt in this episode."

"You two aren't so comedic anymore." Sadie patted his forearm. "Come on everyone, let's sit down and relax."

"Nathan is brilliant and modest," David said. "Did you know he was in the Stanford Terman Study?"

"No, what is that? Sounds like my dad was a guinea pig."

"Not at all. Basically, it's a lifelong study of people who have IQs of over 130. Your dad remembers all the important things he has ever heard or read; you've experienced his genius. I think the government used the Terman list to recruit people for specific jobs."

"My curiosity might get me into trouble." Heidi tensed and ran her hand through her newly permed hair. "What kind of job?"

"Miscellaneous security work. I think…"

196

Sadie interrupted, "Heidi come into the kitchen and help me with some snacks."

The two women left the room and began to prepare a tea tray at the small kitchen table.

"David and I adore your dad." Sadie ate a cracker. A crump dropped on her blouse, and she wiped it away. "Did he ever tell you about the hatpin mishaps on one of his flights to California?"

"No, I didn't realize he flew out there."

"You were very small at the time. It was one of many stories we exchanged after you and Claudia were asleep. In this story, your father was sitting on the plane next to a middle-aged woman who pulled out a three-inch straight hatpin from her hat. She wrapped her fist around the decorative end and was about to stab herself. Your father took a chance and put his hand on hers. Understandably the woman was offended by a stranger touching her, but before she could voice her objections, two over inflated falsies peaked out of her blouse by the top buttons. Turned out the air pressure in the plane overinflated them. Needless to say, he was quite embarrassed that he even looked toward her bosoms to realize they weren't nearly as large as she tried to pretend."

Heidi smirked. "I get the overinflating bit. My air pillow over expands when I fly. The story sounded like it was going to turn violent but then got silly."

"Certainly did." Sadie chuckled. "Here; carry the tea tray. I'll bring the plate of cucumber sandwiches and scones."

The women walked back into the living room.

"You sounded like you two were having fun in the kitchen," Walt remarked.

"We were," Sadie said. "Excuse me for a minute. I'll be right back." Sadie disappeared through David's office door and returned with a wrapped box. "Walt, I bought a little something. It's for your outdoor adventures with Heidi."

She smiled as Walt accepted the package and gingerly removed the ribbon and beige wrapping paper. Inside sat a folded flannel shirt cocooned in white tissue paper. "How did you know green is my favorite color? Thank you, Mrs. McGwire." Walt's hand moved across the fabric.

"Oh, *please*, call me Sadie. *Everyone* calls us by our given names unless it's a formal business meeting. We like to keep the atmosphere around us light and easy."

"I don't think I've ever heard anyone call you aunt or uncle," Heidi reflected.

"No one ever does. Not even my actual nieces and nephews. I think you were around ten when I asked you to stop. Your mother didn't approve, but I told her it was my choice, and that you wouldn't be ruined." Sadie puffed up like a peacock. "I'm not a fan of titles of any sort between friends and family members."

"Thank you for including me," Walt replied.

"How did you and my dad meet?" Heidi asked David.

"During our initial enlistment and training. We were from the same area in California. One thing led to another, and we became steadfast friends. It's never mattered that I'm fifteen years his junior. We've been through a lot together over the years."

Heidi took another sip of her tea. "This is delicious." She needed to take a moment to carefully think over her next question. "Perhaps I shouldn't bring this up, but I'd like to learn more since he rarely talks about his past."

David raised one eyebrow. "About something in particular?"

"Mmm, yes. Dad told me he went to Stanford, then Harvard to become a lawyer. Afterward, he served in the Second World War. He never told me any details.... Oh, and he was married before. What can you tell me about his first wife?"

"Aw, right to the heart." David placed the tips of his fingers together and then released them before he answered. "I never met her, but he told me she was both gorgeous and intelligent. They were doing all right while Nathan practiced law. Then, later on, he enlisted in the Army Air Corps, and their relationship went through some unresolvable rough patches."

"Wait. Army Air Corps?" Heidi hadn't ever heard her dad mention the specific branch.

"In those days, the Air Force was part of the Army. They figured out his skills and, before we knew it, he went from sergeant to major. Almost all of his time in the war was spent in North Africa."

"Wow, all news to me!"

"After the war, they were divorced." David picked up a cucumber sandwich. "Such things were never spoken about out loud in those days, only whispered—the 'D' word."

"Why were they divorced?"

"I'm sorry, if he didn't tell you, I shouldn't betray his confidence. You need to find a way to ask."

"Someday, I'll manage. My parents are struggling, and I don't want to make Dad's life more complicated by asking questions. Mom's pretty uptight about Walt."

Sadie puckered her lips into a tight point. "Your mother's opinion of your living arrangement isn't glowing. I know she wants the best for you, but no man will fit her criteria." She glanced at Walt. "No offense intended. If Heidi trusts you, that's good enough for me."

Before the women could explore her mother's troubles any further, David changed the subject. "So, Walt, I've heard about how you met Heidi. What do you do for a living?"

"I work for the government." He hesitated. "I'm a correspondent of sorts."

"Aw, enough said. My work with the State Department isn't something I can explain either. I have only one question for you. Are your intentions honorable?"

"David, please don't embarrass him. I'm practically thirty. I think I can make my own decisions. Nowadays, it's not unusual for unmarried couples to live together. Believe me, I thought it all out."

Walt interjected, "Heidi, I'm not embarrassed. Of course, he's asking. Yes, sir, my intentions are honorable."

"Good to know, Walt, good to know," David said and shifted his attention to Heidi. "Honestly, I don't know how you've turned out so well. Your mom has been troubled for years about so many things." David made a clicking sound with his tongue.

"I think Mom was okay with Walt for a while, but—ever since we moved in together—she thinks he's a bad influence on me. Like he brainwashed me or something. She doesn't seem to believe I can think for myself."

Sadie piped in, "Of course you can. Your mother hangs on too tight because she thinks she's losing you and has to blame someone, might as well be Walt. Living with someone outside of marriage wasn't something she considered, since she was counting on the religious values your dad instilled in you through the church to keep you under control. For her, everything is about preserving appearances. I'm not sure she'll ever get over your leaving home to be with Walt."

David's face reddened. "Sadie, settle down…"

"I didn't mean any harm."

"It's all right, I understand." Heidi could never fault Sadie for anything.

David put his hand on Walt's shoulder. "Walt, come and see my miniature lead soldier collection." He guided Walt to the other side of the room while Heidi sat next to Sadie drinking tea and listened to the men's conversation. David explained, "I painted each one to resemble a soldier I knew during the war."

"Sounds heart wrenching."

"Would you like to paint a modern version?" David took one out of the cabinet.

"I admire your dexterity. I could try, but I'm likely to make a mess. I'm better at working on larger projects."

"Quite all right." David put the little figure back and closed the cabinet. "We all have different hobbies. Painting the soldiers is therapeutic for me."

"Yes, sir. Thanks for sharing your collection."

"My pleasure. You can drop the sir. Call me David, please."

"Sorry, just habit. My dad was a Marine."

David patted Walt on the back while they walked across the room. "I've enjoyed our visit."

Heidi peered at Walt with a slight turn of her head and raised one eyebrow. "I'm glad I could bring Walt over to meet you without my parents."

Walt appeared more relaxed, but his stance was still rigid. "I enjoyed hearing more about Mr. Schwartz."

David squinted at Walt. "I should warn you that Mrs. Schwartz won't ever allow you to call her Gwen. Once she's decided you're an enemy, there's little chance of changing her mind."

"I wish I could find a way to alter their opinions."

"Nathan likes you, but he won't go to battle with his wife. She's stubborn—a tough nut to crack."

"Great wording, David." Heidi's sarcasm was unmistakable.

"Sorry." He let out a long sigh. "You're such a love."

Heidi didn't hold back and said, "Mom has always been able to stick a knife in my side and twist it. I can't figure out how to ignore her emotional explosions or her constant pleading to get rid of Walt."

Sadie added, "You had plenty of lectures long before Walt appeared in your life. I assumed you had learned to sluff them off."

"Yes, you're right, I should've by now. I'm feeling vulnerable lately, and Mom's taking advantage."

"You need to put an emotional wall up," David said.

"I'm trying," Heidi responded. "I'm glad we came by today."

Walt eyed Heidi. "Haven't you forgotten something?"

"Never." A smile covered her face, and her eyes felt like they were dancing.

"Be brave." Walt cleared his throat.

Heidi put her hand in her pocket, wiggled her fingers to maneuver the ring back into place. "Okay." She took a deep breath.

"Here goes… we've only told a few people." She held out her hand. "Walt proposed last weekend."

Sadie grabbed her hand. "You are full of surprises. Your mother didn't tell me."

"She doesn't know. I figured I needed to tell you first, so you'd be prepared when Mom calls. She's going to blow up. It's going to be huge, and not in a good way."

"Well, it's a gorgeous ring! So, tell the story, how did he propose?"

"Walt was a bit of a rat at the time," Heidi said and poked his side. "A couple weeks before, he talked about his great-grandmother's ring. He dangled me along, making me think a proposal was coming, which included my ring size. Next thing I knew he said he wasn't ready for marriage and closed the subject." Heidi hesitated. "I sulked around for days wondering what to do next. Pretending nothing was bothering me was almost impossible. Moving out wasn't an appealing choice and loving him for years without marriage wasn't what I wanted. A week later, after I'd been stewing on everything, we went out to a movie and back to Anglers Inn; that's where we had our first date. After the meal, he asked me to marry him. His escapades are sometimes infuriating, but I said yes."

"Heidi did, but I thought she was going to lunge across the table and punch me for stringing her along," Walt added.

Sadie hugged Heidi. "I'm happy for you."

David shook Walt's hand. "Congratulations, you have a gem of a lady. Take good care of each other."

"Thank you, we will," Walt smiled.

"Let's have a drink to celebrate!" David pulled out a bottle of Courvoisier Cognac from a cabinet.

"Thank you, but Walt and I need to go. I'm sorry we can't stay, we're meeting some friends in Harper's Ferry." Heidi moved toward the door.

"Another time then," Sadie said.

"I'm glad to have met you both. Your opinions are very important to Heidi. Thanks again for the flannel shirt."

Heidi hugged David and Sadie goodbye. "I plan to tell my parents alone, so Walt isn't horrified by Mom's temper. "On a more positive note; I plan to ask Claudia to be my maid of honor."

"I'm sure she would love to," David said.

"Sometimes I wish you were my parents."

Sadie's face softened. "You don't mean that, not really. Go on, enjoy your time at Harpers Ferry. Once you've told your parents your news, I'll see if I can calm your mother down."

"You're the best! We want to get married in less than a year, and I'm hoping Mom can settle into the idea." She sighed with disdain. "You know, I do love her, but I need her to accept me the way I am." Heidi reached out and took Walt's hand. "See you both soon." She waved on their way out the door.

Chapter 22

1986...

With considerable hesitation, after another work week had passed, Heidi drove over to tell her parents about their engagement. No surprise, her mother was incensed. Her father stood by, merely watching the fireworks ignite without making a remark. All he said was to go easy on her mother since she wasn't well. This excuse covered everything from physical to mental ailments and always had. Things were so unpleasant that Heidi left within thirty minutes of her arrival.

Heidi didn't waste any time. The very next day they began planning their wedding. They thought about marrying at a chapel at the National Cathedral but decided it was too grand and reserved a date at the Norwood Parish where she'd attended Sunday school as a child. With Walt's encouragement, she gave her parent's the information hoping to eventually receive some support. If she had to, she'd marry without their approval but hoped her father would at least walk her down the aisle.

The phone rang, the caller ID flashed *Nathan Schwartz*, but she knew who it was; her mother only called in the evenings. She only talked to her father on Sunday mornings. The phone wasn't her friend anymore, the words that came through the receiver brought negative vibes into their home. She wanted her world with Walt to be a sheltered place, but Heidi let her mother in every time the phone rang. They no longer spoke at work, that issue had been resolved long ago, but a palpable tension remained between them.

Heidi reluctantly picked up the receiver. "Hi, Mom. How are you?"

"Well enough," her mother said in a curt tone. "Heidi, I called the parish today. The receptionist wasn't very accommodating, so I spoke with the minister. Once he found out you were living in *sin*, he crossed you two off the church schedule," her mother said victoriously. "Your wedding is off."

"What! You can't... this is my wedding." Heidi felt like steam was pouring out of her ears and knew the pastor wouldn't have done such a thing. "You had no right! What did Dad think?"

"I didn't tell him."

"Seriously?" she said in a barbed voice. "Now you've totally humiliated me. My friend's mother is a receptionist at Norwood, and I'm sure I can find out the details. Mother, you know, I'll just find another place if I can't marry there!" Heidi paused to compose herself. "My wedding is supposed to be one of the best days of my life."

"Yes, well, it isn't the best day of *my* life!" her mother sneered.

"That's beside the point. It's not up to you to decide where I take my marriage vows."

"You haven't been to that church for services or any other church since college."

"I'm still a spiritual person, and I've always wanted a formal wedding. Why do you care where I marry? You only went to church for Christmas services. Sundays Dad and I went together the rest of the year. Last time we talked about God it sounded like you'd rejected Him. Now, you decide to have a say?"

"Yes, I'm your mother, and I can say what I like even though I have doubts about God. You're abandoning me just like He did when I was a child." Her mother's disgust or perhaps jealousy seemed to be oozing out of the edges of the phone.

"This isn't about any of that, so don't make excuses. I'm sorry you don't approve of Walt, but I'm marrying the man I love."

"I just…never thought you two would…" Her mother didn't finish the sentence, then started another. "You must not love your mother! No self-respecting daughter would ever disappoint her mother like you've disappointed me!"

The words rattled around in Heidi's brain and seared into her heart. "Really? You're being cruel. I have to hang up before I say something I can't take back. Goodnight, Mother."

After disconnecting, Heidi got out a telephone directory. With any luck, she could find another spot before telling Walt what had happened. Whenever she got into disputes with her mother, Walt always supported Heidi's position while rightfully never choosing to argue on her behalf. He'd told her he was sure her mother would never approve of him so he would not put fuel into a confrontational fire. Twenty-four hours later, she found and booked a new Episcopal church within a reasonable distance from the reception spot. The church was perfect, with an arched double staircase at the entrance and chandeliers hanging down the aisle from the high vaulted ceiling. She arranged an appointment with the new minister and knew Walt would like the location if she did.

Heidi picked up the phone and dialed her parent's number. "Hello, Mom. It's all settled."

"What's settled?" Her mother's voice sounded like ice.

"I found another place for our wedding. I've had a long chat with the pastor, and he understands my situation."

"Give me the name of the church," her mother demanded.

"You must be joking!" Heidi's voice was escalating. "You ruined things before! I'm not trusting you this time."

"So, you won't be talked out of marrying that-that man?"

"No." Heidi felt like screaming but controlled herself. "I spoke to Dad yesterday morning. He said he's paying, and that you and I should plan the event together. We should try."

"I see. Well, your father and I will have a long talk."

"And then what, Mom?" Heidi was sure she didn't want to be near that conversation.

"I'm not happy about your decision, but—to save face—I'll help you create an elegant event," her mother grumbled. "I'm coming to your appointments. I can't have you choosing the menu or picking flowers or anything if I don't approve. I plan to invite my friends to this wedding, and I won't be humiliated by inferior products." She curtly announced, "Since we are paying, I get a say—you can't plan this on your own. I won't allow it."

"I've been involved with parties all my life, and now you don't think I can plan one properly!" She cursed under her breath. Luckily her mother didn't hear.

"Regardless, I'm helping, and there's nothing you can do about it other than eloping or calling off the wedding."

"I'm not calling it off, we love each other. I don't want to elope and hide Walt from anyone," Heidi asserted. "You can help, but really help—don't try to undermine my wedding again. I'm going to be married in less than a year... husband and wife, just like you and Dad."

"Walt is nothing like your dad!"

"Stop!" Heidi said, gritting her teeth. "Mom, give me a break, my patience is all used up. This nastiness between us has to end!"

Her mother responded after a long pause. "Very well, I can't lose my only daughter over this. Let's plan a proper wedding together."

"We can try." Heidi rubbed a tear off her cheek and wondered what it would be like to have a mother who could help without being unpleasant.

Her mother's breath came through the receiver. "What am I going to wear? I want to be glamorous, but I've gained thirty pounds since I last wore anything chic. My waist has ballooned."

"Oh, Mother, please! You're still *glamorous* with your Revlon blonde hair and curls." Heidi intended the compliment to be an offensive, sarcastic remark. Instead, it produced the opposite effect, and her mother calmed down.

"What kind of gown do you want to buy? We should go shopping."

"I've asked Claudia to be my maid of honor. The three of us can go out together and pick out her dress and the bridesmaids. I haven't decided who they are yet." Heidi hadn't been shopping with her mother in years and wasn't looking forward to starting again, especially not for her wedding. Yet, she hoped that the experience would help her mother feel more included in the event and perhaps change her negative point of view. "Mom, you don't need to worry about my gown."

"What! What do you mean?" Her mother's voice elevated.

"I'm not buying one. I have been making it behind closed doors, no one has seen it. I'll surprise everyone on our wedding day. I bought an off-white satin fabric, and I'll be appliquéing lace onto it. My days in theater costuming are coming in handy. The design isn't as complex as some of the things I've made."

"Well, at least you haven't forgotten your theater days," her mother scoffed. "Off-white… an appropriate color for an impure bride."

"You're being mean, again. I can't talk anymore right now."

Heidi gently placed the receiver in the cradle, and then picked it up again to make sure her mother had disconnected. Heidi slammed the receiver down so hard that it almost broke in two. She'd never felt so angry in her life. Her mother's barb about the dress color emphasized how disapproving and mean she could be. The emotions had been building up inside Heidi for months, and she collapsed on the floor, pulled her knees to her chest and wrapped her arms around them. The tears came, and she sobbed like a hysterical child. Walt rushed into the room and sat next to her on the floor. He handed her his handkerchief. Heidi drenched the cloth before recovering herself. She looked into his deep brown eyes and wiped the last of her tears from her face, assuring him she was all right. There was no need to explain her mother's latest offending remarks. He was compassionate enough to be there by her side without question.

The morning of the wedding, Heidi stood alone in her childhood bedroom. She'd been at her parents' house for the past three days to adhere to some kind of tradition—the groom not seeing the bride before the wedding. It all seemed a little strange since she'd already been living with Walt. Why she honored her mother's request, she didn't know, but she tried to hold herself together while she stood in front of the mirror preening herself. The dress looked perfect. Earlier that morning, the beautician curled her hair, pinned it up, and sprayed it until the strands felt like cardboard. The woman had also applied Heidi's make-up in multiple layers. She felt like an overdone cake. In disgust, Heidi scrubbed the layers off and replaced them with a softer version of the same shades. She wanted the photographs to look like her natural self, not a fragile china doll. The moment felt surreal. Heidi wiped a tear from the corner of one eye. Before she cried even more and ruined her make-up, her father walked into the room.

"You look stunning!" Her father's eyes were full of pride. "Walt and I just finished meeting at the country club. He asked me to bring this red rose to you with a note. You look magnificent!" He kissed her forehead.

"Thanks, Dad."

"Of course. I'll be waiting downstairs."

The red rose smelled like a piece of heaven. Walt's words on the note echoed through her body—*A rose to symbolize hope and new beginnings for us, Heidi Rose. We are strong together. You are my world—I vow to be loyal and love you always—Walt.* In a matter of hours, her life would truly change forever.

Heidi stood at the end of the church in her long gown with the hand-sewn lace all up and down the net sleeves and along the edges of the satin train. Mendelson's *Pachelbel Cannon D* filled the church, but she ignored the music in spite of how loudly the organ pumped out the notes. Her father came to her side, and she slipped her hand into his bent arm. All the guests were staring in their direction. She squeezed her cascading rose and stephanotis bouquet a little tighter.

Her eyes swept past the blush-colored roses that lined the aisles and met with Walt's eyes at the altar. His smile was so broad that she could see his dimples. Everyone else in the pews vanished, she focused only on him. Tremors passed through her body. Her heart leapt as she walked down the red carpet holding onto her father's arm. At that moment, she realized that all the planning wasn't important. This day, this perfect day, was the day they would commit themselves to each other before God. She left her father's arm and linked arms with Walt.

The minister recited First Corinthian's 13:1 – *Love is patient and kind…* Heidi knew that the entire basis of her relationship with Walt was stable because of those two words; patience and kindness. They both spoke their vows with quiet voices that only they could hear and placed a simple gold ring on each other's fingers. The minister pronounced them husband and wife. Heidi turned her chin up to Walt, and he tenderly kissed her trembling lips.

She was now Mrs. Bailey and felt like a dancing star as she walked back down the aisle with Walt—her Mr. Bailey. The photographer captured them with his 35mm camera as they moved toward the exit doors. Heidi was sure they could do anything together.

In the receiving line, just outside the church, Cousin Edward walked up to her and leaned in toward her ear. "I watched your mother and waited for her to stand up when the minister asked if anyone had any objections."

Heidi felt elated and wasn't in the mood for tragedy. "And what happened?"

"Well, she had a tissue in her hand, and her face was all squished." Her cousin grinned.

"I guess she didn't dare." Heidi tickled Edward's side, and whispered, "Mom would've embarrassed herself if she'd publicly objected. After all, she has her glamorous image to protect."

"Yes, she does." Edward kissed her cheek and shook Walt's hand. "Good luck, you two. And, Heidi, thanks for wearing the pearl necklace my mom gave you."

"I like to keep her close to me." Smiling, Heidi squeezed Edward's arm before he could get away. "Hey, have you seen Claudia? She has the family toasting chalice."

"The what?"

"Oh, come on, how could you forget? The lucky German Nuremberg bridal cup? It was at your wedding, too. Your dad showed up last night at the rehearsal dinner and brought the cup. My mother looked incensed."

"Oh, right, the groom drinks out of the skirt, while the bride sips out of the cup. The thing didn't bring me any luck." Edward snickered. "If Claudia has it, don't worry—she'll get it to the reception."

Next, one of her favorite people appeared in the line. "Nanny Maddie! It's good to see you. I'm so happy you're here. I've been getting your birthday cards every year with your updates. I treasure them. How's your daughter? I haven't seen her since she was a baby. I think I was ten or maybe eight at the time. How old is she now?"

"Corinne is twenty and doing well. She just finished school and found a job near our house."

"That's good news. Where's your husband? Is William here?" Heidi's eyebrows went up, and she scanned the crowd.

"No, he couldn't leave work to come with me." Maddie embraced Heidi, then Walt. "Heidi, you're beaming." She bent between them and said, "Be happy. I know Mrs. Schwartz can be difficult, be strong together."

Heidi winked at Maddie and said in French, "I love you. I'll phone you soon."

"I'm afraid you can't. We're moving overseas, and phoning won't be possible for some time. I will write when I know more."

"Thanks again for coming to our wedding!" She kissed Maddie on the cheek. They had talked for too long, the other guests in line were fidgeting. "I'll look forward to your letters."

After the receiving line dwindled down, Walt and Heidi left the grounds in a chauffeured antique car on loan from a man Heidi had charmed at a party three months earlier. Out of the back window, Heidi could see a parade of cars following them down River Road to the Kenwood Country Club.

Everything seemed perfect at the reception with dancing, cutting of the cake, and general merriment. At the end of the evening, the photographer asked the crowd to gather outside. Heidi and Walt changed into their travel clothes and walked into the lobby. Without warning, her mother grabbed her and hugged her with a vice-like grip. Hugs of any kind were rare, and this one was unbearable. She looked over her mother at Walt who stood rigidly behind them with a grimace smeared across his face.

"Mom, please, I can't breathe." She peeled her mother off and gently, but deliberately, pushed her away. "Give me a break."

"No, no, I can't." Wailing, her mother cried, "Don't leave me! Walt's family isn't like us. They have no boundaries, and they'll be a bad influence on you."

The contempt Heidi felt at that instant toward her mother almost overcame her sense of reason. What she said to herself pulled at her soul; *no, Walt's mom isn't like you. She accepts my decisions. I can't believe you're saying these things when he's standing right here. I'm happy today, and you're not going to ruin things.* And then, out loud she said, "I'm still my own person no matter what. You've done your part, Mother. It's time for me to be in charge of my own life. How you react to my choices is entirely up to you. I have to go."

Taking Walt's hand, she noticed her father standing near a table filled with roses and walked away from her mother. Glancing back, while Walt led her forward, she saw her dramatically glaring at them before disappearing down a hallway. Heidi was thankful that the only other person in the lobby was the front desk clerk and he was undoubtedly embarrassed by her mother's outburst. He dropped the papers in his hand and disappeared behind the counter before reappearing to answer the ringing telephone.

"Dad, thank you for my beautiful wedding." Heidi kissed him on the cheek.

"I'm sorry about your mother. She's feeling her age and taking it out on Walt's family. They must be twenty years younger. I think she might even be a little jealous of their youth. I hope you two get past this."

Heidi took her father's hand. "Dad, I love you so much. I don't know what I would've done without our relationship. I'll phone you when we get home from our honeymoon."

He put one of his hands on each of her shoulders and kissed her forehead. "I love you. Have a full and happy life with Walt. I put a box of your childhood photos in the trunk of his car. I will always treasure our times together. Your devotion to us is admirable, but don't worry about your mother. Go… live your life." Much to her surprise, he shook Walt's hand heartily. It was quite apparent he approved of the match even though he'd never said a word to that effect before, but then he did pay for the wedding which she knew was his way of giving his consent. She clasped her hand in Walt's, and they walked out of the lobby's front door.

The fanfare outside felt unreal with the guests cheering and throwing birdseed in every direction. Rice would have been easier to pick out of her hair, but the club wanted something more natural on the sidewalks that the birds could pluck away. Heidi and Walt waved. She stood by the passenger door for a moment. He opened it, and she slid onto the seat. Watching him rush around the front of the car to sit beside her in the driver's seat made her smile. She was eager to get to the airport.

As they drove away, she felt a twinge of sadness for her father. He was much older now, but still so full of love and kindness. Despite her annoyance with her mother, she worried about her parents' future and how things would turn out for them.

The car stopped at a red light, and Heidi felt Walt's eyes on her. She hadn't said a word for quite some time.

"Hey," he said, reaching over to take her hand. "You okay?"

"Yeah, just… worried."

He gave her hand a little squeeze of reassurance. "Your parents will be fine. Today is our day, and the first day of the rest of our married life together."

"I know, I'm excited and terrified." She smiled coyly. Walt filled her heart with optimism. He always knew how to brighten her mood. "Walt?"

"Yeah?"

"What is that pungent smell? Pull over after the light changes."

Once the light turned green, they pulled into a bank parking lot and got out of the car. Heidi pulled out a Kleenex from her dress pocket and covered her nose as Walt lifted the front hood. Laughter burst from somewhere deep inside him. "It looks like there's Limburger cheese on the manifold! Damn!"

"Well, which one of your groomsmen did that?"

"Who knows." He smirked.

"Well… I think we know it was your best man," she teased.

"Pete! He never was a good sport about me winning you over when we first met on the canal. We better check the rest of the car."

Walt walked around to the trunk, pulled it open, and Heidi peered inside.

A dozen blown up condoms surrounded the photo box.

She laughed so hard that her stomach hurt. "Oh God! I hope Dad didn't see these."

"Your face is all red." Walt chuckled. "Not likely, he put the photo box in there this morning. My other prankster groomsmen probably added the condoms during the reception."

By the time they got to the National Airport, Heidi felt light and giddy.

Their honeymoon in the Cayman Islands was filled with scuba diving and exotic all-you-can-eat foods. Scuba diving felt like perfect silence beneath the surface, with just the gentle whoosh of their breath going in and out through the regulators. Heidi brought a mesh bag of hot dogs down with her and fed broken pieces to an eel who promptly looked like an overstuffed, lumpy pillow. A muffled giggle came through her mouthpiece. She recalled how much she hated eating hot dogs as a child contrasting with how much the eel adored them. Walt floated nearby. He pulled up a rock and then finned over, grasped her hand, and brought a small octopus from his other hand over to hers. It entwined their wrists and hands and, with a tiny bit of prodding from Walt, the creature emitted a cloud of purple ink before it jettisoned away.

After hours of travel Heidi and Walt returned from the Caymans and drove home. Heidi took his hand as they walked up the sidewalk to their townhouse, but something didn't feel right. It was almost as though the street was too quiet. Without warning, Walt scooped her into his arms, and she giggled from the romantic gesture that made her feel like a bride. Draping one arm around his neck as he carried her to the front door, she pulled out her key from the front pocket of her jeans. Leaning forward a tad, she touched the key to the lock, but the door swung open. Heidi gazed over at Walt with a questioning look. Abruptly, Walt released her onto her feet, then snaked her around his back as he pushed the door further open. Heidi stepped into the foyer with him, and they both hesitated. The drawer of the side table was upside down on the floor next to an exposed heating vent out of place. The carpet edges were pulled back. The plate over the electric socket had been removed and leaned up against the wall. Walt disappeared in the bowels of the house leaving her behind to stare at the minutes ticking by on her watch while she mulled over the situation.

"Oh, finally, there you are, it's been ten minutes. I was beginning to worry you'd been chloroformed and dragged off."

"This isn't a movie, I don't think that happens often in the real world."

"Yeah, sure. What did you find?"

"Most everything looks fine. Nothing's missing that I can see, but there are a few things out of place in my office."

"How can you tell? Your papers are always scattered on the desk."

"You know me, I can find everything in there and can tell if things have been moved."

"Yes, yes, I understand." Heidi tried to keep her mood light, but it wasn't working.

Walt put his hand over his lips and mumbled while reexamining the debris by the wall. "I would say someone was searching for something specific. The phone is unplugged not only in the office but also in the kitchen, and the tape was removed from the answering machine."

"We don't have anything to hide," Heidi stammered in an equally hushed voice. "Maybe it's some kind of prank. All I want to do is go to bed, and now we have to deal with this stuff."

"I don't think our friends would do this. Can't stay, this feels wrong." Taking her hand, he guided her to the car. He opened the passenger door, and she stepped inside.

"The neighbors didn't call the police. If they had, they would have left us a note or something. Whoever did this must have looked like they were supposed to be here."

"Let's just drive to the station and file a report." Walt pushed the gas pedal hard, and the car squealed around the corner.

"I need to call my Dad on the way to tell him we're home. Please stop at the pay phone on Jefferson."

Heidi got out of the car, put a quarter in the slot, and dialed her parents' phone number. Her father answered. Her mother's voice came through seconds after he said hello. She must've picked up the other line. Heidi decided not to tell them about their trip or the break-in and began a brief conversation about the weather. Her mother interrupted and launched into complaints about the wedding guests.

"Walt's family fumbled about in their tuxedos and gowns. Everyone stared at them and hardly spoke to me. The country club complained about the noise; his family is just too loud. They kept laughing and dancing with happiness. I didn't feel happy at all."

"Mom, I'm sorry you're so miserable." Heidi recalled her mother's loud outburst in the lobby. The guests were happy and not unusually boisterous.

"I emphatically told you not to marry him... I told you. Why didn't you find a State Department man? Why? Why? Stay away from his family! Heidi, promise me." Her mother's pleading sounded like an unhappy child trapped in a cage.

"Mother, please." Heidi's neck tensed into a huge knot. This conversation on top of the break-in was almost too much to deal with.

"Let's try and be civil to each other," her father groaned.

Heidi tried not to react to her mother's tirade and said, "We've been over Walt's family dynamics before! He's my husband now. The wedding was beautiful. Please stop fussing. I just wanted to tell you our phone is out-of-service. I will call you after it's repaired. I'll talk to you another time." She gently pushed the lever down on the payphone and disconnected the call.

Walt drove to the station. The police said the circumstances were unusual and sent a team to investigate. To keep out of the way, Heidi and Walt went to rest for a few hours in a nearby park. They grabbed two small blankets out of the trunk and sat cuddled up on a park bench. Walt dropped off to sleep. Heidi kept watch.

A homeless man rolled by with a shopping cart covered in brown canvas concealing a high mound of undisclosed items. He settled down across the path on a bench next to a tree. His hair was long, and his skin was brown from the sun. Heidi tried not to stare at him, but it was impossible. Somehow, he seemed familiar. She wondered what his story was, and she couldn't imagine how to start a conversation with the man without being intrusive.

Heidi turned away and leaned against Walt wishing their last hours hadn't been so trying. Thinking about the break-in made her nervous, but Walt's eyes were closed, and he appeared to be napping. Her husband could fall asleep anywhere. On the other hand, Heidi was always acutely aware of her surroundings, especially in public places. She'd never quite gotten over her college encounter with the strangers giving her packages for David. She squinted at a phone booth down the path to her right when a loud cough startled her from the other direction. It came from the homeless man. And, then, she realized who he was.

"Walt, Walt. Wake up." She nudged his shoulder.

"What is it? I'm tired."

"Yes, yes, I know. Let's get out of here."

"What's the rush?" he said sleepily.

She put her head on his shoulder. "That guy over there is drooling. He's eating something out of a brown bag and looking this way. He's holding a manila envelope, too."

Walt glanced across the path at the other bench. "What? He looks like a standard homeless man, but there aren't many in this area—he must be new around here."

"We should go." Heidi's heart started to pound.

"Relax. Don't get all paranoid."

"Easy for you to say!" She clutched at his arm. "What's that brown envelope in his hand? I wish he'd stop staring at me." She tried to divert her eyes and failed. "I—I've seen him before." She slumped closer to Walt. "Oh, God, this is too much. He's the guy from my university theater department, but something is different about him!"

"What are you talking about?"

Heidi's voice came out low and so quiet she could barely hear herself talk. "At the end of my senior year at the university, I walked into my costume shop to finish a project. The guy, the guy over there on the bench, was in the shop. He asked me if I'd ever had sex with a stranger. Of course, I left and got a security guard, but he was gone when we got back. I didn't notice right away, but there was an envelope on the table with David McGwire written across the top. I didn't overthink it at first, but then I got a second envelope later in the day from another guy who jumped in my car and nearly scared me to death. I went to the McGwires' and confronted David."

"I'm sorry, that sounds awful. What did David say?"

"Never mind." She gasped. "Walt... the guy's falling off the bench..., I don't know, and twitching. Is he having a seizure? We need to phone the police or an ambulance."

"Crap! Get up, slowly," urged Walt. "I sense there's something very wrong going on. We need to walk away without bringing suspicion to ourselves and get to a phone."

Heidi stood up first and playfully pulled Walt off the bench in an effort to act nonchalant. Together they started to stroll in the opposite direction of the scene of the alleged crime toward the payphone on the corner. Heidi stepped into the phone booth behind Walt and closed the door. He snatched up the receiver and dialed 9-1-1. Out of the corner of her eye, she glanced at the park bench. "Walt, Walt!"

"What now? I'm waiting for emergency services to pick up."

"Don't turn around. There are two guys in black jumpsuits carrying the man away. An envelope dropped out of his hand."

"What?" Walt started to turn around despite her warning, but he kept the phone to his ear.

"Don't turn around! One of the guys just snatched up the envelope," she hissed, grabbing Walt's arm. "Oh, God, they threw the man in the back of a van!"

Walt placed the phone receiver in its cradle. "Play along with me." In one swift motion, he embraced her in a passionate kiss before pulling back. "Okay, I think they're gone. I memorized the license plate. Things are getting stranger by the hour. We need to think this through and talk to David in person since you're sure that guy in the van is one of his connections."

"I'll call him now and arrange a meeting." Heidi grabbed the receiver, scooped out the quarter that had been returned from the failed call, put it back in the slot and dialed the McGwire's house. It rang three times before Sadie picked up. After explaining she and Walt needed to speak with David, Sadie told her he was on his way home from Europe.

"He's not available for a couple days. We'll have to wait."

"Okay, that was worth a try," Walt rubbed his scalp.

"I think I need a glass of wine or something stronger. This situation has gotten out of hand. I wonder why the guy keeled over, maybe he was poisoned by whatever he was eating. I wonder if the person who broke into the house was involved. I don't think I would even consider this if he hadn't looked at me with that damn brown envelope on his lap."

"It's been years since you were involved with the other package. How can this be related?"

"I don't know—I just think it might be. I can't deal with this until David returns, so I'll focus on the house. All I know right now is that after the police are done at home, I want to stay in a hotel tonight. The idea of going back in the dark scares me."

"Sounds reasonable to me."

"I want this entire business over with! I can't believe we've come home from our honeymoon to all this nastiness." Heidi felt flustered. "So, I'm struggling, should I wash everything at home when the police are done?"

"Noooo," Walt exclaimed. "You can't turn into your mother!"

"I guess that does sound like something she'd do. I'll just wash the kitchen counters and my lingerie, that's not too drastic a response. Maybe we need a dog for security?"

"A dog would be nice. Everything will be fine."

"You sound like Dad, that's his favorite line."

"Everything will be fine." Walt smiled ever so slightly. "I don't understand why someone broke into our house; we don't have anything worth stealing other than our wedding presents.

"Oh, right." Heidi wondered for an instant how she'd write thank you notes for unopened gifts and laughed at herself. "Claudia said she'd move them out of the club to her apartment while we were on our honeymoon."

"We don't know for sure what the thief took other than the phone cassette. Maybe our credit card numbers from the filing cabinet? To be on the safe side, we need to get new ones issued."

Heidi exhaled. "We're quite a pair, handling this so rationally without shouting. Never happened with my parents. I hope we always handle troubles this way."

"So far we're doing great. Let's go to a hotel and deal with the house tomorrow."

Chapter 23

They had only been home for forty-eight hours when Heidi received a frantic call from Claudia. "He's dead, he's dead!" she sobbed convulsively through the receiver. "My dad... was shot! I don't know what to do."

"Where are you? Your place?"

"No, I'm at my parents' house." Claudia's voice trembled. "I can't talk about this on the phone."

"I'll be there in half an hour." She hung up, grabbed her purse, and ran out the front door to the car. The engine started up right away. She rushed over to Harrison Street and parallel parked in front of the McGwire's house. Men in suits checked her identification. Inside, she found her mother sitting next to Sadie on a straight-back chair. There were also two men she didn't recognize standing in a corner with her father. One man in a black suit, and the other in an Army camouflage uniform.

"I'm so sorry." She leaned in and hugged Sadie.

"Heidi, bless you for coming."

"I was at home tidying the house when Claudia called, I came right over. Hello, Mom." Heidi felt almost catatonic. "What happened?"

"Hello, Heidi." Her mother stared at her with a grim expression, with her neck arched in a way that accentuated the wrinkles that creased along her throat. Her blue eyes pierced into Heidi's as though they were daggers, and—with a smirk—she added dryly, "Where is Walt? Too busy to support us?"

"Oh, Mother, please! This isn't the time to be nasty. He's on an errand. I left a note on the hall table. I'm sure he'll be over soon."

Sadie stopped nursing her wine and spoke in-between her tears. "I can't believe David's gone... Claudia is upstairs. Go! She'll tell you everything."

Bounding up the stairs, two at a time, was not fast enough. "Claudia?" she called down the hall.

"Here, I'm here in my room."

Heidi passed by two bedrooms, with unmade beds, on the way to Claudia's room. Her best friend was in bed with her back up against the wall, and her knees tucked up to her chin. She appeared to be encased in her blue blanket as she clutched at the corners. Claudia's words came out through choked sobs. "I've always hated Dad's work."

"What happened? Who are those men downstairs?"

"They are work associates of Dad's, but I'd never met them until today." Claudia choked on her sobs. "The man in camouflage was at the range with Dad, and the other guy came from the office."

"Hold on, I'm having trouble understanding. Let me get you some water or, better yet, a glass of wine. Stay here." Heidi raised her hand like a stop sign. "I'll be right back."

Heidi went down to the first floor. Pulling the curtain by the door away, she saw more men in suits outside by the curb. Sighing, she trudged through the kitchen to the cellar for a bottle of wine and started to scan the racks. In the dark space, something was rattling around next to a stone wall.

"What the hell! Who's there?" challenged Heidi.

Her father stepped out of a niche in the shadows.

"Jesus, Dad, you scared me. What are you doing?"

"You caught me." Her father's hair was covered with old webs.

She put her hands on her hips. "Wipe the spider webs off your head, Mom will go crazy."

"That's not important." Her father brushed the webs off his head and then wiped his hands on his navy-blue trousers.

"What's going on?"

"Sorry, I didn't mean to alarm you." He slipped a narrow-elongated canister into his pocket.

"There can't be anything more alarming than David's death. What is that thing you stuffed into your pocket?"

"Here's some wine. I presume that's why you're down here." Her father grabbed the nearest bottle off the wrought iron rack and started speaking in French. "I shouldn't say. I don't want to put you in danger."

Naturally, she responded in French while wondering why he chose not to speak English. "This isn't even your house!" She squinted in the dim room and flicked on a second light. The room glowed yellow. "Why are we speaking in French?"

"No one else in the house can. I need to keep this conversation private. David and I had an arrangement."

"What sort?"

"If anything ever happened to him—I was supposed to complete his assignment."

"I don't understand." Heidi's eyes seared into his.

"Promise me you won't tell a soul what I'm doing down here! Not Claudia, not Walt, not anyone. Do you understand?"

Heidi felt faint. "Yes, I promise."

"David was an important man in the government, and his actions will change history over the next few years." Her father patted his pocket. "I have to deliver this before anything else happens."

"But you haven't told me what this is *really* about." Her eyes darted back and forth across the room trying to focus on his words.

"The Soviets and communism. I've said too much already. Please, forget you saw me down here."

"This is all about politics," she gasped. "Never mind, your right, I don't want to know anymore. Please, be careful. I have to go, Claudia needs me."

Heidi hurried back upstairs to the kitchen and stood holding onto the counter gasping. Taking in a deep breath, holding it for ten seconds, and then slowly releasing it regulated her breathing. She grabbed two glasses from an upper cabinet and a corkscrew from the countertop. Fumbling with the bottle, it almost fell to pieces on the counter. Pouring the wine into the first glass didn't play out well either. She'd filled it to the top instead of halfway. Giving up she drank the red liquid in four swallows and barely noticed the tannic aftertaste. Placing both glasses in one hand and the bottle in the other, she headed back up to Claudia's room.

"I'm back." Heidi put the glasses on the dresser and poured the wine. "Here, drink this. It'll calm your nerves."

"Thank you." Claudia gulped it down and puckered her lips. Her tears stopped with the distraction. "This tastes like Mom's wine, too dry. Yuck! Whatever, I'll drink it anyway."

Heidi stared at the glass and poured more. "Sorry, I was a little freaked out in the dark cellar. I grabbed the first bottle I got my hands on and didn't read the label. Now, tell me, what happened to your dad?"

Claudia sipped more wine before she began to explain. "Last night, Dad and I were talking on the phone. He told me he was going to the range in the morning and wanted to meet me here for lunch. No big surprise, he went out there all the time."

"He's an excellent marksman."

"It wasn't an accident; he was executed. Murdered! Gunned down!" Claudia grabbed a handful of tissue out of the box on the nightstand and fiercely blew her nose.

"Take a breath. Tell me what happened."

"Mr. Camo saw Dad arguing with someone. He couldn't hear what they were saying, but he heard the guy's accent and became suspicious." Claudia wiped her eyes.

"Accent?"

"Heidi, he was Russian."

"Damned Cold War! Will it ever end?" Heidi didn't expect a response.

"Mr. Camo heard a high-powered rifle. There was a lot of added confusion because those types of guns aren't allowed on the range. They saw my father on the ground. At first, no one knew who fired the shots, but they heard gravel flying around when a car sped away and figured it out."

"Sounds like chaos. Guessing the shooter wasn't a club member." Heidi rubbed her friend's back. "This doesn't make sense. Your dad was in the military. How could he miss all the clues?"

"Tell me about it." Claudia brought the wine glass up to her lips and emptied it. "Dad was shot in the head!"

"God, this is all so unbelievable!" Heidi shivered. "He's gone."

"This can't be real. It just can't! I was always afraid for him, but I didn't think he'd ever be killed. He was so close to retirement! You are so lucky your dad's been out of the State Department for ages."

"Yes, right, State Department," Heidi said caustically. She pulled herself together. "But today isn't about my dad. Some men are standing watch outside. We need to go downstairs and see if we can find out anything else…"

"Right. Give me a second to touch up my face." Claudia ducked into the bathroom across the hall.

Heidi stood nearby, completely still, with unblinking eyes. Calling through the door, she said, "Claudia, I wish I knew the right things to say. This is a nightmare."

Claudia came out, and Heidi followed her down the hall. On the first floor, they stood side by side near the front door waiting for one of their mothers to say something. Heidi could see her father through the window, by the curb, talking to the men she'd seen earlier. Walt was there! Heidi watched them as they turned around, walked up the slate sidewalk, and entered the house. Heidi jumped to Walt's side the instant he came through the door.

"The guys out front are serious about keeping this place locked down," Walt reported. "I had to show my identification and get a pat-down before they'd let me come in. You holding up okay?"

"Well enough, considering everything that's going on." Heidi squeezed his arm.

Her father hugged Claudia. "Today has been a tremendous shock. Your father loved you so much."

"Thanks, Uncle Nathan." Claudia appeared to relax a little.

He walked over to Sadie. "I'm concerned about your safety over the next few weeks. A task force will investigate David's death, and I'll make sure they do a thorough job."

"You are a godsend," Sadie bravely replied.

"I don't know about that. David will be put to rest with honors for his government service. I know he would want me to take care of the details for you."

"Thank you, but please, only a flag—no gun salute. I wouldn't be able to stand the sound," Sadie stoically replied. "I'm so relieved you and Gwen have been here with me these last hours, but please go home. I need to—I don't know what—the guards will watch over us."

Heidi couldn't stop thinking about David's last moments of life, and she couldn't understand why he had to die. Her dad knew, she was sure of it, but he wouldn't say anything beyond his incomplete explanation in the cellar. Heidi's work at the office became more difficult because she couldn't concentrate on editing the documents for the company's latest fundraiser. Her boss depended on a timely turn-around, and Heidi was determined not to let her personal life interfere. Tapping her pencil on the desk didn't help. Brooding, she wrote an adjustment on a rough-draft, but she still wasn't able to focus. The only solution was to step outside for a brief walk. Two blocks away she stopped at a payphone and called Claudia.

"Hey, Claudia, I'm at work. How are you holding up?"

"I keep running everything through my mind," Claudia said. "When I'm not, I'm looking over my shoulder, thinking something else horrible is going to happen."

"I know what you mean. How's your mom?"

"She's in pieces. Staying at the house with her is making me feel worse, and I don't think it's helping her either. We're wallowing. I go to work to distract myself. When I get back, Mom looks like she's been crying all day. Last night she finally took a shower and said she couldn't cry anymore. She said it was time to put on a different face, and that Dad would want us to remember him but not let this ruin us. Mom and I have been telephoning people all week giving them the news and asking only specific ones to the graveside and Cosmos Club after the main service. I've never been to that club, they have a dress code."

"My mom told me, I'll wear a suit. Let me know if I can help you with anything."

"Thanks. The phone calls you made already helped. I'll see you at the house tomorrow. We're being chauffeured and escorted by a security detail to the ceremony."

"I'll see you then." Heidi turned on her heel, and it momentarily wedged into a gap in the sidewalk.

It was time to pick up the pace, finish the boss's documents, and get out of the office on time. She phoned Walt before leaving, and only said, "Tomorrow's service is going to be rough."

Heidi asked Walt to drive them over to the McGwires. She buckled her seatbelt both literally and figuratively. He parked behind Harrison Street, in the alleyway. Heidi thought about the last time she parked in the same spot and gone in the house to confront David about the envelopes she'd received at Catholic University. That day seemed easy compared to what their lives had become.

She took Walt's hand, and they started to walk along the side of the house where they were promptly stopped by a security officer. He checked their IDs and let them pass, noting he and his partners would be watching out for the family during the services. He continued to explain that Mrs. and Miss McGwire were waiting in the car out front, and they should join them. A separate vehicle would follow behind, with Mr. and Mrs. Schwartz.

Heidi and Walt walked the rest of the way to the car with the guard. She exchanged glances with Walt before he got into the passenger seat next to the chauffeur. She slipped into the back next to Claudia. Sadie was on the far side of the seat, gripping her daughter's hand.

The silent trip to the cathedral took an agonizing twenty minutes. Heidi wasn't sure she, the McGwires, or her parents would be able to hold their tears at bay for the ceremony. The cars pulled up along the side of the building. Heidi got out first before helping Claudia and Sadie.

Walt joined them, along with her parents. Silently, they all walked together into the chapel and positioned themselves in the front pews. David's American flag was draped across his casket in front of the altar. She listened to the minister, the fragmented eulogies didn't comfort her heart or ease the worries that crept in. The speakers talked only of David's exemplary character and didn't mention any significant aspects of his career. After the scant things her father had said in the cellar, Heidi was sure the speakers weren't allowed to say more.

Neither Heidi nor Claudia said a word for the next hour, other than nodding to accept condolences from the myriads of mourners who exited at the back of the chapel after the service. People said things like, "He was a good man," or "He was so young," or "So tragic, we'll always remember him fondly," or "Let us know if we can help." Heidi was relieved only a few of these unknown people would be at Rock Creek cemetery where David's remains would be lowered into the ground.

Back at the curb outside the cathedral, Heidi smiled weakly at her parents, knowing full well her mother would sit in the car at the cemetery while everyone else stood by the graveside. Heidi knew her mother couldn't act her way through the role she should play since her fears far outweighed her obligations.

Heidi and Walt got back into the chauffeured car with the McGwires and accompanied them to the cemetery. The cars pulled through the gates on Webster Street in Northwest, D.C. and wove around the roads within the property; one grave after the other passed by Heidi's line of sight and her sorrow almost overtook her. Outside of the car, she interlocked her arm with Claudia's. Her friend shivered with what Heidi imagined was a mix of sorrow and anxiety. She hoped Sadie, who had Claudia's other arm, hadn't noticed.

They approached the graveside together and stood waiting for the pallbearers to bring David's casket. The minister said a few choice words from a prayer book. Two men in dress Air Force uniforms, complete with white gloves, folded David's flag into a ceremonial triangle. They walked over to Sadie, placed it in her open palms and saluted.

The reception for close friends and family followed at the Cosmos Club. Heidi remembered Claudia mentioning the club at her father's retirement party and how only people with exceptional qualifications could be members. She sat by Claudia during the meal and absentmindedly glanced at the columned archways, the chandeliers, and the décor inspired by classic French styles. The two-stacked plates that sat on the table surrounded by multiple forks and spoons for the various courses they'd be served seemed so meaningless. The situation with the McGwires was far more important than the old-world ambiance. The evening at the club ended in a blur with the drive back to the McGwires' house.

When they drove down Harrison Street, Heidi felt uneasy. Her mother said she had a migraine and wanted to go home. Her father insisted that he and the other men go inside the McGwires' to make sure the house was secure. They came back out and reported that, much to Heidi's chagrin, that the house was not okay. Heidi went inside with Claudia and Sadie to find everything in shambles with books and the contents of drawers strewn about. Sadie broke down in tears and collapsed into David's chair.

"I will find out what I can." Heidi's father put his hand on the chair. "The girls can help sort out the mess. If anything is missing let me know."

"Dad, I didn't tell you, but when Walt and I got back from our honeymoon our house had been broken into as well. Could it be related?"

"Yes, it could, that's not good. Anyone connected to David is at risk. I'll take your mother home and set the alarm system. When I get back, give me the details."

Heidi and Claudia met at Clyde's in Georgetown and sat at the bar closest to the entrance's glass-paned windows. Everything in their lives had changed over the last eight weeks.

Heidi swirled her rum and Coke around in the glass. "Claudia, I'm so nervous about your safety."

"Yes, I know what you mean, but I'm trying to relax. Mom and I are struggling. She understood the life she signed onto when they got married, but what choice did I have? None, none at all."

"Born into danger, but your dad kept you safe." Heidi repositioned herself on the bar stool. "Is your mom planning to leave town?"

"Yes, and she wants me to go with her to Cape Cod." Claudia pushed her hair behind her ears.

"Walt and I have decided to move to California; work said they wanted him back."

"Wanted him back?"

"Yes, he worked there a bit after we started dating," Heidi replied.

"Oh, that's right. Everything is changing too quickly." Claudia snacked on the peanuts in the bowl at the bar.

"Don't eat those, gross! They look stale—I'm sorry. We've been through so much. It's good we're both moving. Dad says it's better that we all go away. He's not leaving because Mom won't budge."

"I understand." Claudia sounded bitter. "What the—look outside the window. Your dad is passing by with a man in tattered clothes and long hair."

"What? Let's follow him, this isn't right! I bet Dad just came down the road from Martin's Tavern. He likes that place, but the guy he's with wouldn't be welcome there; too raggedy." Heidi threw some money on the bar.

They slipped out of Clyde's and followed the men from a safe distance through the humid air, toward the canal.

"What's your dad wearing? Old ratty jean? I've never seen him dressed like that away from home," Claudia said in a hushed voice.

"I know, right. He never wears jeans out of his garden. His shirt sleeves are turned up unevenly too. So not, Dad."

The men hopped onto a mule-drawn ferry. Heidi held onto Claudia's arm and sputtered, "Keep moving and ignore them so Dad can't spot us." The unnamed man looked like the guy at the costume warehouse who'd taken her money. This time, his face was clean-shaven.

Heidi guided them onto the bridge that overlooked the canal. They crouched down and peered through the railing.

Claudia exclaimed, "What is going on? This doesn't make any sense!"

"I bet he's pursuing leads into your dad's death."

"This guy is from some other world," Claudia said. "I thought your dad only dealt with people in suits."

"Apparently, not this time."

"We better stop watching him." Claudia's nails dug into Heidi's arm. "Wait! The dude scanned a small piece of paper and ate it!"

"I guess both our dads' work was hush, hush. I won't ask, I'm not ready to hear the answer." Heidi pulled Claudia down the road.

"Maybe there was more to their desk jobs at the State Department than we thought. CIA work, too?"

"I'm trying not to think about it. Crap! I think he saw me. I'm done for. We shouldn't be stalking him, let's get out of here."

They fled the area.

"What's he going to do to you? I'll tell you, not a damn thing!" Claudia said, changing the subject, "So, when are you and Walt moving?

"In three weeks. What about you two?"

"Next Saturday. All the arrangements have been made. Your dad helped."

"Figures," Heidi moaned. "We'll never learn who our fathers really are, and maybe that's best. I've had enough intrigue for a while. I need to go home and start packing our house. Walt's renting a moving van, and we're driving cross-country pulling one car behind us."

"Heidi, I'll miss you. We've lived in the same town forever."

"Other than our time apart, when I went to Bradford, we haven't lived in different cities since we were babies in France."

"I forgot about Paris. We should go back there together someday, but I can't imagine when."

"Find some happiness in Cape Cod." Heidi hugged her fiercely. "Best friends forever. We'll talk on the phone soon."

"Yes, best friends forever. I'll write when I can, but I think we won't see each other for a long time." Claudia's chin dropped down, and she walked off.

Chapter 24

Eighteen months later, 1988…

It happened… Heidi and Walt were expecting a baby. Heidi flew from California to Maryland to tell her parents in person. Her mother had been unpleasant to deal with over the years, but Heidi kept hoping things would change. They were elated when she arrived at the house.

"Mom, Dad, I want to tell you something important."

Her father piped in, "Good news?"

"Yes, I think so, I'm pregnant."

He smiled with obvious contentment.

Her mother's jaw muscles visibly twitched. "It's bad enough that you live so far away and now this! I thought you were coming home to tell us you were getting a divorce!"

"Mother, you can be such a bitch!" Heidi's mood shifted to despair.

Her mother collapsed into one of her new tufted, brocade dining room chairs in hysterics. "How can you talk to me that way! A baby. Do what I did with my first husband, get a medical D&C and a divorce. Get both of them out of your life!"

Heidi glared at her mother and wondered how she could survive the ordeal. "What did you say? D&C?"

"Never mind. I don't want to talk about it. This isn't about me."

"Oh, but it is. You've chosen to make it about you. For God's sake, Mother, why do you always have to be the center of attention? You've turned into an unhappy, cold person. I hardly remember what you were like before… when you weren't so angry. This is an all-time low for you, get rid of the baby and my husband! I don't know you anymore!"

Heidi walked straight out of the room with the intention of leaving the house. It was late, and she didn't know where to go. Claudia could help, but Heidi was too stunned to even think of calling her friend with another crisis. For an instant, she'd forgotten Claudia was still living on Cape Cod. Heidi went to her room seething and closed the door. She thought about calling a taxi and going to a hotel or her mother-in-law's, but she was sure that would make the situation worse over the long haul. Two unbearable days passed before she was able to board the plane back to Walt.

It had been five months since Heidi walked out of her parents' house. Work at the public relations firm in California kept her mind off the terrible blow up on Brookside Drive. She wasn't sure she'd ever get over her mother's spiteful behavior. Yet, oddly, Heidi still felt the tug of parental commitments. While she sat at the breakfast table with Walt, she placed her hand on her round belly and said, "I want to stay home with our baby."

"We can't manage financially. Everything is super expensive on the West Coast."

"I know you're right. When the baby's here, we'll have to consider daycare costs and how that'll eat up most of my income.

ELSA WOLF

Then there's my age and the complications that might bring. You know, doctors don't like women having babies so late. Then in the future, I'll want to go back to working in an office, and that'll be tough after being away for years. I'm not sure anyone will hire me." Heidi liked her public relations work, but she was torn on how to juggle her upcoming responsibilities.

"Yes, that makes sense. I can request a transfer back to D.C. We can sell this house for double what we paid and have more than enough to buy a small place in the suburbs."

"I like the idea of raising our own children. Daycare sounds so impersonal." She rubbed her temples. "What about our families? My mother is unbelievably nasty."

"Being here or there doesn't seem to change your mother-daughter relationship. She still phones here every day pouting, and you talk to her."

"You're right."

"It seems like she's trying to push you away and leech onto you all at the same time. She needs to find another project to focus on instead of you." Walt filled two mugs with coffee. "Are you sure you want to go back to their world?"

"I don't know, I guess. I love them, warts and all. They're in their late seventies, I can't stay away for the rest of their lives, I just can't. We'll have to manage somehow. If we don't, I think the guilt will kill me. I want our kids to be able to spend time around their grandparents. It's odd I never met Dad's family."

Walt took both her hands in his. "All right, but please don't get too entrenched with them."

"I'll try not to. Dad sounds like he's managing, but I think he's discouraged. Mom is struggling with everything, and he has trouble leaving the house for simple errands without her worrying. He's not incompetent, but she treats him like a child. I think she's afraid his life will end like David's and she'll be completely alone. She doesn't go out much."

"I feel sorry for him." Walt got up from the table and went back into their corridor kitchen to get another bowl of cereal. Their place was less than a thousand square feet, but it was enough for the two of them. They could hear each other talking no matter how far apart they stood.

"Sad—last week Mom called and said Dad went out to Woodward & Lothrop's to buy some new shirts, and he didn't return for hours. There was nothing majorly wrong, but Mom went ballistic."

"Details?"

"Mom panicked. I told her she was overreacting and to calm down, but that went over like a ton of bricks. She hung up on me. Less than an hour later the phone rang again, and she told me she'd contacted the store's security. It turned out Dad was in the parking lot with a mechanic working on the dead battery. He called me the next morning and told me that from now on he would sneak out of the house while Mom was sleeping. He sounded annoyed."

"What's going to happen if we move back?" Walt poured himself another coffee.

"I don't know. I hope she'll relax and Dad can catch a break. She turned into a complete nitwit after David died and we left town. Eileen's gone, and Sadie seems to be permanently on Cape Cod. I guess my parents' other friends aren't filling those voids. Speaking of friends, I'm going to miss the ones we've made here."

"I don't think you can turn back the clock for your parents." Walt rubbed the top of his head. "The babies are going to keep us busy."

She groaned, inspecting her belly. "Babies? You think we're having twins?"

"Who knows, you have no idea if you have a twin gene in your heritage. We want more than one, right?"

"Yep, I've always wanted four."

"Oh, whoa, four? Maybe three." Walt chuckled. "Funny, we've never talked about these details."

"I always wanted kids since I know nothing about my birth family. Having some would make me feel more connected to my lost genetics. I'd feel more complete." Heidi finished the waffle on her plate.

"That makes sense, but I don't think I can ever completely understand how you feel. I can probably manage a transfer this fall. Let's move back East and hope for the best."

Chapter 25

Nine years later, 1997…

T he years had flown by, and before Heidi knew it, she and Walt had four children. First, there was Tessie, perfect in every way, straight down to her brown doe-eyes and adorable curls. When she was first born, Heidi believed that the key to a successful marriage included setting time aside to go out on dates with Walt without a child. This allowed them to spend just a couple of hours together outside of the house once a week. As the months passed, they decided to have another baby. Less than two years after Tessie's arrival, Claire was born. Heidi spent many a sleepless night tending to the baby's colic. Then and there she decided not to have any more children. But much to their surprise, when the girls were in elementary school, the twins, Kyle and Caleb, were born. Heidi often recalled how she and Walt laughed about having twins when they were expecting their first child, so the boys' arrival was obviously meant to be. They quickly hired and a second babysitter to help the first. Having two sitters was expensive, but Heidi wasn't about to give up their dates. She cherished their time away from the children, and it truly didn't matter where they went.

One of Heidi's favorite spots was the Gadsby's Tavern for dinner followed by the Crown Books in Alexandria. On this occasion, she and Walt meandered toward the bargain shelf. A title caught her attention, and she picked it up.

"Hey, Walt, check out this book. *The Other Mother* by Carol Schaefer." Heidi leaned it in his direction so he could see the title.

Walt was a bit distracted by his own find. "What's it about? Mine's a spy thriller."

"Your favorite type, good. My book's jacket says it's about a young woman in 1965 who had to give up her baby for adoption."

"You haven't talked about adoption in a long time. Do you want to read other people's stories?"

"Yes, I think I should. Having our own children has put a new spin on adoption."

"Well, if you're sure. I'll take the books up to the register and pay."

They went home, and the children were either settled or asleep in their rooms. Heidi sat on the couch and began reading her new book while Walt went up to bed. An hour in, she was so engrossed that she stayed awake all night reading the book from cover to cover. The story helped her understand what it was like to give up a child. The next morning, Heidi was exhausted and fell asleep on the couch only an hour before the children woke up wanting breakfast. Walt emerged from the bedroom and offered to make pancakes, which Heidi welcomed. Once they'd cleaned up the dishes, the children ran out into the backyard to play.

"Walt, I think I want to search for my birth mother."

"I figured you might. Anything I can do?"

"Thanks. If I find out the truth, just be there. I can't imagine why she gave me away. I don't think I could ever do such a thing."

"I know what you mean. It would be devastating to give away one of our children, but maybe it's for the best in some cases."

"Who really knows. My *current* mom is such a pain. It might be good to find my birth mother and fill in some of my missing history. I won't be able to share this with anyone."

"How about our kids?"

"No," Heidi said emphatically. "They're too young to understand a secret this big. I don't want them to tell my parents by mistake. When I was thirteen, my mom left a newspaper article on my desk about adoption after she told me. It said searching was a bad idea; that was Mom's way of making it perfectly clear rekindling my past was not acceptable. I'm pretty sure it was a weekly advice column from Ann Landers or someone similar. I kept the clipping, but it's hidden somewhere in my old drawers."

"What would your dad think? Surely he is sensible enough to understand."

"I think he is, but I don't want to put him into a difficult position. Let's keep things simple and to ourselves."

"As you wish," Walt acquiesced.

In the back of *The Other Mother*, she examined the appendix, which provided several suggestions. The International Soundex Registry seemed like an excellent place to start. Through them, Heidi found a retired researcher who had immigrated from Germany in her youth and was still a fluent German speaker. The kind woman asked if she had her adoption papers, but she didn't. The woman told her to ask the German government for a 'complete copy' of her birth certificate. Heidi was not to explain why she needed the document because some record-keepers might still be compelled to refuse if they didn't agree with her search. She wrote her certificate number in the letter and sent an unregistered copy saying she needed an original and signed it—Heidi Rose Schwartz.

"You okay?" Walt said.

"Mm-hmm, yes. I bet I started out with another name. *What's in a name? That which we call a rose by any other name…* Hah, Shakespeare said that I think! So many names. I'll stick with my married name—Heidi Schwartz Bailey. Except I kinda wish I'd left my middle name in the official documents. Oh well." She kissed Walt.

"I like your current name. You can add Rose back in at some point, it's a simple change. Not sure how you didn't get confused with your parents giving you nicknames, too." He smiled slyly. "Lucky you don't have some kind of identity disorder or split personality."

She punched him in the arm. "Be serious."

He fluttered a hand in the air. "Levity keep us sane."

"Whatever. You're such a weirdo."

After a month of waiting, Heidi gave up her frantic daily trips to the mailbox. The back and forth, from the front door to the end of the driveway, became mundane. One day, without a care, she grabbed the mail and threw the rubber banded bundle on the counter before her chores. When she returned, she rolled off the band and sorted through the mail. There it was; a brown rectangular envelope with a postmark from Germany. Would it be a rejection or new information? She flipped the envelope over a few times in disbelief. Stalling over a cup of tea, the grandfather clock ticked behind her for another thirty minutes before she grabbed a knife and slid it under the edges of the envelope flap. Holding her breath, Heidi inched the papers out and found the birth certificate.

What?! The top of the document resembles the one I have, but the bottom is new. I've got to call Walt. No, I should wait until he comes home. No, I can't. I'll call him and make it short. She flitted about like a hummingbird. Settling down enough to concentrate required an enormous effort. With shaking hands, she picked up the telephone and pushed the buttons. *Oh, God. I keyed it in wrong. Slow down, do it again. The numbers have been the same for years, hold yourself together, Heidi. Or whoever you are.*

Her heart pounded harder with each beat. He finally answered the phone. "Walt, hope I'm not catching you at a bad time, but my birth certificate arrived."

"Don't keep me in suspense, what does it say?"

With her throat constricting, Heidi said, "The top of the certificate still has my adopted name and birth date, but the bottom says my birth mother's name and my original name."

"Wow! And?"

"My name was Mariana Maria; my birth mother is Rita Baumann Regent. It also says I was Catholic." Heidi took a deep breath and let it out. "I'm amazed I was given a name. I was practically a newborn when I was adopted."

"It's nice you weren't nameless, maybe there was a reason." Walt sounded upbeat. "This is exciting, you feeling all right?"

"Yes, but Catholic! At least I went to a Catholic university, but it was only because I liked the place. I wonder what my birth mother would think of me being Episcopalian." Her cheeks flushed. "Maybe Lutheran would be better. Anyway, German-French-American. I'm a real international since I've lived in all three places. Well, not really Germany. But, hey, I'll count that since that's my heritage."

"It's time to celebrate. I have a meeting I can't miss. I'll come home around three. Call the babysitters, and we'll go out tonight. Love you."

"I love you, too." Her heart jumped with excitement. Even though she was alone, Heidi spoke out loud. "Sit down, sit down. Stop pacing. Call the sitters. Oh, right, I have to wait until they get out of class. What am I supposed to do while I wait? Right, keep busy. Um, the German woman who's helping me wanted my birth mother's name so she can find her. I'm panicking. Call Claudia— she'll help me calm down. No! This is supposed to be a secret. I can't ask her to keep... God, I sound like my mother talking to myself. Argh, I have to stop."

An hour scooted past. Opening the front door, Heidi stepped out into the hot afternoon sun and started walking around the long block. Her thoughts rattled in her head.

It must be ninety degrees out here. I'm on top of the situation now! The kids will come home, the sitter will feed them, and get them started on their homework. I'm glad it's Friday. Everything will be fine.

Walt's car appeared next to her half-way up the street during the last lap of her walk. He rolled down the window. "Hi there."

Heidi blurted out, "Hi… what if she wants a relationship—what if she doesn't?"

"Your face is a little flushed." He handed her a bottle of water through the window.

She drank half the bottle in seconds. "Oh, that helps." After she finished the rest of the water, she walked around the front of the car and got in next to him.

"Maybe nothing will happen if I write Rita."

"Or maybe, something will. Try to be more optimistic."

"Okay. I'll start writing tomorrow. I hope her last name hasn't changed."

"If it has, I bet your researcher friend can figure it out." Walt's voice was upbeat and full of encouragement. "The kids will be getting off the bus soon. Did you get in touch with the sitters?"

"Yep, their school only had a half-day today. I called, they'll be here about six."

"Great! It's time to celebrate."

Heidi wrote a letter to Rita a week after hers arrived. She had a million questions, starting with; *Why did you give me up? And who is my father?* Instead, she decided to start with a short introduction. She would mail it to her researcher, who would translate the text and send it to Germany once she found the correct address.

April 6, 1997

Dear Rita,

We haven't seen each other since March 15, 1958—my birthday. I realized I needed to find you after having children of my own. My search for you began after I read a book about adoption, and it explained how difficult it is to give up a baby.

When I was adopted, I was named Heidi Rose, but you should know me as Mariana Maria. Until today, I only had part of my birth certificate; even though it looked complete, it actually wasn't. The one I've always had only stated my adopted name, the German town where I was born, and my birthdate. I've felt incomplete without knowing more about you. With the help of a very generous German–American woman and the German department of records, I was sent my entire birth certificate that listed your name.

Do you have more children? Could you send me pictures? I have included a recent photo of me. I have a lot more to tell you and many questions to ask. I hope it's all right that I wrote to you and this letter wasn't a mistake.

All the best,

Heidi

Again, the waiting seemed to go on forever. For weeks, Heidi went up the driveway to the mailbox every day hoping for some kind of response. She made sure to go before the children got off the bus, often pacing back and forth. The pacing wore out the grass and left a track of brown earth below her feet—a human version of a deer path. Finally, a letter came a month after she sent her original letter. It was written in German with a translation attached.

11 May 1997

Dear Heidi,

I don't know where to begin. I am surprised and thankful you found me. It was wonderful to get your letter and the picture of you all grown up. Please forgive me for sending you away.

I wanted to look for you many times, but I was afraid you would reject me because I gave you away. Believe me, I didn't have much choice. My husband died. I had a baby before you and you were born a year later. My mother already had to take care of Mina (my first baby), and I had to go back to work to support the family. My mum refused to take care of you, too. I went to the Catholic sisters for help. I didn't feel like I had another choice.

I was happy the nuns let me name you after you were born. That's not the usual way with adoptions, I don't know why they did it. When I named you Mariana Maria, after Saint Mariana, I prayed she would protect you during your life. It's strange, I know, but when I watch television, and there is a girl with dark eyes and hair, I think of you.

I hope you like the album of photographs I've included of the family. I labeled them. They should show you what our life is like. The first picture in the book is when I was twenty, and the next one is how I look now. There's also a newborn picture of you.

I hope we can talk on the phone and meet soon. I speak English, but my friend translated my words and wrote them down here.

Your mother,

Rita

When Heidi read 'mother,' her stomach felt queasy. The newborn photograph matched the one in her baby album. She put the letter on the table, sat down, and put her face in her hands. After many deep breaths and a half bottle of wine that didn't produce the expected euphoria, she began writing a reply. Looking up at the calendar on the wall she wrote the date on the top of a sheet of scratch paper. After several drafts, she was satisfied and wrote out the final version on a piece of fine Crane stationary from her collection.

June 10, 1997

Dear Rita,

My heart was racing when I received your letter. I felt happy and tearful. I can't believe we have found each other after being separated for almost forty years. I'm scared about what this new connection means. I think we should go slowly. I want to meet someday in Germany, but for now, we should just write. My husband—Walt—knows everything, but no one else. I'm sorry I'm asking you to wait. My parents don't know we reconnected and I can't tell them. I need to take care of them before myself, they are very old and would never understand.

I will write more in a couple of days and tell you about my life.

Thinking of you,

Heidi

The photo album Rita sent Heidi began growing, and her heritage was becoming clearer with each new letter and photograph. She wanted to write to her older sister, but Rita initially resisted the idea. Eventually, Heidi received an unsolicited letter post marked August 3, 1997 that started a chain of exchanges between them.

Dear Heidi—my sister,

I am excited to be able to write to you. I have known about you all my life but didn't know how to find you. Mum told me you found her and now I want to write. I am happy Mum told you some things about me. My husband is happy I'm writing.

I don't like talking about my childhood. I went through tough times. I had to live with my Grandmother Magda. She had always been there for me. I was lucky to have a grandmother like this, she saved my life. When she died, I moved in with my mum and stepfather.

My stepfather was mean and made me do a lot of work. When I didn't listen, he hit me with a cane. One day he tried to get rid of me in a children's home for orphans. I did not have a good relationship with Mum after all that, and things are not better now. I think she sees a heartbreaking memory when she looks at me. No matter what I do or say it never seems to be right.

Mum told me about my father and gave me a picture. Except she won't tell me anything about your story. I asked my son, Sam, to translate this letter. I am now paying for not learning English in school, and it is too hard for me to start.

Your sister,
Mina

Chapter 26

Two years later, 1999…

A fter the children had left for school on the bus, the clouds crept across the sky during Heidi's walk with five other stay-at-home moms in the neighborhood. By ten o'clock, she was back in the house straightening up and making the beds. The phone rang and interrupted her routine. On the other end of the line, a woman's voice formally identified herself as Miss Landings; Mr. Nathan Schwartz's trust officer from California. Heidi was taken aback at first and asked the woman to 'hold on' while she put Miss Landings on the speakerphone. She's seen her father's financial statements and related letters on his desk many times, but they'd never discussed the contents.

Heidi rustled around the room for another thirty seconds and pulled the quilt up over the sheets, "Okay, I'm all set. Miss Landings, how can I help you?"

"I presume you're aware you're next in line to inherit considerable funds from your grandmother Schwartz?"

"Dad told me, but why are you contacting me? I thought this was between you and my father at this point."

"We need to do some verification for legal purposes. Do you know where your sister, Joan, is?"

Heidi put her hand on her throat and swallowed hard. She made up a plausible response. "No, I have no idea. My father doesn't talk about her." She reflected, *Sister? What sister? What's this woman talking about? The only sister I know about is Mina. Who the hell is Joan?*

Miss Landings kept talking through the speaker. "I thought it was strange your father didn't know where his other daughter lived." The woman's voice echoed through the room.

"No, I can't help you." Heidi's words came out more briskly than she intended. This seemed like some kind of sick joke. "I don't know why you called me."

"I'm just following protocol. I will find out another way. Sorry to trouble you."

The line went dead, and Heidi put the phone back in the cradle. Sinking down into the bed, her heart felt heavy. Her father had another child, and she never knew! At first, anger emerged, but the agitation dissolved into disappointment.

Heidi rubbed her tense shoulders and said to no one in particular, "Joan, Joan… And, I'm hiding that I found my birth family. Maybe we should leave our stories buried."

Pacing and discussions with Walt over her recent discovery became an evening routine. Since she knew her mother would be asleep until noon, she resolved to talk to her father alone and arranged to see him the following Wednesday.

At the appointed time, Heidi met her father outside his front door, and they walked around the garden among the singing birds. A pair of doves sat on a branch of the only apple tree at the head of the garden. Their heads tilting left and right as if they were investigating Heidi's motives.

"Dad, I never asked, why the roses and apple tree?"

"Long before your mom and I met, I developed a fondness for both in Europe during the Second World War. To me, the roses represent beauty in a world that isn't always beautiful. The apple blooms help me remember the people I knew and will never forget. The plants need love and care to thrive just like we do."

"Flowers never felt like that to me, I'll think of them differently from now on."

As they settled down on the stone bench, Heidi wiped the cut grass off the tops of her sneakers and leaned back. The apple tree truly complimented the budding cornucopia of roses. "Dad, lately I've been thinking about a lot of things I wanted to ask you about. What happened with your California family?"

"Aw, that's ancient history you're digging up. I hardly even know anymore."

His answer was troubling. His tone sounded like he thought Heidi knew everything, but no—she felt confused.

"I can't imagine how I would have made it through life with Gwen without the light you brought into our lives. I've always been very proud of you," her father added as his words almost floated away.

Heidi decided to tackle the real reason she came over. "Dad, I received a phone call from your trustee, Miss Landings."

His entire face turned down into a frown. "What did the woman want?"

"I was completely blindsided. She asked if I knew where your other daughter was living, and now I'm asking you. Tell me about Joan."

"No!" His face turned ashen.

"Is it true?" Heidi said. Her lips tightly closed and twisted.

"Oh, God!" A long lull followed. "Only partly. I'm sorry, I never thought I needed to explain. Miss Landings had no business

255

calling you. The bank contacted me last week asking questions. I had no idea they'd have the nerve to bother you."

"Well, she did. I feel broken." Drama seemed appropriate.

"You're my only daughter. I wasn't able to create children. I divorced my first wife because of her infidelity, but I wouldn't embarrass my wife by telling my mother the complete truth. Mother was very unhappy with me for my failed marriage. In the end, from our families' and community's point of view, I took all the blame for the marriage falling apart. To keep the peace, I agreed to pay child support until my first wife married the baby's father, which was within a year after our expedited divorce. I was emotionally exhausted from working in North Africa during the war and coming back home to betrayal made my recovery all the more difficult. It all took a lot out of me. Admitting my shortcomings was not easy. My family doctor recommended not marrying again until I came to terms with my situation—doing so took quite some time. I met Gwen, I mean your mother, in the middle of my recovery and we had to wait longer than either of us wanted before we got married. At the time, I praised her patience. She's changed a lot since those days. Do you understand why I didn't explain before now?"

"Yes, but I'm hurt you never told me on your own."

"I'm sorry. I never thought the information would make any difference."

"Dad, it does matter. I know so little about you and more about Mom. I've always hated missing out on your life story. Well, hate may be too strong a word."

"I made a mistake, but I don't like dwelling on the past."

"Yeah, I guess that makes sense."

"Let's talk about something lighter."

Heidi hesitated while she composed her thoughts. "I can't, there are more things I need to ask."

"All right, since I'm on the hot seat. Go ahead."

"Does your ex-wife's daughter know she isn't yours by birth?"

"Yes, she contacted me when you were five—she was in her early twenties—to inform me her mother had died. Soon after, she traveled to D.C., and we met for lunch. I told her about the beginning of her life. At first, she didn't believe me. Eventually, once we'd discussed the situation some more, she realized I was telling the truth. Before we said goodbye, she thanked me for not disgracing her mother."

"Did you go back to California after the divorce?"

"A few times, before your mother and I lived in Paris. A year after we moved, my mother died. I went back for the funeral, but not many times afterward. She left a specific one-time gift to Joan, and the rest was intended for Mother's descendants. I've specifically excluded Joan in my will and included you by name. You will be quite comfortable with my assets. My mother didn't leave much wiggle room in her documents. The dividends go from generation to generation in pre-set monthly distributions. The entire amount will come out of the trust during your children's lifetime. Half will go to them and the other half to my sister's grandchildren, who are also adopted.

Heidi tried not to choke on her words. "Oh, my! Really?" She hoped he wouldn't try to talk about her adoption. Then she looked up at the sky. "Thank you, Grandmother. Our children are going to be surprised."

"Yes, I expect so, but don't tell them until they've established themselves in the world. They need to build their own lives rather than counting on an inheritance."

"That makes sense. That was very generous of your mother, considering I never met her."

"These things happen all the time. Well-to-do families want their descendants to have the same luxuries they enjoyed."

"What happened to your father?"

"He died of a stroke when I was twelve. My sister, Beatrice, I call her Bea, was only nine at the time. After Dad died, my mother dug her heels in and made sure we received the best education. We had mandatory times each day for study and pleasure reading, and French lessons. She found out about a research group at Stanford University that was accepting candidates with exceptional IQs and had us tested. It was called the Terman Study. I passed, but Bea didn't. We traveled down to Stanford a few times with Mother, but the rest was done through phone calls. They still call me once a year to see what I'm up to."

Heidi decided not to mention she'd talked to David about the Terman Study and done some research on her own. Instead, she said, "That's horrible you and Mom both lost a parent at such a young age." Heidi rubbed her temples and sighed. "I've never heard about Bea. What happened to her?"

"My sister and I grew up and went our separate ways. We wrote, but not often. I went back a couple of times and visited friends, but I didn't see her every time. Bea became quite annoyed. Eventually, I gave up going out there because I always came back to D.C. in a rather glum state of mind. I'm sorry you didn't grow up around Bea."

"Me too."

"After decades passed, her grown children brought her to Maryland to visit. They're quite interesting. The last time I saw them, they were children. Now, one's a professional musician and the other a textile artist. The reunion in 1989 and long overdue."

"1989? Walt and I had moved back from California by then. Why didn't you mention the meeting to me? It seems like I should've been told a lot of things."

"I'm sorry, I was preoccupied. Your mother didn't understand the visit and was rather cruel to them; I kept future contact with them a secret. Your mother has a fierce desire to protect us from all harm but often does more damage. When she's not in control of her world, she spins herself into an emotional frenzy, which doesn't help anyone. But, that's not news to you."

"Yeah, I know." Heidi looked into his eyes and held his gaze. "I still think you should've told me your family was coming to town."

Her father pulled his eyes away from hers. "You had your first baby only two weeks before their visit, which was a difficult adjustment for your mother on top of having to cope with my family reunion. Telling you was another hurdle I didn't want to jump at the time, and then I never made of point of bringing it up. There's no good excuse."

"I wish you had. It's been strange only having Mom's side of the family actually in our lives. I would've liked to have met yours."

"Yes, I think I made a grievous error that should've been repaired a long time ago. It's too late to meet Bea. She died a couple of years ago. I wish I'd told you about this before, but some things can't be changed. Maybe you'll meet your California cousins on your own someday. I'd rather not talk about this anymore."

"All right, back to Mom." Heidi felt perturbed but needed to keep the conversation going. "I've thought a lot about my life with her, too. Lately, whenever she tells stories, they are almost always about her life before she met you. I wonder if she's depressed."

"I wonder, too. We have had such an amazing life, and she barely speaks of it. She talks about her childhood and her acting career. Other times she talks about what I've done wrong on any given day. Her memory is quite slanted. She used to think I was the cat's pajamas."

"Yes, I think she's changed, and you've stayed the same."

"Thank you, but I'm not so sure I'm the same." He sighed. "I'm used to Gwen's emotional troubles and live with them daily, but something else is wrong."

"Oh?" Heidi's shoulders drooped down.

"At the onset, her sudden vision loss was traumatic, but the last couple of years have been even more stressful. She won't agree to go to the theater or out to dinner no matter how many times I ask.

It's quite sad, we always loved going to shows together. I don't think I ever told you I was an actor when I went to Harvard."

"No, no, you didn't. I always wondered, but the topic never came up."

"Shakespeare was my forte. Anyway, the isolation she's chosen has made her moods and phobias worse. There are plenty of resources to help, but she won't try any of them."

"But, Dad, we still love her."

"Yet, love hasn't been enough. She and I have dealt poorly with her vision and many other challenges, but it's her digestive system that I'm concerned about now. Her insides haven't been right for a while."

"What did the doctor say?"

"We haven't found out what's wrong." Her father flicked a ladybug off his knee and mumbled something about good luck before he said, "Convincing her to go to the doctor hasn't worked so far."

"Oh, Dad, I'm so sorry."

"You're such a sweetheart!" Her father cast his eyes down to the ground, before looking up and going on. "Everything has been so difficult for all of us. It's miserable that you, and now Walt, are plagued by her insecurities."

"Well, I haven't helped calm her down or boost her mood up, either. We should've gotten professional help years ago."

"Let's not linger on this anymore today."

"You're right, I already spend enough time mulling over Mom's issues."

"I know the feeling." Her father put his hand on hers. "Is there anything else on your mind?'

"Yes, there's one more subject I have to bring up—David's death."

Her father fidgeted and inhaled sharply. "I was hoping the topic wouldn't reemerge. Before I begin, your mother and Sadie aren't aware of what I'm going to tell you. I'd like to keep it that way. They're too fragile at this point to know the truth."

"I understand. What about Claudia and Walt? Can I tell them?"

"Walt, yes, but Claudia's got enough to deal with these days with her mother's newly diagnosed dementia. Someday, when I'm gone from this world, you can tell Claudia."

"If that's what you want, I'll wait to tell her. I don't like to think of your passing. Okay, now can you explain?"

"Yes, yes. Today certainly is my day for confessions. What do you want to know?" He raked his hands through his black hair, and the wrinkles on his face appeared more pronounced than usual.

"The day David died, I promised I wouldn't tell anyone I saw you in the wine cellar snooping around. There's more to his death than anyone's let on. Tell me… why he was killed."

"That was one of the worst days of my life, followed by expecting you to keep my secret. It didn't help that I saw you and Claudia following me by the canal some weeks later, which was even more disturbing. I never said anything because I didn't want to have to explain myself."

"I thought you spotted us, but I couldn't bring myself to confront you either."

"Yes, saying nothing is often the best choice. The guy I met was doing some work for me related to David's death."

"He looked pretty shady."

"He's one of the two men who left you packages to deliver to David when you were at Catholic U."

"What, I didn't realize you even knew about those incidences."

"David and I didn't keep things from each other and didn't have to because we had the same security clearances at the office. Regardless, those men both crossed an invisible line that day. You never should've been involved. One of them died in a Virginia park the year you were married, he was poisoned."

Heidi stifled a gasp. Immediately she presumed her father was referring to the man she and Walt had seen collapse in the park. She never wished him dead, but his methods for delivering packages still made her suspicious of scraggly looking characters.

"Losing David is something I'll never get over." Her father dropped his head into his hand before bringing his eyes back to hers. "David died over a decade ago, and I still think of him every day. Among other things, I should tell you... I was at the range when he was shot. I'd gone off to the bathroom, and he was on the ground when I returned. I held him in my arms; I don't even know why. He was already dead. My shirt was covered in blood. A stranger gave me a fresh shirt. The only people who knew were the witnesses and the investigators. I haven't shared this with anyone."

"Dad, you've kept that to yourself all this time? That's even more tragic." Heidi paused, then persisted with her questioning. "What was that canister you put in your pocket in the cellar about?"

"World history... I can tell you the connection now; enough time has passed. Do you remember what I told you the night David died?"

"Not much. To keep my promise, I had to let your words slip away."

"A sensible woman. Several weeks before David's death, we met. He was extremely agitated. He had found out vital information about the Soviets that could help end the Cold War. I promised to take what he'd found to the right people if anything happened to him before he could report to his superiors. The information was in his head, but he also stored it on microfilm and had a sample of the antidote in his wine cellar in case something went wrong. If the Soviets pressured him, he would tell them something that sounded important, but actually wasn't. I can only presume he never had that chance since they ended his life."

"His death didn't change the world."

"No, but his actions contributed to major victories. Come to think of it, I'm not sure what the history books will reveal. They never tell the entire story."

Her father wiped his temple with his handkerchief and fell silent.

"Go on—please."

"Remember the scuffle at my retirement party?"

"You barely mentioned it back then, but yes. David was talking to someone in Russian."

"That man later became his informant; the mole. David told me his name, but it's not prudent to mention. He was disenchanted with the Soviet government after his daughter was in a major car accident. She didn't receive proper care, and he was sure the medical community could've done more because he was a high-ranking member of the Communist Party. He became bitter and found a way to regularly visit D.C. to give David government secrets to use against Moscow. A few times David went to meet him in Russia except those liaisons proved to be too risky."

"What happened to the mole's daughter?"

"She died under suspicious circumstances."

"Aw, being the daughter of an important person is dangerous." Heidi felt grateful he was no longer in the business. "Okay, then what about the canister in the cellar?"

"When you caught me, I said it had to do with communism. The canister held the formula for the antidote for a biological weapon the Russians had spent a fortune on to back up their nuclear arsenal. David didn't turn it in right away because the mole had given it to him. He believed that if he handed it over too soon, the informant would be killed. In the end, the Soviets found out anyway and executed them both. I don't think they realized he had a backup plan. By the time they did, it was too late. I'd already given the canister to our government. The amount of money the Soviets spent on nukes and reformulating their biologics affected the country's economic planning. This all led to a crisis and a revolution in Poland and Hungary. Most of the members of the fifteen Soviet republics declared independence, and the USSR crumbled along with the Berlin wall."

"I thought you and David worked for the State Department."

"We did, but he had some other things on the side. David was an important man with an agenda. So many events surrounded him."

"Yes, I see, but if you hadn't passed the information along, our government would've had to find another way."

"True, but this way saved more lives."

"Mmm." Her mind was overflowing. "So, did these events have anything to do with some of our houses being broken into?"

"Yes, that was proven. The Russians came searching to see if they could find anything David secretly stashed…"

"I think I've heard enough," Heidi scoffed. "And I thought learning the truth about Santa Claus was tough."

"Well, my dear, you did start this conversation today."

"Yep, I did. I think you and David are unsung heroes."

"It took a huge collaborative effort to succeed. We were pieces of a bigger puzzle."

"I think you're too modest." Heidi sat silently, staring at her hands. She couldn't think of anything else to say and wondered what other secrets he concealed.

Chapter 27

A year later, 2000…

Christmas was long over. It was mid-February before Heidi was invited with Walt, and the kids, to her parents' house for dessert and the customary gift exchange. Heidi didn't understand why they had delayed the celebration since they'd always insisted it should be held on Christmas night.

On the appointed Saturday, the Bailey's hopped into the car with Walt behind the wheel. An hour later, the car pulled into the Kenwood development and stopped on Brookside Drive. The kids piled out of the car and ran up to their grandparents' front door with Heidi and Walt trailing behind carrying a few gifts for her parents.

Heidi wiggled through the crowd of kids and knocked on the front door. Her mother opened the door on the chain, called through the crack to make sure it was them, and then opened the door. "Hello, come in everyone."

"Hi Mom, Merry Christmas," Heidi exclaimed, not knowing what else to say.

"Your dad is upstairs, and I think he's still in bed. Heidi, take the family into the sunroom and then go see what's going on."

"Yes, Mom. Okay, everyone into the sunroom." The kids didn't have to be told twice. Walt, the Nintendo is already set up on an old television—I did that last summer. Have fun getting them to take turns. There should still be some cards or board games for the stragglers in the TV cabinet, but I doubt they'll have that much time before gift opening."

In the room, Heidi noticed wrapped gifts peeking out from under a cloth-covered table in the corner instead of under a Christmas tree. She placed her parent's gifts on top of the table. On another table leaned the ever-present display of artistic costume renderings from her time in the theater.

"I stopped designing those things years ago. Every time I want to take the drawings, Mom says I can't." Heidi shook her head and smirked. "I should just steal them. Never mind, I'm going to see what's going on with Dad."

"Okay, I got the kids." Walt pulled up a chair beside the television and helped the twins with the game console. The girl opened up a deck of cards and got started on their own. Heidi smiled thinking she loved him more now than the day they married and gave him a quick kiss before leaving the room.

Taking two steps at a time up the stairs, Heidi found her father curled on his side in bed. "Hi, Dad. Everyone is here. Are you getting out of bed?"

"Hello." His voice sounded sleepy. "I'll get up and come downstairs."

"You sure you're okay?

"Yes." Her father sat up and ruffled his short hair and stretched. "Don't worry. I lost track of the day. Please, make me some oatmeal."

She was concerned as she watched him drag his eighty-six-year-old body out of bed. He cinched the strings on his pajama pants a little tighter.

"Okay, do you want Postum and orange juice?"

"Yes, thanks."

Her parents hadn't had a live-in maid for years, and her father had taken over the cooking. Quite a challenge for a man who'd never cooked a day in his life. Their menu consisted mainly of oatmeal, sandwiches, and Stouffer's Lean Cuisine dinner entrees.

Heidi went back downstairs to report her findings to her mother, who stood next to the hand railing at the bottom of the stairs. "Dad's getting up, he'll be down soon."

Her mother seemed to relax and wandered off to the sunroom.

In the kitchen, Heidi poured some orange juice in a glass and boiled enough water for a cup of Postum and a bowl of oatmeal. Pacing between the counters in the room, Heidi waited for her father to appear. She heard something in the dining room and pushed through the swinging kitchen door. He looked fine, and she breathed a sigh of relief.

"Good evening." He smiled and winked at her. "Sorry about that, I had to take a nap."

"I'm glad you're all right," Heidi replied.

"How's my breakfast coming along?" He emphasized the word *breakfast* and laughed. "It's dark out, maybe we're in the North Pole."

"Funny, Dad. I'll bring everything right out." She disappeared into the kitchen and grabbed a silver tray from under the counter. Quickly she placed the bowl of oatmeal, the glass of orange juice and two cups of Postum in the middle. She knew he'd want the two cups of fake coffee and brought them all out at once to speed things along. The evening was dwindling away, and she wanted to get on with the gift exchange before the children got restless for ice cream. Her father looked at the oatmeal and declared with a playful growl that there wasn't any honey on top. It wasn't *just right*, and he sent her away to try again. His remarks made him sound like one of the characters from *Goldilocks and the Three Bears*.

"Perhaps the next batch will work out." Heidi smiled, picked up the bowl, and passed through the swinging door again into the kitchen. Heidi reheated the oatmeal, added a dollop of honey, and took it back out.

"Oh, thank you. That looks good. I'll eat quickly, I want to see my grandchildren."

The doorbell rang, and she popped around the corner to find Edward at the front door. Heidi lamely waved and kissed him on the cheek. They walked into the dining room together.

"Hi, Uncle Nathan."

"Evening, Edward."

"Mom was in the sunroom, but I saw her walk by in the hallway a few minutes ago. I'm not sure where she went," Heidi said. "I imagine she'll make a grand entrance shortly. As far as I know, Walt is still out there with the kids. Go on out, Dad and I will be there soon."

"Will do." Edward ducked out of the dining room.

Heidi watched her father pull out pill bottles from a shoebox in front of his placemat. He opened each one, place a pill on a saucer, and laid the bottles back down one after the other in the box.

"Dad what are you doing?"

"I have a system. If the bottle is on its side, it means I've dispensed the pill I'm supposed to take. Some pills are for my heart and others are for my lungs. By the time I swallow them, I'm so full of pills, I rattle."

Heidi chuckled at his attempt at levity, and said, "Yes, that's a lot of prescription pills. Your system scares me. I'm going to write these down since I don't have a clue what you're taking."

She grabbed a pencil and paper out a drawer in the kitchen. Then, sitting at the table with her dad, she absentmindedly grabbed his other cup and took a sip of the brown liquid. She puckered her lips and scrunched her nose in disgust. "Oh blah!"

"It's not so bad." He took another sip of his cup of Postum.

She slid her tongue against the bottom of her front teeth to scrape off the unpleasant taste. "Postum doesn't even taste like coffee, more like diluted molasses. Since I'm on a roll, I'll try your salt substitute." She picked up the cardboard cylinder, turned the slat in the plastic top, then sprinkled some on her hand and licked it. "This isn't any better. Yuck!"

"Not fair, why are you picking on me?" he said playfully. "Besides, I'm used to it. You don't have to partake."

"Well, this *stuff* doesn't seem like it's good for you."

"Hey, go easy on the old man."

"Sorry, Dad, just worrying."

"Thanks, you don't need to. I'll just finish here and go to my grandchildren. Your mother and I wrapped their gifts months ago. The year before last, Kyle and Caleb didn't understand Christmas since they were so much younger. I think they'll like what we got them."

In the sunroom, Edward handed out the presents as her mother instructed. Everything seemed fine initially, but her father got slower and slower. He sat there with a gift in his lap and didn't perform his usual careful opening of the package. Heidi helped by pulling on the ribbons and unfastening the tape.

"What is this? What is this? What do I do with it?" He didn't admire the hand-knit sweater she'd struggled to knit to precisely the right size and proportions.

Edward leaned toward Heidi and croaked, "Do you think he's had a stroke?"

"He has a doctor's appointment tomorrow," her mother said. "We won't do anything tonight. Heidi, don't forget, you're driving him."

"Is that okay, Dad?" Heidi wasn't sure he was capable of making any decisions.

"Yes. doctor, tomorrow." His speech slurred and sounded like he was drugged.

They all left later that evening with a false sense of security after her father began sounding more like himself.

In the morning, Heidi drove the forty-minute drive back to her parents. She went into the house through the garage, using her key.

Her father was eating his oatmeal topped with a shallow lake of honey. The pill bottles were on their sides.

He put down his spoon and said, "Good morning, before we go to the doctor's, let's go into the den."

Heidi felt relieved that he sounded more like his usual self.

They walked out of the dining room and into the den together. He ran his hands over the leather office chair before sitting down and opening a drawer. "Take this packet, it tells you how to handle everything after I'm gone forever."

"Aw, Dad, don't talk like that."

"Always good to plan ahead, I should have given it to you ages ago. Read it over and let me know if you have any questions."

"Not today, okay?"

"That's fine, at your leisure." He squeezed the arms of his chair. "I like this chair and my manual typewriter. Do you remember when you tried to teach me how to use a computer?"

"Yes, you didn't like it at all. The buttons were too easy to push. You liked the solid feel of your Smith-Corona better than..."

"I do," he interrupted. "It's quite satisfying hammering my fingers down on the keys. Please, keep the old relic to remind you of me."

"Dad, you'll be around a long while."

"Please, keep it, won't you? It's at least fifty-years-old. I have no idea what happened to the carrying case."

"Okay, I'll keep the typewriter."

He rolled away from the desk and tilted back in the chair. Across from him, on the wall over what was left of some faux burlap wallpaper, hung a poster size auburn chalk portrait of Heidi in her wedding gown. He said, "Anytime I'm depressed, I look at your picture, and I feel better. Keep that, too."

"Yes, sir. I'm glad you still like it. I think the artist at the Renaissance festival would love to know he's appreciated."

"Perhaps, but it's the woman in the portrait I adore. You've brought me so much joy through the years."

"You give me too much credit."

"Credit well deserved."

"Thanks—I wish the room wasn't such a wreck."

"I think this room has a lot in common with my current condition," her father chuckled.

"Dad, you deserve better."

"This place was doomed after the pipes broke and the water passed through to the lower levels. If you recall, your mother wouldn't allow me to shut off the water while we waited for the plumber. Half the den's ceiling fell down, and the carpet was ruined by the time he arrived."

"Yes, I know. The pipes were repaired, and the maid's room was redone, but she quit anyway. You never hired another. I kept thinking more plaster was going to fall on your head."

"Me too, but I eventually pulled most of it down. Instead of looking up at the awful ragged rafters, I focus on your beautiful portrait. Believe me, if I could've found a way to call a contractor, without having to disinfect everything after the workers left, I would have. I'm relieved your mother didn't try to stop me from taking care of the outside of the house, but then we didn't have a choice since there's a neighborhood covenant."

"Dad, the color is draining from your face. I think there's something wrong with your medications. I'll bring the box of pills with us."

"Yes, we should go. I'm feeling woozy."

The walk down the thirty-foot hall to the garage took longer than it should've. Once he was in the car, Heidi raced down the road to the doctor's office. She grabbed a wheelchair from the lobby and rolled him into the building. His eyes closed and his head tilted forward. Heidi sat staring at a magazine without reading a word.

Doctor Yance, much to Heidi's surprise, personally appeared in the waiting room. He said, "I hear we have a problem?"

"Hello, I'm very worried. Dad said he took his pills right before I got to the house and he started to decline within an hour. I don't understand what's happening, here are his meds." Heidi handed over the shoebox filled with her father's pill bottles along with the itemized list.

"Let me check." He scanned the list and bent over the wheelchair. "Both of you, come into my office."

The chair's movement woke her father when she rolled it around the corner. The doctor examined him in the wheelchair.

"Mr. Schwartz, you've neglected yourself, and now you're in trouble," Doctor Yance scolded. "Your medications aren't working properly, and your blood pressure is too low. You were supposed to come in for an appointment two months ago." The doctor said nothing for a few minutes.

Heidi felt like he was glaring at them as a parent does to a naughty child.

The doctor started up again. "You'll need to be hospitalized, and it could've been avoided if you weren't so busy taking care of your wife. Her condition may be taxing, but it's not life-threatening."

"I know, I know. I'm cold," her father groggily replied.

"I can call an ambulance, but they'll only take you to the nearest hospital, which is Sibley. I have privileges there and can visit after you're admitted. If you choose to go to Suburban, you'll have to get there on your own. The staff doctors can consult me over the phone."

Her father groggily said, "Suburban. Gwen… likes better."

"Not the best idea, but you need to feel comfortable. Take the pills with you, so the medical staff knows what's going on."

Heidi struggled on her own to help her father back out of the wheelchair into the car. By the time they arrived at the emergency room, his fingers had turned a pale shade of blue. Now, it was an emergency. She cursed to herself and wondered what his primary doctor was thinking when he sent them away. The staff at Suburban wrapped him in blankets, injected him with some sort of stimulant, and put him on an intravenous drip of electrolytes. His vitals returned to normal within half an hour.

"Dad, you scared me, but you're looking better." Heidi put her hand on the bed rail and lowered herself into a chair next to him.

He glanced at the intravenous line coming out of his arm and up to the saline bag. "Humph, I don't remember any of this."

They were interrupted by a nurse talking about advanced directive forms and what her father would want if he were unable to speak for himself in the future.

He responded with a wink and said, "No extraordinary measures, but I sure would like to continue living. Thanks for the boost in my IV bag."

Next, a staff doctor appeared and explained that her father had been dehydrated upon arrival. They had already examined the pill bottles and discovered that the Metropol heart medication had been duplicated into a container that was supposed to be filled with baby aspirin. As a result, he had taken twice the prescribed amount, causing his blood pressure plummeted. Heidi thought back to the poisoned 'homeless' man in the park and David's death. She worried that someone who didn't belong at her parents' house had snuck in and tampered with the bottles. Maybe she was just feeling paranoid, and her father had mixed things up on his own, but why didn't the number of pills add up?

The doctor interrupted her thoughts and said her father needed to stay in the hospital for a few days for observation. He didn't object.

"Dad, they have a room for you upstairs. I'm going to inspect it and wait for you there."

"Thank you. See you later, Mousey."

Heidi found the nearest elevator up to the cardiac wing. The room he'd been assigned looked more like a hotel than a hospital, with its dark wood wainscoting, moss green painted walls and plush burgundy lounge chairs. It even had a connecting room for relatives. This wasn't a typical hospital room. Heidi wondered why he had been assigned the executive suite.

Once her father was settled, he asked, "What are we going to do about Gwen? She needs meals and companionship while we're apart."

"Forever thinking about others. I love you for that, but you have to concentrate on getting well. I'll divide my time between Mom, you, and the kids. Walt will do his part, and I'll ask Edward to help, too."

The nurse walked in and picked up her father's wrist. "How are we feeling?"

Heidi felt depressed and nonsensically said, "Life is a revolving door."

"Mr. Schwartz, we'll need to monitor you for a few days, and the doctor wants you in a room closer to the nurses' station. As soon as one becomes available, we'll roll you down there." She frowned while checking his vitals.

"Can it be a private room, too?" her father asked.

"Yes, sir." She took his temperature while Heidi watched. When the nurse was done, she helped him out of bed, but he couldn't walk more than two steps before exhaustion set in. He lay back down and fell asleep.

"Your father is in good hands," the nurse said. "Go on home, and we'll see you in the morning."

"Thank you, I need to check on my mother. Please, when Dad wakes up, tell him I'll be back before lunch tomorrow." Heidi tried to smile to show her gratitude to the nurse, but her lips trembled with the effort. Turning away she left the room.

On Brookside Drive, Heidi dealt with her mother roaming around the house all night with the television on full blast in the background. She found a pair of ear-plugs in the den drawer, but they only helped a little. In her world, noise during the night usually meant the children were in some sort of distress. Heidi preferred quiet in the dark hours, which was the complete polar opposite of her mother. All and all she only managed to get about two hours of sleep with the surrounding commotion. By morning, the house was finally quiet, but Heidi couldn't allow herself to fall asleep given the time. Tired and cranky, she went back to the hospital.

"Morning, Dad. Look what I found in the closet of my old room." She held up a stuffed rabbit. "Sorry, it's a bit worn out. When I'm not here, you can hold the little bunny. I'm surprised it's still in one piece after all these years."

"Thanks, how's your mother?"

"Mom is doing all right. We've got a system in place. Edward is coming over after work, and I'm going home for the weekend."

"Edward is a good man." He squeezed the bunny ever so gently. "Oh, look, here comes a nurse. Earlier she said I'd get a real shower today." Her father handed the bunny back and stood up with help from the nurse and struggled clumsily into the wheelchair. The nurse rolled the chair out of the room.

Heidi sat near the bed and wrote six thank you notes to the people who'd already sent flowers. The arrangements were spread across the window sill. She was pleased she could write so quickly with perfect penmanship. Thirty minutes later the nurse brought her father back into the room.

"How was your shower?" Heidi tried to sound upbeat, but it wasn't easy.

Her father replied with a saucy roll of his eyes and a contented smile. "It felt wonderful! Cute nurse, too."

The nurse let out a giggle and helped him into his hospital bed.

"Dad, you're naughty," Heidi jested.

Someone brought in a breakfast tray. It didn't look appetizing. Without a word of complaint from her father, she spoon-fed him scrambled eggs and a side-dish of oatmeal. Each bite was tiny, and he took a long time to swallow.

It shouldn't be him laying here, it should be Mom. She's the one with the physical and emotional problems. I'm a beast! I have no right to think these things.

Heidi continued to drive back and forth between her mother and father. Her father seemed to be improving, but by the end of the week, he had curled himself into a little ball of pain. The technicians rolled his bed out of the room and into another for a CAT scan, while she paced in the hallway waiting. A doctor appeared and informed Heidi her father needed to be moved into ICU for more comprehensive care since his condition was declining. The doctor wanted to put him on a respirator, to provide him with more oxygen than what he could take in with the regular nasal cannula, but the hospital would need the family's consent. He said the scan showed that her father's brain was fine, at least, but they would have to wait longer for the results of various other tests. Heidi phoned Walt. "Can you believe it! They say his brain is fine! The doctors sound insane. He's not fine! They're moving him to ICU. The doctor wants to put him on a respirator."
"Should I come?"

"No, stay with the children. I have to phone Mom." She disconnected. Heidi called her mother and spoke carefully while her nails dug into the counter at the nurses' station.

"The doctors said to put Dad on a respirator and to keep him sedated until there's a full diagnosis or he'll be gone in an hour." Heidi's stomach rolled into a tight knot. For the first time in Heidi's memory, her mother consented to the doctor's recommendation without any discussion or emotional drama connected to the decision. She handed the phone to the doctor for verbal verification.

After the doctors finished the intubation, Heidi picked up the nearest phone and dialed home. "Walt, he's on the ventilator. During the procedure, one of his lungs collapsed. The doctor said that happens sometimes, but both of them are working now. This is a private hell I will never forget."

"You made the best decision at the time. That's all anyone can ask." Walt's voice soothed her nerves.

"Everything sounds like a cliché. My world is spinning around me." The hysteria was building up inside her.

"Should I come now? It's Saturday, I can call the babysitter."

"Nooo, I need you to stay at home. The boys are too little to know what's going on, but the girls aren't, and you need to help them understand." Heidi choked on a tear. "One of us there is better than none."

"I'll keep asking, just to be sure. When you get a chance, get yourself a glass of wine, it'll help you relax."

Walt hung up, but Heidi kept the phone beside her ear until the computer voice on the other end said, "If you'd like to make a call, please hang up." She jolted back to reality. Everything she did seemed to be happening in slow motion.

During the days that followed, Heidi sat next to her father and read uplifting articles to him from the newspaper even though she didn't think he could hear her under sedation. Sometimes she held his hand, and he would squeeze hers, but she had no idea if the gesture was real or a nervous twitch. At night, when she left to take care of her mother, she'd leave the stuffed bunny rabbit under his hand.

One morning, the rabbit sat askew on the nightstand. Heidi felt frustrated and crossed over to the nurses' station in the hall.

Heidi asked the woman on duty, "Why can't the night nurse leave the rabbit with Mr. Schwartz when I'm away? This isn't a difficult request, he seems calmer when it's under his hand even though he's sedated."

The nurse replied, "Yes, ma'am, I'll write it on his chart. Sorry, we didn't mean to upset you."

Just as Heidi was about to go back into her father's room, the doctor arrived with a diagnosis. He took her around the corner away from the nurses' station.

"I'm sorry to say, your father has suffered a number of small heart attacks he wouldn't have noticed at his age. The attacks disabled his heart to half of its normal capacity. The ventilator will prolong his life, but he's too old to be eligible for a heart transplant. It would be best to take him off the machine. We can give him oxygen and some medication to keep him comfortable." The doctor put on his eyeglasses. "I've already called Mrs. Schwartz, and she authorized us to remove the ventilator. He'll be with us for at most a week but be assured we'll keep him comfortable."

Heidi put her head down and tried not to cry. She looked up at the doctor and said, "I understand. Thank you for your support."

"I wish I could've done more. I suggest you go get something to eat and rest. Come back in a couple hours, it'll take some time for him to wake up. This will be a difficult journey, but he'll need you and so will your mother."

"Yes, all right." She shook the doctor's hand and walked as fast as she could down the stairs to the cafeteria to relieve some of the...she didn't know what.

Blinking hard over and over to keep herself from fading away, she pulled a cream cheese bagel and a coffee onto her tray, then paid, before sitting at a table by the window. Absentmindedly she ate while staring at nothing in particular. In between, she glanced down from the window to her watch. The bagel was soon gone, and the tray pushed away. The doctor said to rest, so she put her head down on crossed arms on the table and tried to follow his orders. When she woke up, fewer people were sitting around than there were before. Her watch said she'd been sleeping for an hour. The coffee had cooled off, but she gulped it down anyway. It was time to head back up to ICU. Hopefully, he'd be able to communicate with her. Taking the stairs two steps at a time, she turned the corner and walked down the hall to his room. The television was on, and the remote was resting on the bed by his hand.

"Hi, Dad. You're watching TV?"

"It was on when I woke up."

"How do you feel?"

"I feeeel woozy," his voice slurred.

"You sound drunk."

"I'm stoned on drugs." One eye appeared normal and the other drooped. His voice was scratchy and slurred.

"Are you in pain?"

"No, don't worry. I'm here waiting for what comes next. This is the end of the road. No one has to tell me."

"Oh, Dad, what should I do?"

"You're doing all the right things—love you, always. Heaven's going to be…"

"I love you." Heidi's lips twitched into a tear-filled smile. "God's gonna make you a star."

"That's a nice image."

Over the last three weeks, his skin had become as thin as the tissue paper that once wrapped around the gifts in Heidi's childhood Christmas stockings. Dissolving under the sheets, he lay weak and quiet, with plastic tubes and bags extending in all directions. His olive, deeply wrinkled skin stood out against the white pillowcase.

They talked for a while before he prompted her to leave for the night.

The next day her father was breathless when he tried to speak. He beckoned in pantomime for a pen and paper. She rifled around in her oversized bag, pulled out a notebook with a pen and positioned them on a swivel, bedside table within his reach. The words he wrote were large and child-like, but Heidi understood them. Up until that point, is writing had always been precise. She focused on his pen as it moved across the page. He requested a radio.

Heidi drove out of the hospital parking lot gripping the steering wheel so tightly that her knuckles turned white. Despite the radio playing an upbeat tune, she barely heard anything outside of her own rapid heartbeat.

After driving for half an hour in congested traffic, Heidi pulled into the closest CVS near Montgomery Mall. With an image of her father seared into her mind, she rushed into the crowded store, grabbed the nearest radio from the general merchandise shelf, and slid her credit card through the card reader at the cashier stall without even a second glance. Back in the car, she encountered red lights at each intersection before arriving at the hospital. She parked the car and took the elevator to her father's room. Thankfully, he was still hanging on, and she could tell he hardly noticed her absence.

"Hey, Dad, I'm back. Mission accomplished." She set up the blue radio and turned it on to his favorite classical music station, WGAY.

He hugged the bunny with a pleased look on his face and fell asleep. Heidi sat in the chair by the window and closed her eyes, but only for twenty minutes. She stood up and stretched before wandering out into the waiting room to find a copy of The Washington Post. Needing a temporary escape, she flipped to the *Arts and Entertainment* section for some light reading, but she got pulled back in time to her childhood Sunday memories with her dad. She gave up and walked back into his room. He was awake, and cousin stood by his side.

Edward spoke gently and calmly with nothing but affection in his voice. Her father wrote notes in response, and Heidi interpreted the lopsided scribbles. Edward took her father's hand and talked to him about faith. He sounded like a minister giving last rites.

"Uncle Nathan, you have always lived in a way that showed the kindness and love Jesus conveyed. He must be smiling at you now for your faith in Him as well as for the good you have done in this world. Can we say a prayer together?"

Her father moved his lips, but no words emerged. Instead, he squeezed his eyes closed and then open them again several times in apparent agreement.

Heidi turned to the window to view the cars parked in the asphalt parking lot several floors below, to avoid intruding on the prayer. She sniffled, wiped a tear from her eye, and tried to absorb what was happening. Edward's voice stopped, and she turned to face him.

"You're wonderful, Edward. I'm going down to the hospital cafeteria while you're here. Can you come and find me before you leave the building?"

"Sure, see you in about an hour." Edward put his arms around her, and she leaned into his shoulder.

"Dad, I'll be back in a little while. Love you." She kissed his forehead and hesitated at the door before walking out. Every time she left she worried that he'd be gone when she returned.

Chapter 28

The chicken dish she pulled off the cafeteria conveyor belt tasted like it had been overcooked and someone had forgotten to add seasoning. Heidi weighed herself on the scale in the corner, she'd lost eight pounds since this crisis began. At the table, twirling her peas in the pot pie was more soothing than anything else. Before she knew it, Edward pulled out the chair on the opposite side of the table.

"Oh, hello." Caught unawares, Heidi's knee popped up and banged into the underside of the table.

"Didn't mean to startle you." Edward cleared his throat. "Those peas look tasty. You should eat some before they become mashed."

"I know, I was zoning out again." Heidi blinked and rubbed her eyes.

"I'm sorry about your dad."

"You've been so good to my parents."

"Hey, they're my aunt and uncle, so I wouldn't have it any other way. Did anyone ever tell you how your dad helped me in Paris when I was a lad?"

"No, tell me. I need a distraction."

"You and I met for the first time in Paris when you were about four months old. You were so cute, propped up against pillows in your playpen, waiting for a bunch of women to come meet you for the first time." His unusually long eyelashes blinked several times.

"Mmm, what do you know about that time of my life?"

"I knew you were adopted and came to Paris when you were almost two months old. Nothing else though. I was too preoccupied with being seventeen at the time. Babies were the last thing on my mind."

"Makes sense. Wait, what were you going to tell me about Dad helping you?"

"Right, sorry. The winter before I met you when I was at my boarding school in Switzerland, I got a bad case of pneumonia. Your dad found a doctor who made house calls, so I didn't have to go out in the cold to a hospital. That was just the first of many times he helped me. He was the glue that held our families together."

"Yes, Dad's a kind man. These last days he keeps saying, 'Take care of your mother.' I'm not sure how to manage. It's no secret that my relationship with her isn't great."

"You've put up with a lot of nonsense from her. Most daughters would have walked away years ago."

"Well, I didn't because I couldn't cut Dad out of my life. They're a package deal. I've come to terms with her in my heart, but that required me to isolate her from many parts of my life."

"I've seen you do that over the years, and it's been hard to watch, but I know you had to for self-preservation. Yet, it seems only natural that he wants you to make sure she's taken care of. We've been managing so far, but we'll need a long-term solution."

"I know, I know." Heidi adjusted the buttons on her sweater and scooted her chair away from the table. "I need to go to the chapel alone before heading back upstairs."

"Call me if you need me. I'll stay with your mother tonight."

"You're a gem. Talk to you soon." Barely holding herself together, she hurried out of the cafeteria straight to the chapel with tears washing down her face. She dropped onto a pew, and the old wood groaned.

Sobbing, Heidi prayed, "God, I know you see everything, but I'll ask anyway. Please take Dad soon. His heart isn't working. They won't give him a new one. I don't want him to suffer. Thank you for watching over us, amen."

While Heidi sat in the chapel trying to compose herself, someone dozed on another pew. Looking around she saw sound-proof tiles in the ceiling and an altar that appeared to be a desk with a solid back facing into the room. Behind it, on a blank illuminated wall, hung a framed stained-glass sun surrounded by blue sky and scattered clouds.

She thought back to Aunt Eileen's death when she had asked God, "Who will you take next?"

She had been behind her parents' house under the den window, next to the poplar tree that loomed 50-feet above her head. She had stood and concentrated. It seemed like a guardian angel spoke to her. The voice inside her soul said, *Your father and, two years later, your mother*.

The whispers were coming true even though Aunt Eileen had been gone for ages.

Heidi finished meditating and worked her way back to her father's room.

He wrote on a page of the notebook, *Go home to your children, see you tomorrow*.

"Promise?" Heidi was reluctant to leave.

Yes, I promise.

The next day, Heidi returned. She sat with him for hours. Some of the time he was awake and wanted her to read excerpts of the *Washington Post* out loud.

Around two in the afternoon, Heidi's father only spoke one word and pat the bedsheet next to his hip several times. He said, "Gwen."

"I'll go get her, but it'll take some time."

The right side of his lips twitched.

Heidi rushed out of the hospital to the car, jumped in, and rattled the steering wheel. She shouted through her tears as she drove. Her throat clenched. "Why did Mom leave the hospital vigil all to me? Why? Why?"

She yelled some more before pulling into her parents' driveway and pushed the remote to the garage door. Getting out of the car was a struggle since she'd parked too close to the boxes on the left wall. Rather than repositioning the car, she crawled over the passenger seat and walked across the concrete floor. The door to the house stuck when Heidi turned the key, but she shoved it with her shoulder. It flew open, she lost her balance and almost smashed into one of the paintings on the side wall. No one was around to hear her curse.

As she walked into the house, she felt the silence, and it weighed her mood down even further. She grabbed hold of the white wrought iron railing on the central staircase with her right hand and forced herself upward. Turning into the hallway and then into her parents' bedroom, she saw her mother nestled under a pink woolen blanket.

Heidi said, "Mom, sorry to wake you."

"I'm not asleep, just resting."

"You have to go to the hospital. Dad wants to see you."

The response was brisk. "I can't, who will help me up the hospital stairs?"

"Mom, we can do this, we have to." Heidi was trying to be patient.

"No!" her mother cried. "My husband is dying... I need Edward."

"Edward left here this morning. He has to work today. We can take the elevator."

"No! I'm not going in those contraptions. After they stopped having operators thirty years ago, I got trapped, and I didn't know what to do."

"Yes, I know, I was there. All right. Try and call Edward." She wanted to drag her mother off the bed.

What if Dad can't hold on? Focus, I have to focus.

Heidi paced back and forth across the bedroom. She felt like a pent-up animal, and she was sure her energy negatively radiated out of her body with every step.

Her mother picked up the telephone on the nightstand. She said into the mouthpiece, "Edward... The auto-dialer is working today... The phone is ringing." Her voice elevated. "Heidi, while I'm getting up, go to the garden and cut a yellow rose."

"What?" Heidi wanted to shout at her mother, but she didn't. Instead, she paced back and forth across the room some more.

I can't believe this, Mom's thinking of flowers. Edward must have picked up the phone, she's talking again.

"This is your Aunt Gwen." She pleaded, "I need your help to get to Nathan."

Signaling toward Heidi, she said, "Go on, just do it." Her mother began to talk to Edward again, but Heidi didn't stick around to listen.

Heidi ran down the stairs and outside the front door to the garden.

Heidi, her mother, and Edward went on their way to the hospital. Standing at the bottom of the three sets of wraparound stairs, with landings in between, Heidi waited while her mother grasped the tubular railing and prepared for the ascent. Edward held her mother's free arm, and Heidi walked behind them holding the rose, without any hope of catching her mother if she fell. After a grueling half hour, they arrived on the third floor. Passing through the door into the ICU hallway, they continued arm-in-arm, three across, down the ward. Outside her father's door, they disconnected themselves from each other and entered the room.

"Stop the beeping!" The monitors got through to her mother's mostly deaf ears. She said, "How do you expect anyone to rest with all that noise? Please, put the rose on the night table."

Her father's face contorted, his eyes flickered open and turned into saucers as her mother struggled onto the bed with Edward's help. Her parent's lay together with their heads touching and held onto each other. The silence stretched into minutes until her mother sat up and recited one of her poems. It had always been his favorite.

A Rose

Oh, darling, you were so amorous when you told me I was so glamorous and luscious and delicious and wouldn't I please be yours?

I didn't say yes, but I didn't exactly say no.

Your dark eyes did so plead as you told me how desperately me you did need.

Your voice was filled with emotion as you spoke of your devotion and said you thought you would go mad if me you soon did not have.

You expressed your passion in such a romantic fashion.

You laid a long-stemmed rose on my lap and put a kiss in the palm of my hand and closed it tightly in yours, and softly you whispered, "Couldn't it be tonight? Oh, darling, you don't understand."

And I said, "Oh yes I do because I love you, too."

Her mother kissed him on the cheek just before he fell asleep with an almost imperceptible smile on his face. With help from

Edward and Heidi, her mother struggled off the edge of the bed ignoring the rose.

"Bunny—Heidi," her mother said, "please, stay here tonight."

"Come on Aunt Gwen let's go down to the lobby," Edward coaxed.

"Edward, thank God you're here to help." Heidi pointed to the heavens. "Apparently, He thinks I have a little more than I can handle on my own."

"You'll be all right." Edward squeezed her shoulder and walked out with her mother.

Heidi sat beside his bed staring at the soft plastic IV bag that dripped an infusion of saline and morphine down a tube into his arm. While thinking about his departure, she said a prayer wishing for a peaceful transition. His spirit seemed to be hovering by the ceiling even though his chest still moved up and down. She walked out of the room and turned to look through the glass. She thought; *God is surely holding him up. I'll go get a bite to eat, then come back and sit with him tonight.*

Throughout the night, Heidi sat in a chair close to her father with her hand under his. He woke up for a few minutes in the middle of the night and clutched at her hand. He said something, but she couldn't hear and put her head close to his. He hadn't been able to speak the last few days, and she knew she needed to hear whatever he said now.

"What, Dad? What did you say?"

"Forgive my secrets," he said into her ear. "I love you, good night."

She tried to stay awake but fell asleep in the chair. By seven in the morning, Heidi woke up with a jolt, pulled out of sleep by the heart machine's alarm. A nurse bustled into the room, and her father seemed to exhale.

The nurse checked his vitals. "I'm sorry, ma'am, he's gone. Do you want me to call someone?"

"Yes, please, my husband." Heidi passed a card with his number to the nurse.

Walt appeared in the corridor an hour later. She ducted into his embrace and continued to look through the glass at what remained of her father. A fresh white sheet covered his entire body.

"In the middle of the night, before Dad closed his eyes for the last time, he said, 'Forgive my secrets.' I wonder what that meant."

"We'll never know for sure." Walt hugged her, and she melted into the warmth of his arms.

"What about the kids?"

"They're at school. I drove them in before coming here. The neighbor agreed to look after them when they get home from school. She said she'd bring some dinner over tonight, so I don't have to worry about anything but you today."

"I'll have to do something for her."

"The kids have been so good." Walt massaged Heidi's shoulders. "I'll go home later on. I think your mom will need you. Let's go tell her before the doctor calls. On the way over, call Edward. I'm sure he'll agree to continue helping while things get sorted out."

"Dad is gone! I can't handle this." She was shaking.

"Yes, you can." Walt reached into his pocket and brought out a small flask. He said, "You can sip on this. It'll get you through today."

She took a sip. "Whiskey. I needed that."

They drove over to her parents' house and walked up to the front door rather than through the garage. Heidi put the key in the lock, and the chain on the other side only allowed her to open it a few inches.

"Mom? Mom?" She heard her mother shuffling the walker across the room. A little louder Heidi said, "Please, open the door."

From the other side, her mother shoved the door closed. Heidi heard the chain jingle, and she pushed gently on the wooden door until it opened. Their eyes met. Heidi knew, from the expression on her mother's face, the doctor had already called.

"Mom, I can't believe he's gone." Heidi hugged her, but her mother stood rigidly and didn't move her arms.

"Where are the children?"

"I wanted to come here first. The kids are in school. We haven't told them."

"Oh, why not?" Her mother seemed confused.

"We'll talk to them later."

"I see. Come in and wash your hands. Make some coffee and put some pastries on a plate."

Heidi made the coffee and Walt set out the pastries. Her mother stood blankly staring in their direction. In a haze, they found their way to the sunroom and sat in front of steaming cups of coffee in an uncomfortable silence until Heidi couldn't stand it another minute.

"Mom, I have to collect Dad's belongings and go to the funeral home."

"I loathe those places. Go, do what you like with your father's things. Make the cemetery arrangements. We'll do the memorial service next month. I'm not ready." Her mother's voice was uncharacteristically flat. "Just *go* and do what must be done." Her mother escorted them to the front door and closed it behind them.

Back at the hospital, they went to the front desk to pick up a paper bag containing her father's trousers, shirt, shoes, and his wallet. Inside there was a small photo of Kyle and Caleb. Had she neglected to give him a picture of the girls? No, she hadn't, but she wondered why Tessie and Claire's photos weren't there. Searching some more, she found a small piece of her mother's hair resting under a flap along with his driver's license. He seemed to be looking back at Heidi from the government photo, eerily smiling. Digging back into the bottom of the bag, she brought out the last meaningful thing—the stuffed bunny. She buried her face in its crumpled fur.

The woman at the desk interrupted her thoughts. "Ma'am, I'm sorry for your loss. Mr. Schwartz was transferred to the funeral home. Before heading over there, please go to the business office across the corridor." Heidi knew the woman didn't mean to be insensitive, yet she sounded callous. And, how did they know where to take him? She didn't remember giving them any information, and she hadn't signed anything to release him.

They walked across the hall, and the clerk handed them two bills. This woman was worse than the last. One printout was what the insurance company would be charged, and the other was for people who didn't have any coverage.

Heidi couldn't believe her eyes. "Uninsured people can't pay double for all the services. This doesn't make any sense."

The clerk took back the higher bill, and said, "I'm sorry for the confusion. I should have only given you one of those papers."

"This process is absurd. Walt, let's go." Heidi picked up her dad's belongings and threw his worn-out clothes into the nearest rubbish bin. His wallet and the rabbit would go home with her. Frantically, she pawed through the bag searching for the radio—it was gone. Letting it go was the only viable option. Going back upstairs to the wing where her father died to confront the nurses was out of the question. Instead, they drove over to the funeral home.

A man respectfully greeted them, and they followed him to an adjacent room they called a parlor. He said, "This is a difficult time, but a natural course for all of us. Even though we collected Mr. Schwartz from the hospital, you'll still need to identify him. It's our protocol."

"We understand." Walt stood tall and his nose wrinkled before he said, "I will do it."

Heidi looked at him, bewildered. "Are you sure?"

"Positive, you don't want this to be your last memory of him." Walt bent over and kissed her forehead before he left the parlor.

She sat and waited in a chair trying not to cry over what Walt was doing, but it was no use. By the time the men returned, she was sobbing a river of tears into her sleeve and choked out the words, "Thank—you—I—I—love you so much! You're amazing!"

The following Saturday, hundreds of mourners arrived at Rock Creek Cemetery's diplomatic section. Her mother didn't attend, but she gave Heidi some poems to put in his grave, along with a long string of pearls. Heidi hadn't visited the cemetery since her Aunt Eileen's death, and a sense of unimaginable dread filled her heart.

At the graveside, Edward read the familiar *Rose* poem, and guests stood in their finest mourning attire under a tent, as raindrops began to fall. Heidi imagined God crying in recognition of their loss. Her father's earthly life was over, and his rose etched urn sat on a green cloth on the ground.

"Walt, he looks like a little bit of nothing," Heidi whimpered.

"You know better. Your father was exceptional."

Kneeling down, she placed her hands on the vessel. "Goodbye, Dad."

"Come on," Walt said, ever so gently. He helped her up off the ground. "We have a reception lunch to host."

"Yes, you're right." Her voice cracked. "Walt?"

"What is it?"

"No one showed up to perform Dad's flag service—someone was supposed to bring a flag. The funeral home said they'd take care of this!" She felt frantic and clutched Walt's arm.

Walt put his arm around her and led her to the car. "You're shaking, and it's eighty degrees out here. Why don't you call the funeral home after the luncheon?"

"No, I need to take care of this now." Once they were in the car, she snatched her mobile phone out of her purse, scrolled through the phone log and hit send. "This is Heidi Bailey. My father's flag is missing."

Papers crackled through the phone line. "I'm sorry," said a voice. "We'll mail it next week."

"That isn't the point. It was supposed to be at the graveside service... I understand it's not entirely your fault, but I'm very disappointed no one contacted me with this information before the funeral... My father worked keeping this country safe his entire career! This isn't right!" Heidi exclaimed. "Please, just mail it."

Heidi pushed the disconnect button on the phone and stared through the front window. "I feel horrible."

"Well, what did they say?"

"They apologized and blamed the government. Dad gave much more of himself than he ever got back in this world."

"I'm sorry." Walt's hand landed on hers. "We'll get through the reception, and then you can rest at home. Edward's already told me he's staying with your mother this weekend."

That night, Heidi fell into a deep sleep. She woke, rubbed her eyes, reached for Walt's arm, and squeezed it. "I had a strange dream about Dad."

"Ouch! That hurts!" Walt released her fingers. "Write it down in your journal before you forget."

"I won't forget." Her voice sounded hoarse when she said, "The hospital phoned and told me to come right away. When I arrived, Dad's wispy, translucent spirit levitated over a bed. He said, 'Tell Gwen to come, this is a magnificent place, I will wait for her.' In an instant, he vanished, and I woke up."

Heidi continued to feel haunted by her father's death. She drove back to Rock Creek Cemetery to check on the progress of the headstone but regretted the decision the second she arrived. The stone hadn't been put in place. The bare ground matched the raw feeling in her heart. She got back in the car gasping for air, realizing she shouldn't have come alone. Her fingers started to tingle, and her chest hurt. She thought the symptoms would pass, but they didn't. The cell phone sat on the console next to her. After momentarily staring blankly at the keypad, she revived herself and called the doctor. After she described her symptoms and where the event occurred, the doctor didn't seem alarmed saying it was likely a 'panic attack.' To be sure, Heidi drove to the hospital with the doctor's encouragement. The drive didn't feel real. It was as if she was on auto-pilot for at least half of the time. Thinking about Walt helped her relax, but she wouldn't telephone him until the diagnosis, whatever it might be, was confirmed.

After parking the car and checking herself in at the emergency room, Heidi changed out of her clothes into a loosely-tied hospital gown that crossed over her chest. On the gurney, she gazed up at the ceiling of the examination bay and tried to focus on the sounds of the piped-in classical music. The doctor appeared, examined her, and ordered some tests which included an EKG with twelve, cold, sticky leads attached to her body and a quick blood draw. She waited with her eyes closed and tried to empty her mind. An undetermined amount of time passed.

"The tests results said your heart is in tip-top shape," the doctor said out of nowhere, and she opened her eyes. "Tell me, what happened before you came here?"

Blinking hard to shake herself back into mental awareness, she explained, "My dad died a couple of weeks ago. I went to the cemetery alone and felt swallowed up by the void. It was as if

someone grabbed my chest and squeezed the life right out of me."
She stopped talking and took a deep breath. "I promised Dad I
would look after my mother. She's disabled and housebound. I
can't figure out how to live my life with my family while keeping
the promise. My husband has been taking care of our four children
for the last two months. I'm tired. I want to go home, but Mom
needs me, too."

"How old are your children?"

"Tessie is twelve, Claire—eleven. The twin boys, Kyle and
Caleb, are six."

"Aw, the boys are still quite young. And, how old is your
mother?"

"Um, let me think—she's eighty-six."

"Oh, older than I'd expected." The doctor put his hand on
Heidi's and patted her reassuringly. "Can you get help at your
mother's house or move her to a care facility?"

"Mom will let me hire a maid and nothing more. It's
frightening to watch her in the kitchen fumbling with the dials on
the toaster oven while she holds onto her walker. She shuffles from
place to place and blindly gropes around on the counter until she
finds what she needs." Sighing, Heidi continued, "Mom can't adapt
to a new environment and will become combative. It's best to let
her stay at home."

"You need to consider your health. One person can't be in two
places at once. I can prescribe an anti-anxiety medication for the
short-term, but I recommend finding another solution with your
primary care doctor."

"Thank you, I'll start the pills now and make an appointment."
Heidi didn't think they would help. Only managing her time better
would bring her peace of mind.

Two weeks later…

Heidi and Walt got their four children out of bed, made six breakfast plates and bagged lunches, then hurried the kids out the front door at one-hour intervals to two different buses. After they were gone, Heidi sat relaxing with Walt on the back deck chatting over mugs of coffee. They sounded like any other family with both parents leaving for work, except Heidi never thought that eldercare would become such a large part of their existence. Clearly, something had to be done to stabilize their lives. Heidi continued to feel blessed to have a husband as supportive as Walt.

"You look pretty," he said. "I haven't seen you in a dress in a long time."

"Yep. I kind of like them. They look sharper than jeans and more professional. Funny, as a kid, I hated dresses and mom thought trousers of any kind weren't feminine. The only time she wore pants was on horseback, but that was long before I came into her life. Anyway, my list of duties for Mom is huge. I feel totally unprepared even though Dad left me that 'to do' list right before he went into the hospital. It still feels like he's around even though I know better." She reflected on the thought and pushed her mind back into the day's tasks. "Oh my gosh," she gasped, "my Gladiator van won't fit in the garage at the bank. I'll have to trade it for my parents' Cadillac. Besides, if Mom knew she'd be embarrassed if I took our beastie van."

"Where's the meeting?"

"At Friendship Heights."

"Where?" he said quizzically.

"Oh, you know, down where the D.C. and Maryland line connect."

"Ah."

"I've lost count of the years since I'd worked in an office." She sat and mulled it over while eating her scrambled eggs. "It's been over ten."

"You stopped a couple months before Tessie was born and we moved east. So that would be closer to fourteen years."

"Give or take, it doesn't really matter. When I woke up this morning, I realized working in an office back then was easy compared to raising children. Mom's eldercare is yet another challenge. I'm nervous about all the added responsibilities, and this upcoming financial planning meeting is making me even more on edge."

"Do you need me to come to the meeting? I can take the day off."

"No, no." She took a swig of her orange juice.

"You can do this. You're a strong woman."

"Sometimes I don't feel like it." Another swallow of coffee warmed her throat. "I had another dream about Dad last night. I was in my parents' living room. He was in the hallway standing next to the narrow table with vases full of flowers. Dad looked like his younger pictures and was wearing a suit with a rose in the lapel. He stood there gazing at me, but his lips didn't move when he said I was doing a fantastic job taking care of Mom. I felt like he was actually standing there. Then he vanished."

"Remember, that's the third dream you've had about him. The other one was almost exactly the same, except it happened in our front hallway."

"That's right, Dad said he was proud of me, and I had a good life with you."

"Glad he noticed." Walt winked and kissed her. "Go to your meeting. Everything will be fine, eventually."

"We'll see. I'll be home later. Edward's going to stay with Mom after I leave and he'll commute to work from there. For all our sakes, I need to hire a live-in maid fast."

Driving into in Bethesda with her van, Heidi parked around the corner from Brookside Drive and walked up her parents' driveway. She wasn't sure whether to call the house her parents or her mother's. The place would never be the same. Her stomach churned uncomfortably. She slipped quietly into the Cadillac, started the car, and drove into town to a high-rise garage in Friendship Heights. Walking around the other vehicles in her unfamiliar heels, she almost twisted her ankle looking for the elevator. Inside she pushed '2' and waited, the doors opened, and she stepped out. Mr. Warren's estate management firm was across the hall. The lobby was decorated in dark woods and burgundy brocade fabrics that reminded her of the first room her dad was in at the hospital.

Mr. Warren walked over to greet her. "Hello, good to finally meet you in person."

Heidi smiled and discreetly wiped her moist hand on the side of her dress before shaking Mr. Warren's massive hand.

He escorted her into his private office and passed her a cup of coffee. "How are you and your family getting along?"

"Mom is having a difficult time managing her disabilities without Dad. I need to hire someone to help when I'm not around. When she's out of bed, she can't be alone in the house. I'm afraid she'll trip over something and fall or get hurt in the kitchen."

"Your dad has left plenty of funds to provide for her needs."

"I wish my parents did more entertaining and traveling after Dad retired." She frowned. "I don't think they enjoyed the last twenty years of their life together."

"I'm sorry, that must have been difficult to watch. Let's go over the portfolio and discuss your mother's monthly budget. She'll have to do without your paternal grandmother's money, as that will be given to you each month instead. This isn't a problem because the house is paid off, and the other bills should be low."

The presentation portfolio was well organized and easy to understand. Even so, by the time they were done, Heidi's head was pounding.

Edward and Heidi worked together and, within a month, they hired Gabriella. After Gabriella started living with her mother, Heidi only visited once a week, for less than twenty-four hours at a time. Until now, Heidi hadn't appreciated all the things her father had done to support her mother's physical disabilities. They'd hidden many details that she was slowly uncovering. Each visit was like going back in time. Her mother had a rich history, but the same history was trapped within her soul, and a self-created imaginary wall kept new experiences out. It was a sad existence, and Heidi was often drawn into the sadness. If she knew how to move her mother into a happier place, she would.

On one of Heidi's weekly treks to Bethesda, she arrived at the house about one in the afternoon. As she drove into the neighborhood, the cherry blossoms were dropping their blooms on the road and the adjacent lawns. She entered through the back door of the garage and went into the house. Each time she passed by the oil paintings hanging on the back-hall wall, she made sure to close the doors in the temperature-controlled area before entering the rest of the house. In hand, she carried grocery bags full of food and a six-pack of paper towels that were used up by the end of every week. They were used in the kitchen to wipe the counters, the first-floor bathroom for quick sponge baths, and to wrap around water glasses and walker handles to act as germ barriers. Heidi left the shopping bags on the floor for Gabriella to put away in the yellow Formica kitchen cabinets. The outsides of the bags were considered dirty. Her mother wouldn't allow them to be placed on the counters. Even though she was upstairs asleep, Heidi still abided by the rules.

She climbed the main stairs to her mother's room. "Hello… hello," she sang many times. In person, Heidi spoke loudly in a low-alto voice. Sometimes she spelled the words or repeated them multiple times to be heard over the loud, high-pitched screeching tinnitus that her mother said resonated in her ears. The hearing aid, which would make life easier, only left the den's desk drawer for visitors, never for Heidi.

While Heidi waited for her mother to wake up a little more, she cleaned the bathroom, and then sat in the rocking chair and watched. Her mother groaned, and the covers wiggled around as she pulled herself out from under the blankets and shoved her crooked toes into the golden wedged slippers that waited on the floor. And then, reaching out into the air her hands groped around until they connected with the walker. The slippers concealed the front half of her feet and were lightly dusted with a coat of baby powder that Heidi wiped off every week. It seemed a rather pointless exercise since the carpet was only vacuumed with her mother's consent once or twice a year. The carpet dust hopped on the slippers as she shuffled across the room and into the bathroom. They were only worn in her suite, and she professed to never put her bare feet flat on the 'dirty' bathroom floor, even when it was clean. Each week, she said the same phrase, "Everyone should have a pair of golden slippers." Heidi would affably agree.

"Mom, can you go barefoot if you need to?"

"No, I have high arches. It hurts to put them flat on the floor, see?" Her mother put her feet down next to the tub to demonstrate before stepping over the side. Her feet were as flat as pancakes.

Heidi didn't understand the problem and kept her thoughts hidden. *Mom is cursed and blessed with her poor vision. She can't see her own physical decline. Maybe that's good since she wouldn't be able to cope with her appearance.*

While her mother sat on the plastic shower chair soaping herself with a washcloth, Heidi held the shower spray wand over her back and repeatedly moved it back and forth until her mother was done. The room steamed up over the next half hour, and Heidi felt like she was suffocating in the heat. She wished she was somewhere else, anywhere else. After her mother dried off with a towel, she stepped back over the lip of the tub straight into her golden fleece-lined slippers.

"My slippers are sticking, I can't move. Please, rinse the floor. I need to put on fresh powder and perfume. Oh, and comb my hair. My short hair is so easy; a little dab of a stiffener, and then I squeeze it into waves and it's done. I'm so glad I'm not grey. How do the roots look?"

"Mm, they're peeking out about a half inch." Heidi didn't mention that the once light brown roots were indeed mostly grey—she was sure her father had never divulged the secret either.

"No, that won't do, I'll make an appointment for the next time you're here."

"Let me know, so I can plan." They'd need to take a trip to the hairdresser carrying a box of the favored blonde, Revlon, shade. Appropriately named; golden blonde. These expeditions were the only time Heidi could convince her mother to leave the house.

"Yes, I will. Can you fix the sticky floor?"

"Mom," Heidi pause, "can you pick your feet up a little more?"

"I am picking up my feet. Don't blame me! The baby powder is the problem!" The soft powder smell wafted out of a nearby cleaning bucket, but there wasn't any on the floor anymore.

Right after they left the bathroom, her mother complained, "My carpet is old and lumpy. I can't walk. We should take it up along with the lumpy padding to make it easier to walk to and from the bathroom. But only a path, not the entire carpet. Once it's up, tape it down on the wood floor by the edges." Heidi snickered to herself at the 'we' remark.

"Mom, that will take time, I can do it when you're downstairs." Heidi pulled a plum colored dress out of the closet.

Her mother slipped the dress over her head but then panicked. She blurted out, "No! Wait! Just thinking about the old carpet is depressing. Don't bother. Let's get out of here."

Moving down the hallway to the top of the stairs next to Heidi's childhood bedroom took a good five minutes. Heidi glanced in her old room and counted the years in her head; seventeen. The décor hadn't changed since she'd left to move in with Walt.

"Okay, I'll leave the carpet along. Maybe that's better, and less of a trip hazard."

"My walker feels heavy today."

Leaving the upstairs walker behind, her mother pivoted around the railing and walked down the stairs backward. She explained, "It's easier to go down this way. I can hold on with both hands."

"Can't we just get a chair lift installed? And, a walk-in shower?"

"No! No repairmen in my house! We'll leave things as they are."

On the main level, her mother grabbed onto her downstairs walker and shuffled around over the tiles. The rest of the day was spent in the dining room at the faux marble table.

"I designed this table and had it made, isn't it wonderful! Many dinner parties were enjoyed in this room." Her mother boasted, for the hundredth time, about the table that Heidi recalled had arrived shortly before her eighth birthday.

The custom-made, tufted brocade chairs with plush-padded seats had always been comfortable for guests. Although, per Heidi's mother's instructions, Gabriella had removed one of the chairs and had replaced it with a plastic lawn chair. Everything Heidi's mother needed each day was within reach. Her mother's chair faced away from the table toward an adjacent wall where the television sat on a cart. The screen was covered with several brown paper bags to diminish the glare that hurt what was left of her mother's eyesight; she chose only to listen to the words that emanated out of the unit's speakers. Her mother's prized marble table was to the left and served as a desk. To the right, a bookshelf. A variety of items were on each of the three shelves. On the first; a box of Kleenex tissues, a flashlight, and a telephone. The next one held several sets of audiobook cassettes and a bulky player from the Library of Congress. On the last, sat a private hat box filled with absorbent incontinence pads. Sadly, at times, the sweet smell of her mother's L'Air du Temps perfume was replaced by an odor of urine.

Every visit, Heidi became her mother's second eyes. They went over the order of the audiobooks and sorted the mail. During the afternoon, they took several breaks to eat small meals. Heidi transcribed dictated letters, and poems, into her laptop. A particular poem was about an apple tree and the beaches of Normandy, France. Through the years her mother hadn't said much about WWII other than that she'd served in the USO and helped wounded soldiers. The stanzas of the poem were about a man who sat and rested his back up against an apple tree on D-Day while he thought of his family and died of his wounds. By the time Heidi finished typing in the poem, she was crying silent tears. She didn't know which man the poem referred to, but she did remember her father talking about his apple tree and the memories it invoked.

As the evening dwindled away, Gabriella brought in a try with a glass of Gordon's gin on the rocks, along with olives, nuts, and crackers. Once everything was in place, the night would keep going without Heidi.

"Mom, I've been awake since six this morning. It's almost midnight. I need to get some sleep." Heidi got up from the dining room chair. Her impatience grew. The fatigue was taking over her sense of reason.

"Before you go, please turn the television on for me. I want to listen to the news."

"Yep, yep." Flicking the switch brought instant pain to Heidi's ears. She sighed, pulled earplugs out of her pocket and rolled them in her palm before setting one in each ear canal.

"Good night, Heidi. Thank you for your help. Drive carefully through the rush hour traffic."

Heidi turned and rolled her eyes and tried to find some humor in the situation. Her current 'rush hour traffic' would consist of leaving the dining room, turning left, and stepping over the den threshold straight into the La-Z-Boy chair that was calling her name. The real rush hour in the morning would be more challenging. She yawned and stretched her arms out.

"Okay, I will. Good night, Mom," she called over her shoulder.

"Keep your mobile with you."

"I always do. It'll be on vibrate on my lap tonight." Heidi tried to keep her exasperation in check. "I wish you could go to your bed at night instead of sitting in the dining room until morning."

"And, Heidi, I wish you could sleep in your bed upstairs, but you can't for some reason. The truth is," her mother called out in a desperate tone of voice, "I don't want to die in my bed, in the dark. I can't get in bed until the sun comes up—I just can't."

"Mom that's the saddest thing I've ever heard. Try and get some rest, I'll call you tomorrow afternoon." Heidi walked away and settled into her chair hoping the night would pass by quickly so she could get back to Walt and the children.

Chapter 30

A year later, 2001…

Whenever there was an opportunity, Heidi asked her mother to tell a story about her past. On this visit, her mother declared she would never tell another story as they all reminded her of happier times and did nothing but depress her. Instead, she asked Heidi to pull a box out of the basement from the ones that were sorted and categorized. Heidi found a box labeled 'Gwen's memorabilia' and brought it to her mother's feet. Blindly she shuffled through and drew out a piece of paper for Heidi to read out loud. Heidi began reading the headline, and her mother stopped her in mid-sentence. It wasn't much of anything, just an old advertisement of a woman doing laundry in the 1950s.

"Are there any photos of my younger self? It is time to write my obituary. You know, I'm going to die of old age soon. I have to face reality."

"We can wait, no rush." Heidi's heart felt like it had moved into her throat.

"No, we must do this today, but let me rest for ten minutes in my chair. I forgot to put a coffee cake on your shopping list. Please go to Safeway and pick one up. If they don't have any hop over to the bakery across the road. Bunny, please?"

"Okay, rest for an hour or so."

"Why so long?"

"Um, I need to tend to the roses before we work today."

"Yes, you should. Go on then. I'll be right here."

After the quick stop at the store, Heidi went into her father's garden on the side of the property. She noticed the rose bushes were tall and straight with only one magnificent yellow bloom. Over the last year, she'd barely managed to keep the plants healthy, and most of the flowers either wilted or were plagued by insects without her father's touch.

A jogger, whom she had never seen before, ran by and commented, "Beautiful roses, my dear." The man had a wrinkled and sun-parched face.

Then another man of similar looks, who couldn't jog since he was even older, strolled by. He called out in a wispy voice, "What lovely yellow roses."

Wait, there's only one. I'm confused, what's going on? Why are these people coming through the side yard, and into the neighbor's property? I must be imagining things.

She stood there looking at the single rose, then looked down at herself and realized she was wearing a yellow blouse.

Could I be the other yellow rose? Maybe I'm my mother's angel, fulfilling the promise to my father. That sounds absurd and egotistical. God isn't talking to me through these old men; or is He? I don't deserve to be called an angel. I never help enough.

She remembered a long-gone neighbor who once had the most exquisite rose garden she'd ever seen. The bushes lined the backyard in rows. Each stem had perfect glossy leaves, with beautiful fragrant blooms. When the old lady's property was sold, the roses vanished, and the house was demolished. Heidi heaved a sigh. After *Mom is gone, I'll take my father's roses to our garden.*

When she went into the house, her mother was moving about with her walker. The cut tennis balls jammed on the ends of the contraption's legs helped it run smoothly across the tiled floor, but it still made a thumping noise when she picked it up to turn left or right. Once her mother settled down in her plastic cushioned chair, she began to dictate her obituary and all the instructions for her memorial service. Heidi tried to stay focused, but her shoulders and neck tensed with every word she typed. The task was almost too much to bear.

That night, Heidi slept for a few hours in the den La-Z Boy before her mobile vibrated in her lap. Rubbing the clouds of sleep from her eyes, she struggled with the lever on the recliner to help her get up and stumbled over to the dining room.

"What's wrong, Mom? Can I do something for you?"

"Call Edward before he goes to work." Her mother's breath was ragged. "Call Dr. Tomlin when the office opens."

"We shouldn't wait. I can call an ambulance." Heidi tried to speed up the process, but the effort created less cooperation and heightened resistance.

God, I think Mom's having a panic attack. Help! What do I do? Maybe a paper bag to blow in—no, she's claustrophobic.

"I'm *not* dying today," Her mother snapped defiantly and sipped some water from a nearby glass. "I want to finish my poems." Her mother breathed in and gagged on a cough that didn't quite erupt. "Call Edward! No, don't. Wait until eight o'clock."

Heidi did as she was told.

∽ꝺꝎ

When Edward arrived, Heidi started the car in the garage so he could help her mother down the hall. Heidi worried that a pattern was emerging and that this would be a one-way medical trip like her father's. It didn't take long to get over to the office. As soon as they were inside, Doctor Tomlin's nurse escorted her mother into an examination room. While Heidi waited with Edward, they sat and read magazines without any discussion of what might lay ahead. After some time passed, the doctor appeared in the waiting room, and spoke directly to Edward and instructed him to wait with his aunt in her office, rather than leaving Heidi's mother alone. Edward obliged.

The doctor explained, "Last year when your mother came to the office, the tests showed she had a treatable heart condition. I tried to medicate her then, but she refused. Now, she needs a diagnostic scan of her torso."

"I don't understand. What's that for?"

"On this visit, I found a lump in her abdomen. We might be able to help her, but so far she won't consent to the tests."

"That sounds bad. I should tell you, against my mother's wishes, that her bowels are rarely right. She refuses to sit on the toilet seat, and I have to clean up messes when I go over every week. Mom also uses insufficient pads in her bed rather than getting up and going to the toilet. The sheets should be changed daily, except she won't allow the maid in her room. I've suggested alternative pads or methods, but those ideas aren't going over well either. My dad briefly mentioned that he had to deal with this too, so it's been going on for quite a while. He didn't know what to do, and now I have no idea either." Heidi felt rather desperate about the situation and ashamed she'd violated her mother's trust by confiding in the doctor.

"I see, that's a problem, but it was right to tell me. It's not easy to convince her to get proper care. Believe me, I've tried. Whether we agree or not, she knows her own mind, and won't be swayed. Don't lose sight of the fact that your mother's in her late eighties and has many disabilities that she's fully aware of."

"Yes, I realize. You're the professional, what should we do?"

Doctor Tomlin handed Heidi some scripts. "Tell you what, fill these prescriptions down the hall and see what you can do when you get your mother home. Make sure she takes, at least, the diuretic. She's got to get off the extra fluid that's built up in her system. Her heart's more critical than the lump at this point. I gave her an ultimatum. Either go to the hospital today to have them supervise her medications or have a nurse come to the house tomorrow. Unbelievably, she agreed to one visit from the nurse. Maybe that's a start in the right direction, and more visits can be added. I'll make the arrangements, and we'll see what happens." The doctor shook Heidi's hand and disappeared.

Edward drove them back to Bethesda, but he couldn't stay.

Inside the house, her mother announced she was tired and instructed Heidi to cover a chair with green plastic bags in the dining room to keep the area free of germs from the doctor's office. After some more conversation, Heidi convinced her to take one baby aspirin, plus a heart tablet. The diuretic was dismissed because going to the toilet every twenty minutes was a 'nuisance.' Heidi tried earnestly to convince her mother why it was important.

"I can't hear you," her mother said in a sing-song voice while covering her ears.

"You heard what I said," Heidi spoke through clenched teeth.

"You're being bitchy," replied her mother.

"I do not appreciate being called a bitch."

"I did not! I used the adjective form, which is bitchy. I wouldn't forgive myself if I called you a bitch."

Under her breath, Heidi growled so low that no one else could possibly hear. She said, "Yes, but once, I called you that; I wonder if you remember. I still haven't forgiven you for telling me to divorce Walt and get rid of my unborn child."

"Do you understand?"

"Oh, for heaven's sake! I just want you to take your medications." Heidi shook her head and got back on track. "Life could be so much easier for you. Why are you so resistant?"

"Go easy on me; I'm old and fragile," her mother whined.

"I'm only trying to help, and sometimes you're hard-headed."

"I never thought my life with your father would turn out the way it did—and now I'm terribly decrepit—being pleasant is often beyond me."

"You and Dad were together more than fifty years. There were tough times in your lives, but you had each other."

"That's true, but he was difficult to get along with sometimes."

"We all have struggles," Heidi replied instead of saying the words that ran through her head. *You charmed everyone, but Dad and I knew the truth. He was a saint to deal with your constant nonsense, but he's gone now, and you don't even seem to miss him.* Heidi reined in her emotions but was eager to go home and leave her mother alone with Gabriella. Instead, she took the more sensible approach and stayed overnight.

The nurse's visit was staged right down to the last detail. Her mother applied outdated baby blue eyeshadow thickly from brow to lashes, then caked mascara on the fine lash hairs that remained. Followed by a dash of red on her lips, and—for the last touch—she firmly clipped one pearl earring onto each earlobe. The nurse arrived, and they sat in the hall. Her mother on one garden chair and the nurse on another, next to the hall table covered with green plastic bags. The woman didn't seem at all fazed by the odd situation throughout the examination. Heidi stood with her back up against the nearest wall without blinking.

The front doorbell rang. Heidi was startled out of her daze. She headed to the door and opened it after she was sure who was on the other side.

Her mother hissed, "Who's there, what do they want?" She escaped the nurse, moved across the room with her walker faster than she had in ages, and forcefully pushed Heidi out of the way. The postal worker passed the mail over and fled.

Heidi glanced at the nurse and watched her scribble on a pad of paper.

After the nurse left, her mother disappeared into the hall bathroom. While Heidi waited, she opened up her laptop on the dining room table and prepared for whatever task might come next. Her mother appeared and rustled around the bookshelf before sitting down in the adjacent chair.

Heidi rubbed her neck and came to a decision; the timing seemed ideal. She began, "Mom, you need daily visits from a caregiver to help with showers, changing your sheets, and other stuff that will help you stay healthy. Gabriella will cook your meals, and I will keep coming once a week to transcribe your writing and bring your groceries. I'm always rushing about, and there aren't enough hours in a day. My children need more of my time—especially the boys."

"You knew your father and I were struggling. I don't understand why you waited so long to have the twins. You were practically forty by the time they were born!"

"Mom, what can I say? Life is full of surprises." A nerve in Heidi's eye twitched. "Hey, you were practically fifty when I came along."

"That's beside the point," her mother roared. "Your children will have to tolerate my needs, and furthermore, my personal care is your job. How do you expect me to be exposed to a stranger?"

"I see, but they're trained to look after people, like the lady who came today. She was very nice. But, if that's how you feel, how about going to a smaller place that's a little closer to my house?"

"Don't worry," an odd smile popped on her face, "I'll be dead soon, and you can spend all your time with the children."

"Ouch, Mom, that hurts." Heidi thought; *dead comment, thanks! You know how to unhinge me more quickly than anyone else in the world.*

"I love my home, and I refuse to go anywhere else!" Her voice cracked. "I don't want to follow other peoples' rules or be with anyone when I'm not feeling well. Nathan tried to talk me into moving a decade ago when my eyes failed. I didn't want to leave then, and I still don't. Your grandfather lived in a nursing home the last years of his life; those places aren't for me."

"Mom, things have changed since then. There are other places you can live that are nothing like that."

"I'm staying here. We are managing fine without changing things. Don't bother trying to talk me into anything else. Edward and other people I know, who are still alive, have told me all about retirement communities with assisted living."

"Okay," Heidi sighed. She withdrew into her thoughts while her mother fussed with her audiobooks to further side-step the topic. Moving was scary for anyone, but for a woman like her mother, it was terrifying. Perhaps Heidi understood, maybe a little. She lamented over how sad it was that her mother couldn't read any of the books on the shelves in the den that she'd intended to read in her old age. But her eyes prevented her from seeing words that were less than three inches tall and held up close to her face. She was like an older model of Helen Keller, living in a restricted world, mostly blind and deaf. Add anxiety and OCD to the recipe, and you get a woman shut in her home. Heidi still wanted a better life for her mother, but there was nothing left to do beyond helping her feel at ease. It was time for her mother's cleansing shower, and Heidi dutifully followed her up the stairs.

After the usual bathing procedure, Heidi sat in the adult sized rocking chair in the bedroom and waited.

She watched, thinking to herself, *Mom's never been shy about parading around the upstairs like a nudist. Poor, dear. She moves across the room, old and sagging, yet her words and behavior have never changed over the decades. I see her, a young soul trapped in an ancient body, struggling through the middle of the room clinging to her walker.*

Her mother dried herself while sitting on the edge of the queen bed. The empty spot where Heidi's father once slept forever vacant. On the edge of Heidi's consciousness, she heard her mother say, "I'm going to get dressed…"

"What?" Heidi jolted back from her contemplations. "I'm sorry, I didn't hear you."

"Don't question me. I don't want to go up and down the stairs alone anymore. Besides, I don't like being so far away from Gabriella. I feel so isolated when she's in her room in the basement. Move a twin bed downstairs. I can't sleep up here anymore."

"Sounds like a good idea. I should get a portable phone for you too."

"We can try but you know I'm not good with gadgets. Also, take my dresses down and hang them in the hall closet across from the powder room. I'm happy you made me so many in different colors—they're fashionable and easy to put over my head."

"You're welcome." The dresses weren't her mother's usual high-fashion garments, but they were classic and comfortable. These latest ones were loose, with a shirt collar, and rolled sleeves. Each made of a crisp, no-iron, washable Pima cotton.

"Oh, and I have one more job for you," her mother continued. "Take the plastic bin downstairs with my underclothes and put it on the sofa. I need to be able to reach them when I'm sitting on the bed."

"Okay, Mom, I'll fix everything when you're downstairs eating."

"Thank you. Write yourself a check for twenty-five hundred dollars. I'd rather give you the money than have someone else care for me. I'll make my own way down the steps." Her mother shuffled along and disappeared.

Hadn't we been through enough the last couple days? Now, this! I'll use a piece of plastic to slide the mattress along to keep the carpet dust out. Why doesn't Mom understand? I'm being torn apart inside. I don't think this is what Dad had in mind when he asked me to look after her. I hope I never put our children in the same position. Heidi stopped mulling over the 'what ifs' and got the job done.

"Okay, Mom, I've moved everything. Today went by quickly, and I need something to eat." She popped into the kitchen and asked Gabriella to heat up the casserole she'd brought from home. Heidi ate and then got to work helping her mother by reading the mail, discussing her audiobooks, and going over which charities to donate to by the end of the month.

It was ten o'clock before Heidi realized, and she felt worn out. "Mom, you need anything before I go to sleep?"

"No, not really. Can you ask your computer a question for me? It's incredible that you can type in queries without ever going to a research library. Technology confounds me! I can't even use a television remote without struggling. Ask the computer about Van Gogh paintings."

"Van Gogh?"

"Yes. I recall liking his paintings; they were quite captivating. I never read about his background when I could see well enough to visit museums. Your dad and David loved art. Every time they got a chance, they were off to exhibits and auctions. They only bought a few things, but they're on the walls in the back hall."

"I know, I know. Okay, I'll help you, but I can only find the answers on the internet from home. I can't access it from here. When I phone tomorrow for your wake-up call, I'll tell you what it says about Van Gogh." She sympathized with her mother's need for companionship, but such stalling tactics kept Heidi awake longer than she wanted and grated on her nerves. She reminded herself to be patient.

Chapter 31

One year later, 2002…

Heidi spent yet another Thursday afternoon and evening with her mother. On Friday morning, before Heidi got into her car and drove away, she checked on her mother who was sound asleep on the bed in the living room. The bed seemed out of place in a room which was once used for lavish parties.

Three days later, mid-morning, the phone rang, and the caller ID read, 'Schwartz.' Heidi was concerned right away since her mother never called until after seven o'clock to hear about the family's day. She picked up the phone and was surprised to hear Gabriella's voice on the other end of the line.

"Morning, is everything okay?"

"No, Ma'am. I was eating my breakfast and heard Mrs. Schwartz calling for help from the living room. When I got there, she was on the floor. I tried, but I couldn't lift her."

"Does she want an ambulance?"

"No, she said to call you."

"I understand, tell her I'm coming. Call an ambulance if she starts slurring her words or goes unconscious."

Forty minutes later, Heidi found her mother sitting patiently on the floor, with her back up against a velvet loveseat across from the bed. Gabriella and Heidi hoisted her up onto the mattress. Her mother was quite embarrassed and didn't know how she fell, but she was more concerned about bathing. She pulled herself back up with the walker, shuffled across the floor, and up the stairs with labored determination.

Getting over the lip of the bathtub and into the waterproof chair challenged her mother even more than usual. Heidi grabbed her when she started to fall and tilted her into the chair. In the process, her mother reached out with one hand and hooked onto Heidi's waist to stabilize herself. "Oh, my, Heidi, you've gotten fat."

"Gee, thanks. Did you have to mention that right now? You almost fell again, and my back is still spasming from earlier. We're quite a pair today." She couldn't remember when her mom had last had a sensitivity filter and then scolded herself for grumbling about such things when there were more important things to fret over.

The entire process of getting her mother ready to go downstairs took three hours. Once she was settled into her cushioned plastic chair, her mother wanted to eat, but couldn't put a bite into her mouth without feeling nauseous.

"Mom, you need to go to the hospital. I'm calling Edward."

"He was here the other day. I don't want to bother him again. I'll ask Gabriella for soup and toast."

When the soup was heated, Gabriella placed it on the table within reach. Her mother attempted to eat a spoonful but couldn't. She placed the spoon down on a napkin, then tried the toast.

Shaking her head, she said, "No, I can't eat this either."

"Mom, you look gray." Heidi put the back of her hand on her mother's forehead. "I'm going to call an ambulance."

"I'll get up; you can drive me." Her mother couldn't stand. "Oh, dear. What's happening to me? My tummy feels hard."

"I'm calling for help." Heidi phoned for emergency services, then Edward—he would meet them at the hospital.

The paramedics arrived fifteen minutes later and gently picked her mother up out of the chair and placed her on a wheeled gurney. During the process, she appeared to be paralyzed with fear and verbalized her distress with groans and awkward objections. The ambulance drove off, and Heidi followed with the Cadillac.

In the emergency ward, her mother was moved to a curtained-off triage area. Heidi held back and proceeded to fill out the necessary hospital forms. When she was done, she moved closer to the curtained off area where her mother was being examined. From the opposite side of the corridor, Heidi could see shadows of the staff and hear everything. It felt like a horrible dream, and she wanted to wake up.

Over and over her mother cried out, "Leave me alone! No, no!"

Heidi wanted to help but stood frozen in place and resisted the urge to run. Her stomach felt queasy. Eventually, a doctor appeared and took Heidi to her mother's bedside to discuss his evaluation. Keeping her mother's fears in mind, he said, a barium x-ray would be the least invasive diagnostic tool he could use. Her mother consented, but only with Heidi's persistent encouragement.

"Okay, Mom, now you need to drink some flavored water before the test." Heidi felt guilty because she didn't say the fluid contained a substance that would make the scan clearer. She purposely left out that information because she knew her mother would become combative again.

"I'm drinking, see—" her mother held up the jug— "but it tastes peculiar." She continued to sip it through a straw and drank half of what was required, with the doctor excusing her from drinking the rest.

The tests revealed that an area in her mother's GI system had shut down somehow and she'd need a bowel resection. Her mother briefly asked if she could go home and wait a few days, but the doctor said she wouldn't survive if they delayed.

"All right, Doctor, you may operate." Her mother reached out for Heidi's hand, and said, "Promise me you'll publish my poetry if I die."

"Mom, please—you'll make it—but yes, I promise." Heidi felt a huge knot in her throat. Promising her parents things hadn't turned out well so far.

"One more thing." Her mother slid her wedding rings off her finger. "Take these. They're yours now."

"Mom, please, don't." Heidi took the rings and scrunched up her face to try and stop the tears.

A nurse wheeled her mother out of the emergency room into surgery. Edward and Heidi waited in the family room and drank vending machine coffee.

Heidi spoke in a low monotone, "Edward, I have a bad feeling about this. Can you stand vigil while I close my eyes? I won't be able to do anything later if I'm exhausted."

"Of course," Edward responded.

There wasn't any place to lay down other than next to the ATM bank machine on a cushioned bench. She put her empty coffee cup down on the floor, rested her head on her carpetbag purse and closed her eyes. A little while later she jolted upright. In the cup there sat a couple of quarters. She knew Edward was trying to lighten her mood, but the humor escaped her. Eyeing her watch, she noticed almost three hours had gone by since her mother had been wheeled away.

The swinging double doors opened, and the surgeon emerged. The tension in the room was palpable. The doctor said, "Things were touch and go." He wiped the perspiration from his forehead. "We found things that didn't show up on the images. A cancerous mass was growing in her appendix. It became inflamed and ruptured. We cleaned it up as best as we could before Mrs. Schwartz's heart became unstable. If she can recover enough, we can go back in and do the needed bowel resection. I'm sorry we couldn't do everything at once."

"I had no idea! I thought appendicitis caused excruciating pain. Mom didn't complain about anything over the last few days."

"That's not unusual for people her age."

"When can I see her?"

"She'll be in recovery for the next hour or so. Take some time to collect yourself. She's going to need a lot of support."

"I understand." Heidi watched the doctor pass back through the swinging doors. She looked over at Edward, and he put his hand on her shoulder and spoke some reassuring words. Sighing, she slid her mobile out of her pocket and told Edward she needed to take a walk alone. Then, catatonically she flipped the phone open to call Walt as she passing the nurse's station.

An attendant interrupted, "Ma'am you okay?"

"No, I'm not. My mother is very sick."

"I'm sorry. There's a chapel down the hall if you need some rest."

"Thank you." Heidi closed her mobile, deciding she'd make the call later.

Sitting in the chapel, Heidi wept. Too many tears had been shed over the past few years. This chapel—the same one she'd sat in before her father died—didn't bring her any consolation. After some time, her tears dried, and she escaped reality by drifting off into a dreamless sleep.

Startled, she woke to mumbling sounds. A man in hospital scrubs was praying. She thought again of the people who act like angels to the needy. People who appear at the most unlikely times, strange—yet familiar—who do or say something helpful. Unexplainably, this praying man soothed her soul. She rubbed the kinks out of her shoulders. Her electronic watch flashed in the dim light, and she noticed another hour had gone by.

Upon leaving the chapel, Heidi found out that her mother had been admitted to a private room and hurried in. Edward was standing by the bedside. Her mother's eyes fluttered open, but she only remained awake long enough to grab Edward's hand and release it before she fell back asleep.

"The doctors said she should be fully awake by morning," Edward said. "There's nothing we can do other than taking turns sitting with her. She'll feel more vulnerable than most with her vision issues."

"Thank you for being here. It's hard to believe we're going through this again. It seems like yesterday since we teamed up to help Dad."

"It's been nearly two years," Edward whispered. "Poor Uncle Nathan. We all miss him so much."

Every time her mother woke, she began mumbling about events from years before. "Tell Nathan to buy theater tickets for Macbeth... The dog is making a mess of the trash cans. I'll tell the maid to clean it up... Bunny, stop biting your nails." On and on, day after day, remarks from the past reemerged. The staff called them temporary post-surgical psychosis that were supposed to dissipate but remained. Heidi became more worried and frustrated with each passing day. She tried kept her emotions under control, but being called Bunny made her feel weak and exposed.

Heidi and Edward each took eight-hour shifts. For the other eight, she left her mother with the hospital staff. Two weeks crawled by, Heidi felt utterly lost. Unexpectedly, Claudia appeared in the doorway. In a controlled whisper, she said, "You're here! Mom's sleeping." Heidi hurried across the room and wrapped her arms around her dear friend. "I didn't think you were moving back to D.C. until next month?"

"Surprise! The plans changed. I drove here right away after I talked Walt. I'll need to go back to finish packing, but that should only take a couple of days."

"Thank you for coming. It's been ages since we've seen each other. Mom's suffering from hallucinations. The episodes should have been over soon after surgery, but they're not. It's been ten days. The doctor said we shouldn't role-play, but there's nothing else to do. When I talk to Mom about current events, she's only present for a short time before her eyes glaze over. You'll see what I mean when she wakes up."

"It can't be any harder than talking to my mom."

"Yeah, that's true. But, it's rougher on you since it's been going on for years. I'm glad you're both moving back here. Sadie is so sweet, even with dementia."

And, then, Heidi's mom woke up and began talking. "Please tell Nathan to put the liquor bottles in the cabinet when he comes back." Her mother continued to talk about chores and inconsequential things. Finally, she revolved around to her daily repetitive script, and said, "Help me upstairs, I want to take a shower."

Heidi held out her arm. Her mother grabbed on and tried to pull herself up from the already raised bed, but she was too weak and fell back onto the pillow.

"What is this? Too tight. Get it off me!" Her mother tugged at the edges of the pressure bandage that stretched across her mid-section.

"Mom, you had an operation. Please, leave the bandage alone."

"Operation? An operation for what?"

"A burst appendix," Heidi said.

"Oh." Her mother spread her palms across her belly. "I need to go upstairs."

Heidi and Claudia played along with the charade, but Heidi was sure her mother wouldn't have agreed with the word, charade.

This situation was nothing less than tragic and could've been avoided if she had been treated earlier and her appendix hadn't ruptured.

"I'm sorry, Claudia, I have to ask. Can you stay with Mom while I run away? I need a real shower."

"Sure."

"Thanks, I'll be back in a bit."

Heidi drove the twenty minutes it took to return to her parents' house, knowing it would be a quiet and private place to shower. Despite the peace and privacy, she couldn't escape the dread that crept into her subconscious. At the house, she slipped through the garage door into the hallway, closing the door behind her. Only the kitchen lights were on. Quietly, she walked into the room and paused at a yellow notepad sitting on the counter. It was from Gabriella stating she'd gone to a friend's apartment until she was needed again. Also, she hoped that Mrs. Schwartz would recover soon and left a phone number, which Heidi appreciated.

In the old bathroom, Heidi had shared with her father upstairs, she turned on the tub spigot to the highest temperature she could tolerate and pushed the button to engage the shower. The room began to fill with steam. She stripped off her clothes and ducked behind the frayed shower curtain. The hot water spilled over her head, she could feel the tension in her neck ebb, and her mind began to clear. She recalled the days she used to have breakfast with her father. How she'd sit on the other side of his newspaper, waiting for his attention. It struck her that maybe she hadn't taken the time to properly mourn after his death. Day-to-day obligations, childcare, combined with eldercare, and everything else in between used up so much energy. She hadn't taken time to focus on her own emotional needs. Little by little that pent-up, suffocating feeling of loss overwhelmed her, and she struggled to maintain a levelheaded attitude until her convulsive tears mixed in with the water and disappeared down the drain. All too often, she refused to succumb to tears. This was her moment to sort out her feelings, and to get herself centered again before going back to the hospital.

With a renewed sense of determination, she scrubbed her face with a washcloth until it felt raw. Thinking back to every little thing that irked her about her relationship with her mother, she mused, *I'm too damn sensitive! I need to forgive Mom… Just forgive her and go on with my life!*

The water ran cold. Heidi wrapped a threadbare towel around herself, dried off, and got dressed.

What am I sensing in the house? No lingering souls, nothing. Everything that ever happened here seems to have vanished. Think, Heidi, think. I wish our dog were here to help fill the emptiness I feel in every corner. I remember bringing Dante once, but Mom said I had to tie him up on the same tree Dad and I had hung twinkle lights on for his retirement party. The only other memory I can stir up revolves around Dad and me painting my room pink. Really? I'm lame. Why can't I come up with any happy thoughts about Mom? Maybe I need time, and I'll think of some. Enough! Just get out of this house.

Heidi drove back to the hospital. She found Claudia sitting in the corner reading *Harry Potter and the Goblet of Fire*—J.K. Rowling's fourth book. "Your mom passed out. Heidi, it is time for us to do the same. I plan to stay in the hospital tonight."

"I'd rather talk about your life's adventures, but you're right. We should rest."

Heidi stared at Claudia as she adjusted and blanketed the hospital room's recliner. Claudia then said, "Goodnight, I'm going to read in the waiting room for a bit. Harry's getting into all sorts of trouble."

"I know, I know," Heidi replied. "I love reading the series to the kids."

Claudia turned away and walked out.

Heidi stood at the window. How many days had she and Edward taken shifts in this room? She'd lost track. This particular night seemed very dark.

Claudia came back into the room. "Hey, you're not sleeping in that beautiful recliner."

"Funny."

"No, really, what are you thinking about?"

"Everything and nothing. My mind isn't settling down. That, and I'm sick of reclining chairs. I'm going to the bathroom down the hall." Heidi walked past her mother's bed and private bathroom.

"You have fifteen minutes." Claudia cajoled.

"You're a goof. You're right though, I should hurry. We never know how long Mom will sleep, and I need to catch as many z's as possible." Heidi left the room.

She finished in the public bathroom and diverted to the nearest elevator. The door opened, she stepped in and pushed the button for the ground floor. She wanted to go into the maternity ward and admire the newborn babies. The entrance door was locked. Walking soothed her but seeing the babies would've helped more. Heidi went back upstairs to the 'sad' ward.

"How did I do? Did I meet my fifteen-minute deadline?"

Claudia's eyes looked stern. "Almost," she purred. "Goodnight."

Heidi watched her best friend walk toward the lounge before getting into the recliner and dozed off until midnight. After a few restless moments in the chair, she wandered out to Claudia's spot, but she was gone.

The next morning, she stepped into the hall and found Claudia back in place with breakfast for two on the table.

"Morning. Where'd you sleep?" Heidi asked.

"In my car with a blanket. I don't think car camping's my thing; too cramped."

"Thank you. I don't know how I'd manage without you and Edward, but what about your work?"

"I'm transitioning down here from my New York firm and arranged to have a couple weeks off. Truthfully, it was purely coincidental this happened before I called your house and talked to Walt. My new apartment in D.C. isn't available yet, but I'll find another place to stay. I'll help wherever you need me; here or with the kids. It's a balancing act, but we'll get through this together."

"Thanks. You can stay at my parent's house or maybe Edward's place."

"Hmmm, I'm not sure. I'll figure it out later."

Heidi's mother was awake when they re-entered the room. Again, Heidi explained about the surgery.

"Nooo! An operation?" Her mother's head turned. She squinted at the wall. "Wait, those people in the corner, I think I recognize them. Who are they?"

"Mom, I can't identify them. Who do they look like?"

"My parents." Her mother spoke to the invisible people. "Hello. It's wonderful to see you." Her eyes came alive, and her joy filled the room.

"God, what is happening?" Heidi whispered. Then louder, she asked, "Mom, your parents are over there?"

Her mother didn't respond.

Heidi surmised that angels must be in the room. Yet, it seemed like an illogical explanation.

The doctor appeared behind Heidi and whispered, "I don't think this is the medication anymore. People often see things we can't toward the end of their lives. Let's go out in the hall and talk. If your mom says anything else, you can pop back in."

Following him, Heidi almost cried out but restrained herself. "What? I thought you could repair the damage?"

"She's frail, and her kidneys are failing. There's nothing more we can do at this point. The best choice is hospice care. I'm sorry."

In a state of disbelief, with the help of a social worker, Heidi went through the motions of making the needed arrangements for her mother to be transferred by ambulance to a room in a center called Brookdale, in Alexandria, for palliative care. It seemed strange to Heidi that they'd found a place named similarly to the name of her parents' street in Bethesda. Then she discovered that her father had put them on a waiting list years ago, which made the admission process less painful—it was a strange twist of fate. They hired around the clock nursing care. Heidi was relieved to know her mother would never be alone. During her conscious moments, she only drank Ensure protein shakes with the hospice medications and continued to appear unaware of her surroundings.

Before Heidi decided to go home three evenings later, Edward arrived. Heidi wanted to stay longer, but she needed to sleep at home and explain the current situation to their children even though Walt was there for them. She kissed her mother on the forehead and left her with Edward and the attending nurse.

Heidi received a call four hours later. Edward said, "Hi, I'm on my way home. Aunt Gwen is fine with the nurse. You won't believe what happened. I sat with her for a while and then she changed. We had a real conversation. She sounded more like herself. At one point, she even asked where you were. I said you were sleeping. And she said you like to sleep a lot." The phone crackled. "She said something else... She said you're a good daughter, which is no surprise, but then she said, you have a good life with Walt." Edward paused. "I never thought I'd hear her utter those words."

Heidi's words caught in her throat. "She *really* said that?"

"Yes, and she was fully conscious." Edward's words came out emotionally charged. "This is what you wanted to hear all these years. It's her last gift to you."

Heidi raised her head to the heavens and took a deep tearful breath. "Thank you, God!" Then spoke over the phone line. "Edward, you're a jewel of a man. I'll see Mom in the morning."

The private nurse phoned later that night. "I'm sorry to bother you in the middle of the night."

"What time is it?"

"Two in the morning."

"What's wrong?"

"A short while ago, your mother said she was dying."

"Yes, well… wait, what? I'm sorry, what is happening?" Heidi rubbed the sleep out of her eyes.

"I'm sorry, but your mother passed away ten minutes ago."

"She…" Heidi was fully awake and pushed on Walt's arm. "Wake up. Mom's gone." Even though she expected her mother's life would end, she was unprepared for the call.

Heidi wanted the nurse to be quiet, but the woman kept talking on the other end of the phone. "Her passing was peaceful. Your mother is with the angels now."

"Thank you, can you stay?"

"Of course, I'm sorry for your loss," the nurse replied. "We will see you soon."

Heidi got dressed and got in the car with Walt. He drove her back to Brookdale for a last goodbye. The nurse had brushed her mother's hair and tucked the blankets around the rest of her lifeless body. She seemed thinner than the day before, and her full cheeks had sunken and wrinkled; her soul was gone. Until that day, her face had never looked a day over sixty, but there was death hiding behind her mother's sealed eyes. Heidi felt a breeze wash across her face from somewhere distant.

At the funeral home, Heidi picked out a marble urn. It looked like the marble dining room table her mother adored. They would bury the urn next to her father's and place one more name on the tombstone.

Chapter 32

The service was scheduled at Saint Albans' Episcopal Church, followed by the reception in a banquet room in Edward's apartment building. Heidi's father died two years prior, during the first week of March. Every year, Heidi knew that when she'd see the cherry blossoms, she would think of both their deaths. She hoped that her own birthday wouldn't remain clouded by their loss and that in time the raw spot in her heart would be replaced by comforting memories.

Heidi went over to Edward in the hall. "Thank you for all the help. I want to give you my parents' Cadillac."

"Really?" he said with surprise. "Are you sure?"

"Of course, I want you to have it. The car's parked out front and you can take it today. I'll send the paperwork next week." Heidi hugged Edward and noticed he felt thinner.

"I can park the car in my garage around the corner. Do you have a way to get back home?"

"Yes, Walt brought our car. Oh, before I forget to tell you, I took the Cadillac through the automatic car wash yesterday. The brushes whooshing over the windshield made me think of Dad.

When I was a kid, we went there twice a month. He used to say the water was like being in a magical rainforest."

Heidi left Edward and found Walt strolling around idly talking to the guests while their children sat at the bar drinking sodas. She crumpled her unspoken eulogy script in her pocket. Speaking in front of groups was always a nerve-racking experience and, at the last minute, she backed out of sharing her mother's private life with the congregation.

Someone called her out of her thoughts for a family photo. Walt, Heidi, and their children—Tessie, Claire, Kyle, and Caleb—stood on a set of stairs with ten other relatives who dispersed right after the photograph. The moment blurred in her heart. All at once she mourned the loss of both parents and wondered what would come next.

She scanned the room looking for Edward. "There you are. I have a verse Mom recorded about rabbits. Can you tell the story about naming my furballs before we play it?"

"Not a problem." Edward walked to the front of the room. "Everyone, may I have your attention? I understand the buffet should be ready soon. In the meantime, Heidi asked me to tell a story. Some of you know, my Aunt Gwen composed poems and verses. Because her eyesight was failing, she memorized each one until she knew them by heart. She could shuffle them in her mind and randomly recite one of them whenever she had an audience.

"Heidi didn't have any pets until she was around eleven-years-old. She picked two soft, white rabbits out of the display case at the country club. The family had gone there every Easter, and each time the scene was the same. A raised platform edged with a foot-high fence, grass sod, plastic Easter eggs, miniature houses, and a new group of baby rabbits.

"Gwen and Nathan invited me over for a baby rabbit naming ceremony, but I didn't realize I was the master of ceremonies. There I was, standing in my black suit, unprepared, and I instantly became a fur magnet. I named one Peter and the other Kate before lowering them into the outdoor, bamboo playpen Heidi had constructed. My Aunt Gwen wrote dozens of verses on a variety of topics, but today, Heidi and I would like to share her recording about rabbits. Many of you know my aunt affectionately referred to Heidi as Bunny from time to time." Edward pushed the button on the tape recorder. Heidi's mother's voice echoed through the hall.

"A Rabbit Dines Out—

Bunny had a bad habit of riding her bike to Peter's house every night at dinner time.

Mum replied, 'That's not right. Have dinner with me tonight. Ask Peter to come at seven.'

'I can't! Your food is so humdrum. Do you remember succotash stew?'

'Oh, Bunny, that icky sticky goo.'

'And Mum, sassafras soufflé? And, your nasty parsnip pâté?'

'Bunny please, no more no more!'

'Peter's mum cooks better. It's her food I adore.'

'I'll tell you what I'm going to do. I'll go to Paris, to L'école Cordon Bleu.

Little Bunny, I'll do anything for you.'"

Edward pushed a button on the machine before another verse began. There certainly wasn't a dry eye in the room. Edward dabbed the corner of his eye with his finger.

"Thank you all for being here. Please, help yourselves to the buffet. Some of the dishes are French and inspired by the poem."

Walt put his arm around Heidi, and she silently leaned into him while they sat side by side. She was soon interrupted by a tap on the shoulder.

"Excuse me, Rosie?"

No one had called her Rosie in a long time. Heidi's eyes grew wide. She turned abruptly away from Walt and saw Nanny Madeline.

She squealed, "Oh, God! Maddie! Is it really you?"

"Yes, Rosie. I'm older and wiser, but it's me."

Heidi jumped out of her chair and hugged Maddie. She didn't want to let go and felt like a little girl again. After a few minutes, she straightened up and stepped back. "Maddie, I've missed you. We haven't seen each other in a long time. What's it been, fifteen years? You haven't said much in your letters lately. How are you? Tell me everything."

"No, truly, I shouldn't. We're here to mourn your mother."

"I'll bring my plate." Heidi grabbed her plate from next to Walt's. "Let's get one filled for you from the buffet, come on."

"All right."

"Walt, I'll be back."

Heidi and Maddie walked across the room and Heidi encouraged Maddie to take generous helpings of all the buffet had to offer. As they walked further into the room to an isolated table in a corner, Heidi asked again, "How are you, really?"

Maddie began to speak in French. "Rosie, things have been difficult for me. My husband died in a bicycle accident two years ago. William was almost home when it happened, and I saw it all. The car hit him, and he landed on the windshield."

"Oh, Maddie," Heidi said, crestfallen. "I'm so sorry! How awful for you. I can't imagine how I'd feel if I lost Walt."

"Thank you, but I shouldn't burden you with my situation."

"It's okay. I want to know. How's Corinne managing without her father?"

"After William died, she moved out of state for a higher paying job. We talk on the phone once a month, but I haven't seen our daughter since she left. She sounds like she's managing, but I really don't know." Maddie ate some of the chicken cordon bleu on her plate. "This was your mother's favorite dish in Paris."

"I hope you and Corinne can see each other again soon."

"Me too. Tell me, what's been going on with you?"

"I've struggled with my parents, but my life has been good overall." Heidi noticed the staff moving about. "Oh, the dessert just arrived. Stay here."

She stood up and crossed the room, grabbed two plates of crème brule from the cart, and headed toward Maddie. A few people tried to start up a conversation, but she politely excused herself saying she'd be back.

"Here you go." Heidi sat down. "After we eat, I'd like you to properly meet my family, but first I need to ask—did you know I was adopted?"

"I knew, but it wasn't my place to discuss, and you were so young when we lived together."

"What do you remember?"

"I was in my early twenties, and I was working for Madame Kendrick. Her husband was moving the family to South Africa, and I didn't want to go. So, when your mother approached me about taking care of a new baby, I agreed. I became your nanny about a month later... I remember thinking how unusual it was for an older couple to adopt a baby."

"My life was rather confusing with older parents. Sorry, go on. I didn't mean to interrupt."

"That's all right. When it was time to pick you up, I traveled with your father to Mainz, Germany with Michel—the chauffeur. Madame Schwartz didn't feel well, so she stayed at home.

"What was the place like?"

"It was a cathedral, with a school, but I didn't see the orphanage. We were only in the Reverend Mother's office. When we got back to Paris, I took care of you for more hours each day than I'd expected. Your mother had a lot of headaches and anxious times."

"Yes, she told me about her dental troubles, and I lived around her migraines."

"I don't think I ever told you that I met William when your mother was sick. The house phone wasn't working, and she sent me to the embassy to get your father. She couldn't take care of you, so I took you on your first secret Métro ride that day."

"What? Secret Métro?"

"Your mother wouldn't have approved, but I was in a hurry, and there weren't any taxis."

"Oh, of course. Germs! Sorry, tell me more."

"William was the embassy guard and helped us find your father. Two weeks later, William and I went out on our first date. That was in 1960. I moved with your family to Maryland when you were three, and my dear William followed. He got a government job in D.C. We married when you were going into first grade at the Maret school. That's when I moved out of your parents' house. Occasionally, I came to stay with you in the afternoons and sometimes in the evening when your parents went out. A few months later, William and I left for South Carolina. Once we were settled, I stopped being a nanny and only babysat part-time."

"Thank you for telling me what you know about my adoption. When you left, everything changed. I'm sorry about William. I'm sure you and Corrine miss him every day."

"Yes, that's true. I think I loved him from the first day we met in Paris, and I have never wanted anyone else." Madeline gently put her hand on Heidi's arm. "Rosie, make sure you go through everything in your parents' basement. Many important things may still be hiding in boxes. I suspect they continued the habit of keeping everything long after I stopped working for them."

"Yes, there are many things tucked away in the attic and basement. Mom never could let Dad take anything out of the house that might be of value or bring a memory to mind. I'm not sure anyone really knew to what extent she collected things since the main parts of the house were kept tidy. The attic and some of the basement looks like a pack rat lived there. Are you talking about any specific items?"

"Nothing really, but I remember one time there were several items delivered to the house in one week. It's as clear as if it happened yesterday because that was the day I told you I was getting married and moving out. It was also right before you were going to Maret for the first year. You wanted me to stay, but your parents said you didn't need a nanny after you finished kindergarten."

"That was a big change for all of us. What were the deliveries?"

"All I know is a courier came to the front door while we were eating ice cream with your mother. I shooed him away to the basement door and met him down there with an envelope from your father. The man moved a box inside and went on his way. I lied to your mother and told her the package was for me when she'd asked who was at the door. Your dad asked me to conceal things from her when he first hired me. He said I'd be helping you in the long run." Maddie's eyes glazed over long enough for Heidi to notice.

"Well, my mother was an odd dramatic character, and maybe he had a little in him as well." Heidi wanted to ease Maddie's mind. "Alright, I'll look carefully. I started going through papers the last few years, but so far most of it has been Mom's stuff."

"Your father was an important man. I helped him with many packages and enveloped when I lived with you, but I never asked what they were. It was none of my business."

"Mm-hmm sounds familiar, but I only dealt with envelopes related to David McGwire. Our families are still very close. I'm sure you remember Claudia, she's here somewhere."

"I'd like to say hello to Claudia."

"After we've finished our dessert, I'll look for her so you two can reconnect."

"I'd like that. Tell me, how's her mother?"

"Poor Sadie, she's had a rough life, but that's a long story I won't get into today. She has dementia." Heidi slipped a piece of dessert off her fork into her mouth.

A few days after the memorial service, Heidi decided to sleep alone in her childhood room at her parent's house for one night and to never sleep in a La-Z-Boy chair again. At first, she felt swaddled in her old bed, but thinking about her mother's traumas kept her awake. The wound she'd seen on her mother's stomach when the bandages were changed, kept coming back every time she closed her eyes. When sleep took her, she didn't dream happy things like she did after her father's death. Instead, she dreamed that her mother was lost, then dirty, and finally angry at the world. Heidi prayed it was her own mind playing tricks. The afterlife for her mother sounded like hell and for her father, heaven.

The next morning, Heidi walked down the stairs, gripping the wrought iron banister she'd gone down so many times before. At the bottom, she turned the corner, and a picture on the hall table caught her eye. It was of her parents with Jerald Ford in the White House. The edges of Heidi's mouth turned up, and moisture brimmed her eyes. She walked into the kitchen and filled up a glass with water before going down to the basement into the crowded laundry room. Looking in a random box, she pulled out a letter written to her mother in 1937 when she was an actress in New York. Heidi read the entire letter for the first time and felt more connected to her mother than she'd ever been before. The day progressed better than the night before as she got on with sorting through things in the house. Satisfied she drove home to Walt and the children, and feel sound asleep without regrets.

For the next three weeks, she only went to Bethesda during the day while the children were in school. Each morning she helped them get ready for their day before driving away, promising herself to be home before they got off the bus at the end of their street.

Edward offered to help with sorting through the house, but Heidi felt he had already done enough. He didn't need to help with anything else. Calling around, she found a disposal company and rented a twenty-foot long dumpster. The manager indicated it would be too big and cumbersome for most driveways. They worked things out with the Kenwood Association and arranged for the container to sit along the curbside but they were only permitted to leave it there for a month. Heidi would have to work quickly to meet their deadline.

After finding a surprise guest, a possum, sleeping in the corner of the garden shed, she made sure to be careful while filling her father's wheelbarrow with broken or useless things before pitching them into the dumpster. She left a good shovel, rake, and clippers behind for digging up her father's roses later on. Once the shed was tidy, she abandoned the wheelbarrow and grabbed garbage bags from the car and went into the house. She filled the bags with junk and dragged one bag after the other to the dumpster. Some of heavier items would have to wait until later. She wanted to get the bulk of the useless things out before anyone else got involved. The first full dumpster was emptied ten days into the process. The second remained empty for the time being while Heidi lugged whatever else she could carry into the garage. The muscles in her arms were feeling the stress of moving so many things around. By the end of everything, she wondered if she'd look like an Olympic athlete. At some point in the three-week process, Heidi wasn't sure when, she telephoned Claudia and asked her to come over on day twenty-one when Walt and the children would be there to help as well.

The last day of the clear-out finally arrived. Heidi lifted the boys into Walt's truck in front of their house. She smiled to herself when they asked to ride in the trailer he had attached to the back. Of course, the answer was no. Sometimes it was hard to believe the twins were already eight years old. Kyle and Caleb's surprise arrival all those years ago still brought a smile to Heidi's face. Tessie and Claire had been so accepting when they were born despite the chaos they brought into their sisters' orderly world.

Following Heidi's instructions, the girls walked over to the Gladiator van and hopped in. During the drive, Heidi told them they would have to haul the trash bags out of the garage and pitch them over the top of the dumpster with their dad. She wasn't sure what the boys would be able to do but knew they would help in any way they could. During the process, Heidi and Claudia would work in the attic. The drive took a little longer than usual. Both vehicles arrived in front of the house at the same time after a lengthy bumper-to-bumper drive caused by a Saturday morning accident on the highway. Everyone piled out of the cars.

Heidi saw Claudia sitting on the front step, and called out, "Good morning, Claudia."

Thankfully everyone seemed pretty chipper under the circumstances. Having the seven of them there together warmed Heidi's heart.

"Hey, the gangs all here." Claudia hugged each of them individually.

"You can all catch up with Claudia over lunch later. I'll get it delivered. In the meantime, your dad will help you. Okay, team get to work."

Heidi grabbed Claudia's arm and took her to the attic. "I've pulled out most of the junk in the front, the good stuff's in the back, I think. I haven't gotten into any of it yet."

"It still amazes me you weren't ever allowed in here."

"Yeah, I've been in the front with my parents, and alone that one time I snuck in and found Santa's gifts."

In the top drawer of a cabinet, Heidi pulled out a note written in her mother's hand, pinned to an emerald dress. "Wow! We could have a dress-up party with all these."

"Or a museum display." Claudia laughed.

Heidi straightened her back. "These notes are fun, but all of these outfits can't be intact, some of them must be disintegrating after years in the attic. The temperatures in here must rise and fall constantly. We'll go through them later and throw out the bad ones."

"Make sure you take photos of the clothes and make copies of the notes," Claudia pleaded. "You'll regret it later if you don't keep a record of things. If you don't want any of them, I'm sure we can sell the ones that are in good shape or donate them to the Smithsonian."

"Um, you're probably right. I'll get Walt to carry the drawers downstairs to the car later."

Each fashionable garment had an explanation pinned on top. The note papers were intact, but the writing was somewhat faded. The earliest note was from 1940, but Heidi didn't want to go back that far today. She pulled open another drawer.

"Claudia, look—this note Mom wrote says, 'November 1962. I wore this when Nathan took me to the dedication of Dulles airport. The dress looks like a coat. Such a marvelous mustard.'"

"This is so cool." Claudia pulled out another, and read, "'I wore this glittering silver-flecked, off the shoulder gown to meet Lady Bird Johnson at a fundraiser.' This is great!"

"Okay, one more," Heidi said. "She wrote, 'I wore this suit, with oversized buttons down the front of the fitted scoop-necked jacket, along with the pencil skirt, to the White House to meet Vice President Ford.' Mom was so organized in those days. I wonder what happened."

"Life overwhelmed her at some point," Claudia said in a speculative tone.

Heidi bent one garment after the other forward against her shirt and skimmed through the pile. The old tissue paper was scented with pungent mothballs and took her mind back in time to the long-gone gifts in her mother's closet. To her delight, at the bottom of the chronologically ordered collection was an item smaller than the rest. "This one says, 'Bunny, you wore this pink jumper when we brought you to America for the first time on the SS United States.' Hey, look, underneath the pile there is a menu from the vessel's dining room along with a passenger list."

Claudia took the menu and began to read out loud, "L. J. Alexanderson was the captain. This menu is incredible; curried lamb, green kale, Swiss chard with cream, and mango sherbet. It must have fifty options just for lunch! What's happened to the world? Most of our generation doesn't eat like this. We spent our childhood eating processed foods during the week and only got the good stuff on weekends. I'm glad we're eating healthier foods full-time now. Check it out."

"It's all amazing!" Heidi took the papers. Tears filled her eyes as she gazed at the ship's log. "Look, the port of entry was in New York City, and my name is on the passenger list! I immigrated on this ship. This is awesome."

"Maybe we can find the ship and visit someday?" Claudia rubbed Heidi's shoulders."

"Perhaps… I'm okay, don't worry." Heidi laughed, and said, "I don't know why, but this reminds me of the time my parents drove to Canada when I was a young kid. According to Mom, I refused to eat food from a foreign country. My parents gave me the applesauce Mom brought from home for three days straight before I gave in and ate Canadian food."

"That's a hoot," Claudia said with a chuckle.

They explored some more, and Heidi saw a different sort of box. It sat in the farthest corner of the attic on some exposed floor beams that weren't covered with hardwood like the rest. Heidi balanced on the beams and pushed her hand through the cracked, dried out tape on the top of the box.

"Hey, Claudia, I bet this is one of the things Maddie was talking about."

"Careful, don't fall." Claudia held out her hands and grabbed the box, while Heidi stepped to safety. "I thought Maddie said there were things in the basement?"

"Yes, but this one looks special. Dad must've hidden it up here." Shivering anxiously in the warm attic, she read a few of the papers on the top of the stack. "They're about his career." Heidi continued scanning the documents, and her eyebrows lifted.

"What's going on? You look weird."

"Some clues were given at his memorial, but these documents will tell us more about his entire career. Some of his younger peers said he was part of the 'Greatest Generation,' and I think this is why. Look, these papers mention his intelligence liaison work. I don't understand any of the code words or abbreviations."

Claudia pulled out a stapled packet from the bottom of the box. "This one's from the 1930s and is stamped 'Top Secret and Cleared for Release.' Looks like your next research project."

Heidi backed up and dropped into a wooden rocking chair, but she didn't quite fit. It was her old childhood 'punishment' chair. She laughed, squirmed around, and wedged herself into it—music jingled from deep within the box. She pulled it onto her lap, rooted around, and found her old Raggedy Ann doll playing *Rock a Bye Baby*.

Heidi was miffed. "Why is that playing all of a sudden? I'm guessing rattling the box around disturbed the creepy thing." She pretended to toss it across the room and abruptly stopped. "Wait, check out the stitches across its stomach. I forgot I used to operate on dolls like I was going to be a doctor—yeah, right."

"That's weird coming from the artist you turned out to be."

"Ha, ha. The stitches look creative. Hey! I'm going to open her up. Now that I'm thinking about it, I recall putting a key inside to hide for Dad." Heidi pulled a Swiss Army knife out of her pocket, unfolded the tiny scissors, and snipped at the stitches. "He asked me to keep it hidden and said that I'd need it one day, but I didn't know why." She pulled on the loose threads, found the key where she'd left it under the music box, and passed it over.

"Must be his love of Sherlock Holmes mysteries that made him do such a silly thing. It looks like a travel key." Claudia walked around checking the suitcases. "The only one it fits in is this steamer trunk."

"Claudia, I'm having trouble wrapping myself around this situation." Heidi stood up, and the chair followed her hips. Giggling, she pried herself out. "How will I ever piece Dad together?"

"I don't know." Claudia pulled on the front of the upright trunk, and it squeaked opened like a book on the long hinge. A pearl-tipped hatpin wove through a note and the fabric liner in the trunk. Claudia read the text, pausing in between each word. "These family pieces are for you Heidi Rose, love Dad."

The trunk was full of sterling silver bars, teapots, and tableware.

"O-kay, this is nuts. I want to ask him so many questions, and now I can't. I'm grateful for the gifts, but what am I going to do with all this silver?"

"I think, in the old days, people kept silver housewares for daily use knowing they could sell the stuff if they needed money. The current-day dealers are going to love the silver bars best since they won't need to melt them down like they'll have to with the teapots and such. I wonder how much this one weighs?" Claudia pulled out a bar. "This one has 0.925-Sterling-24.8 tr. oz. etched on it—haven't a clue what it's worth."

"I guess we'll find out. This is all making me queasy inside. I don't understand."

"I didn't understand my dad, either. At least yours lived longer."

"Oh, I'm sorry, Claudia. How thoughtless of me." Heidi hesitated before picking up another document out of her dad's box.

"Don't worry. Everything will be fine."

"Ha, ha. You sound like Dad." Heidi skimmed a line on the document without comprehending the codes. "I have a lot to go through. I think we should put the papers, letters, and pictures into new boxes. The silver can wait. Walt will have to lug it downstairs, too."

Claudia craned her head up at the peaks of the uninsulated ceiling. "We need to pick up the pace. This area is getting hotter by the minute. Hang on. I'll be right back." She hurried down the stairs and returned with half a dozen large plastic storage containers. "I only have two more hours before I have to go to an impromptu meeting in D.C. It's annoying, having to go in on a Saturday, but there are some glitches with the next fund-raiser. Oh well, let's keep moving forward with this project."

"Right, okay, I won't dawdle." Heidi arranged the bins in a straight line and got to work. Another hour or so passed by.

"If you need me, I can come back tomorrow for the entire day."

"Okay, thanks." Heidi's neck started to tense up. "I meant to mention something. Remember the boxes in the basement laundry I told you were moved there when the recreation room was done during high school?"

"What about them? Do we have to deal with those, too?"

"No, not really. In the weeks of sorting through things, I didn't find more than a dozen boxes with photos and letters. Some of them were moldy and ruined, the others I've already moved to a small temperature-controlled bin in Laurel. It's big enough to use for a private office for a few months. I'd rather finish going through stuff there instead of bringing that musty old-book smell home. The other boxes have china place settings, crystal, small porcelain figurines, and other knickknacks. The things I've left on the first floor here aren't coming with me. Mr. Warren is going to bring an antique dealer in from Christie's auction house. Whatever remains after that will be part of the on-site estate sale. Thankfully, I don't have to deal with buyers. Whatever money they bring in will go into my accounts."

"Wow! You've been busy."

"Yep," Heidi concurred. She stopped and stared straight ahead at the built-in attic fan recalling the year a raccoon nested in the corner of the giant box and, to her surprise, safely had a litter of babies. "Claudia, I need to share something with you that's more important than any of this stuff. I'm scared though, not sure how you'll react. It's way past time."

"Time for what?"

Heidi struggled with her thoughts before speaking. "The day your dad was shot I went into your cellar to get some wine. Remember?"

"Not really." Claudia moved her hands to the back of her neck. "Go on."

"At the time I found my dad rummaging around in the dark. I asked him why and he gave me a rather sketchy answer and made me promise not to tell anyone he was down there. I left the room and pretty much let the information drop out of my mind. The 'official' story came much later."

"What!" Claudia chirped. "Christ, why didn't you tell me?"

"Three years ago, my dad told me everything and asked me not to tell you while he was alive. I need to tell you now. Your dad died because he was involved with highly volatile events connected to national security."

"Why?"

"Your mom had just been diagnosed with dementia, and he didn't think it was right to tell you then. He confessed because I insisted, and he said it was safe to tell me. I think, even though your mother's still around, it's time to tell you what I know."

"Poor Mom. She's not unhappy, but it's so difficult to watch her living in her demented world." Claudia leaned on the steamer trunk, and the silver rattled.

Heidi's pulse elevated. "This is all crazy stuff."

"Go ahead! Tell me."

Heidi wasn't feeling very confident, but she knew she had to get this out. "Before your dad's death, he received classified information from a disgruntled Soviet mole—informant. The loud man, who created trouble at my dad's retirement party, was the same person. After the event, he started giving your dad information about the Soviets. This went on for years, and eventually, things turned ugly."

"Yeah, I remember that guy at the party. Sometimes he showed up at our house and Dad seemed on edge. They'd sit in the backyard or go on walks. I remember thinking it was strange that I never even knew his name."

"There was definitely something going on." Heidi rested her hips against the attic stair railing. "I don't know any details about their meetings. All I know is that your dad hid the last, and most critical information, in the wine cellar of your house on Harrison Street. He thought it would be secure there while he figured out how to get the mole to safety."

"This is incredible! What was it?" Claudia's voice elevated. "Where was it?"

"A small canister. He hid it in an alcove." Heidi looked at her watch. "Oh, oh, look at the time. What about your meeting?"

"Is that all? If not, I've got to hear the rest. Go on." Claudia's face scrunched up.

"Are you sure?" Heidi coaxed.

"Get on with it!"

"What I eventually learned was that the canister had an antidote for a chemical weapon inside, along with a formula on microfilm. They killed your dad because of what he knew, and they wanted to stop him from transferring the damaging information. All the money the Soviets spent on the project was wasted once the information was disclosed, and they had to spend even more money to develop alternative toxins. Ultimately, all their combined financial loses on this project, and other failings that we've all seen on the news at the end of the Cold War caused the collapse of the Soviet Union."

"Ok-aay. Now I get it. It seems foolish to think about using chemical weapons. They could create a domino effect and hurt their own citizens." Claudia took her hand off the steamer trunk. "I have to digest all this. Is there anything more you're not telling me?"

"I don't know anything else. If we're missing pieces, they're likely lost. We could try the internet or a government library."

"Who am I kidding, we'll probably never know everything. I need to take a walk before my meeting to clear my head." Claudia moved across the room.

Heidi called after her, "Wait, don't go, what about lunch?"

"Never mind that."

"I'm sorry I kept Dad's secret from you."

"It's not your fault. I need time to think. I'll see you later." Claudia disappeared down the stairs.

While Heidi and Walt moved around the rest of her parents' belongings, she sent the children inside to comb through the first floor and pick out a few items they wanted to keep. Getting rid of most of her parents' belongings was harder than she expected. She felt like she was symbolically discarding them, too.

She knew Mr. Warren would take care of selling the house once it was swept clean, but she expected it to be torn down and replaced. It would likely go quickly since properties in Bethesda, particularly within Kenwood, were highly sought after and not readily available. Long ago, she'd fantasized about renovating and taking over the house, but she'd had a change of heart. Her parents created their home in the 50s, and it would leave after them—maybe that was best. Much to Heid's relief, without being asked, Walt and the children worked together to dig up and bag her father's roses to add to the rest of the memorabilia in the cars.

Not long after Heidi ordered pizza and the family finished eating, Mr. Warren's crew arrived. Heidi watched the men put the paintings from the back hall in crates and take them away. A tinge of regret came over her once the art was gone. There was no valid reason for her angst because she'd already decided to pay for the children's university education with the money she'd get for the paintings. It was the right answer.

As the children rummaged loudly about the house, Heidi and Walt sorted through the cases of wine under the basement stairs. Heidi realized the bottles had been standing upright for years which seemed rather odd because her father understood the complexities of wine even though he preferred Scotch whisky. She opened one bottle, and it tasted so bad that she had to spit it into the laundry room sink. Every one she tried resulted in the same reaction. Some of the others weren't worth tasting because they smelled like wet cardboard or vinegar, or had a brownish cloudy appearance when she held them up to the hall light. She wanted to find one wine to share with Walt, but there weren't any. They collected the nasty bottles in cartons and carried them outside. Heidi climbed up the ladder that rested up against the dumpster. One by one she took the bottles from Walt's outstretched hand and threw them against the internal walls of the bin. The glass exploded with liquid splashing in every direction, drenching the trash bags her family had piled into the dumpster earlier that day. With each pitch, she felt the tension in her body release.

Everything they wanted was now in the cars. Heidi handed each kid a broom and sent them to work. The task was somewhat futile, but it gave Heidi some time to walk through the house with Walt one more time peering in every space. She didn't want to leave anything tangible behind. Much to her surprise, they saw a small double plywood door under the basement stair landing that blended in perfectly with the adjacent walls. Walt pried it open and found a wooden case laying horizontally on the floor with a wine label attached. Beside it, there were three wooden crates. He pulled a penlight out of his pocket and illuminated the dark cubby.

"Heidi, check these out, they aren't addressed to your parents."

"Huh? Let me see. Odd, I've never noticed that door before." She put on her black-rimmed reading glasses and crawled next to him under the stairs, wishing she was thinner. They were like two sardines in the space, and he was the leaner of the two of them.

"The crates are addressed to David McGwire." Heidi wiggled back out. "What am I going to do now?" Standing up, she straightened her shirt and brushed off some old, dusty spider webs.

"The only thing you can, call his daughter!" The corners of Walt's mouth turned up.

"When Claudia hears about this find, she'll flip. Well, maybe not the way she did when I told her about David's death."

"Oh? When?" Walt looked at her sideways.

"In the attic earlier today."

"At this point, it's old news to me. I bet she was more stunned than I was."

"Yep, moving on…"

Walt dragged the pine crates out from under the stairs.

She watched from the other side of the hall. "I wonder if Claudia has any ideas. Go ahead and open the wine crate. Now I'm curious. Never mind that it says David on the outside."

"Will do. It looks like my pocketknife will work on the wine, but not the others."

"Okay, keep at it. I need to call Claudia, and I'm stalling. After our last conversation, I'm a bit scared to talk to her."

"Get it over with. She'll be totally distracted and won't rag on you about what you told her in the attic."

"Oookaaay. We'll see." Instead of getting her cell phone out of the car, Heidi darted up to the den to call on the landline. Her hand shook as she dialed.

When she returned to the basement, her face felt flushed. "How's it going?" Heidi asked, trying to catch her breath.

"Fine, fine," Walt replied. "What did she say?"

"Claudia said to open them and call her back. She's a little calmer than she was earlier. What's in the wine box?"

"It's a 1945 La Tache," Walt said.

"Well, that might be a prize." She rested her hands on her hips. "And the other crates?"

"One of them is quite heavy. The other two are light by comparison."

"I still can't believe I never noticed the door, but I didn't come down often, and it's so dark under there." Heidi rubbed her neck.

"I'll find some tools in the truck and grab your cell phone. I think a hammer and crowbar should do the trick." Walt took the stairs two at a time. He returned in less than five minutes and opened the other crates.

What they saw inside took Heidi's breath away. "Oh my God, this is insane, don't touch them with your bare hands. I threw a bag of random stuff on the front seat of the truck, there should be some gloves in there and Dad's old magnifying glass." She pulled a small spiral notebook and a pen out of her back jeans' pocket.

"Okay, I'll get them." Walt stomped up the stairs.

It took him longer than she liked for him to return, but she was able to write a few notes down while he was gone.

"Here you go; gloves and a magnifier as requested." He handed them over. "Oh, and your cell phone. What's this all about?"

"Thanks." She shoved the cell phone in her pocket and put on the gloves. Looking through her glasses wasn't enough, so she moved the magnifying lens over the items and examined them closely, jotting down detailed notes as she went along. "I think

Claudia just hit the jackpot! I'm not a historian per se, but these things are in pristine condition and will likely fatten Claudia's wallet."

"Don't just stand there," Walt encouraged. "Call her again." Heidi needed to steady herself and grabbed the nearest stair railing.

"Right." She pulled out her cell phone, flipped it open and called. "Claudia, you have to come back to my parent's house. Your father left you some priceless gifts."

"What now? The info about my dad's death is hard enough to stomach. Spill the details."

"You sitting down?"

"Yes, yes. Make it quick. I'm tied up." Claudia's voice cracked.

"The first item is made of marble and looks like a bust of a woman with a veil across her face. The note in the box says circa 1863."

"Is it real?"

"I guess."

"The second is a golden musical ship with painted sails, cannons, and a crew of miniature men—circa 1858."

"Where did they come from?"

"He's your dad, figure it out. The last is a drawing by Van Gogh called *Sien under Umbrella with a Girl*."

Sounding bewildered, Claudia exclaimed, "This is madness. I'll come back over now."

Heidi was excited, and her words tumbled out. "Walt, she's on her way. She'll drive back from D.C., but the roads are being worked on, so it'll take extra time."

"How did she sound?"

"Dazed. She plans to telephone Sadie on the way over in hopes that her mother will remember something. Not sure how well that will work since Sadie hasn't been in her right mind for the at least three years."

"Hope there aren't any more skeletons in the closet." Walt chuckled at his own joke.

Chapter 33

Six weeks later…

Heidi arranged for Claudia to pick up the children right after school. She needed an evening with Walt before they spent a week with the kids on spring break in Florida. It was almost too quiet at home without them. They had just started discussing their plans when the phone rang. Heidi hopped up and answered it on the second ring.

"Hello, Heidi. This is Mr. Warren, how are you holding up?" She heard him clear his throat.

"Most of the time, quite well," she said. "Although my new-found independence from my mother unsettles me some days, I take long walks and feel better. Then, Walt and the kids keep me busy, and we're thinking about moving to a quieter neighborhood out in the countryside by the end of the summer."

"I should tell you, the final private auction bids for your parents' house are in. The given amounts are well over a million dollars, actually closer to two million. Every bid is solid, and we should settle soon. With sensible investment strategies, it will grow exponentially."

"It's all so unbelievable." Heidi sat down with a thud and Walt looked over inquisitively. She clamped the phone between her ear and shoulder. With her hands, she made the shape of a house and drew the number in the air.

"You still there?" Mr. Warren asked.

"Yes, yes, I'm here. I hoped this would happen, but now I'm stunned."

"None of this has been easy for you. Tell you what, before you make any decision about your future, I need to give you something in person. Can I come by your house this evening?"

"Tonight?" She sucked in as much air as she could take in.

"Sorry, I should have called earlier."

"No, no, that's all right. We'll be home, and the kids are with my friend, Claudia."

"Oh, yes, David and Sadie McGwire's daughter. I'm sorry her mother passed away. It's only been two weeks?"

"Yes, that's right, Sadie passed away in her sleep. Claudia had made all the arrangement for her mother to be moved from Cape Cod to a care-facility in D.C., but it never happened. She died two days before the move. Claudia was quite shaken and decided to hold a private service on the Cape. How did you know?"

"Since she'd been a resident of D.C. years ago, there was a notice in the paper after the fact." Mr. Warren paused, but not long enough for Heidi to process why he might be interested. He said, "Your father instructed me to—to do a few things for Claudia."

"Oh?"

"I'll explain later."

She looked at Walt and shrugged. "Sure, come on over. Can you be here at seven-thirty?"

"Perfect, that'll work."

"See you soon."

He disconnected.

Heidi couldn't imagine what Mr. Warren had in mind. She wanted to relax and have a quiet meal on the patio with Walt while getting used to the idea of suddenly becoming a millionaire. Her mother, not long ago, said she'd be one someday. At the time, Heidi balked at the idea, now it was true. Instead of celebrating she could do nothing more than gaze out into the backyard and take in the instrumental music Walt had turned on in the background while thinking about what she and Claudia had lost.

The knock on the door came too soon. Heidi and Walt went to the front door. She unlocked the latch and pulled on the curved handle.

"Hello, Mr. Warren." She shook his hand and noticed he had a package wrapped in brown paper under his other arm.

"Come in, come in." Walt firmly shook Mr. Warren's hand. "Thank you for all you've done for the Schwartz family. Heidi and I look forward to working with you on long-term investment strategies."

"Well, that's wonderful! Thank you, sir. Sorry to disturb you this late in the evening."

"No problem. Please, come sit down in the living room." Walt patted Mr. Warren on the back.

Heidi wasn't concerned about the hour, but more about the reason. "I'll get you some coffee."

Walt followed her into the kitchen, and said, "Did you see? The package he's carrying has a yellow ribbon tied around it, like a present."

"Yes, I know. I'm nervous. Go back and make some small talk. I'll be there in a minute." In honor of what her parents once were, she brought out one of their silver trays and rested three warm cups in the middle on individual saucers. She filled them with coffee and imagined each cup represented a person.

Heidi walked back into the living room with the tray balanced on one hand for effect. "May our cups runneth over." The package sat on the coffee table in front of the couch.

"Here you go, Mr. Warren—Folgers. It was Mom's favorite day-to-day brew. She always pre-heated the cups before adding the coffee to keep it piping hot. Dad loved it, too, until he felt he had to switch to Postum, which wasn't coffee at all."

Mr. Warren took a sip. "Mmm, it's quite good this way. I'm not sure how you'll react to what I'm going to give you." He inhaled audibly. "I'm following your father's instructions down to the last detail."

"Oh, I wonder what he's up to now." Heidi tucked one hand into her jeans pocket while she held her cup with the other. "Maybe I need something stronger to drink. Never mind, what is it?"

Mr. Warren picked up the package and handed it to Heidi. "This comes with three keys." In slow motion, he placed each one on the table in a line. She'd never seen such oddly shaped keys and focused on the package. Written across the middle in her father's hand were the words, 'Do not open until I am no more – Nathan Schwartz.' Inside were two letters labeled with consecutive numbers. The first envelope contained a typed letter paper-clipped to a Bar Mitzvah certificate with *Nathan Schwartz* written on the recipient's line.

March 5, 1999

Dearest Heidi Rose,

Funny, I never address you as Rose, but you are as lovely as any I've ever seen, minus the thorns of course. Today I want to tell you about the attached certificate of Bar Mitzvah. I was born into a Jewish family and followed that lifestyle in my youth. We always went to Synagogue and celebrated all the high holidays. In my early thirties, I began to drift away from my traditions.

In 1941, when Pearl Harbor was attacked, I left my law practice in California and joined the Army Air Corps. I was determined not to make my background too prominent due to society's developing anti-Semitic attitudes. Many Jews did, in fact, fight in the war against bigotry, but that's for the history books. By the time the war was over, I had learned quite a bit about Christianity, and then I met your mother who was raised by protestants. Neither of her parents were troubled by my roots, but they were delighted I wasn't Catholic. Their point of view seemed strange to me at first since they were German. But the truth is, not all Germans hated Jews, except it was unusual for people of different faiths to marry. I was relieved her family liked and accepted me.

In my culture, women were the matriarchs of the family, and their religion was to be given to their children, so I saw no reason to change that practice. Hence, you were baptized as an Episcopalian. I came to believe in Christ, so I officially converted when you were Confirmed as a teenager. If you recall, you asked me why I wasn't baptized before, and I told you I hadn't gotten around to it. I have no idea why I didn't tell you everything then.

I should add here that my mother felt betrayed when I announced my second marriage would be to a Christian woman. And, then, she was so upset that I was twenty-eight hundred miles away from home on the East Coast. She went on and on trying to change my mind, saying I should only be married to a Jewish woman and live in California. My poor mother; when she failed, we didn't speak for a long time. As a result of the rift between us and the complications created by my first marriage—you and I spoke of before—I didn't go back to my hometown often. I applaud you for finding a way to stay in our lives here in Maryland after your mother created troubles for you and Walt. I should have counseled you since I knew the pitfalls, but I said nothing. Please, forgive my many failings.

I love you, Dad.

(typed with my Smith-Corona typewriter; now yours)

Heidi twirled a strand of her hair around her finger. Her frustration came out in a strident response. "We talked about his divorce in California, but this new information is unexpected. But it only matters because he didn't trust me enough in life to tell me everything."

Mr. Warren explained, "That's understandable. Your father said I was only to give it to you after both he and your mother had passed on. He didn't want you to start asking her questions."

"I'm overwhelmed. Anyway," she drew out the words, "what are the keys all about?"

"Read on."

"Dad, what now?" She plucked the second letter off the table, opened it, and slid out two pieces of paper and a photograph. Squinting at the pages, she read each one and passed them to Walt along with the photo.

"Walt, look at this first one. I can't believe it." Heidi's eyes filled with tears. "I've become such a weepy thing."

"Heidi!" Walt was flabbergasted. "This is a deed to a house in Paris. In Paris!"

"Yes, and it's…" Her face felt hot."

"22 Rue Desborde Valmore!" Walt marveled. "The house you lived in when you were a baby?"

"Yep, that's the one. I better read on. I feel like I'm playing a hide-and-seek computer game. What was Dad thinking?"

Mr. Warren interjected, "He hoped you'd be surprised and pleased."

"I am, I am. Here we go. And behind door number two?" Heidi laughed in between her tears.

March 7, 1999

Dear Heidi Rose,

Today, you have been presented with a gift—your Paris home. You should be in possession of this letter because your mother and I are gone. Mr. Warren, who you undoubtedly have already encountered before today, is the executor of my estate and will help you with the details. If for some reason he's no longer able, he will hand over these responsibilities to an associate.

I amended the original deed to 22 Rue Desborde Valmore decades ago and added your name. I want it to be yours with all its charms. I realize you won't recall much about the house—you were so young when we left—but, since you've been back to Paris as an adult, I'm confident you will like my gift. Make sure you explore the surrounding countryside, especially Monet's garden and the beaches of Normandy. There are so many marvelous places in France, Europe and all over the world to visit.

For a little house history; during events surrounding WWII, I purchased the building with money my mother gave me to put into a safe investment. I chose to keep this information to myself because, when I met Gwen years later, she was overly concerned about big-ticket items. The Great Depression of 1929 made some people extremely sensitive about saving one's pennies.

When we left Paris with you, I rented the house to the McGwires while they finished their tour. Later, it was leased to other State Department families who were stationed at the embassy. It was only recently that I left instructions with the State Department to stop renting it out and put Mr. Warren in charge until you could take possession.

Whatever you decide about Rue Desborde Valmore, promise me you'll go there before making any decisions, and take the three keys from Mr. Warren with you. Two of the keys are for different doors at the house. The third is for a safety deposit box at a bank called Société Générale on Rue Montorgueil. Your name and mine are registered at the bank. To access the contents, you'll need to provide the bank with my death certificate and your passport, to prove your identity. Whether you choose to keep the house or not, is entirely up to you. If you do sell, offer it to former renters or their descendants before putting it on the open market. This isn't an unusual thing to do in Europe. Mr. Warren has the list of people. And make sure you stop by the neighbor's on the right side of the house. His name is Monsieur Rousseau, and he's kept watch for decades. I send him wine every year, and Mr. Warren will keep up the tradition unless you tell him otherwise. Rousseau is in his seventies now; we've known each other since the war.

By now, Mr. Warren has made you well aware of your inheritance. Take Claudia with you to Paris, using some of those funds—I must

insist on this point, it's vital she enters
the house with you. Ask Mr. Warren to speak
to her. Please, allow him to reserve a hotel
for Claudia when the time comes near the Arc
de Triomphe. She can stay there for a few
days and then decide whether or not to take a
room in the house instead.

    I imagine Walt and the children will have
a great time in Paris—expect to spend a month
in France. I am blessed to have had you in my
life. I love you more than words can express.

Signing off - Dad (Nathan Schwartz)

PS. Of the dolls I gave you after my travels,
I know you kept your favorites (the German,
the Russian, and the French). I saw them in
the curio cabinet in your home on my last
visit. You need to look inside their heads. I
know this sounds peculiar, please just do it.
Also, if it's not too late, find the Raggedy
Ann doll in the attic at our house on
Brookside Drive, and retrieve the key inside.
It fits into one of the steamer trunk locks.

    Heidi gazed through the window across the room before she
spoke. Dropping the letter on the table, she said, "I'll be right back.
I have to find a couple of dolls."
    She went up to the guest room and opened the curio cabinet. It
never occurred to her that they were anything but sentimental

trinkets. Her father was such an unusual man. After a deep breath or two, she eased the dolls off the shelf and carried them back to the living room.

"Find what you needed?" Walt said in an inquisitive tone.

Butterflies jumped in her stomach. "Um, yes, I'm carrying them. I never noticed their heads were this off balance before. We have to behead them."

"Really?" Mr. Warren moved to the edge of the couch and smiled coyly.

"Yes, yes. Come on, we all have to participate." She handed one doll to each of the men.

"This is a bit extreme, don't you think?" Walt said.

"Just... do it," Heidi encouraged. "Oh, and pulling doesn't work—I just tried."

"Taking things apart and reassembling them is my specialty." Walt worked the doll's head back and forth.

"Wait, I'm getting it." Heidi was perspiring. "The heads are screw tops. All together now; one—two—three."

The heads all came off at once.

"Oh, it's like my childhood Christmas stockings with white tissue paper inside," Heidi declared.

"Heidi." Walt winked at her. "Look a large diamond ring with a note that says it belonged to your great-grandmother."

Both Heidi and Mr. Warren unwrapped their prizes.

Mr. Warren said, "I wish I could have told you about the dolls a while back, but your father's orders were strict. My dolls note says, 'This ring was your grandmother's.'"

"You didn't have a choice, Mr. Warren. Dad had his reasons. Anyway, my note says, 'Heidi this band encircled with small diamonds is for you. Wear it on your finger or loop it through a chain. Remember, no matter where I go after this life, I'll always love you.'" Heidi rubbed the tears that rolled down her face.

"Your dad never ceases to amaze me." Walt held her great-grandmother's ring to the light, it sparkled blue within the facets.

"I don't understand how he knew I wouldn't give the dolls to charity. I guess he didn't worry about that since he knew each one of them meant something to me. I got rid of all the others long ago, but I can't think why. I just knew I wanted to keep these particular display dolls."

"Take this." Mr. Warren pushed yet another envelope across the table. "The value is noted inside from three years ago, but I expect they're worth more at this point. A blue diamond is rather rare. I can connect you with an appraiser."

Opening the envelope, she gasped. "They're worth tens of thousands of dollars." She craned her chin up toward the ceiling. "Thanks, Dad, wherever you are. Oh God! I have Mom's rings, too. Mr. Warren, she gave them to me right before she went into surgery. What am I going to do?"

"This is all too much," Walt said.

"I can't deal with these rings today." Heidi took a deep breath and then emptied her coffee cup. "Let's get back to the trip. How do I explain why Claudia needs to travel to Paris?"

"Call her and tell her about the letters and the things Mr. Warren brought over," Walt suggested. "She'll be intrigued. I can't imagine her turning down an all-inclusive trip to Paris."

"Mr. Warren, I'd like you to talk to Claudia before you leave."

"Sure. I'd be glad to. By the way, your father suggested one of two hotels. Either Saint James or Hotel Raphael. Both are delightful, and a bit more extravagant than Claudia might like, but he left precise instructions."

Walt took the tray of coffee cups off the table and walked toward the kitchen.

Heidi picked up the phone in the corner of the living room and dialed. Claudia answered on the fifth ring. "Hi, Claudia, new information to share. I have some letters from Dad. His banker, Mr. Warren, brought them over. There's a gift for you."

"I'm sure I don't need any more gifts. The art under your parents' stairs from my dad set me up for life."

"I know, right. Today I just found out, among other things, that Dad left me some diamond rings." She drew out the words. "Anyway, Dad's gift to you is a trip to Paris with us."

"No way!"

"Yep, it's true, talk to Mr. Warren." Heidi passed the phone over.

Mr. Warren spoke a bit too loudly into the receiver. "Hello, Miss McGwire... Yes, that's right, Mr. Schwartz has put some money aside for you, but he has a condition attached... Yes, basically. Heidi now owns a home in Paris, and Mr. Schwartz wants you to enter it when she does... No, I can't give you any more details... I'll hand you back to Heidi. You two can coordinate dates, and I suspect we'll all be in touch again."

"Claudia, hold on a second, Mr. Warren has to leave." She shook hands with him and got back on the phone as Walt escorted him to the door. "Claudia, you still there?"

"Yes."

"This trip will be awesome, but don't tell the kids anything. I'll clue them in after spring break."

"What's the plan?"

"We will take the kids to Germany first, and then meet you in Paris later.

"Why Germany?"

"I want to meet my birth family."

"Huh! What am I missing here? When did you find them?"

"I'll explain later. Oh, and the kids don't know about my German relatives, so don't say anything about that to them either."

"Don't worry, I won't say a word about the trip or the other family, just the diamonds."

"Thanks. Let me know when you can take time off this summer. We'll need to buy plane tickets soon." Heidi paused a minute. "I'll be over in the morning to pick up the kids. See you around ten?"

"Perfect, and thanks for the gift."

Chapter 34

The plans for the European vacation were set. Hopefully, the journey would help Heidi heal and bring a new perspective to her life. First, she had to tell their children more about her adoption.

Walt brought the girls into the living room.

Heidi began by saying, "It's time for a meeting. Sit down on the couch."

This rarely happened, and they wiggled on the cushions.

"What's going on Mom? Are we in trouble?" Tessie asked. "Where are Kyle and Caleb?"

"You're not in trouble, and the boys can keep playing in their room. What I have to say is hard to explain, and some of it is for mature girls. I will only tell your brothers part of the story another day. They're too young to hear everything."

"Hear that, Tessie? We're mature," Claire declared with confidence.

"We have all been through a lot with my parents over the last few years. Your dad played a big part in helping keep your lives on track. I particularly appreciate how responsible you've been when I was away from home."

365

ELSA WOLF

The girls tickled each other.

"Calm down, please." Heidi waited until they held still. "You asked me for details about my adoption when you were smaller, but I couldn't tell you very much. Now, I'm ready to explain. Some years ago, I found a book that helped me find my birth mother in Germany."

"Mom, that's amazing." Claire smiled. "What's her name?"

"Rita, her name is Rita. I found her using the information on my birth certificate. It didn't take very long. Once I learned her address, I wrote her a letter. She wrote back and was excited I found her." Heidi paused to let the information sink in. "Here's the tricky part... I have a sister. Her name is Mina. I'm sorry I didn't tell you when I found out, but I just couldn't."

Claire just sat and listened.

"Mom, a sister?" Tessie said and smirked in Claire's direction.

"Yes, and it's been tough growing up without a sister or brother. You're all lucky to have each other. Mina stayed with our birth mother in Germany and is her first daughter. I was the second and the only one given up. Rita told me her husband died, and her mother helped with Mina. I was given up at birth because they didn't have enough money to take care of me, too."

"This sounds awful," Claire said.

"I've been writing to both Mina and Rita for quite some time."

"Why didn't you tell us sooner?" Tessie said, crossing her arms over her chest.

"I didn't want either of you to blurt out my news when we visited your grandparents."

"We wouldn't have."

"You were so young, I felt you would. Little kids say stuff they're not supposed to all the time."

"Okay, Mom." Conceding, Claire put her hands in the air and wiggled them around.

"Claire, if you're trying to be funny it's not working." Heidi felt miffed. "I want to meet my first family. Your dad and I have talked things over, and we decided to take you and your brothers to Germany and then France this summer. We've made the arrangements, but we have a few more details to take care of before we go.

"How long will we be away from our friends?" asked Claire.

"We'll be gone for six weeks. In Germany, you'll also meet a new cousin. His name is Sam."

The girls looked at each other. Tessie said, "We need to talk, be right back." They went out the front door and returned five minutes later.

"We don't want to leave our friends for that long—we're mad you didn't tell us about your sister before, but we'll go." Tessie yawned.

Heidi sarcastically responded, "Oh, thank you." She didn't think she needed their permission to take such an important family trip.

"Is there anything else you should tell us?" Claire meekly smiled.

"Yes, one more thing. I don't want any secrets between us. My dad had too many. Mr. Warren brought me a couple of letters from him while you all were at Claudia's house the day your spring break started. For some reason, Dad couldn't tell me while he was alive that he was Jewish. He officially became a Christian when I was a teenager." She gazed out the window at a dove flying past the glass. Their appearance in her life usually signaled a change was coming. Today she had no doubt.

"Is that all?" Tessie grumbled. "Doesn't sound like a big deal."

"Well, in reality, it is. In my parents' time, it was rare for people of different faiths to marry." The girls sat silently, and Heidi continued. "If you have any more questions, let's save them for another day. And, remember, I'll explain my adoption to your brothers in my own way."

"We won't, they can be so annoying." Tessie pulled on Claire, and they left the room.

The adventure began in July with an early morning airport shuttle to Dulles International airport. Heidi and the rest of her family emptied their pockets and took off their shoes to go through the metal detectors at security. They boarded the plane for their long journey in small cramped seats. The airplane taxied down the runway and ascended into the skies toward Germany.

When they arrived in Europe, they stood in the passport and customs lines before they were released onto the streets of Berlin. The city had changed so radically since President Reagan had said, "Tear down this wall," in 1989, that Heidi no longer recognized the place. She had also changed and was no longer the timid high school graduate standing in front of the wall with Claudia.

Helping the children understand what Berlin had been like before David died was important to her. They talked about how the concrete wall came down, and how it had been replaced by a memorial path that wrapped around the city along with historic artifacts and monuments. The East had been completely rebuilt. The gray section had melded into its counterpart. No more eerie tanks, no more forbidden photographs. What had been would never be forgotten by those who lived through the Nazi and Soviet regimes. Future generations would have to rely on museums and books or on stories from their elders. The new Berlin was stunning architecturally. They spent the next ten days exploring the revitalized and unified city until it was time to board a train to Frankfurt. It would be a matter of hours before Heidi met her lost blood relatives.

They exited the train and rented a car barely large enough to fit the six of them along with their backpacks. The next sixty kilometers of their journey to Schlangenbad, to find Mina, took longer than expected. Walt drove around with Heidi trying to help him maneuver through the European streets with the aid of an old traveling map. It didn't take them far before Heidi realized how outdated their map was, as new developments that weren't depicted in their directions confused her navigating, sending them well off course down twisty roads. Heidi didn't mind since the circuitous routes added to the adventure. The children bumped around the back seat, laughing, which helped Heidi calm her jittery nerves. She had told Mina in advance which day they would arrive, but not the exact time.

Walt circled the village of Schlangenbad three times before Heidi saw a person walking down a path who resembled her photo of Mina. The woman didn't respond when Heidi called out the window. Walt parked the car in a community lot. The family wandered around until they found Mina's house. Heidi raised her hand to knock, but—before her hand contacted the wood—the door squeaked open.

Heidi's stomach lurched. "Hello, Mina?"

"The pictures." Mina squinted. "Heidi, is it you?" A broad smile spread across Mina's face. Reaching out she enfolded Heidi into her spindly arms.

"Yes, it's me." Heidi was practically speechless. Her eyes widened, and she smiled but didn't shed a tear.

They stepped back and looked at each other. Mina was crying and choked out English words in a strong Bavarian accent. She said, "I have waited a lifetime to see you."

"Forty-five years apart is such a long time." Heidi stepped back and bit her lip before a smile fluttered across her face. She interlocked her arms across her own stomach and held on tight. Further inside the house, Heidi heard dogs barking. They quieted down when they reached Mina.

"Come, let's go inside. I want to phone Sam."

Walt encouraged Heidi to follow with a hand in the small of her back.

The Baileys walked into the house behind Mina. She pushed her two Dobermans to the side.

Pulling Walt's shoulder down to her level, Heidi spoke low in his ear. "I want to run away like a little kid."

"Hang in there. You couldn't have asked for a better reception."

"Yeah, I know. This is awkward. I should have brought Claudia along."

The dogs flanked Mina. "Here, come, have a beer." After opening three, Mina picked up the phone.

Heidi was glad she'd studied some German, but not enough to understand all of what Mina said to her son.

Mina spoke at a clipped pace. "Sam, Heidi and her family are here. Please come over. I need you to translate… Call your father… *Ja, ja*. See you in thirty minutes."

Heidi sat at the kitchen table sipping her beer with Walt and Mina while the children began watching a Harry Potter film in German, with English subtitles, in the attached room. She tried to speak with her sister with long pauses in-between. They gestured, pointed and tossed both German and English words back and forth. It seemed Walt was the best communicator of the three of them even though he knew less German words than Heidi. She was thankful Sam would be there soon. Eventually, a tall, lanky man with a mop of curly brown hair and tan skin walked in through the doorway with the dogs jumping around him.

"Dad will be here for dinner. He can't leave work until later," he stated in German as he kissed Mina's cheek. He turned to face Heidi and held out his hand. "*Hallo*! I'm Sam, your nephew." Appearing quite at ease, he also said hello to Walt and the children individually.

The conversation traveled back and forth—once in German, once in English—drawing out every interaction into a painful pace.

"Mom, you and your sister look alike," Sam said. "Your hair is different, but the shape of your faces are almost the same— definitely sisters." He tousled his mother's hair. "But you have blue eyes and blonde hair. Heidi has brown hair and eyes."

Mina pushed her hair back into place. "Obviously Sam," she responded impishly.

Heidi exclaimed, "Wow, we are finally together, it's hard to believe!" Heidi felt shyer than she'd ever felt in her life. *What am I doing here? I feel like my brain has turned to mush. My heart's a puddle at my feet. Writing letters was supposed to make this meeting easier. We're still strangers. Walt and the kids are being friendly. I have to talk, too! I think I'm in a daze or something.*

The two families walked, talked, and ate meals together, over a three-day period. Heidi couldn't figure out how to relax. The neck massages Walt gave her didn't help much. She continued to feel uncomfortable. Nothing seemed real. By the second evening, the conversations with Mina became strained and turned negative when Heidi realized Mina didn't want either of them to be involved with Rita. Mina had explained that their relationship had become so strained that they hadn't spoken in over a year. Mina said that promises had been broken between them, and she didn't trust her anymore. Heidi pleaded with Mina until she finally agreed to let Sam help. Sam disappeared into another room. When he returned, he said he'd reached his grandmother on the phone and arranged a meeting. They would all go to Mainz in the morning without Mina.

After being stuffed in the tiny car, which was more cramped with Sam, everyone was cranky. The family pried themselves out of their seats and stumbled out the doors. Claire gave Kyle an extra push to get him off her lap. They walked briskly through the narrow shop-filled streets. Before Heidi could catch her breath, she was face to face with Rita—her birth mother.

"*Oma*, this is Heidi, Walt, and the children." Sam pointed to each of his cousins individually and said, "Tessie, Claire, Kyle, and Tyler."

"Nice to see you," Rita said in perfect English.

"I need to leave and meet a friend down the road. Meet me at the toy shop in two hours." Sam winked and leaned toward Heidi. "*Oma*'s English is good."

"See you soon, Sam" Rita replied.

Heidi didn't know quite what to do. Shaking hands wouldn't be right, so she hugged Rita instead. Both their postures were stiff. Heidi pulled back into herself and took a step away. They looked into each other's eyes for an awkward moment. Heidi was relieved that they had written each other for years, but she felt like an alien in a bubble she couldn't escape. This was more difficult than meeting Mina. Neither Heidi nor Rita shed a tear.

At a local café, the children sat quietly in their chairs and answered questions when asked, but they didn't say a word otherwise. While they ate ice cream, the adults talked about casual, unimportant matters. Once everyone's bowls were empty, Heidi began to tap her foot under the table. "Let's go for a walk through the village."

"Yes. I would like that," Rita replied. They stood and strolled along next to each other while Walt and the children lagged behind them. "Why are my grandchildren unfriendly? They don't smile. I don't understand."

Heidi tried to explain. "They are here for me and want to let us talk. This is all new—I only told the girls about everyone last month, and the boys only know they're meeting cousins. Remember, I told you in a letter before we came?" A brief, emotionally charged, thought flitted through Heidi's head while she waited*; why does she expect the kids to call her anything but Rita? I'm going crazy. I have a family. Why am I doing this? Rita dumped me, and now she wants the perks. Oh, behave. I'm the one who sought her out.*

"Oh, yes," Rita's face twisted like she'd swallowed a lemon. "Did you get the letter I wrote right after you were born?"

"No, where did you leave it?"

"I collected some things for you in a canvas bag and put the letter in the bottom. I'd hoped a nun would pass it along to your new parents."

"No, I'm sorry. I've never seen it."

"I wonder what happened." Rita placed her hand over her heart. "You were my last baby. I couldn't have any more after you were gone. I tried when I married again, but the doctor said my insides were broken. I still think I was being punished for giving you away."

"I don't know what to say." Heidi tried another subject to avoid discussing female anatomy. "When I was a teenager, I got an American passport. Do you know if I can get a German one, too?"

"I don't think the laws will allow it. If you find a way, let me know, and I will help. Maybe you're too old to do it now."

"Maybe. I would like to have two passports, though." Heidi stopped in her tracks, and the children almost ran into her.

"Go along," Walt said. "We'll be in the toy shop over there when you're ready." He pointed at the shop across the street and began to prod the children in that general direction.

"All right, see you later." Heidi walked away with her birth mother. She decided to stop in front of different shops. The window displays would help distract her long enough to keep her emotions in check while they talked. She didn't want to break down.

"You said you would tell me about my birth father when we met."

"Yes, I did." Rita walked another block before speaking again. "It's a long story."

"Okay." Heidi moved a little faster, and Rita matched her pace.

"What I have to say may be hard for you to hear." Rita put her arm around Heidi's waist.

"I'm ready." Heidi tried not to pull away.

"I have not always lived in Mainz."

"Yes, I know, you lived in Wiesbaden when I was born."

"At the time, I worked just outside the military base caring for American children, while their parents were busy. But on the weekends, I worked at an ice cream shop." Rita sneezed.

"Bless you! I mean, *gesundheit*."

"I met Mitch while I was making a new batch of ice cream in the shop. I was confused because he kept looking up at me. He had dark hair and deep blue eyes. I've always liked a man in uniform. I went to his table to see if he needed anything. He was drawing a picture of me in his journal. I learned his name was Captain Mitch Regent from the Army Air Corps."

"Is Mitch my father?"

"Please, let me keep telling the story. Mitch asked me for chocolate ice cream in German with an American accent. He only spoke a little German at the beginning. My English wasn't very good either. When he realized I wasn't understanding, we wrote in German and English in his journal to see if we could understand each other better. We also drew silly pictures. It worked, and we laughed a lot. Ice cream is special to me because it makes me think of Mitch. I have my own ice cream shop, so I never forget."

"What happened to him?"

"This is difficult for me." Rita touched her wet cheek and walked on in silence until the end of the block. "Mitch and I had many days walking in Wiesbaden together. We talked about the war and other things. He understood my struggles. We walked through the ruins of bombed buildings. Even today, I still think about how frightened I was in those days."

"Did your parents help any of the Jewish people or were they Nazis?"

"I thought I told you in a letter that my father died at the beginning of WWII. There was only my mother and me," Rita said with a perplexed tilt of her head. "But no, Mama didn't hate or help the Jews. She didn't agree with Hitler's way of ruling Germany, but she was too scared to rebel." Rita exhaled softly. "Please... back to the main story."

"I'm sorry I interrupted."

"Mmm. Mitch and I had beautiful times together and were very much in love. Six months after we met, we were in the beer garden eating and drinking. We sat and watched an artist painting an impression of the guests. I was so focused on the painting that I didn't notice Mitch leave the table. He came back and smiled at me with a foolish grin on his face. He went down on one knee and asked me to marry him, and then a man behind Mitch started playing romantic music. Later in the evening, we went to tell Mama. She wasn't happy and said Mitch would take me away when work needed him somewhere else. We married two weeks later in a small ceremony."

"What happened next?" Heidi felt impatient.

"Mitch and I stayed at Mama's during the first months of our marriage because we couldn't live on the military base together. He was working on finding a house to rent. Everything was perfect until work sent him away on a mission. Mitch said he would be back in six months. While he was gone, I learned I was pregnant with our child and would have the baby before he came home."

"I saw his picture on Mina's hall table."

"One evening, while I was resting, a soldier named Davey came to the house. He told me Mitch had been killed and gave me a box of my husband's things. Before Davey could tell me anything more, I started to feel sick. Mama showed him out the door. Losing Mitch destroyed me."

"I'm sorry." The soles of Heidi's thin shoes flexed uncomfortably over the cobblestone sidewalk.

"Our baby was born a day later. I needed a lot of help from Mama because I had to have an operation to get Mina out. She continued helping me with Mina after I went back to work to earn money for our family. When Mina was six-weeks-old, I went out with some friends to a beer house. At another table, I saw Davey and went to ask him questions about my husband. He was very kind to me and told me how he died in a plane crash. We spent a lot of time together and became friends. One night we drank too much." Rita hesitated. "We were both lonely, but we never meant... I got pregnant with you."

"Oh... I was an accident. I'd imagined a nicer version." Heidi's shoulders sank; *I shouldn't be surprised. I think I just dropped into a black abyss. Try to keep focusing on Rita's words.*

"Yes, I'm sorry. Mama wouldn't help me. She was ashamed of my behavior and said no man would marry me with two babies. I told Davey I was pregnant, and he got very upset because he was already married. He said he would help me with money, but I said no. My pride was speaking. I should have accepted his offer. His wife and another child were in America. His commanders sent him home. I gave you to the nuns for adoption the day you were born. I was in pain. I felt so sorry I couldn't keep you."

"Mina stayed with you, and I..." Heidi's voice trailed off. She mulled over the explanation and Rita didn't say anything. Heidi stopped in front of another shop. After a deep breath, Heidi said, "You loved Mitch more than my father. I'm not sure what to do with this information. What is his last name?"

Rita answered, "I don't remember, I'm sorry. I realize I have hurt you, but you wanted the truth. I think when I finally married again, I was being punished for my mistakes. I chose such an awful husband. Both of us were married before, and our partners died young. Because of this, my new husband and I had a lot in common at first. When we were first married, Mina continued to live with my mother until she died. Later, we desperately needed more money and took in foster children. He became so bitter over time. My husband felt Mina was a constant reminder of my life with Mitch. He couldn't get over it, and it didn't help that we couldn't have a child together."

"Where is he now?"

"He died, too, but from alcohol poisoning. I don't talk about him much." Rita's hand came up and rested on Heidi's shoulder. "Are you okay?"

"Sure." Heidi didn't feel okay. "Thank you for telling me." Rita could be forgiven but her actions never forgotten. Heidi felt crestfallen after hearing the truth.

"I have made a lot of bad decisions in my life. Mina doesn't talk to me very much. I wasn't nice to her when she was little. I should have been happy around her because I could remember Mitch, but I was sad all the time. My husband didn't make things any better."

"What about your foster children?"

"Sometimes they come to visit me, but never Mina. I only have a few friends."

They turned the corner and walked over to the toy store. Heidi pulled the door open, and a bell brushed over the top and jingled to announce their entrance. Inside they found Walt and the children. No sooner than they had greeted each other, the bell sounded again, and Sam appeared.

"*Oma*, I need to get home. Sorry, I have to take Heidi away."

"It's all right, Sam. We've had a nice visit." Rita sounded content. "Thank you for your help."

"You're welcome."

Rita turned to Heidi. "I hope I have helped you understand. I'm happy you found me, and I hope we keep in touch through the years to come."

"Yes. Thank you for your honesty." Heidi leaned in and hugged Rita, who patted her back and gave her a little squeeze. She stepped away and smiled at Rita before leaving.

Would Heidi write Rita again? She wasn't sure, but if Rita wrote first, she'd answer. The meeting was eye-opening and answered many questions. Heidi didn't feel connected to Germany due to the language barrier and other unknown reasons, even though she was welcomed into the family. All she could do was feel sorry for Rita, and disappointed. There seemed to be a lonely void in her birth mother, but Heidi didn't think she could fill it. She felt fortunate to have had a home with her parents, and then created a home with Walt and their children. Perhaps Rita wasn't odd like Gwen, but they were both quirky in their own ways.

Heidi thought she and Mina would keep in touch—at least she hoped so. No, she had a better idea. They drove back to Schlangenbad. Heidi rushed inside, dragging Sam along for translation purposes. Heidi said, "Mina, Mina. Please come to Paris with us. Can you?"

"I don't know. The dogs can't be alone." Mina froze in place for what seemed like an hour. "Maybe my husband can take care of things if I go."

"Please, we will have fun. I'll buy your train ticket, and I have a place for us to sleep. Have you ever been to Paris?"

"No, I have lived here all my life. What about our language problems?

"My friend, Claudia, will meet us in Paris, and she speaks German. Oh, and I speak French."

Sam and Mina spoke back and forth without translating. Mina finally said in English, "I will go."

Heidi and her family snuggled together in their rented car with Mina squished against the door with her small suitcase and purse on her lap. With the additional occupant, Kyle was forced to sit on Claire's lap again, which made the long ride to Frankfurt all the more cumbersome and uncomfortable with their constant bickering and poking.

They caught a train to Paris. On the journey, Heidi silently sat and thought about her life, while Mina fidgeted in the seat next to her. Sensing Mina's discomfort, Heidi pulled out her journal and flipped to an empty page. She drew a picture with some English words next to it and Mina did the same in German. They also tried speaking short sentences in their native language. Somehow, as their mother did all those years ago with Mitch, they were able to communicate better on paper. Except, there were times Mina just nodded, and Heidi wasn't sure she actually understood. Walt spent the time keeping the four children entertained with card games. Halfway through the trip, the sisters stopped scribbling in the journal. Mina joined the card game across the aisle. Heidi tucked herself into the corner of her seat and began to write;

Parents are strange creatures. I freely admit this since I'm one. It's alarming to realize how little children think of parents as their all-knowing ruler. I'm not sure why they are programmed that way. I'm not an all-knowing being. It's such a huge responsibility to guide and protect our kids. They're exposed to much more information with computers, and they grow up too fast. Television isn't always G-Rated, and there are too many channels to choose from.

Writing in a journal all through the years truly saved my life. I think I equated it to praying in many ways. I was never hungry or in need of a roof over my head, but I needed to understand my life and how to deal with my dramatic and often distraught mother. The challenges plagued me, and in my innocence, I was devoured. I was so naïve. Yeah, Sadie and Aunt Eileen helped but my mom had a vice grip on me, and I don't even know how that happened. Mom stuck to me like crazy glue, and I resented her weaknesses. She was so obsessed with everything. It was as if she thought I would be taken from her by my German ancestors. That seemed like a silly concern, except ever since Mom told me, I've wanted to find them. Maybe she shouldn't have told me. To add to all that, she believed Walt took me away, and I couldn't make my own decisions. She showed the world such confidence but was insecure.

In the end, it turns out neither of my mothers were or are truly happy. Maybe I should feel worse because Rita abandoned me, but I don't for some reason. I am hurt, and a bit numb, yet knowing the truth helps me feel more complete. My mother's illness made our life harder, but I think the lessons I learned from her [Gwen] helped me become a better mother. I've got to stop writing about my childhood and get on with being an adult. I wish Walt hadn't had to suffer along with me. I'm so lucky to have such a devoted man in my life.

Heidi drew a quick sketch of her family scrunched around the table playing cards, then teetered across the train's aisle, and tucked the book under her husband's arm. "Walt, I want you to read what I wrote. I'm not sure I can explain what I'm feeling out loud."

He took the journal and silently read the entry. He was quiet for what seemed like forever to her, but he finally said, "This has been a long time coming."

"I know, I'm sorry," she whispered. "Thank you for all the emotional support. You've had to put up with a lot."

Chapter 35

The train pulled into Gare du Nord in Paris. Heidi crossed the platform with Walt, Mina, and the children to find Claudia waiting on a bench in the main hall of the station. Claudia had arrived in town the night before, courtesy of Mr. Warren. He'd arranged for her to stay at the Saint James Hotel on Avenue Bugeau, near the Arc de Triomphe.

"Hello, everyone!" Claudia reached out toward Heidi and hugged her before hugging the rest of them. "Oh, Heidi, who's this? Is she with us?"

"Mina, my sister." Heidi gave her a little nudge in Claudia's direction.

"*Aw, gut. Wie geht's?*" Claudia's accent sounded off, but effective.

"Hello, I'm fine," Mina replied. "I'm happy you speak German!"

"Excuse me a minute." Claudia pulled Heidi away from the family. "You should've warned me Mina would be here. I wasn't prepared to be a translator. Never mind, I'll get over myself and carry on."

"Oops. Thanks." Heidi grimaced. "I'm sorry, but this is going to be great." She pulled Claudia back over to the group. "How was your flight? Is the hotel all right?"

"Yes, yes. First-class seating on the plane made the trip easy, and the hotel is top notch!"

During their interaction, Heidi ignored Mina who stood awkwardly next to Walt and the children.

"Is everything okay?" Mina said and adjusted her shoulder bag.

"All is good!" Claudia switched to speaking in German and said, "This is wonderful. I didn't know Heidi was bringing you to Paris. I'll help translate your conversations."

Mina smiled. "Thank you. I'm very nervous. I've never traveled away from my village."

Claudia stepped between Heidi and Mina. Heidi looked over at her friend, who looped one hand into the crook of her arm and the other into Mina's. Guiding them around the family, Claudia led them all forward down the road. This time she spoke in English followed by an abridged version of German. "You won't believe the hotel I'm staying in. I've never slept in such a luxurious place." Claudia turned her head toward Heidi and spoke over her shoulder to Walt and the children. "You all must be hungry. What do you say we get some lunch before we go on?"

The four children chimed, "Yes!"

Claudia continued, her voice rose and fell to offset the traffic noises. "Okay, let's eat. It will take us a while to get to the Arc de Triomphe and then to the house."

"Hey, look, let's eat over there at that café," Walt said and shuttled the kids along. "We can stuff our backpacks under our feet."

"Hurry up!" Claudia exclaimed.

"Hey, slow down," Heidi retorted.

"The furniture at the hotel is right out of a Victorian novel or a piece of Versailles! Well, not actually, but the place feels like a queen's suite," Claudia prattled away in English, and in her excitement, she neglected to translate her words into German. "High ceilings, with a double staircase in black, white, and red. The bar even has a huge library of books from floor-to-ceiling. And my room! Well, it's golden. There was a dress—just my size—waiting for me on the bed, with a rose."

"That's a little touch Mr. Warren arranged, per Dad's instructions."

"He's the best! The dinner they served last night looked like a piece of artwork on my plate, with the sauce drizzled around the edges and a sprig of dill across the salmon. It was delicious."

"It doesn't sound like anywhere we've ever stayed, with or without our parents. Mina and I should duck out with you alone in the next few nights before you check-out."

"I have three more nights." Claudia danced a little jig.

"Yes, yes." Heidi wagged her free finger at Claudia. "And then you can stay at Rue Desborde Valmore with us."

"We'll have to go back to reality when we return to the States. I'll never be able to stay in a hotel like this one again."

"Think of it as the ultimate gift from Dad. Not sure what his motivation was, but I'm happy he did this for you."

In a swirl of confusion created by the four children, Heidi's family left the café with happy bellies and walked down to the nearest Métro station. It took them a few minutes to orient themselves before everyone hopped on the appropriate train. Heidi made sure to grab one of each of the twins' hands. After a couple of transfers, they arrived at the Muette station and walked ten minutes to Rue Desborde Valmore. Heidi found number twenty-two on the left side of the street, near the end of the block.

The row house was tall and narrow. The windows seemed to stare back at Heidi. She pulled out the photograph in her bag and made sure the house number matched the image. It was difficult to see the front door through the black, decorative wrought iron fence entwined with ivy. Putting her hand in her pocket, Heidi flipped the set of keys from one finger to the other while a tingle ran up her spine. She looked up at Walt before pushing open the gate. Heidi glided up the path to the marble-stepped double staircase with her family following in her footsteps. Her hand trembled as she slipped the key into the lock.

"Mom! What are you doing?" Tessie pulled on Heidi's arm, while the boys stumbled up the stairs bumping into both of them. "Stop guys, you're being brats. Mom, talk to us."

Claire grabbed the twins' arms. They stood poker straight with twisted grins on their faces. Heidi smiled and let out a small giggle.

Claudia gasped. "You didn't tell the kids?"

Heidi and Walt smiled knowingly at each other. "Nope." Heidi winked. "Surprise! This is your grandfather's other home. I lived here for the first three years of my life before I moved to the States."

"Has it been empty all this time?" Claire asked.

"No, not exactly. Mr. Warren wasn't supposed to tell me about this place until both my parents were gone. Your grandfather wrote me a letter with the details. He purchased this house in 1946 and rented it out to families before he and Mom moved in. Once they left Paris with me, he rented it out again to diplomats until a year before he died. I realize this sounds complicated." She opened the door halfway and continued explaining. "The neighbor, Monsieur Rousseau, kept an eye on things for years. Dad sent him wine regularly to thank him. It's been vacant for the last three years, and Mr. Warren has been a sort of absentee caretaker. I'm not sure how he did it, but I don't need to know."

"Wow!" Claire exclaimed. "Grandpa sure was mysterious. What are we supposed to do?"

Heidi knew she needed to spend time inside before making any decisions about whether or not to keep it. "Your grandfather gave me the house. I don't have to make any decisions today, no hurry."

All seven of them followed Heidi into the foyer. An envelope lay in the middle of an area rug at the bottom of the central staircase. She picked it up and found a note from Mr. Warren inside. It explained that the antique furniture recently came out of storage and that all the pieces were placed where her father had instructed in a detailed diagram. It said that sheets covered the furniture to keep the dust from collecting while the metaphorical 'dollhouse' waited for her arrival. When her father traveled, he picked up more than a collector's doll from other countries for her. The dolls came home in his suitcase, and the antiques were shipped to a storage facility in Paris. She thought to herself, every item had belonged to him, and now it was hers. Heidi leaned heavily on the railing and explained his intent to her followers.

"Mr. Warren's little elves took care of the house," Heidi said through laughing tears and explained what she knew. "Dad did this for me. My quiet father. He collected things for this house like he was filling up a dollhouse, not for his wife, but for his decedents." She wiped her cheeks, took a deep breath, straightened her back, and curled her lips together to calm her heart. It was time to explore.

A piece of furniture stood on the left side of the corridor with flamingo shaped mahogany legs peeking out from underneath a small sheet. Heidi slipped it off and found a narrow table with an old-fashioned, black rotary phone perched on top of a circle of Belgian lace, along with a Waterford crystal bowl filled with wrapped pillow-mints with a bit of paper tucked underneath the candies.

Heidi held the note out

Walt took it, and read, "'Turkish glass from my travels, Dad.' Mr. Warren's been busy." Walt handed it back to Heidi and put a couple mints into the front pockets of his khaki trousers.

Claudia took a mint from the bowl and passed one to Mina.

Heidi was so excited she could barely contain herself. "Mr. Warren also mentioned in the note that I played in a lovely park close by called Jardins du Gallagher that we should visit. He said the famous Notre Dame Cathedral and other wonderful sites are only a few Métro stops away. We'll spend the rest of the month in the house and go out to see the sites." She pulled off another cover. "Everyone, keep taking the sheets off the furniture."

"Let me have the second key," Walt said. "I'll go hunting and see what I find." He took the key from her outstretched hand. Watching him cross the room she couldn't help laughing with delight.

Walt peeked under another sheet, pulled it off, and found a vintage decanter filled with amber-colored liquid. Pulling the stopper, he smelled the contents. "Aw, smells smoky, guessing it's Scotch whisky or something similar. Hey, Heidi, here's another note." He waved it in the air. "Hmm, it says, 'Walt, enjoy the Lagavulin.' Your father's brilliant!"

"I miss him so much. I wish he was here to see our reactions."

"Your father knows what I like." He laughed and poured some of the golden liquid into the glass on the table. A moment later, Walt's footsteps trailed off as he left the room in search of a lock.

Tessie and Claire flurried around, pulling more sheets off the furniture, but they left the ones that covered the dining room table and its legs. The twins crawled under whooping and hollering like they were camping in the great outdoors.

Heidi scanned the room trying to remember the inside of the house beyond the photographs she'd seen in her parents' albums, but understandably nothing felt familiar. While she pondered the situation and moved her eyes from one piece of antique furniture to the next, she saw a pearl tipped hatpin stuck through a note on a chair's cushion. She picked it up and read out loud to any of the kids who might actually be paying attention, "A home, with love."

Tessie and Claire promptly sat on the unveiled sofa.

"Girls, don't sit on the furniture, I'm sure it's quite valuable." Heidi combed her fingers through her hair. "Oh, never mind, this isn't a museum. I'm ridiculous."

"Heidi, come upstairs!" she heard Walt bellow from somewhere deep within the house. "Your father left you a few things."

"Coming," Heidi shouted back up the stairwell.

"Bring Mina and Claudia, along with the whisky," he hollered even louder than before.

Heidi grabbed the decanter and rushed up the stairs with Mina and Claudia in tow.

She called out, "Walt, where are you?"

"The room at the end of the hall," Walt replied. "It's an office."

They went in, and Heidi put the decanter down on the executive rosewood desk. Walt stood with his back to her on the other side of the room peering through a doorway with his hands stretched up on either side of the frame. A tapestry sat folded at his feet.

"Walt, what's the matter?" Heidi ducked under his arm, gasped, and put her hand on his side. Talking into the closet in front of her she said, "Dad, oh Dad, what have you done?"

The room had paintings hung in orderly rows on every inch of the wall. Multiple crates covered most of the floor. "Jesus, one of those paintings looks like a Klimt! How long has this stuff been here?"

Mina and Claudia ducked around on the other side of Walt.

"What the…," Claudia exclaimed.

"Don't worry," Walt said. "We'll figure out everything."

Responding in a hushed tone, Heidi said, "I can't believe my eyes. Dad had secrets, but I never imagined anything like this."

A Victorian parlor chair stood inside the room with two packets of dusty envelopes wrapped in faded yellow ribbons on the seat. The larger one had a dried rose under the ribbon. Heidi gathered up the bundles and turned them over in her hands several times. Written on the top envelope under the rose, in her dad's handwriting—'No 1; Open Me First, Heidi Rose.' And underneath, less precisely, was printed—'A fine wine is under the chair. Enjoy it, and don't consider the cost.'

Claudia pulled a small wooden crate from under the chair.

Walt pried open the lid. Inside were three Waterford crystal wine glasses, a corkscrew, and a bottle of Romaneé-Conti wrapped in a linen cloth.

Heidi gazed at the items. "This wine is a treasure in and of itself. Odd, why three glasses?"

Claudia passed the contents of the box to Mina. "Put these on the table in front of the sofa."

"I don't know what to think," Heidi said. "Guess we should go with the flow."

Walt kissed Heidi hard on the lips.

"Ahem." Claudia cleared her throat. "Hey, you two, get a room. So, I know the note says to drink, but really?"

"Yes... really, let's sit down, and each enjoy a glass. This is what he wanted. I think we should comply. Her mood went from overwhelmed to giddy in a matter of minutes. "Walt, I'll give you a sip of my wine."

"Gee, thanks, but you're right I prefer the whisky. Don't waste the wine on me." Walt's smile overtook his face as he held up his glass.

"What should we do?" Mina asked.

"Give Heidi some space. Go sit down," Claudia said in clipped German.

"Pour Mina a glass of wine," Heidi said.

Heidi moved across the room, putting the envelopes on the desk, and sat in the brown-leather cushioned chair. She scooched the chair up to the desk and worked on untying the bundles. The knots in the ribbons were fused in place, but she managed to peel them off. Inside the envelope, her father's letter explained the contents of the room.

"I'm feeling light-headed," Heidi said. "Hang on. I need to look at the attached envelope. It reads, 'N° 2; Open Me Next for the Proof.' I'll wait to open the others. I'm sure Dad numbered them one through five for a good reason." She painstakingly opened the thick manila envelope.

Walt leaned over Heidi's shoulder as she went through the papers.

Claudia paced around the office. "Is this why we're all here?"

"I suppose so. Keep helping Mina understand what's going on." Heidi fidgeted with her hair. "There are so many items on the inventory list, and they're all described in detail. It'll take some time to go through."

"I can help with everything, no problem." Claudia sipped her wine.

"The first letter says the art is enormously valuable and should either be sold to collectors or displayed on loan at renowned museums. The papers in the second packet are copies of the authentication documents. Here he says, having the original paperwork off-site is for backup security. They're in a safety deposit box at the Société Générale on Rue Montorgueil. Dad mentioned the box in the letter Mr. Warren brought us before this trip, but he didn't tell us what it was about."

Walt interjected, "Now we know."

"Hmm." She put her index finger up to her lips to stop him from talking. "The note says that during the war Dad bought most of the paintings and artifacts from various sources which largely included museums. He used his connections in the world to obtain the art with my grandmother's financial backing. I'm not sure which pieces are which yet, but he said that the money went to help museum curators hide pieces from the Germans."

"Now that's an extraordinary story!" Walt poured more wine into their glasses, added some whisky to his, and walked back to the closet.

Heidi drank deeply from her glass feeling like a detective. "Dad writes that after the war, he and David continued to add to the collection. When he met Mom, he didn't tell her what they were up to because she wouldn't be able to cope with so many valuable things around the house." Heidi rubbed her eyes. Stoically, she said, "I had no idea he was this wealthy."

Claudia was scowling. "Sad, he never seemed to relax around your mother. It's as if he didn't fully trust her emotional reaction to anything. He only had a few paintings in the back hall of their Bethesda house."

"So true on both counts. It's good Mr. Warren had the paintings appraised before they were boxed up. Until then, I had no idea that they were originals. I'm glad he handled that before he took them off to Christie's for auction. Anyway, Dad's letter goes on to say that he never sold the art in Paris because he enjoyed coming into this room to look at it whenever he was in town. It looks like he was here often. He noted the dates he visited on the back of the inventory envelope. He said I should use the funds from any sales wisely. Funny, like I'd do anything else?" She looked over at Claudia. "A few of the pieces have your name on them."

Claudia jolted out of what appeared to be a trance. "I can't imagine why my dad got engrossed in art, but this is a pleasant surprise." She walked back to the closet and leaned over. "We missed a letter. It must've fallen out of one of the packets. It's in German and says in a different handwriting, 'For My Baby.' Under that, in your dad's hand, it says 'N° 3; This belongs to you, Heidi.' Do you want me to read it?"

"Please, I didn't realize I'd dropped it. Read it out loud, in German and English. I guess the baby is me." Heidi wet her lips with the wine.

"There are two sheets of paper in the envelope in two different handwritings." Claudia shuffled the papers around in her hand. "One is in German dated the fifteenth of March 1958, and the other is in English but not dated." Claudia ran her finger under the script and began reading the beginning with the salutation—

15 March 1958

To My Beautiful Baby Girl,

My name is Rita. I have signed papers to give you up. My heart aches, but I can't afford to let you stay with me. Your name is Mariana Maria Baumann. I think it will be changed when you are adopted. I'm trusting the nuns to place you in a good home. I must finish this before they take you. I am sorry you have to go away, but I loved the nine months we spent together, even though I only just saw your face. I live in Wiesbaden. This is my home. I plan to stay if you ever want to find me. Your heritage was severed with the clip of the cord that connected us. I'm sorry. I will always think of you.

Your first mother,

Rita Baumann Regent

Heidi stood up and pulled Walt's handkerchief out of his pocket. It smelled of Old Spice.

He put his hand on hers. "Are you—all right?"

"Yes, I think so." She wiped her eyes. "I know I shouldn't feel stunned, but I'm amazed Dad left this letter for me. I didn't think he wanted me to know my original roots."

"Your dad continues to be full of surprises." Walt swirled his whisky and emptied it before pouring two more fingers worth out of the decanter.

Heidi got up from the desk and paced. "Here we go... 'N°4; Read Me last. Strictly Confidential for Heidi Rose Schwartz' and the other, 'N°5, Private for Claudia Elise McGwire from David McGwire.' Let's see what these are all about." She handed Claudia her letter.

"Careful ladies. Maybe we've had enough shocks for one day."

"Good news comes in threes, or fours, or fives. Right? And, the winner is? I feel like we're at an Oscars award ceremony." Claudia giggled. She tore open the edge of her envelope and pulled out a piece of paper.

"Let's read them at the same time." Heidi robotically opened hers and began scanning through the letter. She squinted at the words with disbelief. Once or twice Heidi sensed Claudia glaring at her.

"Oh, my God!" Heidi let go of her letter, and it fluttered to the floor. Tears rolled down her cheeks, and she rubbed them away in slow motion with her fingertips.

Mina grabbed Heidi's hand, pulling her onto the sofa.

Claudia pinched her letter between her thumb and index finger. Backing up, she bumped into the end table by the sofa before landing on the other side of Mina. Heidi and Claudia stared at each other across Mina's lap, and their tears flowed.

Mina put an arm around each of them. Her eyes turned into saucers. She repeatedly turned her head left and right with apparent confusion.

"Now, ladies, what can be more difficult than what's in the closet?" Walt asked.

Heidi placed her hand over her mouth.

"It's not the art that's the problem!" Claudia waved her father's letter around. "All these years... we never knew. Our fathers didn't tell us..."

"Come on, don't leave Mina and me in the dark." Walt plucked Heidi's letter up off the floor. Heidi watched his head moved back and forth, his eyebrows lift, and his mouth drop open. He pushed his unhinged jaw back into place.

Tessie and Claire walked in from another part of the house with their arms full of folded sheets piled under their chins. Tessie's voice sounded muffled. "Mom? What's wrong? You look like you've seen a ghost."

The girls put the sheets on the floor up against a wall out of the way.

"Yes, Tessie, in a way she has," Walt said on Heidi's behalf.

"Sweethearts, we'll be fine." Heidi collapsed back into the sofa cushions and drank some more wine.

Tessie and Claire stood there motionless. The twins, covered in sheets, kept running in and out of the room like wild-spirited animals.

"What's going on?" The usual sparkle in Claire's voice dwindled away. "Mom? Dad?"

Heidi thought about the artwork, but for now, it didn't matter. "Girls, every time we turn around, unexpected things keep happening. For starters, the art in that hidden room is worth millions." She pointed. "Go look."

The girls disappeared into the back room and returned five minutes later.

"The room is packed," Tessie said.

"Yes, it is." Heidi paused. "We've also learned that Claudia and I are sisters, too."

"Wow! That's great, right? Claire gasped.

"Yes, but we're feeling overwhelmed."

"Tessie, let's leave them alone."

"Thanks, girls, we'll come downstairs soon," Heidi responded in a reassuring voice. She didn't want them to be more involved than they already were.

Heidi took the letter from Walt and held it up. Her voice cracked as she continued the explanation. "This letter says Dad was in charge of secret missions for the U.S. government. He sent two soldiers on a U-2 spy plane mission, and only one survived."

Walt made a guttural sound in his throat. "That was a remarkable time in history, I've done a lot of research on the U-2 plane. It's called 'The Dragon Lady.' Based on this and what we've already read in your dad's boxes back in the States, I'd say he and David were in the thick of things during their entire careers."

Heidi twisted her lip sideways. "Yes, I suppose. I can't think about that right now."

"Claudia, please, translate for Mina. She needs to know what's going on!" Heidi said awkwardly.

"How am I going to say this in German when I can barely deal with it in English?"

"I don't know, please try. We'll get through this like every other crisis." Then Heidi said to Mina, "I'm so sorry your father died during the mission. This letter says Claudia's father—David—took it upon himself to tell your mother in person and that your father was a hero. After that, your mother and David established a friendship that eventually led to an accidental encounter after too many beers. She became pregnant with me."

When Claudia finished explaining the situation to Mina, she gasped. Her face dropped, and she began pacing the room. Mina said several times in German and then English, "Noooo!"

Claudia moved over to the desk, sat on the edge, and put her head in her hands.

All Heidi could bring herself to say was, "We are all sisters! Please, Claudia, I need to tell the rest. Please..."

"All right, all right. Give me a minute." Claudia walked out of the room and returned blotting her face with a wet washcloth. "I'm ready, let's get on with this, sister."

Heidi felt like there were rocks in her stomach and happy butterflies in her heart all at once. "Mina, when your mother and I were talking, I thought it was a coincidence when she mentioned a man named Davey being my father, and she claimed to have forgotten his last name. According to this letter, Davey was a nickname that he gave up! When I got the copy of my birth certificate a few years ago, the line that said 'father' was blank." Heidi paused and nervously fiddled with a button on her blouse while Claudia did her best to translate.

Heidi continued but directed her conversation toward Claudia. "The letter says your father saved two nuns' lives shortly after WWII. They were so grateful that in 1958 they helped with my adoption. David, my adopted father—Nathan, Rita, and the two nuns worked together to arrange everything without our mothers ever knowing what happened. Rita agreed to send me away to an unknown location. It was part of a deal they jointly fabricated to protect David—your father—and supposedly everyone else."

Claudia managed to translate all the words before she exclaimed, "My father—we are all sisters?"

"Yes, we are sisters. All three of us are sisters." Heidi couldn't quite believe it herself and turned to Walt with a questioning look on her face. "Can you—you explain this more logically?"

Walt put a piece of paper on the desk and drew a family tree. "Not exactly all sisters. Mina, you and Heidi are half-sisters because you have the same mother. Claudia and Heidi are half-sisters because they have the same father. There is no genetic connection between Mina and Claudia, but family is more than blood. This entire adventure has been quite a bonding experience, and that's what counts."

"Yes, family," Mina replied after his words were translated.

Heidi and Claudia paced back and forth across the room.

"I don't know what to do," Heidi murmured. "Claudia, what's going on in your head? Forget about translating anything else right now."

Claudia choked out her words, "Our dads... I'm stunned... Dad said he tried to do the right thing, but things got slanted. His initial intention of being respectful to a widow was noble before everything fell to pieces."

"What else did David's letter say?"

"Dad wrote he wanted to give Rita financial help so she could keep you nearby, but she declined and chose adoption. He said he was tormented by the entire situation, but he felt blessed to have a best friend like Nathan to help." Claudia pulled on her cheek. "He loved that you and I could be together even though the truth was buried. He didn't tell Mom because he loved her and didn't want to shred our established family after a night with a suffering friend. Suffering friend! I'm having trouble with that remark. He finished by saying he could've just forgotten about you, but he kept you nearby." Claudia's face reddened. "But still, how could he betray my mother?"

"Hey, go easy. I'm standing right here! The mistake. David carried his guilt with him and didn't burden Sadie. My parents wanted a baby and, without meaning to, he helped them get one. Since Rita couldn't keep me, she could've put me in an orphanage, but instead, she allowed David to get involved with my adoption. In the end, I think he did the right thing. Now that our parents are gone, we know the truth, and we're together. What's that saying, 'let the truth set you free' in this case, us free."

"I'm sorry, I'm losing it!" Claudia raised her voice through her tears. "In your parents' attic, you told me Dad helped end the Soviet regime and was killed for his heroics. Today we find out we're sisters!"

Heidi took Claudia's hands in hers. "I'm sorry, I'm so sorry."

Claudia pulled her hands away and rubbed at her tears. "I can't blame you for any of this mess. I can't. You didn't do anything wrong." Claudia's voice toned down a notch or two. "I don't know how Dad was around you all the time without ever telling us the truth. Then, he locked the confession in a room. I can't yell at a dead man." Claudia brushed more tears from her cheeks.

"Oh, Claudia…" Heidi rubbed her arm.

"There's something else in the letter." Claudia's eyes bored into Mina. After a long pause, she said in German, "Mina, my father knew you in the first months of your life. He's sorry he caused your mother pain. There's a box in the closet for you. He said you should either sell what's inside or keep it; it's your choice. Finally, he hoped that we would all find each other and get along."

"This is…," Mina began.

"Certainly is something," Claudia retorted. "If my mother and Aunt Gwen knew, they would've been devastated. I don't think they could've handled the truth."

"Yeah, it's a mess. So, are you okay with being sisters?" Heidi asked, hoping for the best response possible.

"I like that we're sisters, but I can't stand the deception. It's amazing that you and I grew up together in different houses without a clue!" Claudia draped one arm across Heidi's shoulders and the other across Mina's.

No one moved or said another word for many minutes. They remained linked while Heidi mulled over everything they had discovered. Smiling she mused, "The three of us aren't only children after all. I hope we can find ways to be together for the rest of our lives."

Epilogue

Six Years Later, 2008…

Heidi opened up her laptop computer and logged into Skype before trying to reach Claudia in Paris. The selected number connected and rang—daah whoo, daah whoo, daah whoo. It had a distinctive ring, unlike the dial tones in the United States. *"Bonjour, La Fondation Schwartz et McGwire."* Claudia's voice echoed in French through the computer speaker.

"Bonjour, Foundation Schwartz et McGwire." Claudia's voice echoed through the computer speaker.

"Bonjour, Claudia," Heidi replied. "I'm so proud of you."

"Thank you. I just got back to the house after an evening at ACCORD." Claudia turned around in circles in front of the video feed.

"You look quite Bohemian in that peasant blouse. Why are you still attending French classes? It's been six years since you moved to Paris."

"It was a reunion." Claudia raised a glass of wine into view. "Not to mention, it's another good place to find young artists to sponsor."

"True, true. Who'd you find?"

"Someone named Annika. She's amazing with a pencil and sketchpad. Very intricate scenes with dragons and fairies intertwined with cityscapes. She's only at the school for a month. I've arranged for her to send me more of her work from Massachusetts to feature in our new collection opening at the gallery this coming September. Speaking of which, our gallery's landlord presented me with a new lease agreement. The rent's going up a bit. I'll send you a copy via email. I was hoping it would stay the same except it's not possible. We still get crowds filtering across the street to us from the Musée Marmottan Monet, so I think we need to accept the inevitable rent hike and stay put."

"It's all right. How much longer is Van Gogh's *The Lovers* on loan to Musée du Louvre?"

"Another year, but we're okay. The money from the sale of the Klimt painting and the connected investments will likely keep us going indefinitely. We don't need to sell anything now. If I've made a mistake in calculations, we can always auction off another piece or two in the future."

"Yes, of course." Heidi smiled at the video camera and still wasn't sure she'd ever get used to talking to people through a screen. It did help that the picture could be turned off when she didn't want to be seen. Then she said, "We'll be arriving in Paris on the twenty-seventh of June, but Walt can't be around for more than two weeks at a time this year because of various work-related complications. Kyle and Kaleb will come with me for two months. They're starting to get out of their obstinate adolescent phase and are looking forward to high school next fall. To give you a break from their antics, maybe Walt and I can take them to Belgium and the Netherlands at the end of July rather than hanging around Paris the entire time."

"All right." Heidi watched Claudia wander around the kitchen while she prepared a meat and cheese plate. "I'll be at a conference and can't meet you at the airport. I'll send a car for you. Drop your things by the house and go to the gallery."

"Sounds good, no problem. I'll cut through Gallagher park after I've showered and put on fresh clothes. I'm hoping I can sleep on the plane and there aren't any delays. I'll bring my customary two suitcases. I'm trying to talk the boys into one each, but they want to bring some extra entertainment with them this year. Not sure what they have in mind, we'll see."

"Hey, what do you expect. Let the boys bring whatever they want. The airport driver will manage with the luggage. Stop worrying," Claudia said. "What about your girls, what's going on with them?"

"Tessie is finishing her university studies and has already been offered a job at a law firm in New York. Claire did well in her second year at Oxford. I'm hoping they're able to come to Paris at some point over the summer, but they haven't committed, yet."

"I haven't seen them in ages. I hope they come." Claudia adjusted her chair and sat closer to the screen. "So, what else business-wise is on your mind?"

"The four new artists you found... tell me about them. You didn't say much in your last e-mail."

"Finding this group was more challenging since we changed strategies after our trip last year to the Guggenheim museum in Venice. It may have inspired us to meet overly tough standards, but I think I found four artists I can live with that have different talents. Not sure they'll want to stay in the house for two years, as we'd hoped, but they've agreed to at least one. They'll show their work at the gallery, and then give us a percent of their sales in exchange for publicity, housing, and food. Let's see how that goes. We can always change our tactics again after their contracts are over."

"You still haven't told me who you found to live at the house." Heidi walked out into her garden with her laptop. The roses they'd transplanted from her parents' house were in full bloom. Holding the laptop computer up, she showed them off.

"The roses still look pretty," Claudia said. "The artists; one is a photographer from Southern France who will live in the vintage bedroom."

"Vintage." Heidi laughed. "The entire house is vintage. Guess we can't call it the 'black and white' room since it's decorated with old photographs of people.

This time Claudia walked around with her laptop showing off her decorating skills.

Heidi peered into her screen. "I love the photograph by Kaminsky. Hold on..." Heidi darted back into the house, grabbed an oversize book off a table, found the photo and held it up into the screen. "1949, *The Rain, Woman with Umbrella, Paris*."

"Yes, that's the one."

"Sorry, didn't mean to interrupt your flow." Heidi snickered.

"You're funny. Don't forget; *A Gardener Sweeping Leaves* by Brassaï. There're more prints, but never mind that for now. The second recruit is a graphic artist from Wales. The third is a student of literature studying at the Sorbonne University, she's a book illustrator on the side. They are going to share the Van Gogh room since it has two beds. The blue walls are embellished with a couple of reproductions of his paintings; *The Cathedral in Bayeux* and *The Bedroom in Arles*."

"Hey, keep showing me around."

"Right, right, sorry." Claudia moved the laptop around again. "The fourth artist is a painter; I'll put him in the Jackson Pollack room in the basement next to the kitchen. They're all moving in next weekend." Claudia sounded proud of her accomplishment. It wasn't easy to find honorable and talented artists.

"Well done," Heidi said. "It's great when a plan comes together."

"Oh, and the remodeled studio in the attic is finally done. The artists love the space, the views out the windows are breathtaking and inspiring with the Eiffel Tower in the distance."

"Everything looks wonderful, and it sounds like you found a great combination of people. I look forward to meeting them. You're a marvel, Claudia." Heidi watched her sister's face light up.

"Don't give me too much credit. You were the one who said, 'let's start the Schwartz and McGwire Foundation,' when we first found the art in the house—which, I might add, is mostly still locked safely away in Daddy Nathan's office thanks to my strategies. Every penny Daddy David spent on my marketing degree paid off in spades."

"Daddy Nathan, Daddy David." Heidi paced in front of the laptop. "We're hilarious, but if it weren't for them, we wouldn't be so international or well-to-do."

"Mmm, that's for sure. Did you get the envelope? I mailed it last week."

Heidi recalled the packages she delivered to David while she was at Catholic University. She grabbed Claudia's envelope off the kitchen counter and turned the nine-by-twelve manila envelope around. Holding it up to the screen, she said, "Yes, I got it. We're so nostalgic. Maybe we should stop using these big envelopes and use regular white legal-size for bank deposit receipts, like everyone else."

"You're funny. They're our signature envelopes. We have to use them; it's our family tradition." Claudia held up another envelope, and it blocked her face.

"I can't disagree, although I'd like to at times." Heidi moved through the house with the laptop and placed it down on her sewing room cutting table. "Ouch," Heidi exclaimed. "Hang on a second..." She pulled the straighten pin out of the side of her hand.

"Ouch? What's happening over there?"

"I reached across the new Regency costume I'm making and stuck myself. I love the fabric on this one; it's has tiny rosebuds throughout. I found a base for the hat that I'm going to adjust. I'll add a matching cap over the crown and a satin ribbon so it can be tied on securely."

"You really can't sit still today. You're all over the place. I'm so glad you've made time to do some costuming again after all these years."

"It's been a good thing," Heidi reflected.

"Onto another point, have you heard from Mina?"

"Yes, she'll come for two weeks at the beginning of August. In spite of her lack of confidence about learning English, she does all right without Sam translating every word, but he still stands by her when we have conversations. Every time we see each other on Skype, Sam says we look alike." Heidi scribbled a reminder note to herself about creating a quilted purse for Mina.

"Why doesn't Walt quit work? You don't need the money."

"What can I say, he loves what he does. Once the twins are off to college in four years, Walt will retire early. We'll sell our house and move to Paris, travel around, and help with the foundation."

"Mmm, that's a few years off." Claudia started to sound a bit on edge. "So—for this summer—the house will be crowded if everyone comes. I've added a folding screen to the back half of the living room to conceal the twins' bunk beds. It looks like a separate room now and doesn't obstruct the entrance. If Tessie and Claire show up, we'll have to double up in our bedrooms or set them up in the dining room."

Heidi smiled inwardly and then winked into the camera. "On a more personal level, tell me, what's going on with that Frenchman of yours? You've been dating for two years."

"He's still tops on my list. I think he finally realizes I don't love him for his money. I told him more about our financial background, and he seemed quite relieved. He laughed and said he'd looked up our foundation some time ago and was glad I'd finally explained the entire story."

"Oh, you're ridiculous. You know you told him a year ago."

"Yes, yes. You're right, I did. Just wanted to make sure you're paying attention." Claudia stopped talking, stared straight ahead, and batted her eyelids into the camera.

"What aren't you telling me?" Heidi wasn't going to let this slide. Her sister was up to something.

"Okay, you caught me." Claudia made a tapping sound.

"What was that? I can only see your face on the video chat."

"Oh, right you can't see my hand it's under the table." She giggled and held it up. "It's a cut rock. Half a karat on a platinum band."

"Hurray! You two are engaged?"

"*Oui, oui Madame*. We're getting married next year and will move into one of his family homes along the Seine. Perfect in every way. I'll move out of Rue Desbordes-Valmoure and only work there during the day. When you and Walt come here full-time, everything in our lives will be complete!"

"The foundation is secure." Heidi smiled and disconnected their internet connection.

Acknowledgments

I give thanks to many. Starting with the writers, who showed me how it's done. To my dear friends and my family—who helped me through my journey. To the people whose lives inspired me to write, to my teachers. critique group, and beta readers. Special thanks to—Louise Capon, Amy Colman, and Andria Yu.

38469071R00246

Made in the USA
Middletown, DE
13 March 2019